"PLAYING THE MISTRESS, ARE YOU, GEORGIANA? OR ARE YOU *REALLY* SOMEONE'S MISTRESS?"

Brock flicked a finger across the tops of her breasts, and lifted her pendant up to peer at it.

Georgiana drew in a swift breath. His touch felt like fire. "That wasn't kind of you, Brock."

"I'm not in the mood to be kind," he snapped. "Indeed, I'm less than thrilled to discover my wife dresses like a Cyprian and mingles with London's most notorious demireps. I won't stand for any more bad behavior."

"What of *your* bad behavior? Am I to ignore the way you lured me into marriage with false promises and sweet lies?"

He didn't reply at first. She could see a muscle in his jaw twitching, another sure sign that she'd really set his blood to boiling. "Madam, I do not want the entire assemblage privy to our personal life. We're leaving. You may plead your case with me at Palmer House."

"As you wish," she murmured, lifting her chin.

He grabbed her arm and pulled her close as they walked toward the door. When he spoke, his voice was a mere whisper, meant for her ears alone. "If you want to be a mistress, I'll certainly accommodate you . . . tonight, and every night, until we've satisfied all aspects of your curiosity."

THE CRITICS ADORE TRACY FOBES

FORBIDDEN GARDEN
A *Romantic Times* Top Pick for March 2000

"*Forbidden Garden* is a love story and a thriller. It is one of the most intriguing stories I've read in a long time. Ms. Fobes' forays into the paranormal are on par with Stephen King, her research into her subject matter is exquisite, and her gift of storytelling is superb."
—*New and Previously Owned Books*

"*Forbidden Garden* is an exciting historical romance. The story line is fast-paced while cleverly showing how ironically the freethinking male elite scorns the possibility of a female being their equal. Real persona such as Huxley and Darwin add to the nineteenth-century ambiance of the novel. Tracy Fobes has provided a triumphant tale that will stimulate readers to search for more of her works."
—*Under the Covers Book Reviews*

HEART OF THE DOVE
A *Romantic Times* Top Pick for September 1999

"Tracy Fobes brings a fresh and exciting approach to paranormal romance. Her ingenious plots and engaging characters captivate readers and allow them to give their imaginations free rein. *Heart of the Dove* is a compelling and mesmerizing look at witchcraft from a new angle."
—*Romantic Times*

"A definite keeper on my supernatural shelf."
—*Old Book Barn Gazette*

"Wow! Fans of paranormal romance do not want to miss this one. Tracy Fobes has written a story to enthrall you from the start."
—*Bookaholics*

TOUCH NOT THE CAT

"Tracy Fobes' debut is a stunning novel, beautifully blending the haunting magic of the Highlands with a sensual romance and a love that has the power to confront an ancient curse. . . . You'll be lured into the magical and highly romantic world Tracy Fobes creates in this dazzling debut. . . . She crafts memorable characters and a spellbinding paranormal romance that will appeal to readers seeking something very special."
—*Romantic Times*

"Pulled into a world where mythical creatures, magical transformations, and a legendary love exist, the reader is taken on a delightful journey into the unbelievable, made believable by Ms. Fobes' extraordinary skill as a storyteller."
—*Rendezvous*

"*Touch Not the Cat* is an intriguing and passionate story. The fairy magic of the Scots is woven throughout the tale and gives a mystical atmosphere that will appeal to lovers of romance and fantasy alike. An excellent debut."
—*Writers Write*

Books by Tracy Fobes

Touch Not the Cat
Heart of the Dove
Forbidden Garden
Daughter of Destiny

Available from POCKET BOOKS

TRACY FOBES

DAUGHTER of DESTINY

SONNET BOOKS

New York London Toronto Sydney Singapore

An *Original* Publication of POCKET BOOKS

A Sonnet Book published by
POCKET BOOKS, a division of Simon & Schuster, Inc.
1230 Avenue of the Americas, New York, NY 10020

ISBN: 0-671-04174-6

First Sonnet Books printing September 2000

10 9 8 7 6 5 4 3 2 1

SONNET BOOKS and colophon are trademarks of Simon & Schuster, Inc.

Cover art by Paul Bechem

Printed in the U.S.A.

For my daughters, Emily and Brianna,
with love

Prologue

❦

Welsh Woodlands, 1806

The woman's labored gasp shattered the primordial stillness in the forest. Disembodied, it echoed around the trees, its owner hidden by the mist that floated near the ground.

Moments passed. A light wind blew through the forest, whipping the mist into clutching, gray fingers, allowing filtered sunshine to dapple the ground with patterns of light. It whispered through a large spider web strung between two boulders.

Another gasp. Starting as a hiss, it deepened into an agonized moan.

The wind keened in sympathy as it gained strength and swept across the forest floor, banishing the last of the mist, revealing the woman. Branwyn huddled in a nook by the roots of a fallen tree, the velvety cloak that she wore not quite hiding her swollen figure.

Distant, excited baying drifted toward her hiding place. She froze, her hands shaking as if palsied. The hounds had picked up her scent again. They weren't fooled by the illusions she'd created to hide herself.

Death was coming for her.

She clenched her teeth as yet another cramp ripped through her midsection. When it passed, she stood. Aware the baying had grown louder, she stumbled forward, lurching between the ancient boulders, breaking the spider web into a hundred dewy filaments. She still clutched the faint hope of escape to her heaving breast.

The pain ebbed and released her from its cruel embrace. Knowing that it was but a brief respite, she ran faster yet, weaving between gnarled tree stumps and treacherous, exposed roots. Brambles ripped the hood from her head, and pulled her elegantly coifed hair into a tangled mass of brown.

Branwyn stopped and gauged the distance between her and the hounds that chased her. A few leagues of hills and trees separated them, muffling their baying. Panic began to eat away at the self-control she normally took pride in, and she scanned the trees for a place to birth the babe, for her druid's wisdom warned that her time would be upon her in a moment.

A stream gurgled toward the north. She limped toward it as another cramp began to build, this one the fiercest yet. Waves of pain crashed over her as she collapsed by the stream, her body arching in silent torment. Her eyes were shut tight, her skin flushed hot as she struggled to draw air into seared lungs. The cloak fell back, revealing legs that writhed as she dug her heels into the sandy dirt beneath her.

Exhausted, she pulled her knees up and screamed, the sound an animal grunt of rage and terror—rage over what she was going to lose, terror of the hounds that craved her blood.

The hounds' throaty bellowing also stopped for a moment, but Branwyn gave it little thought. Her trembling legs heaved one final time as she felt the child slide from her, its bony shoulders ripping skin that could stretch no more.

The babe was born.

Lying back against the sodden earth, she heaved a relieved sigh. The infant squalled on her chest, a girl, incredibly frail and small, brought into the world too early. Love, mingled with aching sadness, softened her green eyes as she gazed at the babe. Then, her hands shaking, she tied off the umbilical cord and wrapped the infant in her cloak.

"You will never know me, but understand this," she whispered urgently into one tiny ear. "Even though I hold you for but a moment, I've already loved you a lifetime's worth."

Groaning, she hauled herself to her feet, and stood on legs that nearly crumbled beneath her. More precious time passed as she leaned against a fallen tree, the small bundle held securely in her arms. Her lips twisted into a grim line as she tried to find the strength to continue.

The child squirmed within the cloak, seeking the warmth of her mother's body. But she made not a sound as Branwyn again began to stumble along the stream.

With frightening speed, eager baying now a scant league away broke the stillness that had descended upon the forest. As darkness chased away the last rays of sunlight, Branwyn realized she couldn't elude the hounds much longer. Even so, a bolt of resolve shot through her and she vowed that the infant she'd borne would escape her own fate.

The rippling water next to her reflected a desperate silhouette as she veered from the stream and plunged through a clearing in the forest, trampling tufts of grass beneath her feet. As she ran, she searched the surrounding wood for a nook small enough to hide her child. But when a bevy of geese behind a distant hill took flight, she paused and listened.

Chirping. A bird, perhaps.

Creaking. A tree fighting the effects of wind and age.

She examined the forest edge. Nothing moved.

Had she escaped them?

Listened.

Waited.

Still nothing.

Crash! The hounds charged in an explosion of

sound, heedlessly lunging through the forest undergrowth, almost within view.

The feel of her baby snuggled against her gave her the strength she needed. Oblivious to the trickle of blood that stained her underskirt, she ran out of the clearing, into the field beyond, and almost slammed into a fence. A wooden fence. It bore the mark of the holding it protected—the holding where Gwynllian lived. She was close, so close.

But her ears told her that she wasn't close enough. She collapsed against a fence post, her heart squeezed by hopeless fear. With halting movements, she slipped a necklace bearing a sparkling scarlet egg over her head and dropped it into the folds covering the babe. Then, after lingering a few last moments, she hid the bundle in the green boughs of an oak tree. As she concealed her baby, the pendant slipped from the covers and fell into a nook at the oak's base. Branwyn crouched down to retrieve it, but it had wedged itself between two thick, gnarled roots.

Hounds bayed. They were coming closer.

"Keep her safe, mighty oak," she whispered, knowing she hadn't the time to pry her pendant away from the tree. In a final burst of energy, she hastened back into the forest. The infant mewled only once, very softly.

Deep inside, Branwyn knew there would be no last-second reprieve. Her movements were becoming jerky, uncoordinated, as the blood began to flow down her legs in a steady stream. And yet she staggered forward, lit by a fierce desire to put as much distance as possible between herself and the child she'd delivered.

She'd reached the limits of her body's strength, however. After one last look at the sun that observed her from its serene height, she collapsed. Not even the snuffling noises of the hounds following the trail of blood could prod her into greater effort.

"My baby," she whispered, and drifted into blackness.

Fervent howls roused her from her stupor. She opened her eyes and saw the hounds, their jaws impossibly wide, their eyes baleful with the glare of death. The druid houndmasters stood a few feet behind them, holding their beasts on leashes. The one closest to her prodded her midsection with his booted toe. His face betrayed grim satisfaction. In that moment, she realized he didn't know. He'd felt the afterbirth she'd yet to pass and thought the babe was still inside her.

She'd won.

A smile curved her lips upward.

The houndmaster nodded at his companions, and together, they unleashed their beasts.

Chapter
1

❧

London, England, 1826

Laughter pealed out through the darkened streets and alleys. It mingled with the low hum of conversation spilling out of the doors of the gaming houses and gentleman's clubs on Pall Mall, the Street of Palaces. Moonlight glittered upon three cloaked and hooded figures who slunk their way around the wrought iron fence surrounding St. James's Square, their cloaks flapping like bat's wings in the warm summer breeze. The two larger figures stumbled against each other, and the smallest one laughed again, the sound high, tinkling, at odds with its sinister appearance.

One of the larger figures drew the others against the fence and huddled with them. "Shh, Georgiana, before someone recognizes us. Neddy, you must shut up. You're making Georgie laugh."

Lady Darleigh opened her eyes wide and gave the cloaked man a pleading look, one that had never failed to bring him around. "I can't help myself, Rees. You look too ridiculous."

Rees Viscount Hammond scowled, no doubt trying to frighten her into quietness, but his mask blunted the effect and only made him appear silly. He was a highwayman this evening, complete with a black hat and brace of pistols—unloaded, of course. She fought off another bout of laughter.

"You had *better* help yourself, Georgie," he hissed. "If Brock discovers what we're up to, he'll forbid Neddy and I to see you again. And I, for one, have grown quite used to your company."

Despite the midsummer evening's warmth, Georgiana slung her arms around her two companions' shoulders and pulled them close against her. She'd almost forgotten about Brock, her dear husband. Damn Rees for reminding her. "All right, I'll behave."

A muffled snort emerged from Neddy. "For how long?"

"For as long as I need to," she informed him, then squelched more giggles.

Rees put a finger against her lips. "Georgiana . . ."

She released them both and pushed Rees's hand away. "I promise, no more laughter."

"Let's move on, can we?" Neddy asked. "I'm boiling in this cloak." He pulled at the strings near his throat, revealing a Harlequin costume beneath, white covered with black diamonds and glittering gold thread. In his free hand he held a hat in the style of Napoléon's, long and arched on top and decorated with gold braiding.

Unlike Neddy, Georgiana had little trouble with the heat this eve. Her costume, that of an Italian peasant woman, left her quite cool, no doubt due to the low-cut bodice and the way she'd dampened her single cambric petticoat. The dress clung lovingly to her every curve and made her feel quite daring, if not a little reckless. The stuffier patronesses of the *ton*, such as Lady Cowper, would no doubt faint dead away at the sight of her dressed thus, but Lady Cowper wouldn't dare set foot in Watier's Club, not on this night.

Her smile faltered. How forgiving would society prove of tonight's escapade? Did she even care if society forgave her? She wrapped her fingers around the egg-shaped pendant that dangled from her neck by a chain. Just touching its cool glass surface gave her confidence.

No, she didn't care.

His gaze settling on the pendant, Neddy shuddered. "That's an ugly piece, Georgie. Looks like a drop of blood. Don't think I've ever seen you wear it before."

"I found it in the bottom of my trunk, while rummaging through some old clothes. Thought it matched my costume rather well."

"It does at that. Make sure it finds its way back to the bottom of your trunk tomorrow."

Self-consciously Georgiana tucked the pendant

into her bodice, until only its chain showed. While just a young girl, she'd found it in a Welsh meadow, near the base of an oak tree. At the time, the pendant's strange appearance had captured her fancy and, afraid she'd have to surrender it to its proper owner, she'd kept quiet about her find. Through the years, she'd forgotten the pendant existed . . . until earlier this evening, of course.

She released the scarlet egg and smiled at Neddy. "You're uncommonly chivalrous tonight."

"I'm cranky because I'm hot."

"Take the deuced cloak off, then," Rees demanded.

"I can't." Neddy glanced meaningfully at the cloak's hem. "Georgie's stepping on it. If I remove it I'll sweep her off her feet."

"Not likely," she soberly informed him, and they both laughed, the sound cutting through the night like a whistle on a teapot.

Rees waved his arms. "Devil take it, you'll both be quiet or I'll chase you home."

"Ah, so we're horses, are we, to be herded into stables?" she asked, one eyebrow raised in mock censure.

Neddy took her cue. "Are you jockey or groomsman?"

A reluctant smile curved Rees's lips. Soon he was chuckling, too. "You two will be the death of me. If I wasn't so afraid for Georgie, I'd leave you here to fend for yourselves."

"You know how much we adore your company, Rees. If I had a brother, he would be just like you," she soothed.

She'd needed weeks to convince Rees to come with her and Neddy to the masquerade. Neddy had gleefully supported the idea when she'd first mentioned it. He knew how to enjoy himself. Rees, on the other hand, was too damned serious. He'd talked endlessly about the potential damage to their characters. No doubt Brock had chosen Rees to squire her around for exactly that reason. He'd hoped Rees would keep her out of trouble.

She linked her arms through Rees's and Neddy's. Their cloaks swirled around them as they hurried through St. James's Square, then turned onto Pall Mall, keeping to the shadows. As they walked, Georgiana looked up at the sky and saw the stars twinkling above her. They were a beautiful white, but cold and very far away, taunting her with the promise of the night. She turned away from them, unable to rid herself of a feeling that their outing this eve, while it seemed quite promising in terms of fun and adventure, would leave her equally unfulfilled.

As they passed a church fitted with alcoves and colored glass windows, a barn owl swooped above them and roosted in one of the alcoves. Strident cries, presumably from the prey gripped in its talons, accompanied its long, mournful hoots. The two men glanced at it and hurried on, not even slightly interested. London embraced all sorts of predators; the owl was simply one of the more honest, well-mannered ones.

Georgiana shivered, however. Her sense of impending change—perhaps not all for the good—grew sharper. Unwillingly she remembered the lessons that her Aunt Gwynllian had insisted she learn while growing up in Wales. According to her aunt, if an owl flew over one's head with prey in its grip, someone close would die soon.

She forced the superstitious thought away. Her aunt was full of such warnings and had drummed them into Georgiana at a young age. While other girls had learned to manage household accounts and embroider pretty flowers along the hems of their gowns, Georgiana had discovered the meaning behind a crow's caw and a salmon's insistence on swimming upstream.

Sometimes she wondered what her childhood would have been like if her true parents, Sir John Wesley and Lady Margaret, had survived the carriage accident that had nearly claimed her life, too. Then again, she ought to thank Sir Stanton and his sister Gwynllian for their charity and the love they'd shown her through the years. She could have ended up in an orphanage. Instead, Sir Stanton and Gwynllian had taken her in when she was just a baby, and she'd grown to love them as much as she might a mother and father.

Neddy tugged on her arm. "Come on, Georgie.

Stop looking at the church. You're too far gone to repent now. Watier's Club awaits us."

Rees paused to look back at them. "You're trembling. Is something wrong?"

Georgiana took Neddy's arm.

A frown crossed Rees's face. "Georgie?"

"I'm fine." She forced a smile. "Let's go."

Staying close behind her companions, she slipped down St. James's street and completed the walk to Watier's Club.

The date was July first, at the height of the season in London. The king had asked his royal chef, Jean-Baptiste Watier, to host a midnight masquerade for the nobility of England and their mistresses. Over a thousand guests were expected to attend. Since Watier had selected the dinner menu and the French chef Labourie had prepared the food, his guests would sup like royalty, enjoying various European delicacies the two gourmands had ordered from the Continent.

Still, Georgiana hadn't come for the dinner. Rather, the thought of mingling in these places where no husband ever took a wife sharpened her sense of fun. Since she'd married Brock, she'd made a study of insouciance and a habit of following an impulse to see where it led her. These qualities in another woman might have evoked the wrath of society's *grande dames*. But Brock's fortune and his position in society protected her, while her deliberate indifference and fair looks had inspired a crop of imitators. Despite her behavior, or perhaps because of it, she was accepted in every salon in London.

"Here we are," Neddy said unnecessarily.

Georgiana and her two companions drew to a halt. She took in the building with a wide, considering gaze.

Situated between two townhouses, Watier's Club stretched upward at least three stories high. Its windows were long, mullioned, and curtained with heavy drapes that blocked the view from the inside. No drapes, however, could mute the noise that echoed within its walls: laughter, merry shouts, and the lilting melody of a waltz played by an orchestral ensemble.

Carriages, many sporting noble crests, formed a long queue leading up to the door. Several footmen, dressed in spotless red uniforms sporting gold frogging, were handing masked peers and their Cyprian friends out of carriages. Torches and oil lamps cast shadows upon the aristocrats' faces.

Georgiana wondered how many of their wives thought them safely ensconced at White's, Brook's, or even Boodle's, cards in their hands as they enjoyed a civilized game of faro, as Brock often did. Would some of these gentlemen see through her disguise and blanch at the thought of Lady Darleigh rubbing shoulders with their mistresses? Quite possibly. Of all her capers with Rees and Neddy, tonight's was definitely the most outrageous. Word would likely find its way to Brock, and then she'd see if he finally remembered he had a wife.

Up until now, she'd carefully orchestrated her antics to annoy him without casting a blemish on the family name. Hers was a subtle game of revenge designed to spend the money he'd married her for and make him regret their union. But he never reacted visibly to the gossip she managed to spark. Instead, he treated her with a polite coolness which nearly drove her mad. She'd finally come to the point where she wanted him irritated, angered, even enraged. She wanted to hear him shout at her and call her names.

"By God, I hope we don't run into Brock inside," Rees muttered. "He'll have my head on a plate."

"Don't worry about him." Georgiana lifted her chin. "He may be my husband, but he doesn't know me well enough to recognize me behind this costume. We're safe."

A spark flickered in Rees's eyes. "I've always admired Brock, you know that. But will you permit me to say he's a fool?"

Georgiana shrugged. "Say what you like. I care not."

Neddy leaned in close to them. "What's all this whispering about?"

"We're whispering about an ogre," she muttered. Something inside her twisted at the thought of Brock attending Watier's midnight masquerade.

God knew her husband hadn't visited her bed since the first disastrous month after they'd married. Would he come here with his mistress? Did he even have a mistress?

She frowned. Let him come, alone or accompanied. She'd make sure he noticed the Italian peasant girl who charmed and danced with every man in the room. Perhaps she'd even interest him enough into inquiring about her, with the possibility of making her his mistress. How delightful it would be, to reveal to him that the Italian peasant girl was none other than his very own wife, innocent once but now the toast of the *haut ton*.

"Let's not talk about ogres," Neddy pleaded. "They have a habit of spoiling one's night. Instead, let's mingle our way into Watier's, so I might relieve myself of this blasted cloak."

"Agreed." Rees steered them both toward the door, nodding at the footmen who guarded the entrance. He whispered discreetly in one man's ear. Pound notes exchanged hands. A smiling footman waved them in.

The Marquess of Darleigh glanced lazily at his cards, then at the pile of guineas at his elbow. They were playing for small stakes at the moment, but the night hadn't really started yet. The true gambling at White's began well after midnight, when fools lost whole estates and sharps won them.

He stretched in his leather side chair, his gaze

settling on his gaming partner and good friend Lord Carlisle. Perfectly sober, the man rarely overindulged, preferring to follow his wife's edicts rather than his own whims.

He glanced at the other men around the gaming table. The Honorable Matthew Williams had a glint in his gaze that suggested a certain familiarity with the game. Well-known as a plunderer of women, he'd brushed his brown hair into one of the most recent styles and wore collar points so high he could barely turn his head. While Brock found Williams's predilections wholly disreputable, he at least understood them.

Carlisle, on the other hand, had fallen in love with his wife, married her even though she hadn't a sou to her name, and remained utterly faithful. He was an oddball, forgoing many of the pleasures London had to offer in favor of a passel of screaming children. And while Carlisle's marriage had brought him neither prestige or wealth, the man seemed happy.

Brock glanced at the two peers of the realm who rounded out the fivesome. Their eyelids drooped, presumably with boredom. Brock compared his large pile of guineas to their small ones and decided if he'd lost that easily he'd be far from bored. Panicked, more likely. His father had squandered the family fortune while gambling and departed the earth a few days after Brock uncovered his debts, while his mother had a softness of the mind and required expensive doctors. In short, money troubles had dogged Brock from the moment he'd inherited the Darleigh estate. Now he played for small stakes only.

"Damn it, Brock, you've got the devil's own luck in faro," Williams said as they all threw down their cards.

Brock shrugged and moved guineas over to his pile of winnings. "I watch the cards very carefully."

Carlisle smiled. "Thank God we're playing for guineas."

"You also have the devil's luck with women," the brown-haired man continued, with a sly wink toward Brock. "I heard about the gathering in your wife's salon last week. It's said that a visiting Russian duke spent almost an hour persuading her to return to Russia with him."

His eyebrows lifting in an expression of mild disdain, Brock studied Williams. "And did she go?"

The other men barked with laughter.

When the chuckling died down, Williams picked up a brandy snifter and downed its contents in a single gulp. "If she were my wife, I wouldn't allow her such a long leash."

Brock frowned. "I have no wish to discuss my private life with you, Mr. Williams, nor have I any interest in your opinion."

"Really, Williams, I think you've had too much to drink," Carlisle observed, his blue eyes growing cool.

Brock felt a sour turning in his gut. He didn't want to talk about Georgiana. He didn't even want to think about her. Perversely, an image of her formed in his mind. Beautiful green eyes that held nothing but contempt for him, pink lips that curled with scorn . . . Georgiana didn't like him much. One might even say she hated him.

He pushed the chair backward with a scraping sound and stood. "I believe I'm finished for the night, gentlemen. Had a damned trying day."

"Glad you're leaving, old boy. Now the rest of us have a chance," one of the bored-looking gamblers quipped.

The men dissolved into another round of laughter.

Carlisle lifted a snifter half-filled with ruby liquid. "Have a brandy with me, Brock, before you go."

Brock thought of his cold bed in Palmer House and decided a brandy before leaving would suit him quite well. Perhaps he'd even detour to Figg's Pugilism Academy in Haymarket, and have a couple of go-rounds with the bag before he went home. He nodded his farewell toward the others, then followed Carlisle to a pair of secluded armchairs facing the window.

Carlisle slouched into an armchair, his cravat askew, his black hair ruffled, the very picture of gentlemanly exhaustion. "How is Georgiana?"

"Well enough."

"Is she attending Lady Capshaw's Ball?"

"I'm not certain."

Carlisle groaned and pulled at his collar. "For the last week, my wife's sisters have talked of nothing else. Planned out the evening's wardrobe a month ago, by God. Byron's reading one of his new sonnets and they're excited to think he might have written about one of them."

Brock accepted a snifter from a footman and sipped some brandy. It created a soothing path of warmth down to his stomach and made his regret easier to bear. Unlike Carlisle, he had the ordinary aristocratic marriage—one of convenience—with a woman who lived a life separate from his, although for some time now, he'd been wishing her life wasn't quite so separate.

"I don't keep account of her amusements." He slanted a curious glance at his companion. "Why this sudden interest in my wife?"

Carlisle looked at him, something hidden in his blue eyes. He opened his mouth to speak, then evidently thought the better of it and shrugged. "My sisters were looking forward to chatting with her."

"If she'll stand still long enough to chat," Brock added.

Georgiana, he thought, had a habit of running off from one scrape to another. If he weren't feeling so damned guilty, he would have taken her in hand a long time ago. But memories of her tears and her temporary decline after she'd discovered the true reason he'd married her left him willing to tolerate some very bad behavior indeed.

To keep the family afloat, Brock had gone to Almack's two years ago to find an eligible debutante with a hefty dowry. Taken with Georgiana's large green eyes and the even larger annuity that Sir Stanton, her guardian, had settled upon her, he'd courted and married her within a few months.

Their marriage had seemed a good deal for all concerned. He'd saved the family estate while Georgiana, an orphan without relatives or any real prospects, became Lady Darleigh. Inexplicably, however, Georgiana had wanted more than a noble title out of marriage. She'd wanted love.

A few weeks after their wedding ceremony, she'd overheard a conversation between himself and Carlisle, in which he'd admitted the reasons behind his courtship included affection, but not love. The knowledge had crushed her.

For weeks he'd listened to her sobbing at night and hated himself. He didn't blame her for forbidding him to enter her bedchamber; rather, he blamed himself for trifling with her affections. He should have realized she was too young and countrified to have an understanding of society's ways.

"My wife will no doubt appear at Lady Capshaw's tonight, as well as at a dozen other places," Brock muttered. "We receive so many invitations I can scarce find my mail beneath stacks of scented parchment."

"I'll wager Byron's new sonnet will include Georgiana in some way. She is a spirited piece, if you'll pardon me for saying so."

"I know far too well."

Carlisle's mouth drooped with male commiseration.

Brock took another swig of brandy, thinking back to the weeks following their marriage ceremony. After the shock of the truth had worn off, he'd thought Georgiana would retire to the country to curse him, and the society he represented, in private. Instead, she'd devised a more Machiavellian torture for him. She'd blossomed into a lovely creature capable of trading barbs with the most cynical member of the *ton*, a sultry woman who somehow still retained a charming air of innocence, a wife he could never touch.

He hadn't seen it at first, damn it, that smoldering look of hers which disarmed all who came within ten feet of her. Her large green eyes and pale complexion, offset by full, sensuous lips colored a delicate pink, made a devastating impression on every man she met. Charming, elegant, she became sought after by every society matron and surrounded by gentlemen who curried her favor.

By then she would have nothing to do with him. Worried that she might take a lover, he'd asked his cousin Rees to squire her around. He could trust Rees. He'd known the lad from childhood. Rees would watch her and keep her safe. Still, it irked him that Rees could enjoy his wife's company on a daily basis while he slept in a cold, lonely bed each night.

He placed his snifter on a side table with more force than necessary. "Christ, what a day I've had."

"You sound in need of amusement," Carlisle observed. "Come with me to Watier's Club for a visit. Jean-Baptiste is holding a masquerade for peers and their mistresses. We'll see who has become available."

Brock regarded Carlisle with wide eyes. "Pardon me? Did I hear aright?"

The other man sat straighter and assumed an injured expression. "You did. I'm suggesting a visit to Watier's Club."

"For what? Don't tell me you wish to find a mistress."

"Perhaps I do."

Brock couldn't prevent a bark of laughter. "What would Harriet say, do you suppose?"

An answering grin flashed across Carlisle's face. "She'd pack my bags and tell me to go."

"Then why in God's name do you wish to go to Watier's Club tonight, of all nights?"

Carlisle didn't reply. His smile faded. A minute or so passed in which he obviously struggled for words.

"If you aren't visiting for your own benefit," Brock said, "then I must assume you've suggested the trip for my sake. I assure you, man, I do not need you to play the pimp for me."

Silence continued to lie heavily between them. Brock shifted on his chair. "Do you have something to tell me?"

"Obviously you don't know."

"Know what?"

"It's rumored that Georgiana will appear at Watier's Club tonight."

Brock sat forward. "*What?*"

Carlisle looked uneasy. "So say the gossip mongers."

"Who's been gossiping?"

"Lord Watkins, the young heir to the Stanhope title. A friend of mine heard him talking about her at Boodle's, after downing a few whiskeys. He boasted about escorting Lady Darleigh to Watier's Club on masquerade night."

Brock felt a tightening sensation in his gut, like a fist closing. Momentarily bereft of words, he stared at his friend.

Eyebrow raised, Carlisle broke into the lengthening silence. "Are you going to ignore this latest intrigue, too?"

"I have never ignored Georgiana," Brock managed.

"From my perspective, you seem to ignore her quite often, even if you *are* generous."

"I'm not ignoring her, Carlisle. I've allowed her freedom. It's the least I could do after all the pain I've caused her."

Brock saw the incomprehension in Carlisle's

eyes and knew he would never understand. How could he? He hadn't lived two years as Georgiana's husband.

Early in their marriage, Georgiana had begun testing his limits and hadn't stopped since. She purchased the most expensive fabrics she could find from *Swan & Edgar*, and had them sewn into creations that set his account back for months. She hosted gatherings in her salon once a week and filled her guests' glasses with an unending supply of the finest champagne. Only the finest jewels graced her ears and neck.

Even though he could scarce afford it, Brock paid each of her debts without a murmur. He could deny her nothing, not after having listened to her sobbing for weeks on end. Indeed, he remembered the day she'd truly come into her own. At a soirée, two young bucks had offered her different seats at the same time. When she avoided choosing one over the other, they'd resolved to settle the matter with pistols. Both had come away from the field wounded. While the *ton* agreed Georgiana's behavior remained above reproach, the incident had added to her reputation as a seductress and elevated her to the ranks of an Incomparable.

"Who is this Lord Watkins?" Brock demanded.

"They call him 'Neddy.' "

"I've heard of him once or twice from my cousin Rees," Brock admitted, the fist in him loosening only a bit. "He'd seemed harmless enough by

Rees's account. But I must admit, now I'm wondering. Why in God's name would Rees bring Georgiana to Watier's Club on such a night?"

"Perhaps the escapade wasn't Lord Hammond's idea."

"Do you suppose this Neddy fellow suggested it?"

Carlisle shrugged.

Brock stared at him. "You don't mean to say Georgiana is behind it."

After a slight hesitation, Carlisle nodded. "According to Lord Watkins, she demanded they escort her there."

"What devil has gotten into her? You don't attend the mistress masquerade unless you're planning to take a—" Brock broke off, outrage coiling through him. "She's going to take a lover, isn't she?"

"I don't know."

He stood, sending his chair backward with a harsh scraping noise. "I can only think of one reason for her to attend, and I won't have another man's bastard inheriting the Darleigh estate."

"Bring her in line," Carlisle urged. "It's high time."

"Indeed. We'll have to pay a visit to Watier's Club after all."

This time, Georgiana had gone too far.

Chapter
2

❧

Georgiana and her two companions paused in the vestibule and handed their black silk cloaks to a footman. She cast a proud look at Rees, whose highwayman costume set off his blond good looks, and then at Neddy, whose white harlequin costume with the black diamonds perfectly reflected his amusing nature. Rees caught her look and clasped her arm in his, while Neddy jammed his Napoléon hat on his head, then muttered some nonsense in her ear that made her laugh.

The vestibule opened onto a glittering ballroom dominated by a table nearly one hundred feet long. Georgiana gazed at the dark green panels of velvet covering the walls and the golden embroidered *fleurs-de-lys* that conducted a stately march up and down the heavy emerald draperies. Gold fringes and tassels hung from every conceivable location and chandeliers sporting hundreds of candles cast a lambent glow upon the hordes of merrymakers.

The scents of wine and expensive perfume filled the air. She drew in the intoxicating fragrance and felt excitement catch at her.

"Jean-Baptiste has decided upon a fruit theme," Neddy murmured, indicating the piles of apples, peaches, cherries, and apricots which tumbled in artful abandon in the center of the table.

She eyed the overflowing bodices of the Marie-Antoinettes and the Cleopatras and the gypsy girls. "I find a fruit theme wholly appropriate, don't you?"

He chuckled. "You are wicked, Georgie."

"Not wicked, just regrettably cynical."

Neddy and Rees at her side, she smiled and advanced into the room, searching all the while for a tall, powerful man with dark brown hair. People pressed in on her from all sides, enjoying conversation and Jean-Baptiste's splendid hors d'oeuvres. She didn't recognize her husband among the pirates, Spanish soldiers, and myriads of other costumes which disguised society's finest gentlemen.

Mixed emotions coursed through her. Part of her wished to see him here, so she might defy him to his face and finally draw a reaction from him. Another part was glad he hadn't come. He would only attend for one reason—to find a mistress—and she didn't like the idea of Brock sharing another woman's bed. She fully admitted to herself that she wasn't done with him yet.

In the two years since they'd married, she'd used every trick she could think of to make Brock notice her. She wanted him to acknowledge her, and admire her, and love her as he'd once pretended to do. Once his heart was in her hands, she could do whatever she fancied to it. Only then would the scales of justice sway into balance.

So far, however, her plan had fallen flat. She would have preferred anything to Brock's neglect. Rees, and not Brock, chaperoned her and carried her packages and lent her money when she lost at the gaming tables. He entertained her and flattered her and kept her busy, freeing Brock to run his estate. It was the worst insult he could have dealt her.

Georgiana waded into the crowd, her two courtiers at her side. She deduced the identity of several of the men—and some of the women— despite their costumes. Who could fail to recognize the Duke of Argyll, trailing as he was after Harriet Wilson, his part-time mistress? Henry Brougham, Lord Worcester, Sir William Knighton, the Duke of Wellington—they'd all come with ladyloves whose names were more prominent than those of many noblewomen.

Even the Duke of Gloucester had deigned to attend, his cold blue gaze restlessly surveying the crowd. During the last twenty years he'd reclaimed his vast Lancastrian estates and his English heritage, and had positioned himself firmly with

George IV. Normally the duke appeared at state
functions only, much to polite society's relief. One
of the king's closest advisors, he had a network of
spies more complicated than Napoléon's and ruthlessly disposed of anyone who opposed his policies.

Georgiana found him most unpleasant.

She noticed the duke's gaze lock onto a robed
figure. She felt a surge of sympathy for the robed
man . . . trouble had just discovered him. The hood
over the man's head concealed his features, making
identification impossible; she wouldn't be able to
warn him later of the duke's interest, even if she
wished to. Georgiana studied the wooden staff the
robed man held and the green pendant hanging
from his neck, similar to hers in all but color. Was he
from Wales also?

Neddy and Rees stopped near an alcove, presumably to better observe the crowd. Georgiana
took up post near them.

"Do you know who that robed man is?" she asked
them in a whisper, nodding toward the figure.

"Not that I can say," Rees admitted. "Why?"

"The Duke of Gloucester is staring at him with a
fixed expression. I believe the robed man is
doomed."

"I'm surprised to see the duke at all," Rees murmured. "He rarely attends anything but state recep-
tions."

"Obviously Watier's Club holds something to
interest the duke this evening, and I'm certain it

isn't the thought of gaining a mistress." Georgiana shivered. "Someone ought to warn that poor man."

Neddy shook his head. "I recommend forgetting you've seen anything untoward, unless you want a stay at the Tower."

"The Tower isn't used for prisoners anymore," Georgiana chided.

"Ah, but they say the duke still uses those dungeons . . . secretly, of course."

"You're trying to frighten me," she accused.

A wicked grin curled Neddy's lips. "Only so you might run into my arms for comfort."

She tapped him lightly on the arm with her fan. "I'd likely run the other way."

Neddy returned his attention to the robed figure. "Who do you suppose he's pretending to be?"

Rees leaned close and murmured, "I've seen paintings of Merlin, dressed in similar garb, in the British Museum."

"So?"

"Our man's wearing druid's robes."

Eyebrow raised, Neddy clearly remained unimpressed.

"Haven't you read the tales of King Arthur?" Rees demanded.

"No, and I don't care to hear them." Neddy slung an arm around Georgiana's shoulders. "To the devil with King Arthur, the Duke of Gloucester, and all men wearing robes. Let's dance, Georgie."

"My pleasure." Laughing, Georgiana allowed

Neddy to sweep her onto the dance floor. They whirled around with great abandon, to the tune of a waltz, her peasant skirts flying up to reveal her calves and her hair swinging around her, unbound. The large golden earring she'd hooked in one ear brushed against her cheek and her breasts surged against her neckline as she fought for air. Neddy was a spirited dancer indeed.

A moment later, she caught the gleam in his eyes, and quickly decided the evening would have to be an early one. While Rees remained naught but a brother to her in manner, Neddy sometimes made her wonder. Young, impressionable, and idealistic, he was at the perfect age to fall hopelessly in love. She ought to know well enough. Hadn't she done the same thing, then suffered for it ever since?

"Neddy, stop," she pleaded. "I'm thirsty and tired. Leave me off at Rees's side and go find yourself someone more lively."

He pouted, but followed her instructions nevertheless and steered her toward the edge of the floor. "Nonsense. You're more lively than all of us. Do you recall Byron's poem about you? 'Her dizzying charm so overwhelmed that she made more beautiful women seem plain.' "

Georgiana sighed. "Of course I remember. How like Lord Byron to kiss one cheek and slap the other."

Brow quirked, Neddy moved aside as Rees joined them. "You're less than pleased with the poem?"

"Neddy, he is saying that my charm makes up for my lack of beauty."

Rees smiled. "When Lord Byron wrote your sonnet, Georgie, he had eyes for no one but Caroline Lamb. All women paled in comparison."

She shrugged and fanned herself with a black lace fan. Lord Byron's opinion held little interest for her. She was simply out to annoy Brock, nothing more.

Rees and Neddy continued to hover near her side. A bewhiskered old gentleman whose eyes glittered with lust behind his pink mask strolled past her, his gaze fixed on her bosom. Georgiana fought the urge to shield herself with her hands. She focused on the dance floor and watched Lord Worcester fondle a blond shepherdess's backside. She looked away, only to see a portly woman shifting her bulk around the table, stuffing *pots de crème* into her mouth.

Distaste stirred inside her. She frowned.

A tall man in a clown costume sauntered by with a woman on either arm. When he saw Georgiana's frown, he stopped and affected a courtly bow without letting go of his companions. The women, both dressed as doves in costumes of white feathers, wore hats topped by a long white plume. As the clown dragged them downward into similar bows, one of the feathers poked Georgiana in the eye.

She blinked and took a step backward, her nose twitching with the smell of whiskey. The trio fairly reeked of it. "Move on," she muttered, not really caring if she appeared churlish. The whole scene was beginning to feel very tawdry.

"Oh, sweet peasant," the man slurred, "I see by your Friday face that you are in a very poor mood. Has no one offered for you yet?"

"I'm not available."

"Come with us, then," he enjoined, appearing to have not heard her. "I have Mrs. Bang on my right, and she likes it Frenchified, and I've the dutchess on my left, who likes it with her pattens on." He slipped a monocle from his pocket, placed it in his eye, and observed her face for but a moment before he blatantly examined her bosom. "How about you?"

"I wouldn't like it at all, queernabs. Move along."

He sniffed. "A whore with airs. How very . . . tedious." Accompanied by the doves' snide laughter, the clown walked away.

Georgiana's stomach clenched as his words penetrated. Tonight she had really outdone herself. She had stooped to a level so low that even her Aunt Gwynllian wouldn't recognize her. And for what? To annoy Brock?

Suddenly the laughter seemed far too shrill, the wine on the edge of vinegar, the partygoers denizens of some sexual purgatory. She looked around at the pawing hands and barely covered bosoms and thought, *I've made myself one of them.*

She stood right in the thick of it, dressed as scantily as the rest.

A sinking feeling began in the pit of her stomach and ended in her toes. She hadn't become this person in just one night. It had taken two long years of excess. Once she'd been an innocent girl who lived in the Welsh woodlands. Now she was a woman who accepted praise as her due, one with a jaded wit and hardened heart. She imagined the ghost of the girl she used to be looking at the Georgiana she'd become and felt ashamed.

Rees tried to press a glass of ratafia in her hand. "A drink, Georgie?"

She waved it away. "No, thank you."

Neddy put his arm through hers. "Dance with me, then."

"I believe I'm quite through with dancing."

They both stared at her, their eyebrows drawn together.

"Are you going sour on us?" Neddy asked.

"Don't allow this talk about Byron to turn your mood," Rees quickly followed up.

Georgiana returned their stares. They thought she was sulking because Byron hadn't adequately praised her beauty. By God, she didn't give a fig what Byron said about her. Did they truly consider her that shallow?

"How ridiculous you both are," she said, striving for an even tone when inside she wanted to find fresh air and turn her face to the stars.

"Why not join me at the gaming table?" Neddy pleaded.

"I don't want to play cards, Neddy. Indeed, I'm finding myself a bit overwhelmed by all of these finely-dressed people. Off with you, Neddy. You too, Rees. Allow me some time to myself. When you return, I promise my mood will have improved."

"You won't go running off on us," Rees said. "You'll stay right here and rest."

Georgiana pointed to a chair by the wall. "I'll sit in that very seat until you return."

Rees frowned. Neddy examined her with narrowed eyes. Clearly uncomfortable, yet propelled by her determined expression, they moved off into the crowd.

Hand pressed against her temple, Georgiana swiped a glass of champagne from a passing footman and made for the chair she'd promised to sit in. As she turned to sit down, she saw *her*—the woman she'd so recently met but would rather not acknowledge—reflected in a large, gilt-framed mirror. Her hair was the same rich brown as Georgiana's, and many would consider the oval face fetching.

Still, tiny lines pinched the corners of her mouth, and her lips were pressed together in a hard line. Sadness and betrayal had dulled the spark in her green eyes. She looked like a woman who'd been locked in a stone cell, forever peering out at the sunlight through the bars but unable to feel it on her face.

Georgiana sank into the chair and rubbed her temples. Memories of her childhood pressed in on her, days spent in the meadows and fields of Wales with Aunt Gwynllian. They'd wandered through meadows hazy with sunshine, watching the birds fly and the mice skitter through the grass, and Georgiana had been at peace with herself and the world around her. In those long, lazy days her aunt had taught her how to truly *know* something . . . how to develop an awareness beyond sight and sound and touch, a oneness rooted in love of all things.

That oneness now seemed no more real than a pleasant dream.

Georgiana dragged her attention from the mirror. A drowsy sort of desperation filled her. She'd become someone she didn't know and she hadn't the slightest idea what to do about it. Aunt Gwynllian had always eased the crises of her youth, those moments that now felt silly when she thought about them but at the time had seemed momentous. Still, her aunt was almost two hundred miles away, in Wales. A rush of longing swept through her, to hear Gwynllian's melodic voice, to listen to the wisdom of her words.

Her gaze unfocused, she stared across the dance floor, trying to block it all out. She saw not the partygoers but the shimmer of air around them, heard not their voices but the vibrations their words created.

Her eyes fluttered closed.

The shimmering air and vibrations became a fog of unformed patterns in her mind. She noticed that the fog had a faintly buzzing sound, like a hive of bees. She'd heard the sound before in her dreams, and didn't like it much. It seemed filled with tumult and confusion, and hovered just on the edge of blatant anarchy. Was the sound a reflection of her own inner turmoil? Or of impending madness? She didn't know.

Suddenly it became very important to her to replace that ugly buzz with something beautiful, someone who had brought her happiness. She focused on the mindless whirling of the fog and, in her desperation, molded it into an image of her aunt. A faint pressure built behind her temples.

Slowly, her aunt emerged in her mind. Georgiana relaxed in response. She felt Gwynllian's presence all around her, comforting her. Indeed, she'd never quite realized how much she missed her aunt and the simpler life she represented until this moment.

Guided by some deeply-buried instinct, Georgiana opened eyes moist with unshed tears. Eagerly she focused on the dark green walls and chandeliers of glittering crystal which shone on a hundred laughing faces. There, amidst those faces, one more dear to her than any other stared back at her, the gray eyes wise and filled with love, the brown hair framing a heart-shaped face.

Her heart took a giant leap in her chest. Joy surged through her, tempered by confusion.

Aunt Gwynllian was here. But how?

Hungrily Georgiana took in the details of her aunt's appearance. Gwynllian didn't appear a moment older than the day Georgiana had left Wales for London. Her skin still had that fine, porcelainlike appearance and a rose blush colored her cheeks. Dressed in a round gown sporting distinctive Welsh embroidery, her aunt seemed to have stepped right from her home in Wales, Cadair Abbey.

Georgiana stood up from the chair. In the back of her mind, she still felt that sense of pressure. She could still hear an angry buzz that had smoothed out into pleasing vibrations. And as she stared at Aunt Gwynllian, another odd effect took hold of her: interspersed with her regular vision, she saw flashes of the ballroom from a different perspective.

She seemed to be seeing through Gwynllian's eyes.

She took a step toward her aunt, then faltered. She blinked once, twice. What was wrong with her vision? Could she be imagining her aunt? She must have fallen asleep in her little chair, and surrendered to a dream of her dearest wish.

Then why did her aunt look so incredibly real?

She pressed her hand against a nearby column and steadied herself while her mind fought to grasp the situation. Gwynllian's appearance made no sense at all. What in God's name was her aunt doing here, at Watier's Club? Georgiana knew

Gwynllian couldn't possibly approve of her presence at the masquerade. Why wasn't Gwynllian advancing on her, with the intent to tell her exactly what a muddle she'd made of her life?

At that moment, her aunt beckoned her with an outstretched hand.

Georgiana tilted her head and stared. Suddenly, she saw herself for a moment, through Gwynllian's eyes. Disoriented, she clutched the back of a chair and waited for her vision to right itself. She focused again on Gwynllian.

Her aunt's beckoning motion, she thought, was too slow, almost dreamlike. In any case, the Gwynllian she knew didn't beckon. A sudden fear for her aunt grabbed hold of her, along with the sense that what she was seeing right now wasn't her aunt but a shade of the woman she'd been.

Georgiana felt something constrict in her chest, preventing her ability to breathe.

The man dressed as a druid approached Gwynllian and began to talk to her. Georgiana looked at him, and abruptly he was directly in front of her, giving her a view of a youthful face topped with blond hair. Again, she was seeing through the shade's eyes. She blinked. Her sight returned to normal.

She wasn't certain if she'd really seen the youth's face. If he truly did exist, who was he—some aristocrat's son trying to find his first mistress? Whatever the case, she found some comfort in the druid's actions; if he saw Gwynllian too, then she, Georgiana, wasn't hallucinating.

Her aunt evidently found nothing comforting or even slightly interesting in the druid. She dismissed him and lifted her hand, still beckoning Georgiana over, her lips abruptly curling into a frown.

Almost of their own volition, Georgiana's feet moved her forward. Out of the corner of her eye, she noticed that the Duke of Gloucester was staring at her aunt too. His expression arrested, he looked as if he'd frozen solid.

Fear chased through her. She felt caught in the grip of something beyond herself and didn't know what to do about it. Indeed, there was something sinister about her aunt now. Even the shade of Gwynllian wouldn't act this way. Nevertheless, she couldn't stop herself from approaching. The child in her recognized her aunt's authority and obeyed. She pushed past another harlequin and maneuvered around Queen Mary's skirts, her gaze fixed on her aunt.

Flashes of the ballroom from Gwynllian's perspective made her dizzy. She picked her way carefully through the ballroom, thinking that she could very well be going mad, then paused.

Something was happening to her aunt.

Gwynllian had grown hazy; the proportions of her figure had become distorted. Her edges thinned into a swirl of pretty colors, like the gauzy scarves of harem women. It was, Georgiana thought, like looking at someone through water.

Again she wondered if her eyes had deceived her.

Perhaps she needed spectacles.

Squinting, she realized that she could see a crowd of laughing people behind her aunt. Spectacles wouldn't fix *that* problem. Nor would it fix the different perspectives of the ballroom that continued to appear in her mind's eye, although they'd grown similarly fuzzy. In fact, the pleasant vibrations had begun to fall apart into the ugly buzz again.

Her fear intensified. That thing across the room, she suddenly thought, wasn't her aunt. Gwynllian wasn't dead, either. There had to be another explanation. Hand pressed against her chest, she drew in a shuddering breath.

Growing less solid by the second, the shade continued to beckon. Then, with the abruptness of a curtain coming down at the end of a theatrical production, it winked out. At the same moment, Georgiana felt an easing of the pressure in her mind. The buzz disappeared, along with the odd sense that she was seeing through Gwynllian's eyes.

The druid who had paused to talk to her aunt blinked a couple of times. Clearly the shade's disappearance had surprised him, too. The Duke of Gloucester, for his part, began to walk toward the druid, but in the manner of someone who didn't wish to be noticed.

Chilled, Georgiana backed away. She plopped back into her chair and stared at the place where her aunt had stood. Abruptly she felt a warm spot of skin between her breasts. The glass pendant, she realized, had grown almost hot. She lifted the pendant, her fingers trembling, and examined it from all angles. It didn't look any different, but it certainly *felt* different. She reasoned that her skin must have warmed it. Aware that the explanation didn't quite fit, because the damned thing was hot, not warm, she allowed it to drop against her skin again.

Despite her turmoil, a yawn crept up on her. Surprised, Georgiana let it run its course. After closing her mouth and checking to see if anyone had observed her, she wondered how she could feel tired after such an experience. Regardless, she *did* feel tired. Exhausted, in fact.

Frowning, she fought off another insistent yawn. She could explain the strange lethargy that had stolen through her no more easily than the pendant's odd behavior or her aunt's unexpected appearance. A more superstitious person might ascribe the events to unearthly intervention, but Georgiana wasn't the type to believe in ghosts. While her upbringing in Wales had been rather unorthodox, her aunt had never encouraged her to practice witchcraft or anything of a similar sort. And Georgiana bristled at the notion that Gwynllian had died and visited her in spiritual form. She would know if her aunt had died, despite the miles and years that separated them.

She would *know*.

Across the room, on the other side of the dance floor, the druid turned to face her, his white robe swirling with the motion. Even though she couldn't see his countenance, she had a feeling that the figure was watching her. People jostled him left and right, but he always turned so the black oval in his hood, where his face ought to be, pointed her way.

The skin on the back of her neck prickled. In another moment, she knew he'd begin to walk toward her, perhaps with a desire to converse with her. *Go away*, she wanted to tell him. If he came to her, he'd bring the Duke of Gloucester with him, and those who had even an ounce of sense knew enough to stay clear of the duke.

He continued to stare. She returned his gaze, trying to gather the energy to bolt into the crowd should he actually start toward her. Just when she felt certain he would walk in her direction, however, he turned and strode hurriedly to the front door. She watched him go with a heartfelt sigh and risked a glance at the duke.

The silver-haired man wore a heavy frown.

Counting herself lucky to have avoided a court intrigue involving the duke, she watched the aristocrat walk toward the entrance to Watier's Club, presumably chasing after the druid.

At the door, he brushed past two men who had just arrived. One of the men was Lord Carlisle,

Brock's closest friend. Georgiana recognized him with a start. Carlisle, at a demimonde masquerade? She couldn't believe it. Carlisle had told her many times he loved his wife, securing her loyalty and helpless jealousy of his situation. Even though she wasn't married to him, she felt betrayed in some obscure way at seeing him here.

Frowning, she focused on the other man. Tall, powerfully built, his dark brown hair slightly longer than fashionable, he paused in the vestibule to survey the crowd. Gray hair peppered his temples and a tight smile curved his lips. He had eschewed costume and mask for a severe black coat and trousers.

Georgiana had no trouble identifying *him*. Her heart gave one painful, trapped thump before settling into a rapid beat. Was he here to find a mistress? Or had he come for her?

Brock took a few steps into the ballroom. Acquaintances paused to talk to him. He conversed politely, his dark gaze restlessly scanning the party-goers. When a courtesan dressed as Queen Mary took to the dance floor, Brock fixed his gaze on her. Georgiana noticed the courtesan had much the same size and build as herself. Abruptly, Queen Mary laughed at something her partner had said, and Brock immediately dismissed her.

All doubt fled her mind.

He knew she was here and had come for her.

Her moment had arrived.

Only now she wasn't certain she wanted this moment. In light of her new vision of herself, she realized that she had embarrassed herself as much as him. She'd much rather escape and come to terms with him in the privacy of Palmer House than suffer through a public confrontation.

She cast a flustered glance toward the last place she'd seen Rees and Neddy. Rees had his blond head bent toward a woman of considerable charms. She couldn't find Neddy. In any case, they were both too far away to help spirit her out of the building. She would have to leave on her own.

She emerged from her alcove and started toward the dance floor. The orchestra had struck up a merry tune. Couples twined through each other and hopped around as required by the country dance they were performing. Lower lip caught between her teeth, Georgiana assessed the couples who stood between her and the entrance. First they surged left, then they surged right, alternately opening and closing avenues of escape. She would have to wait for the right moment to dart between couples and speed across the floor to freedom.

Poised on the edge of the dance floor, she took a step forward, then stopped as she espied Brock's dark head on the other side of the dancers. She watched as a blond-haired courtesan staggered against him, then used the opportunity to flutter her lashes at him. He set her aright with rough indifference and turned in Georgiana's direction, his gaze passing by her once, then returning to her and settling on her with riveting intensity.

Their gazes clashed, and in his black eyes she saw carefully controlled rage. His smile became contemptuous. She swallowed and pressed a hand against a breast which suddenly felt far too naked. The threat of a public confrontation hanging over her head, she hurried along the edge of the ballroom toward the entrance, stumbling between a pirate and nun on the verge of embracing. She ignored their scowls and maneuvered around a very old woman dressed as a shepherdess.

Just as she nearly reached the entrance, Georgiana spotted him only five feet away, behind a group of men who assessed the charms of a dark-haired courtesan just as they might a particularly fine mare. He was staring at her again, his smile smooth and assured this time.

Chin held high, she waited for him to come to her.

"Playing the whore, are you, Georgiana?" he asked when he reached her. "Or are you *really* a whore?" He flicked a finger across the tops of her breasts, and lifted her pendant up to peer at it. His touch felt like fire.

Suddenly she had difficulty breathing. "That wasn't kind of you, Brock."

"I'm not in the mood to be kind," he snapped. "Indeed, I'm less than thrilled to discover my wife dressed like a Cyprian and mingling with London's most notorious demireps."

"Why do you suddenly care what I do?"

"You've never gone this far before. I won't stand for it."

Satisfaction cut through the misgivings she'd been feeling. She'd finally gotten beneath his skin! But a more sober part of her asked: at what cost to herself? "Why, that's just grand, Brock. You won't stand for *my* bad behavior. What of yours? Am I to ignore the way you lured me into marriage with false promises and sweet lies?"

He didn't reply at first. She could see a muscle in his jaw twitching, another sure sign that she'd really set his blood to boiling. "Madam, I do not want the entire assemblage privy to our personal life. We're leaving. You may plead your case with me at Palmer House."

"As you wish."

He grabbed her arm and pulled her close as they walked toward the door. When he spoke, his voice was a mere whisper, meant for her ears alone. "If you wish to be a mistress, Georgiana, I'll certainly accommodate you . . . tonight, and every night, until we've satisfied all aspects of your curiosity."

The Duke of Gloucester paused on the porch opening to St. James's Street and stared out into the dark night. He drew the deep, clean air into his lungs and let it out slowly, striving for the calm that had always served him well as a statesman. The scars on his calf were paining him more than usual today, forcing him to carry his cane. He leaned on it now, enjoying the feel of its cold silver grip in his hand.

Somehow, he thought, the Glamorgan Druids had produced another Guardian of Becoming, someone other than David Gwylum. They must have found a druid with latent ability and developed it. He could account for the strength and power of illusion he'd just seen in no other manner. But why had they flaunted this new druid's ability, rather than keep it secret? A guardian was a powerful weapon, one to be used only in certain circumstances. He ought to know—he possessed the ability himself.

The duke was suddenly very glad he'd attended Watier's Club this evening. Normally he avoided events like these because they made him terribly angry. For too long now, commoner's blood had flooded the aristocracy, diluting its purity and dignity. New money embraced old money and fishwives danced with dukes. In short, too many people simply didn't know their places.

When he was king, he'd make certain they learned where they belonged. Indeed, only two people stood between himself and the throne—the king's weak-spined brother William, and the Duke of Kent's little female whelp, Victoria. He planned to deal with each of them in their time, and then England would be restored to its former purity.

A footman, who'd been standing on street level,

walked up the steps to pause hesitantly at the duke's side. He bowed, then fixed his gaze on the duke's chin. "May I have your carriage brought around, Your Grace?"

The duke locked gazes with the footman and saw carefully concealed dislike in the servant's eyes. "Not yet. I'm looking for a man costumed in a long white robe. He left the ball a minute or so ago. Have you seen him?"

"No, Your Grace," the footman mumbled, his voice trembling.

"How much has he paid you to conceal his exit?" the duke asked gently.

"Nothing, Your Grace. I did not see this man whom you speak of."

The duke nodded, knowing very well that the other man had lied and would continue to lie. David Gwylum, the bothersome little gnat, had escaped well and good. Until tonight, he'd thought the youth the only other Guardian of Becoming in existence. He'd very much wanted to question Gwylum about this new guardian. Indeed, he'd like to catch them both—Gwylum and the new guardian—and take them to Cailleach's tomb, where all of his enemies quickly found their tongues . . . and then lost them.

The duke glanced at the shrubs to his left and the tree that spread its branches upward at the corner of the building. They formed a leafy wall around the porch which concealed them from the street. In that instant he decided the footman's fate.

Scanning the sidewalks to make certain his actions would remain undetected, he reflected that this illusion he'd felt and seen tonight had followed patterns he'd never encountered before. The new guardian was very powerful, if unskilled . . . and that made him twice as dangerous. And the duke didn't like threats.

"Will you be returning to the ball, Your Grace?" the footman interrupted, his voice trembling even more than before.

The duke smiled to himself. "I don't think so."

"May I retrieve your cloak?"

"No, but I wish you to lower the wick on the oil lamp above us. I find that the light hurts my eyes."

"But 'tis very low already . . ."

"Lower it."

The servant hustled to obey.

His lips curved in a smile, the duke imagined how quickly the footman's heart must be beating, like the quick pitter-patter of a rabbit trapped between a wolf's paws. He also reeked of stale sweat, an odor which seemed to grow worse by the moment. The duke recognized it as the smell of fear, second only to the smell of blood.

He breathed it in, savoring it, and concentrated on maneuvering the footman away from Watier's Club. He had a ceremony planned for the tomb tonight . . . one that required a beating heart.

The footman's would do.

Cailleach would be pleased.

His mood instantly improved. Ah yes, he'd torn out more than one heart during the course of his druidic studies, and while he found his victims' cries distasteful, he recognized the necessity of his actions. A demanding goddess, Cailleach required such sacrifices from her worshippers.

She was the Veiled One and the Destroyer, the hag of winter, the one-eyed death goddess, an enemy of life and growing things. She'd lived before Merlin, before Christ, even before man himself had walked the earth. Today she stood on the threshold between life and death, and existed in a place without time, watching over the world and waiting for it to end. The greatest sorceress ever to have lived, the duke suspected Cailleach was the first of his kind . . . the very first Guardian of Becoming.

Ugly but wise, Cailleach knew the thoughts of both the dead and the living. For a price, she imparted that knowledge to her most faithful worshippers. Without her wisdom and the visions of the future she'd sent him, he would have died long ago, the victim of some assassin's knife.

"Is that agreeable, Your Grace?" the footman asked.

Pulled from his thoughts, the duke focused on the other man and noticed a light fuzz coating his chin. The footman, he realized, was just a youth, like David Gwylum.

The notion pleased him. A youth's heart beat the

strongest, and Cailleach deserved only the best. He reached into his waistcoat, withdrew a billfold, and dropped it on the porch.

"I'll retrieve it, Your Grace," the footman mumbled, and bent over to pick up the billfold.

The duke spent a moment scanning the street, making certain their little tête-à-tête would remain private. Then he raised his cane, and swung it downward. Hard.

But not hard enough to still the footman's heart.

Chapter
3

Georgiana remained silent as Brock took her arm and led her toward the door. Rees intersected their path just as they reached the vestibule. Lips pinched, his skin pale, the younger man stuttered out a greeting to Brock, then fell silent.

Brock studied him with one raised eyebrow. "Thanks for escorting my wife around town, Rees. Where else have you taken her—to a whorehouse?"

Two spots of color formed high in Rees's cheeks. "My apologies, Brock." He turned a swift, tortured glance on Georgiana. "You must not blame Georgie. It was my idea entirely—"

"Pshaw! I insisted Rees take me here." Georgiana turned to the blond-haired man. "Rees, I know your sense of chivalry demands that you accept blame for our escapades, but I won't allow you to."

Brock's other eyebrow rose to join the first, forming a look of mild scorn. "I'll receive you in the morning, Rees, and we'll discuss, ah, your role in all of this."

The younger man swallowed. "It would be my pleasure."

"Until tomorrow, then."

Rees gave them a smart bow and disappeared back into Watier's Club.

Brock placed Georgiana's cloak around her shoulders. "I believe you ought to wear this," he said, assessing her costume, "despite the temperature. I don't want to start a riot."

Georgiana allowed her lashes to flutter downward, so Brock wouldn't see the surge of triumph she could barely suppress. Still, the sense that she'd also compromised herself had grown stronger, tempering the enjoyment she took in her victory over him.

Silently they walked outside and waited for a footman to appear. Oddly enough, the footman normally stationed near the front door had disappeared, forcing Brock to return to the vestibule. He emerged outside a few moments later with a new footman in tow, and charged the lad to bring his gig around. When it arrived, Brock handed her in none too gently. He drove very fast, and as Palmer House was situated on Brook Street, their ride home would be distressingly short. Throughout the ride Georgiana shivered, wondering what Brock had meant when he'd said he would make her his mistress. She lifted her chin, aware that a queer warmth was spreading slowly through her limbs. *She* would win this encounter, not he.

They pulled up in front of Palmer House. A footman stationed near the door hurried down the steps to assist them out of the carriage. Georgiana refused the footman's hand, climbing down without assistance and starting toward the arched doorway.

The house had always intimidated her. Built by William Kent in the previous century, it was solid, massive, heavily festooned with cornices and friezes, every room an individual work of art. It rather felt like a prison, too. She imagined she would disappear into its ornate interior, never to emerge.

"Inside, Georgiana," Brock muttered.

Abruptly she realized she'd been lingering on the porch. Drawing her cloak tightly around her body, she slipped past the footman who held the door open for her, hurried through the foyer, and made for the staircase. Within minutes she had navigated the stairs and second floor to her bedchamber. She closed her door behind her and locked it.

Her bedchamber was her one refuge from her husband and society. She'd replaced the cumbersome mahogany bureaus and massive four-poster bed with delicate satinwood pieces and a gilt tester bed. Lace rather than velvet hung from the tester and sprigged wallpaper covered the paneling on the walls. She plopped onto the bed and dragged an ivory satin counterpane around her body, taking comfort in the softness it offered.

Her cheeks felt so hot, she wanted to splash water on them. Tension formed a knot in her stomach as she waited for her husband to knock. Now that she'd roused his anger, she had only to seduce him into a softer frame of mind. After all, she couldn't win his heart by keeping him at arm's length. And without his heart, she could have no vengeance.

A soft rap on the door made her jump. "Who is it?"

"Nellie, ma'am."

"Nellie." She breathed the name out as if it were a benediction. "One moment. I'll unlock the door."

She hurried to the door and opened it for her lady's maid, who entered with a basin of steaming water.

"I thought you'd like to freshen up." Her soft blond hair stuffed into a cap, Nellie began to prepare Georgiana's evening toilette. She poured water into the basin on the washstand, laid out a towel, and spread a nightgown on the bed.

Georgiana considered the pristine white cotton nightgown Nellie had selected. This wasn't the kind of nightgown that a woman who planned to seduce her husband would wear. "No, no, not that one, Nellie. I would much rather wear the emerald silk tonight."

Eyebrow raised, Nellie returned the offending garment to the wardrobe and withdrew a vivid green confection that had been part of Georgiana's wedding trousseau. Brock had never seen the emerald silk before—she'd never had a chance to wear it. "This one, ma'am?"

"Yes." Georgiana smiled. Soon, soon, she'd have him exactly where she wanted him.

Nellie placed the gown on the bed and moved behind Georgiana to unbutton her Italian peasant costume. "Did you enjoy your evening, ma'am?"

"Not particularly. I'm afraid Watier's Club isn't for me."

Nellie pursed her lips. "I didn't think it would be. God willing the master will never find out."

"He already knows," Georgiana admitted. "I don't know who told him."

"It wasn't me," Nellie said, her eyes wide. "Good Lord, ma'am, what are you going to do now?"

"I'm not certain." Head tilted, Georgiana remembered Gwynllian. "Nellie, have we had any visitors from Wales while I've been out?"

The lady's maid frowned. "From Wales, ma'am? Not that I'm aware of."

"That will be all, Nellie," a deep male voice announced from behind her.

Georgiana spun around, her partially unfastened bodice gaping wide.

Brock stood in the doorway, his body filling the opening.

"I haven't finished dressing, Brock," she murmured. "Please go until I send for you."

"Like hell I will." He advanced into the bed-chamber and pointed at Nellie. "Out."

Nellie looked from her, to Brock, and back to her again. Her shoulders drooped. Giving her a look that pleaded for understanding, the lady's maid slipped out of the room and closed the door behind her.

They were alone.

Georgiana felt wooden. Everything inside her was tense and stiff. Her heart pounded, she could scarcely think, her legs practically itched with an urge to run. She willed herself to calm down and maintain at least some poise. She had a job to do, a man to punish.

Fighting for composure, she measured him with a single look. He still wore his jacket and trousers, but he'd loosened his cravat, giving him a rakish air. His dark brown hair appeared mussed, as if he'd run a hand through it several times. Still, it was his eyes that captured her attention, brown eyes that smoldered with fury and something else, something that made her heart race faster and her breathing quicken with anticipation.

Damn her body's wayward response to him! It had always been like this, from the first moment they'd met. She remembered an afternoon almost two years ago. They'd been walking through the forest, their horses beside them. Without warning, he'd kissed her with shocking fervor. Her legs had weakened and the oddest feeling had grown in her, a desire to possess and be possessed, something she had never known before.

"What devil lured you into attending Watier's Club this evening?" Brock strode over to her side. "Were you addled, or simply drunk?"

She strove for a husky, sensuous tone but ended up sounding defensive. "Neither, my lord. I was seeking entertainment."

"Ah, we come so quickly to the crux of the matter. What sort of entertainment were you seeking, Georgiana?" He moved behind her and brushed his fingers across her neck, making her jump.

"You prefer to spend your days at Palmer House mired in ledger books, and your nights rehashing old times with your cronies. I desire a livelier existence. Watier's Club proved an unusual diversion."

"A diversion that could have placed you beyond the pale."

"You're making more of this than necessary. My attendance there was marked by no one. Rees and Neddy remained by my side the entire time. No harm was done—"

"Your attendance was marked by *everyone*. Who could fail to identify you, surrounded as you were by Rees and 'Neddy,' your constant companions?"

"Perhaps others guessed my name. What of it? Society has learned to expect as much from me."

Brock snorted. "Are you so bored that you must act in such an outrageous manner? God's blood,

woman, you were dressed as a whore and prancing
around in a room full of demireps."

"What's wrong, Brock? Does it bother you that
your wife would seek pleasure elsewhere?"

She couldn't see his face—he still stood behind
her—but she could feel his reaction in the way he
stiffened. Just as quickly, however, he relaxed, making her wary. His arm went around her and drew
her against him. He touched the back of her neck
again, his fingers slipping around the front of her
gown to skim the tops of her breasts. Her glass pendant fluttered between her breasts.

"What sort of pleasure? The kind a whore
prefers?" His voice was deceptively soft.

A spark of anger flared within her. She spun
around to face him. "You're quick to point out my
sins, while conveniently forgetting about your
own."

"My sins?"

"Have you already forgotten the circumstances
behind our marriage? You didn't marry *me*. You
married my money, and once you got what you
wanted, you forgot that I even existed."

"How could anyone forget you, Georgiana?"

"You forgot me very easily after we first married
and I was but a country bumpkin."

He didn't deny the accusation, insulting her
thoroughly. All of the resentment and anger she'd
harbored against him came bubbling inside despite
her every effort to tamp it down. "Now that I'm an

Incomparable, you've decided I might be worth your notice? You simply want what you can't have, and I assure you, sir, you will never have *me*."

Silence lingered in the room. At length, he took in a deep breath and let it out slowly. "For two years now I've looked the other way. I've paid your debts and indulged your every whim because I felt guilty for misrepresenting my feelings when we married. I've also apologized . . . several times."

Georgiana narrowed her eyes and stared at him. She knew she stood at a crossroads. She could either soften her attitude and attempt to return to the path toward seduction, or spit in his eye.

"I only wish your Aunt Gwynllian had educated you a bit more in the ways of society," he added.

She bristled. Any slur cast upon her aunt was one too many. To hell with the seduction attempt. Now she was spoiling for a fight. "My aunt taught me about the predators who lurked in the forest at night, but she didn't mention the human ones who roamed Almack's, looking for their next meal."

"Dammit, Georgiana, I'd thought you understood. Men and women don't marry for love, they marry for convenience."

"I may have loved you once," she told him, her voice bitter, "but I assure you, I love you no more. Don't flatter yourself otherwise."

He nodded, then faced her squarely. "Whatever the case, I simply cannot tolerate any more scandalous behavior on your part. If I must punish you into acquiescence, then so be it."

"I dare you to punish me," she hissed, her eyes narrowed. "What will you do, lock me in my room?"

A toe-curling grin suddenly curled his lips, setting her hackles up even higher. "I had something a bit more . . . inventive in mind."

"Whatever you plan, I need only send a few missives to my friends explaining the situation, and you'll find your good name more blackened than I could ever make it."

"More likely I'd receive a standing ovation for finally taking my wayward wife into hand. You've gone too far this time, Georgiana. I'm afraid I'm going to have to curtail your activities with Rees and Neddy."

"The hell you will."

He touched her hair, twining one of her curls around his finger. "You are beautiful when you're defiant."

"Get out," she demanded, pulling her hair from his grasp. "Get out before I scream the bloody house down."

He slipped his hand into her bodice and yanked on the delicate fabric, ripping it apart at the seams. Cool air brushed across her breasts. Even so, her skin burned with the heat of his gaze.

She backed away, her arms crossed over her breasts. "Brock, I'm warning you."

"A mouth as luscious as yours was made for

finer things than threats," he purred, closing the distance between them.

Suddenly, his gaze locked on her pendant. Eyes widening, he crossed the remaining distance between them and plucked the pendant from her cleavage. "Who gave you this? Your lover?"

She didn't answer, preferring to torture him with silence. Let him draw his own conclusions, she thought.

"Damn you, Georgiana," he hissed, and threw the pendant in the corner. It bounced against the wooden floor with a muted crack. "You will accept presents from no one but me."

"How dare you," she choked out. "How dare you tell me what I may and may not do. You aren't a husband to me. You're not even a friend. You have no right."

"I have every right," he informed her, his voice tight. "When I married you, I promised your uncle I would take care of you. You're my problem now, Georgiana, and as a result, I have to protect you— from yourself, if need be."

"I don't want your protection." Memories of her anguish when she'd first learned Brock had married her for her monetary holdings, not love, surfaced in her mind. Suddenly she wanted to hurt him as badly as he'd hurt her. "I've accepted another man as my lover. It's his touch that I desire."

He grabbed her shoulders. "Who is he? Tell me, damn it."

She pushed at his chest, trying to keep a distance between them, but he wouldn't let go. Their tussle freed her breasts even more, baring them almost fully. His gaze dropped lower and he cursed beneath his breath.

She fought the urge to cover up. Let him look at her breasts, she thought. She wasn't going to cower before him. "And if I tell you his name, what will you do then?" she challenged. "Call him out? I thought you, of all people, would understand that our marriage is one of convenience only. I received a title, and you gained government annuities, and now we must seek our happiness elsewhere."

His face paled. "You have an obligation to me, Georgiana, to provide me with an heir. I won't have somebody else's bastard inherit the Darleigh estate."

"You shall never have one. Not from me."

"You're *my* wife," he snarled. "You will give me a son."

"I'm your wife in name only."

"You leave me no other option. You are no longer allowed out without me."

"If you dislike me so, Brock, why don't you simply divorce me?" she cried.

His eyes darkened and his mouth twisted. "No. You're bought and paid for with my good name, mine to do with as I please."

Something inside her broke, some invisible dam that had kept her rage from boiling over. Her vision grew red and she flew at him, fingers hooked into claws, determined to rake his eyes from his head, to pull that lying tongue from his mouth. A sound rent the bedchamber and dimly she realized it was her own shriek of rage.

He clapped a hand over her mouth and together they fell onto the ivory counterpane covering her tester bed. Eyebrows drawn low, eyes dark, he removed his hand and brushed her hair back from her forehead. "Shh, Georgiana—"

"Bastard!" She angled her knee toward his groin and connected with his thigh instead, drawing a gasp from him. Even so, he held her tightly, his arms around her like bands of iron, his weight pinning her down as she twisted against him, hating him. Her vision narrowed and became a single point of light, and she thought wildly she was about to swoon. For the first time in her life, she was going to faint, and Brock was at the root of it.

Ornery pride kept the darkness at bay.

"You're mine, Georgiana," he whispered against her ear, his voice raw, almost shaky. "You'll always be mine."

"Never," she hissed, and twisted against him some more, but his touch was soft, and gentle, and so very pleasant.

"Please, Georgie, stop," he pleaded, wearing her down with his tenderness and the pressure of his muscular body.

As the seconds passed, the rage inside her

cooled. She grew tired from struggling against him, for she had just about as much effect on him as if she'd tried to level a tree trunk with her fists. After a few more moments of futile defiance she grew quiescent. Wrung out, her body a quivering mass of nerves, she simply had nothing to fight him with.

Lids half-mast, he sighed and kissed her forehead. Evidently he'd realized the battle was over. "By God, I've wanted you for so long. And yet, I always act the fool around you, driving you away."

She trembled at the warm insistence of his lips. That familiar longing she felt whenever she saw him swelled up in her now, consuming her with need. How long had she wished him to notice her? Was *this* what she'd wanted from him all along?

"In your company," he whispered, trailing kisses along her brow, "I can't think, I can't talk . . . and I grow angry at the slightest provocation."

She made a little noise that was somewhere between recognition and regret. Had any couple been more ill-suited than they? And yet, there was something between them that she couldn't deny, something that scorched her whenever they touched.

"When I look in the mirror," he continued, "I think, 'Brock, you're ten years older than your wife; she needs a younger man, a carefree companion who hasn't the responsibilities that weigh on your shoulders.' And then I want to put my fist through the wall. This is what you do to me, Georgiana."

She was incapable of replying. She could only feel the hard length of him pressed against her, the gentleness of his hands as they stroked her hair, the strong beat of his heart.

"Look at me," he murmured.

Swallowing, she turned her face toward him. His eyes were very dark, his lids half-mast, a sleepy look of concealed desire. Perhaps he thought if he allowed her to see the full force of his need he would frighten her. But she wasn't frightened. God knew she wanted the same thing, regardless of the way she'd cursed him mere moments before. . . .

"Georgiana," he murmured, "may I stay with you?"

"I hate you," she whispered, her voice soft.

He began to sit up.

"Don't leave." She placed a hand on his shoulder and pulled him back to her. She hadn't anything left in her—no strength, no willpower, nothing. He'd taken her pride and anger away from her and left a void only he could fill.

He gathered her into his arms, and lowered his head toward hers, slowly, closer still, until she could see the tiny flares of gold that radiated from his irises, a detail she hadn't noticed before. Her breasts rubbed against the refined wool of his evening coat, sending a sharp, exquisite pang of pleasure through her and she gasped, softly.

He hovered an inch above her, his breath fanning softly against her cheek, until she could barely stand the anticipation. His erection, bulging beneath wool trousers, prodded her thighs. She trembled. It had been so long since the few sweet times they'd made love. Then his mouth closed over hers and he kissed her hungrily, desperately, his lips hard and demanding. She kissed him back with just as much fervor, kneading his shoulders, feeling the hard muscles of his back, breathing in the male scent of him.

They strained against each other, tangling in the counterpane. Groaning, he sat up and pulled her dress from her, ripping the already abused fabric. It fell in a heap of cotton on the floor. Her chemise followed, and then she was naked except for stockings and garters, her breasts swollen and warm, the place between her thighs aching for his touch.

Quickly he yanked his boots and jacket off, followed by his waistcoat and shirt. Half-naked, his skin a burnished gold in the candlelight, he reached down to unfasten his trousers.

She stared with smoky eyes at his broad shoulders and narrow hips. He was very fine, fit and trim, no doubt from his frequent trips to Figg's Pugilism Academy in Haymarket. But he was moving too slowly for her. She slipped her fingers beneath his waistband before he'd even fully unfastened it and, with a little moan, dragged his trousers down, her nether parts burning for him to fill her and claim her as his own.

Once he was as naked as she, he grabbed her

around the hips and pulled her back up to him, their bodies fitting together perfectly. She saw his erection, thick and hard, rising up from a thatch of curly black hair between his legs, and wanted to touch it. The notion shocked her and brought heat to her cheeks. Nevertheless she curled her palm around him and squeezed gently, drawing a deep moan from him.

"Ah, Georgiana," he whispered, his gaze flickering over her breasts, her thighs, the small beauty mark that nestled just above the curls between her legs. "I've missed you so."

She threw her head back and surrendered to intense sensation as he nuzzled her breasts and teased her nipples with his tongue. All the while he rubbed that soft spot between her legs, building the ache inside of her until her thighs became slicked with moisture. Nearly maddened, she wrapped her legs around his hips and strained against him.

"Make me yours, Brock," she moaned.

He drew her on top of his thighs, then settled her down onto him, filling her, stretching her. The sensations brought her back to those early days in their marriage, when she'd still thought he loved her. With him inside her again, she could almost convince herself he loved her still. For now, she would let herself believe it.

Giving in to the dream, she cried out with pure delight. Slowly he began to thrust up into her, and soon she caught the rhythm. She squeezed his waist between her thighs and surged up and down, driving him into her, her hair streaming about her shoulders.

Brock kneaded her breasts and pulled at her nipples, gently, his face sharp, his chest muscles tense. He began to meet her hips with his own, his thrusts strong, harsh, as if he could no longer deny the passion sweeping through him. Teeth clenched, she rode him furiously, the pleasure within her building to indescribable heights.

Suddenly, he swept her under him and claimed her face-to-face, kissing her all the while. Just as the sensations within her intensified until she could hardly bear them, ecstasy washed through her and she fell against him, moaning his name.

With a muffled groan, he buried himself in her to the hilt. She wrapped her legs around his waist and held him close as he began to thrust, slowly and steadily, seeking his own release, and after a few delirious moments she felt him peak with one final driving motion, and shudder, and whisper her name.

He fell onto the mattress and pulled her to him.

Georgiana nestled against his body and kissed his neck and tangled her fingers in the hair on his chest. He grasped her chin with two gentle fingers, pulled her face to his, and kissed her deeply, affectionately, his palm hot against the curls between her legs. Minutes passed, slow delicious minutes as they held each other and their breathing returned to normal.

Brock raised himself on one elbow to look at her. "What are we going to do, Georgie?"

She pressed her face against the pillow, avoiding his gaze. "I don't know."

Now that the heat of passion had passed from her, the troubles between them had returned to plague her full-force. This man she'd married, she hardly knew him. The Brock she'd fallen in love with had disappeared two years ago. The fact that they'd made love hardly changed the situation . . . unless, of course, he'd just gotten her with child, in which case he'd have the son he'd been angling for.

The thought hit her like a slap. She turned on her side to stare him in the eye. "I suppose I should give you my congratulations."

Caution replaced the warmth in his eyes. "For what?"

"For your inventive campaign to seduce me and get yourself an heir. So, this is your way of punishing me."

A beat of silence passed between them, in which Georgiana could feel his surprise in the way he stiffened.

"I hadn't the slightest thought of a son when I made love to you, Georgie."

"Do you expect me to believe you?"

"I'll admit I've given you no reason to trust me. Nevertheless, I'm being honest." He ran a hand through his hair, ruffling it so that it stuck out at odd angles. "We've grown so far apart, I no longer know what to do. At the moment, it seemed right."

His words resonated within her. Yes, something existed between them, but while it scorched her, it was also tearing her apart. "Nothing is right between us. Our marriage has been a farce from the very beginning."

She shifted away from him and covered her nakedness with a sheet. Again she had the notion that she'd become someone she didn't want to be. She'd compromised herself in a vain effort to win a man who'd disappeared long ago. She looked at Brock with new eyes, thinking he and the society which had spawned him represented everything that had gone wrong in her life.

Sadness replaced the pleasure she'd felt moments before as she realized she could compromise herself no further. She didn't belong in London society, and would never be happy with Brock. She wanted to go home to Aunt Gwynllian. To Wales.

"I learned something about myself tonight," she said, hesitating, not certain how to tell him what she needed him to hear. "While my 'scandalous' behavior may embarrass you, it shames me more. I'm no longer going to follow every stray impulse I feel, and seek ways to gain your attention."

Abruptly he sat up and stared at her, eyes wide. "You've been trying to gain my attention? Why?"

"I was hoping to find the man who had courted me. The man I fell in love with."

"*I courted you.*"

"No, you didn't. I fell in love with another Brock, a man you only pretended to be. The memory of this other Brock, and the hope that he might return to me, drove me to the lengths you've witnessed. But now I know he will never return, because I fell in love with an illusion."

He looked away, a spasm twisting his lips, as though he'd just felt a pain. "I've already confessed to misrepresenting my feelings for you before we married. It was a mistake I've come to regret very deeply."

"I know. I'm not blaming you anymore. Just let me go, Brock. Free me."

"I can't."

"Why not?"

His face took on a ruddy flush. Seconds passed before he finally spoke. "Because things aren't finished between us, Georgie."

"Yes, they are. You want an heir, and you want the income from my government annuities, but I need something entirely different—something you aren't able to give."

"How do you know that?"

"Your interest in me is rooted in my financial value to you, and my ability to breed you a son."

He looked at the lace curtaining her tester bed, the muscle twitching in his jaw again. She had the notion that he was trying to find the courage to say something very difficult. But when he didn't respond further, she sighed. "Go back to your own bedchamber, Brock. Leave me alone."

"I'm not leaving."

"For God's sake, why?"

Abruptly, he turned to look at her, his eyes dark, his gaze intense. "Because I sense something between us, something I've never felt before."

Georgiana almost laughed aloud. Bitterness filled her and choked the laugh off before she could do any more than think about it. Brock had said the same thing to her while courting her. Two years ago she'd been thrilled. Now, she was simply saddened. "I sense the same thing," she told him. "It's called pain."

He reared back as though she'd struck him. "It's more than that."

"Perhaps. One might describe it as greed, too. You won't divorce me because you don't wish to give up my income from my government annuities."

"You're wrong." The mattress bounced a little as he stood up. "I'm going to prove it to you."

She didn't look at him while he slipped on his trousers, gathered his remaining clothes together, and left her tangled in sheets that had the smell of their lovemaking upon them. Tears filled her eyes, tears for the Brock she once knew and still loved. He would always be her one grand passion, the man who could stir her as no other—but he was gone, and now it was time to go home.

*   *   *

Brock pushed the door to Georgiana's bedchamber closed and slumped against it. He rubbed his temples. Not a sound leaked from her bedchamber, and that worried him more than hysterical weeping. A few sobs would have convinced him she still felt something for him, but this silence had an ominous finality to it.

He ran a hand through his hair and walked down the hallway, heading for the study rather than his bedchamber. Sleep couldn't have been farther away from him. He knew better than to try. When he reached the steps leading to the first floor, he took them slowly, replaying their conversation in his head all the while.

He couldn't blame her for thinking he'd made love to her in an attempt to secure an heir. She thought him vile and manipulative, and God knew, he hadn't given her a reason to think otherwise. But this news about her trying to gain his attention had left him totally flummoxed. By God, he hadn't seen it, although Carlisle had tried to tell him on more than one occasion.

If only he'd realized it sooner! His wife was the most desirable woman he'd ever known. He would have been proud to escort her around, eager to converse with her—*if* he ever allowed her out of his bed. One would think he'd committed the ultimate folly of falling in love with his own wife, the way he felt about her, and who knew? Perhaps he had, as foreign and outrageous as the idea sounded. Their intimacy *had* satisfied some need deep in him, one that he'd known for so long he didn't even recognize it anymore. Tonight, when he'd held her in his arms, the emptiness that had become a part of his life had suddenly eased.

Frowning at the thought of letting her go, he descended the stairs. She said he'd changed, that he was different from the man she'd once known. Somehow, he had to convince her that the man she'd fallen in love with still existed, but was buried beneath layers of guilt and regret.

He *would* win her back, and together they would plumb the depths of this connection between them.

A sound began to intrude on Brock's consciousness, a low, nearly inaudible moan that swirled through the house like a cold draft. He paused and gripped the banister. Somewhere upstairs, a door opened and shut, and footsteps hurried through the hallway.

He turned on his heel and started back upstairs. Another low moan dogged his steps. Mouth twisted in a resigned line, he passed Georgiana's room and made for the stairs that led to the third floor.

That's where they kept her. In a bedchamber in the third floor.

No one would accuse him of not doing his best for her. She had the finest doctors, the softest linens, a mattress filled with down. He'd spared nothing in his quest to find a cure, without success. She only

grew worse, drifting more regularly into that make-
believe world of hers.

He stopped before a door left open a crack.
Muttering replaced the moans which had drawn
him upstairs. Within the room, he saw Mrs. Steele's
sturdy form encased in a wrapper. For unknown
reasons, only the housekeeper could physically
touch her. Likewise, only he seemed able to draw
her from the mindlessness she plunged into ever
more frequently. Steeling himself for the ordeal
ahead, he pushed the door open and stepped
inside.

Chapter
4

"Mother," Brock said, his voice hushed.

Candlelight created a dim glow that illuminated the crone on the bed. She sat with one hand outstretched, as though she were holding an invisible object. Brock looked at her thinning gray hair held back with a pink ribbon, her bloodshot eyes and yellowed skin, and winced as he always did. Pale, wasted, she had an odd dignity about her. As far as Brock could tell, that dignity was the only remnant that remained of her former life.

"Are you a new doctor?" She fixed a blurry stare upon him for a moment before her gaze skittered away, as though she'd seen something that distressed her.

Brock stiffened, the resignation in him warring with pity. Her loss of memory was a recent development, a sign that her condition had deteriorated further. Oddly enough, as her memory went, so did his. He could barely recall the woman who'd comforted him as a child, holding him against her skirts after he'd scraped his knee.

"No, it's Reginald Evans, Lady Darleigh," he said, assuming the persona of her late secretary, whom she'd once adored and obeyed without question. "Whose hand are you holding?"

"Lord Darleigh's," she whispered. "He's come to take me riding."

Brock nodded. He'd discovered some years ago that his mother saw Lord Darleigh just before she became catatonic. A symbol of his mother's madness, his father appeared in her mind to lead her into a foggy no-man's-land from which she could hardly emerge. He'd learned that if he caught her *before* she left with Lord Darleigh, he could keep her in the present. If, however, she left with her dead husband and became catatonic, Brock had a devil of a time coaxing her out of it.

"Please tell Lord Darleigh that you aren't ready to go riding with him yet," he said.

She jutted her chin forward and stared at him belligerently. "My husband is not a man to be crossed."

Mrs. Steele, his housekeeper-turned-nursemaid, pulled him aside and murmured, "She says he's been sitting on the edge of her bed all morning, right there." She pointed to an empty corner of his mother's bed. "About an hour ago she said he'd taken her hand, poor thing. I think you've come just in time."

Brock turned a helpless gaze toward the shrunken old woman in the bed. A sudden desire to escape her was almost too difficult to overcome. How much easier it was to run away from the madness than to face it and try to see through it. But he couldn't avoid his mother or the sinister, more insidious question her condition raised.

Had he inherited his mother's predisposition toward madness?

Would he, someday, be writhing on a bed just like her?

"Insist that you don't wish to go," he urged, repeating the ritual they went through every few weeks. He knew he'd be wasting his time trying to convince her his father didn't exist. Experience had taught him that he had to make a partner of her, not chide her for seeing demons.

His mother twisted the hand she held in the air. "I've already told him. He won't let go." Her eyes narrowed. "Do you see him, Reginald? Those charlatans didn't."

The "charlatans" were two doctors he'd hired to look after his mother. Both had assisted King George III in his times of madness, and had applied the same techniques to her. They'd restrained her in a straightjacket, blistered her skin with hot glass rims, and made her sit for days in a special chair with straps. Her insanity had grown more virulent throughout the treatment and, despairing, Brock had eventually stopped them. His own amateur brand of treatment, one of talking his mother through her spells, had proven much more effective.

Without warning, his mother nodded. "Yes, Lord Darleigh," she said, her voice singsong. "I simply need to put on my riding habit." She paused and glanced at Brock. "You're most rude, Reginald, ignoring Lord Darleigh as you are."

Brock looked at the empty space at the end of her bed. The calm certainty in her voice had infected him. He could almost see the shade of his father, corpselike and moldy. *Remain detached,* he told himself. *Or you will be drawn into her madness.*

Feeling the perfect fool, he stood and bowed to the empty space. "Pardon me, Lord Darleigh, for insulting you. I wish you all the best on your hunting trip. But I'm afraid Lady Darleigh can't join you today. She has a charity function to hostess."

His mother cocked her head. Her gaze became bright, birdlike, almost eager as she stared at the end of her bed. "He is lonely and wants my company."

Brock pretended to consider. He'd discovered that her sense of duty remained strong behind the madness. If he played his cards right, that sense would draw her out of the pit. "That may be, but the king himself is planning to attend the function. If Lady Darleigh does not play hostess, the function will fail and the charity will be cast into ruin."

"Lord Darleigh says he has already brought my horse around, and our ride will take very little time indeed."

"The king wishes to consult with Lady Darleigh on a remedy she once recommended to him," he countered. "His advisors are on their way to Palmer House now. If she goes out riding, the king may fall ill and forsake the charity function."

"Lord Darleigh's grip is loosening," she informed him in an excited whisper.

"If the king falls ill, he could very well die. England would be overrun by Catholics."

His mother smiled. "He has let go of my hand."

"If England is overrun by Catholics," Brock hurried to add, "the remaining Darleighs will have to move to the Americas or be strung up as heretics. So you see, Lady Darleigh's presence is very much required at the function. She cannot go riding."

His mother dropped her arm to her side. "He's gone."

"And he won't return for some time." He smoothed the bedcovers over her as she curled up in a fetal position and closed her eyes. Quietly he walked toward the door.

Mrs. Steele put an arm around him. "She's sleeping now. You might as well go."

Brock paused at the door. "Send for me if Lord Darleigh reappears."

"The very moment," Mrs. Steele agreed.

Just as he turned to go, his mother spoke, her voice weak but provoking in its lucidity. "Reginald?"

He walked back to her side. "Yes?"

"Tell my son Brock that the other Lady Darleigh needs him. The younger one."

Brock stiffened. "How do you know?"

"Sometimes Lord Darleigh tells me things."

Inside, he reeled. What could his mother possibly know about the situation between Georgiana and himself to lead her to say such a thing? Had she heard them arguing? Sometimes voices carried easily through houses, especially old ones. Before he could question her, however, her chest began to rise and fall with the easy rhythm of sleep.

Confounded, he left the third floor room and made his way to the study, his original destination. Once inside, he shut the door and poured himself a whiskey, straight up and very strong. The painted eyes of long-dead Darleighs stared at him from their portraits on the wall, and busts of the same peered from the rows of mahogany breakfront bookcases. The smell of leather and parchment strong in his nose, he raised his drink to them before collapsing back upon a settee and trying to shake off the pall the episode with his mother had set upon him.

Naturally he thought of his wife.

To her credit, Georgiana sat with his mother at least once a week, paying her respects and entertaining her with stories of her various outings. That had been one of the first times he'd seen the true Georgiana behind the girl he'd married, the sensitive woman who seemed to think of more than soirées and champagne.

Intrigued, he'd felt his first stirrings of an emotion deeper than casual interest in her, but by then it had been too late. She'd already discovered that he'd married her for her government annuities and her uncle's influence at the bank. Helplessly he'd listened to her tell his mother stories of midnight antics and ground his teeth with impotent jealousy.

He certainly hadn't won any ground from her tonight. In fact, he'd virtually made her a house prisoner. Still, what else could he do? She'd already informed him she'd taken a lover. If that other man got her with child, he'd have a bastard foisted upon him. He wondered whom she'd chosen, how many times they'd made love. She'd taken the top position with such confidence tonight. Had she learned that trick from her lover?

What bothered him even more, however, was the thought that she might find a man willing to return her love, and then he'd lose her forever. He rubbed his eyes and put his whiskey glass on a side table. Their lives had become so fixed he didn't see an easy way to change things between them.

But change they would.

She was his wife, and as long as she remained so, a connection would exist between them. He still had a hold on her, as tenuous as that hold might be. They were bound by the laws of society, laws that even she couldn't entirely ignore. Those laws would provide him with an opportunity to win her back.

First, of course, he had to figure out what set him apart from the man she thought she'd lost.

After a while Georgiana found she had no tears left in her. Nor had she the slightest desire to sleep. She pushed the ivory counterpane back and got out of bed, then pulled a silk wrapper over her nightgown. The fire in the hearth glowed with a few embers but gave off little heat. She shivered at the chill in the room, a chill that comes just before dawn, when sun's residual heat has had hours to dissipate. Georgiana glanced at the clock on a side table.

Three o'clock in the morning.

She threw back the drapes and plopped into an overstuffed armchair near the window. From there she contemplated the mist flowing gently across the well-manicured grounds behind Palmer House and the full moon which glittered high above her. Her thoughts automatically led her to Brock.

Judging by his high-handed treatment of her, and his insistence in keeping her under house arrest, he wasn't going to let go easily. And while she wanted to be free to pursue a life in Wales, part of her was the tiniest bit glad that he'd displayed such determination to hold on to her. The emotion in his voice when he'd made love to her told her that more than greed had motivated him.

Perhaps her plan to snare his heart had proven effective after all.

Still, Brock didn't know how to love. She'd

learned as much through painful experience. At the moment, he simply wanted what he couldn't have. She felt certain that as soon as she surrendered to him, she'd find herself placed on the shelf. He'd done nothing to convince her otherwise.

Sighing, she forced her thoughts away from Brock, settling instead upon the mystery of Aunt Gwynllian's earlier appearance. Had she seen the real Gwynllian? Or had she simply seen her aunt's shade? Georgiana curled her feet under her and went over the events leading up to Gwynllian's appearance. Abruptly she realized she'd been wishing for her aunt with all her heart seconds before her aunt had appeared.

Somehow, her wish had been granted.

Her gaze locked on the fog curling around the trees and bushes outside. She remembered the fog she'd imagined in her mind, and its peculiar buzz. She'd imagined the fog slowly coalescing into Gwynllian's form. An idea wormed its way into her thoughts, a preposterous notion which no sane person would lend the slightest credence to. Nevertheless, Georgiana considered it. She didn't know why, but she just couldn't dismiss it.

Had she somehow *created* Gwynllian? With her mind?

As soon as she formulated the question, her rational side castigated her. How could anyone possibly create something with her mind? And how could someone else witness something she'd created with her mind?

She trembled and pulled her wrapper more tightly around her. Again she considered the other possible explanations. First, Gwynllian could have come to visit her in London. But Georgiana didn't think that scenario likely. Her aunt would have visited her at Palmer House rather than attend the masquerade at Watier's Club and stand there beckoning. Maybe she'd seen Gwynllian's shade, then. Still, Georgiana refused to accept her aunt's death. She would *know* if her aunt left this world.

What possibilities were left? Chewing her lower lip, Georgiana wondered if she'd imagined the entire episode. Quickly she decided she couldn't have. The man in the white robe had conversed with Gwynllian, too. He'd obviously seen *something*.

Had she created an *illusion* of Aunt Gwynllian?

Georgiana frowned. Why, if she had the ability to create illusions, by God, she would have created plenty of them before now! Unless, of course, she had done something unusual last night, something that had held no significance to her but had indeed made all the difference. She wracked her brain, trying to think of that key difference, but came up empty-handed. The whole notion was absurd, fit only for those incarcerated in Bedlam.

Then why couldn't she dismiss it?

She sighed noisily. Perhaps she ought to indulge in a little madness, if only to free herself from this insane idea. Who would know? After all, both her bedchamber and her thoughts were private. Lips quirked, she closed her eyes and repeated her thoughts of the previous night, imagining fog that gradually coalesced into her aunt. Bit by bit the vision in her mind became so real that Georgiana almost felt like she could grasp her aunt's hand.

She snapped her eyes open.

The bedchamber remained empty.

She jumped up from the chair and began to pace. She had expected no less; and yet, she still had this feeling that she hadn't put all of the pieces together yet. Something was still missing.

She hadn't heard the peculiar buzzing noise.

Where had it come from, and how could she bring it back?

She paused in her pacing to look out the window and gaze at the moon, at its white face surrounded by a corona of mist. The mist hovering over the land captured the moon's glow and diffused it, making the night seem brighter than normal. Indeed, the moonlight washed across her body to settle against the floor, creating shadows in her bedchamber.

Something sparkled in the corner of the room. Georgiana glanced at it, wondering if a mother-of-pearl button had popped off one of her gowns. She shrugged and had nearly dismissed it when a strange feeling came over her. The glittering object was important, somehow. Slowly she walked toward it and grasped it between two gentle fingers. At once she realized what she'd found: the glass pendant she'd discovered long ago in a meadow, hidden in a niche at the base of an oak.

The chain, she saw, remained intact despite Brock's harsh handling. She remembered how the pendant had grown warm against her skin at the same time Gwynllian had appeared. She'd thought her skin had heated it, but maybe its temperature change had stranger origins. . . .

Georgiana placed the chain around her neck. The glass egg fell into place between her breasts. Cold and hard against her flesh, it felt utterly foreign. Still, she had this sense that she was on the right track. Trembling a little, this time with excitement, she sat back in her chair and closed her eyes.

Taking a deep breath, and then another, she imagined that the fog outside slowly crept into her mind, until mist filled her inner eye. She saw it quite clearly, swirling in a myriad of patterns, as though a mental wind were blowing it back and forth, without direction. As before, the fog had an uncomfortable buzz to it, like a hive of angry bees.

Georgiana felt her skin crawl. She realized she feared the buzz, though she didn't know why. Grimacing with distaste, she began to blow that mist into shapes she understood. She felt a little like a sculptor working with clay, and the fog responded to her mental touch, coalescing according to her will. Even as the fog became more orderly, the buzz began to even out and take on more comfortable vibrations. Slowly, the image of

Gwynllian formed, her oval face first, and then her gray eyes, and then her lean body clad in a Welsh round gown.

As she worked, Georgiana could feel something gathering in the air around her. The glass egg grew warm against her skin, reminding her of its presence, while pressure gathered behind her temples—not a headache, exactly, but a sense of pushing. She hadn't experienced childbirth, but she couldn't put aside the thought that it must feel much like the pushing in her head, a struggle for something to be born.

When the image was complete Georgiana imagined it had substance, not just a flat drawing but a three-dimensional person. She imagined the sound of her aunt's laugh and the smell of the perfume she wore. Soon, she could feel Gwynllian's presence everywhere around her. Georgiana snapped her eyes open.

Aunt Gwynllian sat in a chair near the bed.

Georgiana gasped. All at once, the world around her went dizzy. Several seconds passed before her bedchamber righted itself.

Gwynllian still sat there.

Her chest so tight she could barely breath, Georgiana stood. Abruptly, she saw herself, through Gwynllian's eyes. She looked terrible, with staring green eyes, mussed brown hair, and a face as pale as a sheet. After a moment, her vision cleared. She held onto the back of her chair for support. "Aunt Gwynllian?"

Silence stretched out between them. Gwynllian regarded her steadily.

In the back of her mind, Georgiana heard a pleasing melody of notes, created from the horrible buzz. Another mental image of herself, as seen from Gwynllian's perspective, flashed into her mind and disappeared. She wrapped her fingers around the glass egg, its heat seeping into her fingers.

The egg was the key, she thought.

Her aunt smiled. "The egg was the key."

At the sound of Gwynllian's voice, Georgiana jumped. "Is it really you, Aunt?" she asked, knowing that the real Gwynllian would take her to task for asking such a silly question.

"Why would you ask such a question?"

Georgiana gaped at her. Her head felt muddled. Gwynllian seemed to be saying everything that she, Georgiana, thought. "Are you really my Aunt Gwynllian?"

"Of course."

"How did you get here?"

"You brought me." Gwynllian regarded her quizzically. "Is something wrong?"

For a moment Georgiana had no reply. "I thought I created you," she finally admitted in a small voice.

"Only God creates."

"Then where did you come from?"

"Wales, naturally."

"When did I bring you?" Georgiana asked, her

voice hesitant. Gwynllian was still answering in exactly the way Georgiana expected her to.

"Why, I don't remember. Isn't that strange." Her aunt smiled again, but this time the expression seemed devoid of any true emotion.

"*How* did I bring you?"

"I don't know."

Her movements hesitant, Georgiana walked to Gwynllian's side and tried to grasp her hand. Her hand passed through Gwynllian's hand as if it didn't exist.

Georgiana grew very still and cold. "Are you a ghost?"

"No."

"Am I dreaming?"

"No, you're quite awake. Pinch yourself."

Swallowing, Georgiana did as her aunt had bid and discovered that she was, indeed, awake. "Am I . . . mad?"

Gwynllian simply stared back at her.

"I have to know," Georgiana muttered. *Nellie*, she thought, and turned on her heel. She walked quickly to the bell cord and pulled. If her lady's maid saw Gwynllian, her fears of madness could rest at ease. "I'm going to have tea brought up for us, Aunt. You must be very tired after your journey."

"That's very kind of you."

Georgiana seated herself in a chair and took a deep breath. Suddenly she realized she was bone-weary. Utterly exhausted. She struggled to keep her eyes open and focused on Gwynllian. Flashes of herself kept intruding on her vision. She saw dark circles under her own eyes and thought she might swoon.

In less than a minute, Nellie knocked on her door. Covering a yawn with her hand, Georgiana sprang out of the chair and let her in.

Her robe hastily tied and mobcap askew on her blond curls, Nellie fixed her gaze on Georgiana as she sidestepped into the room. She didn't even glance toward Gwynllian. "Are you ill, miss?"

Georgiana turned to stare at her aunt. Nellie followed the direction of her gaze. Her eyes widened. A small sound escaped her. Immediately she dropped into a curtsey. When she straightened, her face had gained a slight flush. "Miss Stanton, I had no idea you were expected!"

Gwynllian nodded her head. "I arrived earlier."

"I hadn't heard." Nellie's lips remained slightly parted.

Georgiana put an arm around Nellie and ushered her toward the door. She could well understand the maid's confusion, even though it lightened her heart to see it. If Nellie saw Gwynllian, then she, Georgiana, couldn't possibly be imagining her aunt. "Would you fix us some tea, Nellie? We're both sleepless and in need of something to calm our nerves."

"I'll bring it right up," the maid said, her eyes still round. She bolted through the doorway.

Georgiana closed the door behind her and returned to her chair. She curled her feet under her, the tips of her fingers and toes fairly tingling with a need to rest. It might prove interesting, she thought, to ask Gwynllian a question that she, Georgiana, couldn't possibly know the answer to.

"Tell me about the last two years. Is old Harold still alive?" she asked, referring to a widower who lived in Caernarfon.

Frowning, her eyebrows scrunched together, her aunt seemed to wrack her memory for an answer. Georgiana found the lingering silence significant.

"Do you remember anything of the last two years?" Georgiana asked, fighting off another yawn. She had to follow this interview through to its conclusion.

"Of course I do, dear," Gwynllian insisted, but didn't elaborate.

Georgiana cast a bleary gaze toward her aunt. The older woman had begun to grow hazy, just like before. The differing perspectives that flickered in Georgiana's mind had also lost substance. The chaotic buzz was taking over.

Georgiana snuggled into her chair and sighed. She was too damned tired to notice anything else. Unexpectedly, her mind skipped to an old English nursery rhyme her aunt used to tell her, about a little boy dressed in blue who was supposed to blow his horn when the sheep escaped. Slowly, her eyelids drifted downward.

"He's under the haystack, fast asleep," Gwynllian murmured.

Someone was shaking her arm. Georgiana did her level best to ignore it. Wrapped in cotton and floating on a cloud, she felt perfectly at ease, all of her limbs tingling with the languor of a deep, much-needed sleep. After a time, however, she could no longer ignore the sensation and clawed her way from sleep.

"What?" she mumbled.

A high-pitched female voice assaulted her ears. "I'm sorry, madam, I can see you need your sleep, and I would have left the tea on the side table, but I'm afraid we've misplaced Miss Stanton."

She lifted her lids with great effort and stared into Nellie's wide eyes. "What do you mean, you've misplaced her? She's right over there."

"Where?"

"Sitting in that chair. . . ." Georgiana focused on the empty chair near her. Her head felt fuzzy.

"She's not there," Nellie whispered urgently, "nor anywhere else in Palmer House. Shall I wake Lord Darleigh?"

"No." Georgiana sat up a bit straighter. She certainly didn't want Brock involved, not until she'd had a chance to sort this situation out. But what to say to poor Nellie? "Miss Stanton has gone to stay with my uncle, Sir Stanton, in his London townhouse," she invented.

"She left us in the middle of the night?"

Georgiana hesitated. She could feel her little lie growing into a whale. " 'Tis an old Welsh custom. Those who leave at night avoid the painful good-byes that a daytime parting would surely bring."

Nellie didn't look convinced. "And her trunks?"

"She had them sent directly to my uncle's townhouse." Georgiana yawned pointedly.

"Of course, madam." Nellie curtseyed and slipped out the door.

As soon as her head touched the pillow, Georgiana could feel exhaustion claiming her again. This time she surrendered without a fight. Tomorrow, she thought, was soon enough to solve the mystery of Gwynllian's appearance. Tonight she simply needed rest.

Chapter 5

Brock rubbed his eyes and examined his appearance in a small decorative mirror. His cravat had gone hopelessly askew and tiny veins reddened his eyes. He felt like bloody hell and supposed he deserved it, staying up all night with only a bottle of whiskey for company. Light streamed in from the windows, aggravating his headache. He cast a jaundiced glance toward the grandfather clock in the corner of the room and saw the hour was fast approaching nine in the morning.

Rees would be here soon.

He sighed. The notion of confronting Rees was a distasteful one. They'd always been friends; their relationship was based on mutual respect. Still, the notion that Georgiana had taken a lover spurred him on. Distasteful or no, Rees *would* tell him the name of Georgiana's lover.

As though thinking of Rees had conjured him, a knock sounded on the study door.

"Enter," Brock barked, mentally preparing a speech for the young man.

Siddons bowed his way into the room. A fine coating of dust covered his knee breeches and the shoulders of his jacket. Brock found the sight exceptional, as Siddons always kept himself perfectly groomed, as befitting the butler of a marquess.

"Good morning, my lord. Viscount Hammond has come to call." His gaze expressionless, Siddons paused to glance at Brock's clothes. "Shall I put him in the salon?"

"No, send him in. Ask Mrs. Steele to prepare breakfast for both of us."

"Very well, my lord." Siddons inclined his head and turned to go.

"Siddons," Brock called to the butler's retreating back. "Why are you so dusty?"

Siddons halted in the doorway and turned around to face Brock. He opened his mouth, then closed it, his composure obviously as askew as Brock's cravat.

Brock lifted an eyebrow. "Well, man?"

"I've been looking for someone," Siddons admitted after a lengthy pause.

"For whom?" Brock imagined the butler peering into dusty old wardrobes. "And *where* have you been looking—in the attic?"

Siddons frowned and shifted his weight.

Brock's thoughts fixed on his mother. Had she, in her madness, run away and hid somewhere? "Siddons, I demand you come clean immediately."

"I've been looking for Miss Stanton, Lady Darleigh's aunt," the butler said in a rush.

A beat of silence passed between them, during which Brock digested this intelligence with a spurt of surprise. He hadn't seen Georgiana's aunt since he and Georgiana had married. Indeed, Gwynllian had always made him uncomfortable. To this day, he swore she'd known that his feelings for Georgiana weren't fully engaged. "Why wasn't I informed that Miss Stanton had come to visit?"

"Nellie says she arrived late last night, without warning."

"Nellie is Lady Darleigh's maid, is she not?"

Clearly unhappy, Siddons nodded.

"Where *is* Lady Darleigh?"

"Nellie says she still sleeps."

Brock nodded, as if he understood, but he didn't understand at all. "At exactly what time did Miss Stanton arrive?"

Siddons took a deep breath, his expression that of a man mustering what courage he could. "Nellie insists she arrived sometime after . . . three in the morning."

"Good God, that's irregular. Is Miss Stanton awake? I'd like to see her."

"Miss Stanton is gone, my lord."

"Gone?" Brock took a few steps closer to the butler. "What do you mean?"

"According to Nellie, Miss Stanton left shortly after arriving."

"In the middle of the night?" Brock shook his head. "Are you certain Nellie wasn't dreaming?"

Siddons hesitated again. "Lady Darleigh told Nellie that her aunt went to stay with Sir Stanton."

"But you said Lady Darleigh still sleeps."

"Apparently Lady Darleigh mentioned this to Nellie just before she, ah, nodded off last night."

Brock rubbed his chin with two long fingers. He could well understand Georgiana's aunt wanting to stay with Sir Anthony. After all, the man was her brother. Still, the secretive nature of Gwynllian's visit didn't make sense. "Did Lady Darleigh give any reason why her aunt left so precipitously?"

"Evidently Miss Stanton was following an old Welsh custom. 'Those who leave at night avoid the painful good-byes that a daytime parting must bring,' Lady Darleigh said."

Brock spun around and paced away from Siddons. He'd never heard such a load of nonsense in his life. His thoughts darted off in wild directions. Had Nellie concocted this story in an effort to help Georgiana conceal a visit from her lover? Was he even hearing the facts aright? Perhaps his mother's madness had finally set in. . . .

He turned to focus on Siddons. "Inform me

when Lady Darleigh awakens. And have Nellie brought to me after Lord Hammond leaves."

"Yes, my lord."

"You may go, Siddons. Send Lord Hammond in."

The butler bowed his way out of the room. Less than a minute later he returned with Rees.

Hair brushed back from his forehead, his clothes perfectly pressed and a touch grandiose, Rees appeared in fine form. Brock knew all the bucks favored collar points like his young cousin's, so high they could barely turn their heads, but he couldn't see the practicality in it.

Old man, he taunted himself. *No wonder Georgiana took a lover.*

Rees's blue eyes, normally so open, held a shuttered look as he greeted Brock with a smart bow. "Good morning, Lord Darleigh."

Brock returned Rees's bow with a slight inclination of his head. "We needn't revert to formalities, Rees. You're not on Tyburn Hill, and I'm not the executioner."

Rees's shoulders sagged beneath his fawn-colored jacket. "I'm relieved to hear it. Nevertheless, I'm prepared to offer you my deepest apologies for my betrayal of the trust you placed in me—"

"While I appreciate your sentiment, I'm not interested in watching you castigate yourself," Brock cut in. "I'll save my own tongue-lashing for a later date. Only one thing interests me now—the name of Georgiana's lover. Tell me who he is, and our interview is over."

At the mention of the word *lover*, Rees grew quite still. His eyes widened, clearly with surprise. Shock, even. "Lover? Georgie has a lover?"

"Don't try to protect her," Brock ground out. "And don't pretend ignorance, either. You and your friend Neddy have been my wife's constant companions for the last year. You must know the name of the man she's chosen. Is it this Neddy fellow?"

Rees's mouth opened and closed a few times as he attempted a reply. "Neddy?" he eventually croaked.

"Don't make an uncomfortable matter even more difficult. Tell me if it's Neddy."

"No, it isn't Neddy," Rees managed.

"Then who?"

His face pale, Rees swallowed. "Are you certain she's taken a lover?"

"She told me so herself."

"When?"

"Last night, after she left Watier's Club."

The younger man shook his head back and forth, as much as his collar points would allow. "I cannot believe Georgiana has a lover. As you say, Neddy and I have been her constant companions, and never has she mentioned anyone, or spent time with anyone other than ourselves."

Brock fell silent, Rees's statement echoing in his head.

Never spent time with anyone other than ourselves. . . .

His internal temperature plummeted several degrees. Not Neddy. *Rees*. Georgiana had betrayed him with his own cousin. Brock stepped close to Rees and stared him in the eye. "She's selected you, eh, Rees?"

The blond man gulped. "By God, Brock, how could you even suggest it? I would sooner slit my own throat than compromise Georgie in any way."

His spirited defense had the ring of truth to it. Brock stared at him for a moment longer before backing away. "Who is this Neddy fellow?"

Shaking his head back and forth, Rees paced over to the window. "Neddy isn't the one you want. He's already involved with an actress in a theatrical production."

"A man can have two lovers."

Rees stopped pacing and turned to stare directly at Brock. "Neddy isn't the one she's chosen, Brock. I know him too well to suspect otherwise."

"Then she must have fooled you, too," Brock concluded.

A knock on the door interrupted their discussion. Brock cast a quick glance at Rees and saw the pinched look around his mouth, the subdued shock in his eyes. Sympathy for his cousin filled him. "Have you had breakfast?"

"Not as of yet."

A bitter smile on his lips, Brock opened the study door and allowed two serving maids, each bearing a tray of meats and breads, into the room. After they'd set down their trays and left, Brock directed Rees to one tray and then sat before the other.

Rees stared miserably at his tray. "I'm not certain I can manage breakfast. Are you *certain* Georgie has taken a lover?"

"What's wrong, Rees? Are you sorry she's bypassed you in favor of another?"

The younger man flinched. "I would never betray you in that way—"

"I know." Brock sighed. "Forgive me. Ever since she told me, I've wanted to break something. While I've managed to restrain that impulse, my tongue refuses to yield as easily."

Brock uncovered his tray. A cloud of steam hit him in the face. Without interest, he surveyed the tray's contents: buttered eggs, smoked salmon, various marmalades, and a selection of flaky pastries.

Rees followed suit and removed the cover of his tray, but looked equally unwilling to eat. "What exactly did Georgie say to you regarding her new lover?"

"Just that she had selected someone."

"Did she choose someone before our visit to Watier's Club, or that very eve?"

"I received the impression she had chosen a lover before last night. Why don't you tell me what happened at Watier's Club. Did you see Georgiana favor anyone in particular?"

Rees looked at the carpet, his gaze unfocused, his

lips pursed. After a moment, he redirected his attention toward Brock. "Not that I can remember. She spent some time talking about a man costumed in a white robe, but I didn't receive the impression that intimacy existed between them."

"Do you know the costumed man's name?" Brock asked.

"No, I don't." Rees leapt to his feet and began to pace. "I simply can't believe this of Georgie."

"You've already said that, Rees. Several times." Brock regarded the other man closely. "Why do you find the thought hard to accept?"

"She's so, well, honorable."

"My wife attends a demimonde masquerade at Watier's Club, and you call her honorable?"

"She *is* honorable, and much more."

Brock frowned. "Do you know her better than I, or does she merely have you fooled? I wonder."

The younger man pushed back from his tray and stood. His eyes gained a defiant look. "I believe I know her better than you, more's the pity."

About to lift a forkful of smoked salmon to his lips, Brock put his fork down and fixed his gaze on Rees. "Are you mad, Rees, to bait me after all I've been through these past twenty-four hours?"

Eyes wide and face set, Rees nevertheless stood his ground. "I'm simply defending a friend."

"What have I done that's so terrible?"

"You married Georgie only to discard her after gaining her dowry," Rees said without hesitation.

Brock slammed his fork down and stood. "You don't understand the first thing about my relationship with Georgiana and, quite frankly, I'm not willing to enlighten you."

"Why did you do it, Brock?" Rees pressed. "Why did you marry her, then ask me to introduce her into society? I'm husband to her in every way but one."

"Your effrontery is remarkable," Brock observed in clipped tones.

Rees appeared not to have heard him. "Sometimes when she smiles at me, I'm speechless. By God, I want to protect her even as I laugh with her over some nonsense we've embroiled ourselves in. She is beautiful, clever, disarming . . . how could you ignore such a woman?"

"You love her."

"If I love her, then I do so as a sister. I wouldn't allow myself to feel anything else."

Brock looked him in the eye and saw honesty. Suddenly he wanted to laugh. Georgiana had added another feather to her cap. "Evidently you understand all too well my wife's charm."

"Indeed."

"I never saw who she really was until after I married her," Brock admitted with a sigh. He slumped back into his chair and picked up his fork, only to play with his food. "By the time I realized the diamond I had in my grasp, I'd already lost it. I'm trapped, Rees. Trapped by her smile and her sweet nature and the mess I've made of our marriage. She is the woman I'll never have."

"God's blood, Brock, she's your wife! You already have her."

"I have *nothing.* I've hurt her irreparably and I don't believe she'll ever forgive me for it." Abruptly, Brock threw his fork down. It clattered against the serving tray. "She hates me. She's told me so."

The younger man's eyebrows drew together. "And you believed her?"

"Of course I did. Why wouldn't I?"

"Would you permit me to make an observation?"

Brock nodded, a feeling of loss churning inside him, one brought to the forefront by their conversation.

"I've known Georgie for almost two years now," Rees said. "Throughout that time I have never heard her make a single remark about any man but you. When you and she are in the same room, she seeks you out with her gaze, but only when you aren't aware of it. There is such softness in her eyes during those moments that I cannot believe she hates you."

Brock shook his head *no.* Rees's account of the past two years simply didn't match what his own experience had told him.

"And this business with her new lover," Rees continued, "seems very peculiar to me. I would wager any amount that she hasn't a lover but merely led you to believe so, to needle you."

"If what you say is true, why does she possess this relentless desire to cause me grief?"

"I don't think her purpose is to cause you grief. Rather, I think she wishes to draw your attention."

Brock stiffened as though prodded with a hot poker. Georgiana had said the same thing last night. "After we married, Georgiana claimed she hated me and that the very sight of me made her ill. I bowed myself out of her life and allowed her the freedom to do as she wished. But now it appears she thinks I've been ignoring her. Damn the whole female species for its capricious nature."

A smile tugged at Rees's lips. "There's more than hate for you in her heart."

Another knock at the door interrupted them. Assuming Mrs. Steele had returned for their breakfast trays, Brock bid her enter.

Siddons appeared instead and spoke with a sonorous drawl. "Sir Anthony Stanton has come to call," he announced.

Brock pulled the napkin from his lap and threw it on the table. After the business with Gwynllian Stanton, he'd half-expected to see Sir Anthony today. He turned to Rees. "My apologies, Rees, but we're going to have to cut our visit short. I must speak with Georgiana's uncle."

Rees stood as well. "Come to White's tonight, and we'll finish our conversation."

"An excellent suggestion."

The two men exchanged quick bows. Rees then

followed Siddons out of the study. While Brock waited for Sir Anthony, he mused that he hadn't seen quite this many visitors in a single hour since his estate had gone bankrupt and the duns had arrived to collect their money.

Sir Anthony Stanton appeared in the doorway moments later, followed by two serving maids who discreetly removed the breakfast trays.

"Good morning, Sir Stanton," Brock said, surveying the other man's sloppy dress and stubbled chin. "I've been expecting you."

The older man's face had an unusual flush to it. "Georgiana . . . where is she?"

Brock eyed him askance. "She's abed, I believe."

"I must see her."

"She's still sleeping."

The older man stepped closer to Brock, his gaze never wavering in its intensity. "Wake her up."

"Why the urgency? Has it something to do with your sister?"

"Gwynllian? What about Gwynllian?"

"After last night's visit—"

"She's here?"

"No," Brock said, becoming more confused by the moment. "I thought she'd gone to your townhouse. Didn't she arrive?"

One hand on his waist, the other pressed to his forehead, Sir Anthony gave him a harassed look. "I've been traveling all night, and have just returned from Wales."

Eyes narrowed, Brock studied Georgiana's uncle. He'd expected many things from Sir Anthony, but not this wild panic. "Apparently your sister visited Georgiana last night for a brief time before leaving to stay with you."

"I stopped at my London townhouse before coming here. She wasn't there."

"If you haven't seen Gwynllian, then it appears she's disappeared."

Sir Anthony uttered a muffled exclamation of distress.

Brock began to feel angry. "I am completely at sea, man. First your sister appears, then she vanishes, and now I find you on my doorstep at nine-thirty in the morning, without the slightest knowledge of her visit. You must tell me what's going on."

Sir Anthony turned to face him, his gaze piercing, as though he measured Brock to see if he could withstand the truth.

"Tell me. Now," Brock demanded.

"Lord Darleigh, I scarce know where to begin. Still, I must speak to Georgiana first. Privately," he added.

"Why?"

"What I have to say directly affects her. It has much to do with her past. I'm sorry, but I can tell you nothing without her approval."

"She's my wife, for God's sake. I'm entitled to know *everything*."

Sir Anthony hesitated, then fixed him with another intense gaze. "Lord Darleigh, you do not know who you are married to."

Brock swore softly. "Christ Almighty, is everyone privy to the painful circumstances of my marriage? Do you, too, intend to castigate me?"

"You weren't my first choice for Georgiana's husband," the other man told him bluntly. "Judging by the pieces in the scandal rags, your marriage has been less than successful. Perhaps that's for the best."

"For the best? Are you wishing my marriage ill?"

"Things have changed, Lord Darleigh. I'm afraid that from now on, your marriage to Georgiana is only going to cause difficulties."

Brock thumped a hand against his forehead. "I can't believe I'm hearing this. Are you counseling me toward divorce, sir?"

"Georgiana is special in ways you don't understand. As much as it pains me to say this, she's better off without you now."

The sourness in Brock's gut flared again, scorching his insides. "Explain what you mean by all of this."

"Wake Georgiana," Sir Anthony countered. "Let me talk to her. Then we shall see what I can tell you."

Chapter
6

❧

Someone was shaking her shoulder. Again.

Georgiana rolled onto her back, tangling her legs in the bedcovers, and focused bleary eyes on Nellie. She felt as though she hadn't slept a wink. "What time is it?"

Nellie glanced at the window as she folded the top layer of bedcovers back. Bright sunlight streamed through the panes and settled against the floor. "Almost ten o'clock, Lady Darleigh. Your uncle is here to see you."

Fighting off sleep, Georgiana pushed up on one elbow. The grogginess reminded her of the time she'd twisted her ankle some years ago, and had to take laudanum before she could rest. The morning after taking the dose, she'd awoken feeling this way. Had she taken laudanum last night, for some reason?

No. Last night, she'd attended Watier's Club, and then. . . .

Heat flooded her cheeks. She'd made love to Brock. Images assaulted her, erotic recollections of the way he'd kissed her, and filled her, and—

Left her alone in her bedchamber.

Her spirits sank. As an ache settled in around her heart, she wished she hadn't remembered, that somehow, this strange sleepiness would have taken the hurt away.

She closed her eyes and pressed her face against the pillow.

"Sir Stanton is waiting," Nellie reminded her in brisk tones.

Georgiana groaned. Why in God's name would her uncle visit so early? She simply wanted to be left alone to nurse her wounds, but no, now she had to go entertain Sir Anthony. With luck he'd have some news of Wales and Aunt Gwynllian, rather than wanting to ask all of those uncomfortable questions about how she and Brock were faring, and if those rumors he'd heard about her were true.

Aunt Gwynllian.

Georgiana sat straight up in bed. Abruptly she remembered all. Just last night she'd talked to her aunt. Filled with grief and self-loathing, she'd wished for her aunt's comfort and Gwynllian had appeared. But the Gwynllian who had visited had been a pale imitation of the person Georgiana remembered . . . as if someone had created her.

Georgiana's spirits sank even lower. In the cold light of day, her experience with Gwynllian suggested she had gone quite mad. Her desire to yawn vanished, along with the last few wisps of sleep still clinging to her. "How long has Sir Stanton been waiting?"

"For thirty minutes or so. He insists on seeing you immediately. What shall I tell him?"

Georgiana sighed. "Tell him he may come up right away."

Nellie dropped into a quick curtsey. "Yes, ma'am. I'll return in a few minutes with breakfast." She walked toward the door, then paused and looked back at Georgiana. "Miss Stanton *did* visit you last night, Lady Darleigh. I saw her myself."

"You brought us tea," Georgiana confirmed, wondering if she could have infected Nellie with her madness, or if Nellie was patronizing her as they all occasionally patronized Brock's mother, *pretending* to see just to keep the patient calm.

Nellie let out a sigh. "Siddons didn't believe me when I told him Miss Stanton had visited. When he couldn't find Miss Stanton in the house, nor any of her luggage, he thought I'd contracted some sort of mind sickness like . . ." She trailed off and sent Georgiana a guilty look.

Georgiana nodded sympathetically, understanding the reference to Brock's mother. The maid's sincere tone convinced her that Nellie wasn't patronizing her, but in fact thought she had conversed with Gwynllian. Either they were both utterly mad or had seen something very strange indeed. "I'll confirm your story, Nellie. Don't fret about it. Just bring Sir Stanton to me."

Nellie curtseyed again. "Right away, ma'am."

Georgiana waited for Nellie to shut the door behind her before she jumped out of bed and pulled on her silk wrapper. The last few days had proven uncommonly cold and her wrapper did little to warm her up. She huddled within its soft folds and walked to the window, her gaze settling on her uncle's barouche in the carriageway.

Brock, she reasoned, must have summoned him. He couldn't possibly have heard about Gwynllian's visit so quickly otherwise. Her husband's involvement brought new problems. Unless she could convince Brock—and everyone else—that Gwynllian had indeed visited Palmer House last night, he would think his wife teetered on the edge of madness and have all the more reason to restrict her activities. And even though Nellie might corroborate her story, he'd assume the lady's maid was lying to protect her mistress.

Moments later her uncle arrived, curtailing her thoughts. She heard him in the hallway, calling her name. As soon as she told him to enter, the door swung open and he strode in, his faded blue eyes wide.

"Georgiana," he said, expelling a breath at the same time and making her name sound like a long hiss of relief.

She smiled and moved forward to hug him. "Uncle Anthony, I'm glad you've come."

"And I'm glad to discover you're in good health."

They parted, Georgiana taking the opportunity to study his appearance. The gray hair fringing his bald head looked uncombed, and his leg-o'-mutton whiskers needed a trim. His clothes, she noted, seemed well-worn, judging by his disheveled cravat and the wrinkles which creased his trousers.

"What brings you to Palmer House so early?" she asked, thinking how banal the question sounded, given what was on her mind. But how to jump into a discussion where they might end up questioning her sanity? Better to let him lead that particular conversation.

His gaze touched on the various pieces of furniture in her room as he evidently thought about his answer. Georgiana felt as though he could hardly bear to look at her. At length, however, he focused upon her, his gaze so intense she almost shrank from it.

"You wore the serpent's egg."

Completely thrown off, Georgiana stared at him. His statement, delivered so bluntly, had the feel of an accusation. "The serpent's egg? What's that?"

Sir Anthony let out a small, impatient sigh. "You must have worn it, Georgiana. It's imperative that you be honest with me and tell me what happened. We haven't much time."

"Serpent's egg? Are you referring to the old Welsh tales about druid's glass?" she asked, memories from her childhood in Wales coming to the fore.

"Yes. The serpent's egg is a small egg, made of green or blue glass, and is usually suspended by a chain, so a druid might wear it around his neck."

Georgiana grew very still. "Can the egg also be made of red glass?"

He strode forward and gripped her shoulders. "Where did you get it?"

"I found it in a meadow in Wales, many years ago," she whispered.

"Did you wear the pendant last night?"

"For the first time in my life. You're frightening me, uncle."

Sighing, he released her and motioned to a velvet-upholstered side chair. "Sit down, dear. I can see you know nothing."

Mollified only slightly, she settled into the indicated chair. "I know less than nothing."

He nodded and chose a settee by the fireplace, angling it so he might face her. "I had hoped to protect you, Georgiana, as had Gwynllian," he said, his tone heavy. "You're the daughter we never had and are very dear to us. But I suppose it's impossible to thwart destiny. Indeed, Gwynllian and I have both been fearing and anticipating this moment."

Georgiana could feel the tension gathering in the room around her. She held the sides of the armchair and braced for the revelation she knew was to come. "What do you mean?"

"You are very special, Georgiana, the child of two very special people. You have the ability to create illusions, as had your mother and father before you."

Silence filled the room.

Georgiana gaped at him.

Shock leaked through her insides like ice water, making her shiver. For a moment, she couldn't think.

"Georgiana?" Sir Anthony quickly stood and walked to her side. He took her hand and held it. "You know what I'm talking about, don't you? You aren't even going to question me."

"I know," she managed, her voice trembling. "I created an illusion of Aunt Gwynllian last night. But I don't understand how."

"You're ice-cold. Come sit by the fireplace with me," he coaxed. "I'll start a fire."

She stood on legs that felt wooden and allowed him to lead her over to the settee he'd just occupied. He wrapped a blanket around her and sat her down while confusion and a strange sense of foreboding filled her mind like a fog. Just as he began to start a fire, Nellie knocked and entered with a tray of hot cocoa and croissants.

The lady's maid placed the cocoa on a side table by Georgiana's elbow and clucked when she saw Georgiana's countenance. "Poor lamb. First you could hardly wake up, and now you're as pale as a sheet. Should I send for the physician?"

"She'll be fine," Sir Anthony assured the maid. "A few sips of cocoa will warm her up."

Nellie crouched by his side and took the flint from him. "You appear a bit pale too, Sir Stanton. I hope we're not all coming down with something. Let me start the fire."

"Thank you, Nellie." Sir Anthony straightened and sat next to Georgiana. He handed her a cup of cocoa, which she gratefully sipped. After a minute Nellie had a fire crackling in the hearth. Giving one more solicitous cluck, the maid left Georgiana and Sir Anthony alone.

With the hot cocoa, the blanket, and the fire, Georgiana felt warm but far from comforted. She turned to her uncle and placed her hand on his, noting his skin felt unusually moist. "I don't understand what's happening, and it frightens me. Please, start from the beginning, and tell me everything—about my mother and father, how you knew about Aunt Gwynllian's midnight appearance—absolutely everything. But first, tell me about the serpent's egg."

He patted her hand, then placed it in her lap. "The *glain-non-Druidhe* is an oval piece of colored glass, usually green and blue. I know of only one druid who possessed a red serpent's egg. Her name was Branwyn, and she was my sister."

"So I found your sister's pendant all those years ago?"

"Apparently. I'd wager it was your destiny to find it. May I see the pendant?"

Her fingers flew to her throat. She couldn't feel it against her skin now. It must have fallen in the bedcovers while she slept. She unwrapped herself from the blanket, moved to the tester bed, and searched through the sheets until she found the pendant. Frowning, she held it up until it sparkled in a ray of sunlight. As ugly as the night before, the pendant created a blood-red stain of light on the wall.

Sir Anthony walked to her side and gazed at it. "Druid's glass is supposed to protect the wearer from hostile incantations. But it has brought our family nothing but ill luck."

"I remember the old Welsh tales about serpent's eggs," she said, taking a moment to search her scattered thoughts. "When a mass of snakes entwine, their spittle creates an egg. The snakes cast this egg off through their hissing, and a wise druid will catch the egg in a cloth and race away with it, before the pursuing snakes catch him. It's a symbol of office worn by a true druid."

"That's correct."

"Your sister was a druid?"

He nodded his head affirmatively.

Georgiana paused to digest this piece of intelligence. She knew more than the average person about druidism, having grown up in Wales near the Isle of Anglesey, which had once been a druid stronghold. The tales of druidism she'd heard had talked of a gentle people who worshipped the trees and nature in general. In fact, she'd often suspected her Aunt Gwynllian had been a druid. Her aunt's love of nature and her peculiar connection with the outdoors suggested a knowledge that ran deeper than usual.

Overall, druidism had appeared to be a noble, if innocuous, religion. And yet, Georgiana felt certain that the glass pendant lay at the root of her recent peculiar experiences. Perhaps druidism wasn't so innocuous after all.

"And Aunt Gwynllian?" she asked. "Is she a druid, too?"

"She is."

"And you?"

"Yes."

She paused, and shook her head, and then looked back at him. "I may have suspected, but I never knew for certain."

"We didn't wish you to know."

Another thought occurred to her. She sucked in a quick breath and asked, "Do you expect me to become a druid?"

A smile curved his lips, but it was a sickly one. "You can't transform into a druid overnight. It takes twenty or more years of study to become one. You, however, have a very unique ability, one coveted by all druids. I'm afraid that with or without training, you will have to join the order. There is no longer any choice."

"You're referring to my ability to create illusions," she whispered, wonder making her buoyant. "I can create them, no?"

"Unfortunately. If you hadn't found and worn the egg, then you couldn't have created one. But now that you've done so, every druid in England has felt the echoes of that illusion."

"The egg allows me to create these illusions you speak of?"

"It helps you focus your energies. Your mother could create illusions like you, but she grew to the point where she no longer needed the serpent's egg. While few possessed her power, many coveted it."

"So, my mother was a druid, too."

"She was."

"And Sir John, my father? Did he practice druidism?"

"Georgiana, there is something Gwynllian and I haven't told you."

She stiffened, her gaze flying to his face.

"Sir John Wesley and his wife Margaret were not your parents."

"What?"

"My sister, Branwyn, was your mother."

Shock turning her veins to ice, she pressed a hand against her forehead.

"Sir John and Margaret were my good friends. When they died in a carriage accident, their new-born daughter died with them. Gwynllian and I pretended that you were their orphaned daughter to hide your identity. I am truly your uncle, Georgiana, and Gwynllian is your true aunt."

"Is my mother alive, too?" she cried, unanswered questions making her dizzy.

"She passed on many years ago."

"What happened to her? And where is my real father? And why did you have to hide my identity?"

"Answers you shall have." He stood and paced a bit, in the manner of a man about to embark on a difficult tale. When he finally returned his attention to her, his voice was subdued.

"Your mother, your aunt, and I were members of the Welsh Order of Glamorgan Druids, an order which most people thought had disbanded centuries earlier. We were a secretive group. One among us possessed a wondrous ability that many would covet should they learn about it. So we sought to protect ourselves by concealing our existence."

"The wondrous ability is that which produces illusions," Georgiana murmured. Her head still throbbed terribly with the knowledge that the man and woman she'd spent most of her life grieving for weren't even related to her. She felt lost. Adrift.

He nodded. "Your mother, Branwyn, was a Guardian of Becoming, and she passed her ability on to you when she conceived you."

"A Guardian of Becoming?"

"One who protects that which could be."

"I don't understand."

"One of the oldest books of druidry, *Mabinogion*, speaks of special descendents of the *Sidhe*, or fairy people. These descendents are known as the Guardians of Becoming. They stand in the threshold between the worlds of chaos and order, and supervise that which passes through."

"What makes these guardians special?" she asked.

"The guardians can create with their minds. They take unformed energy from the world of chaos, and give it form and direction, placing it in the world of order."

"You mean, a Guardian of Becoming could produce, say, a real apple out of thin air?"

"Indeed."

"And my mother could do this?"

"Not quite. At first, the guardians are unskilled and can only create illusions without substance. But as they practice and begin to understand their ability, their illusions become increasingly solid until finally, they discover how to bring something real into existence.

"Only a very few guardians have progressed to this stage. Merlin was one of them. Your mother came close, but never quite achieved the power described in *Mabinogion*."

Georgiana placed a shaky hand against her brow. "I cannot imagine such an ability."

"It's more a burden than anything else. Think of the temptation! You could have anything you desired, including limitless wealth and power. History tells us that greed and corruption often infect people with vast resources. Unfortunately, mankind hasn't the pureness of soul to act selflessly in all situations."

"Can a guardian create only inanimate objects?"

"So far, the guardians who have walked this earth have only created inanimate objects. But *Mabinogion* mentions one who was able to create plants, animals, and people too. You know Him as God."

A superstitious chill ran through her. She glanced out the window, almost expecting a thunderbolt to rend the lawn in two. Serene blue skies greeted her vision. "Uncle, you speak blasphemy to suggest I could be, well, God Himself with enough practice."

"We were all created in his image, Georgiana. The soul is forever seeking to mirror his perfection. In any case, He *wants* us to be like Him."

"But power like this, in the wrong hands—" She broke off and shuddered.

"Could prove devastating," Sir Anthony agreed. "Most of the guardians have died out. I have mixed emotions about that. On one hand, a great gift has been almost lost, but on the other hand, humankind remains safe. As far as I know, there are only three Guardians of Becoming in the world today."

"And I'm one of them."

"Yes."

"Who are the other two?"

"One is a young man named David Gwylum. Some say he's a descendent of Lugh, the warrior-champion of the Tuatha De Danann and god of light. He's several years your junior, and has been a member of the Order of Glamorgan Druids from early childhood."

Georgiana chewed her lower lip. "Who is the other guardian?"

Sir Anthony's gaze sharpened, as though something about her question bothered him, but inexplicably he remained mute. The silence dragged out between them. For the first time she noticed beads of perspiration on his forehead.

Disquieted, she leaned toward him. "Who is the other guardian, uncle?"

"His name is Cadwallon ab Ilfor Bach, and he is my contemporary," Sir Anthony murmured. "He is no longer one of us."

Georgiana waited for him to continue, but he fixed his gaze on the carpet and said nothing. At length, she ventured hesitantly into the silence. "He sounds rather unpleasant."

"He chose a different path than the rest of us. You know him as the Duke of Gloucester. He is also the Arch Druid of the Order of Caer Llundain Druids."

"Oh!" Georgiana frowned in disgust. "He's an awful man. I'm not surprised to hear he has special druidic ability. How else could such a worm rise to the heights he's attained in court?"

"He worships the Cailleach, an old, elemental goddess with a taste for blood. Some say Cailleach was the first mortal Guardian of Becoming to walk the earth, before Merlin . . . indeed, before Christ himself, who possessed a rather well-developed ability. My druidic order has been battling the duke and all he represents for many years."

Sir Anthony's words had had such a ring of finality to them Georgiana didn't have the courage to question him further. Intense curiosity to know more about her mother burned within her. Rather than pursue the clearly uncomfortable topic of the duke, she focused upon the woman who had borne her. "Tell me what it was like growing up with my mother and Aunt Gwynllian."

He sighed. "It wasn't easy having them as sisters. Branwyn and Gwynllian were cut of the same cloth, two puckish little girls who knew the woods like the back of their hand and enjoyed playing practical jokes on me. Branwyn always seemed to be in the lead, and when she first learned how to create an illusion, hell really broke loose. I cannot count the number of times I stepped in a pile of muck, thinking it wildflowers or whatever Branwyn had decided to fool me with. As she grew, thank God, she suppressed her childish instincts and used her ability in a mature fashion."

Georgiana felt her spirits lighten at the fond exasperation in his voice. He'd often sounded like that during the times he'd charged over to Palmer House to chide her about some tale he'd heard about her. Perhaps she had a bit of her mother's puckish nature in her. She began to feel a little less forlorn. "What about Aunt Gwynllian?"

"Your aunt was the quieter of the two, more prone to introspection and very intuitive. Druidic knowledge came easily to her. She seemed to understand things without formal teaching—like the meanings behind an owl's patterns in flight. People came to her with questions about the future, questions she knew before they were even asked."

Georgiana nodded, her uncle's description similar to her own childhood memories of growing up with Aunt Gwynllian in Wales. The emphasis had always been on trees, flowers, seasons . . . anything to do with nature. "When did my mother begin studying with the order?"

"Just after her twelfth birthday, when she blossomed into womanhood. By that time all three of us were members of the order. As had our parents before us, we learned tales of druidic lore, such as those contained in the *Book of Taliesin*, and practiced the traditions passed down from times before Christ walked the earth."

He hesitated and fixed her with a candid look. "While our youth might sound idyllic, your mother had a heavy burden on her shoulders. The Glamorgan Druids, in an attempt to keep the line of guardians alive, expected her to mate with Cadwallon ab Ilfor Bach and conceive a child."

"Mate with the Duke of Gloucester? Why?"

"Experience has taught us that the odds are quite high that two parents with the ability to create illusions will produce a child with the same gift."

"But I thought the duke was a druidic outcast of some sort."

"At that time, he hadn't yet turned his back on us. Your mother chose to satisfy her obligation to the Glamorgan Druids and mated with him," Sir Anthony said, his expression matter-of-fact. "You are the result."

Georgiana became perfectly still. "I am the result."

"I apologize for being so blunt, but these are things you must understand," he said gently. "The duke is your father."

My father, she silently repeated, a hollow feeling in the pit of her stomach. "Does he know I exist?"

"No."

"Why not?"

"Shortly after your mother became with child, the duke turned to Cailleach, the old hag-goddess of winter. He actively sought both your death and your mother's. While you narrowly escaped, Branwyn's death he achieved. Only through constant vigilance have we concealed the fact that you live."

Georgiana felt tears start in her eyes. "I don't understand."

"As I said, it began shortly after your mother mated with the duke. Occasionally our order exchanged traditions and ideas with an English order of druids founded some twenty years earlier. The trouble started when the druids of the English order attended one of our eisteddfodau."

"Eisteddfodau?"

"Assemblies organized to offer competitions and awards to bards for their poetic work. Our bards, before they could become ovates and then druids, had to prove their knowledge of the ancient traditions by reciting poetry, telling stories, and the like. Often a bard would introduce a poem or tale of his own making, to display his or her adeptness."

"My mother was a bard, too?" she managed.

Sir Anthony nodded. "Branwyn was a very gifted storyteller, second only to Gwydion himself. She owed part of her success to her ability to create illusions, which she used during the telling of a tale. Her audience, so enraptured by her words and the images she evoked, didn't realize she was also creating illusions to support her tales. They literally became so absorbed you could set off a nearby cannon and no one would stir."

Georgiana shook her head slowly. The thought that her *father* had snuffed out the life of this gentle person, and deprived her of her mother in the process, had created a tight ball of anger inside her.

"At one particular eisteddfod," he continued, "Branwyn told her tales, and then Gwynllian divined the future for those who asked. When the duke asked for a reading, she told him that while his ancestry placed him in line for the English throne, he would never achieve such an exalted position. Somehow, you would interfere with his destiny."

"Me?" she breathed. "I wasn't even born!"

"Nevertheless, you *were* conceived, and as long as you remained alive—even inside of Branwyn—you represented a threat."

"So he killed my mother?"

Sir Anthony nodded, his eyes sad. "He left the Glamorgan Druids to join the English druids. The Englishmen, never having seen a Guardian of Becoming, were astounded by his ability to create illusions and quickly made him Arch Druid of their order. Then, as your mother approached her term, he and his minions hunted her down like a hind in the woods. They killed her, but not before she had the chance to hide you in the fields close to Cadair Abbey."

"Aunt Gwynllian found me," Georgiana guessed, her heart aching.

"That she did. The mighty oak protected you, and the duke never realized you had escaped Branwyn's fate. Gwynllian and I concealed you in the Welsh woodlands, pretending you were the orphaned daughter of Sir John and Margaret Wesley, so he wouldn't know that you lived and come after you again.

"If you hadn't used your powers of illusion, we could have kept you a secret forever. But I'm afraid that the moment you created your illusions of Gwynllian, you alerted every druid in England, Ireland, and Wales of your existence. I myself heard it. I've been traveling through the night to reach you."

"How did you hear?"

"When energy passes from the world of chaos to the world of order, it sets off certain vibrations that skilled druids can detect. Your ability is so strong, it's akin to a lighthouse beacon. Even those with only slight knowledge could feel it."

"And the duke . . ."

"Is undoubtedly looking for you. We do have one advantage over him," Sir Anthony pointed out. "While he knows you exist, he does not know your identity."

"It's a small advantage at best."

"I'm afraid I must agree with you. Gwynllian and the Glamorgan Druids no doubt felt the echoes of your illusion as well. They're probably already travelling to England, but I've sent them a note telling them I'll bring you to Wales. Hopefully the note will intercept them before they arrive in London. I don't want any Welsh druids descending on Palmer House—they'd only raise the duke's suspicions."

"What about David Gwylum? Where is he?"

"I've heard he's in London, though I haven't had time to speak to him. No doubt he felt the echoes of your illusions, too. I have sent a note around to his residence, asking him to join us in Wales."

Eyes widening, Georgiana sucked in a breath. "Is there any chance he attended the masquerade at Watier's Club last night?"

"Why do you ask?"

"I saw a young man there, blond-haired, in a

druid's costume. He actually conversed with my illusion of Gwynllian, and then stared at me. At the same time, the Duke of Gloucester fixed his attention on this druid."

A frown creased Sir Anthony's brow. "That sounds like David. Did he approach you?"

"No. He slipped out the front door."

"Well, at least he had enough sense to stay away from you, and avoid focusing the duke's attention on you, too. He's been living secretly in London, watching the duke for me. That young man is extremely capable, and quite handsome, too. You'll meet him in Wales."

Her thoughts darted to Brock. How was he going to react to all this? "When do *we* leave?"

"On the morrow." Sir Anthony paused to take a deep breath. "There is more you must know, Georgiana. Do you remember how I explained that your mother mated with the duke to produce another child of illusion? Well, the Glamorgan Druids will expect you to mate with David Gwylum and conceive a new generation of guardians."

Chapter
7
❦

"What?" Georgiana stared at him, her lips parted. Shock coursed through her. "I'm married! I can't mate with David Gwylum."

"The Glamorgan Druids will not care about your marital status," he predicted. "They are pagans and don't recognize the sanctity of Christian vows."

"Aren't you a Glamorgan Druid, uncle?"

"I am."

"And you care nothing for Christianity?"

"We worship in our own way," he insisted.

"Well, I'm not going to mate with a man I don't love. He isn't even a man—he's a youth! Good God, Uncle, you make me sound like a prized mare."

"The Glamorgan Druids will not give up easily," he warned. "They will also expect you to join our order and prevent the duke from gaining the English throne, as your destiny decrees."

"I won't mate with him," she stubbornly insisted, without even thinking it through. Loyalty to Brock flared in her veins, making them hot.

"Why not? Is your marriage to Brock all that happy? From what I've heard, you two practically lead separate lives."

Some of the fire in Georgiana's veins cooled. Just a few hours ago she had resolved to forget about Brock and return to her former life in Wales.

"The Glamorgan Druids are your people," her uncle pressed. "Now that you've made your presence known to them, I cannot keep them from you. And while they'll place demands upon you, they'll help to protect you as well. That kind of help might prove particularly useful in your effort to prevent the duke from gaining the throne."

"You and Gwynllian are my people. You're my family, Uncle. I don't need the Glamorgan Druids."

"We're your family, but over the years it's become clear to the both of us that we're not enough for you. Perhaps growing up an orphan had something to do with it. In any event, Gwynllian and I have marked your restlessness, which you've displayed since childhood."

"I wish you'd trusted me with the truth," she said.

"We wanted to protect you. We love you and have never been able to withstand your unhappiness."

"I know." She stood and gave him a quick hug. "I love you both, too."

"I'm very worried about you, Georgiana," he said, his voice tight with emotion.

Frowning, she returned to the settee and wrapped the blanket around herself. "Tell me exactly where I stand, Uncle."

He took a deep breath. "You are a Guardian of Becoming. It's your destiny to prevent the Duke of Gloucester, a man we both know as evil, from gaining the throne of England. Of lesser importance, you are expected to assume a life as a druid among the Glamorgan Druids, and mate with David Gwylum to produce another Guardian of Becoming."

"And Lord Darleigh? Where does he fit in?"

"He doesn't," Sir Anthony stated baldly.

Before she could formulate a reply, harsh knocking sounded at the door. She and her uncle exchanged surprised glances.

"That's probably Lord Darleigh," Sir Anthony said. "Would you like me to talk to him?"

"No. I'm going to tell him everything, Uncle."

"It will be difficult," he predicted.

"I know." Almost trembling at thoughts of the confrontation to come, Georgiana stood and walked toward the door. Before she could grasp the knob, the door swung open and Brock strode in.

"I cannot wait a moment longer. You will tell me why you think Georgiana is better off without me," he demanded.

Georgiana's breath caught in her throat. As her gaze locked with Brock's much darker one, an ineffable sadness welled up inside her. Once she'd told him that she was the Duke of Gloucester's bastard and a druid besides, their marriage would be well and truly over.

She stared at his wrinkled jacket and trousers, the same ones he'd worn the previous night, and knew their night together had affected him as much as her. Her gaze shifted to his arms, which had enfolded her deep in the night, and held her so tightly while her defenses crumbled and they joined as one. The old longing swelled up in her, for the man she'd once thought he was. The bluish circles under his eyes and his stubbled chin made her wonder if he could be that man again.

God help her, she wanted him. She wanted him still, despite all that had gone before. She felt the wanting inside her like a shout that she kept suppressed deep within, vibrating with its intensity, rocking her entire being yet invisible to any but her.

There was something between them that couldn't be denied and couldn't be ignored.

Brock looked from Sir Anthony to Georgiana. "Tell me," he insisted, his voice low.

Georgiana cast an agonized glance at Sir Anthony. Suddenly she didn't want to tell Brock anything. She didn't want to create more trouble between them. She wanted to lay her head against his shoulder and feel his arms enfold her again.

"I'll leave the two of you alone," her uncle said, then turned to go.

She held a hand out, silently begging him to stay and help her through this. He hesitated a moment, perhaps thinking of his earlier offer to talk to Brock. Then, with an apologetic look, he slipped quietly from the room.

Brock locked the door behind Sir Anthony, then returned to her side and took her hands in his warmer ones. "You're cold, Georgiana. Sit down by the fire."

"I don't want to sit, Brock." She pulled her hands from his and walked over to the fireplace. Her gaze settled on the flames licking at wood, but in her mind, she saw Brock's face, burnished with candle-light and tense with need, the way he'd looked as he made love to her.

He came up behind her and placed his hands on her shoulders, making her jump. "By God, you're edgy," he murmured, and began to knead the back of her neck.

His touch felt so damned good that every nerve in her body demanded she fall against him and let him work his magic on her. Instead, she pulled away and faced him, knowing the folly of surrender. "And you're being unusually accommodating. Why?"

"I've been thinking about what you said." He dropped his hands to his side and gave her a lop-sided smile. "God knows you've said a lot."

He was different this morning, she thought. His manner held a plea that made him appear open, honest, younger even. It made him look like the Brock she'd known before she'd married. Frowning, she narrowed her eyes; but inside, she despaired. The change, if it had truly come, had come too late. "My words no longer matter, Brock. Nothing is the same as it was last night."

His face tightened. "Nevertheless, I will have my say." He moved to the window and stared out at the grounds. "I married you for your money, Georgiana. I must be brutally honest about that. But I haven't ignored you in the years since our marriage. While I've kept my distance, primarily because I thought you couldn't stand the sight of me, I've watched you incessantly." He spun around and fixed her with an intense gaze. "I've discovered that the woman I've married is a very fine one."

She sucked in a little breath. "Brock, I—"

"I'd like to get to know you better," he cut in, and closed the distance between them until he stood so close she could feel the heat from his body. "I want to court you again."

"You don't understand—"

"I want you back." He put his arms around her and pulled her against him, warming her, making her feel safe and protected. At the same time, the knot of sadness in her swelled and swelled until she thought it might burst. These were the words she'd been longing to hear. But the woman he'd married was about to disappear, replaced by a bastard and a druid. Would he still feel the same way about her after he'd learned the truth?

The knot inside her throbbed. An unreasoning stab of hatred for her uncle shot through her. Sir Anthony had taken her one good chance at happiness away from her.

Or perhaps she'd taken it away from herself.

She began to cry.

"Shh, Georgie," he whispered against her hair. "I know things have been bad between us. I know what I've done to you. Forgive me, and let me try again."

She clenched her jaw. Heaven help her, she had never hurt so badly. Still, she had to tell him. He had to know. First, though, she would savor this moment of tenderness between them, because it might be the last they ever knew. She pressed her face against his broad chest and hugged him tightly, trying to stop the sobs long enough to tell him what she needed him to hear. "No matter what the future brings, Brock . . . no matter how we're separated, know that I'll always be yours."

He stiffened. "We won't be separated."

"Oh, Brock. . . ."

Growing even more tense, he reached behind to his back and pulled her hands apart, then gripped her shoulders and moved her back a foot. Lips set, he stared at her. "What did Sir Stanton tell you?"

She returned his gaze through tear-filled eyes. "I'm not the person you think I am."

"He said the same thing to me. As far as I'm concerned, I know exactly who you are. You're the Marchioness of Darleigh. My wife."

"There is more that you must know."

"Christ Almighty, tell me then. Stop bandying words around."

"It's very difficult—"

"What is so very difficult? Is it something in your past? Something you've done? Were you a thief? Have you incurred impossible gambling debts?"

Her throat felt tight. She couldn't speak. She decided instead to show him exactly what she meant. Silently, she pulled away from him and retrieved her druid's egg, which she'd placed on a side table. She slipped it over her head. Smooth and cold, it nestled between her breasts.

His lip curled. "Why do you put on your lover's token? Are you telling me that you've chosen him over me?"

"I haven't taken a lover, Brock," she managed, finding her voice at last. She would spare him that pain, at least. "When I told you that I wanted another man, I did so solely out of a desire to hurt you. Not very noble of me, was it?"

His shoulders sagged. "Neither of us have shown much nobility lately. But where did you get the necklace, then? It's a damned ugly piece," he added.

"I found it in a Welsh meadow years ago." Heated by her body, the pendant grew warm between her breasts. "In a way, it *is* a token of claiming. It represents my people."

"Your people . . . as in Gwynllian and Sir Stanton?"

"I must show you something." She sat down on the settee and closed her eyes. In her mind, she imagined the fog she had seen on the grounds the previous night: silvery-white with moonlight, swirling, full of potential. Behind the fog she heard an angry, all-too-familiar buzz.

"Georgiana?" Brock's voice held a note of concern.

She thought back to that day in Hyde Park, when Brock kissed her first, before they'd married. Thick streamers of mist had veiled the harshest of the sun's rays, allowing sunshine the color of butter to warm the evergreens around them. Dew, lightly fragranced with pine, dripped from oak trees and gorse bushes, mingling with the scent of warm, sweaty horseflesh.

Her heart beating faster, she molded the fog swirling through her mind to match her recollection. At the same time, the chaotic vibrations that bothered her so smoothed out into tones and patterns she recognized, like orderly music. The druid's egg grew even warmer against her skin. As if from far away, she heard Brock's gasp.

She immersed herself deeper in the memory.

Their horses had walked behind them, both sets of reins in Brock's hand. Several impressions of Brock surfaced one after the other: he'd towered over her, he'd looked very polished in his black Hessians and red hunting jacket, he'd smelled of something elemental like sea spray or grass. In short, he was the most masculine being she'd ever met.

Her breathing came a little quicker. She heard a chair scrape backward with a sharp noise that almost jerked her from the memory. Frowning, she focused on the pictures in her mind.

She'd worn a green velvet riding habit and had a rakish hat perched atop her head. She knew she'd never looked better. The admiration in his eyes told her so. When he leaned forward to kiss her, she held her breath; and when their lips touched delicately, her body surged with yearnings she couldn't name but knew she must satisfy.

After parting, he'd laughed softly, and she'd joined in, so happy she thought she might die of it. He was her knight, her man-about-town, and somehow, he had fallen in love with her.

Georgiana allowed her shoulders to shrug forward slightly. The fog in her mind was gone, replaced by a recollection so precise and complete she could have been standing in that same evergreen forest where she and Brock had first kissed. Music that she'd created from chaos flowed through her veins. Her druid's egg was hot against her skin, almost uncomfortably so, and she opened her eyes.

Shock rippled through her. Although she'd

expected as much, the rational part of her just couldn't accept it.

Half of her bedchamber had disappeared.

Just beyond her tester bed, the walls and carpeting faded into mulch, gorse bushes and pine trees. It was as though a giant axe had sliced her bedchamber in two and transported the half she stood in into a forest. She even heard a soft breeze whispering through the forest canopy.

"I'm dreaming," someone whispered.

Georgiana glanced to her left and saw Brock, pressed against the far wall, his attention locked on the forest. His face had gone quite pale and his eyes were mere slashes of black as he evidently tried to assimilate what he was seeing. She moved toward him while keeping the forest in her line of vision, aware the strange sleepiness that she'd felt the previous night was creeping over her again.

An image flickered in her mind, of Brock's face, then of the forest, and then of her own face. The perspective was very odd and kept shifting. She knew she was seeing through the eyes of the illusions she'd created.

When she stood close to Brock, she grasped his hand, noting his palm felt cold and moist.

"Georgiana," he whispered. "Am I going mad? Or do you see it too?"

Fighting off the urge to close her eyes and sleep, she squeezed his hand once. The lethargy was much stronger now than it had been last night. "You're not mad, Brock."

He didn't answer; rather, his hand trembled within hers. Did he believe her reassurances? She couldn't even guess. But he would have to believe, and accept, or he truly *would* go mad. Feeling some security in the heat of his body next to hers, she stared at the illusion she'd created.

Within the trees, a man and woman were looking at each other and smiling. Brock's red hunting jacket and polished Hessians, her velvet riding habit and girlish smile—they were perfect down to the tiniest detail. Georgiana watched as the man bent his head toward the woman and whispered something into her ear, making her tremble visibly.

Georgiana remembered what he'd murmured: *marry me.* She almost had to look away, the scene was so painful. God, she'd been so stupid, such a dupe. And Brock had acted so damned smooth, he deserved an award for his performance.

Abruptly, her husband of two years squeezed her hand. When he spoke, his voice was raw with wonder. "What is this?"

"Our past." She closed her eyes, depression making her more vulnerable to the encroaching lethargy.

"Are you doing this?"

"Yes."

He made a noise somewhere between a question and a groan. Georgiana forced herself to lift her eyelids and stay awake. He needed her now.

The horses that stood behind the couple breathed soft plumes of mist toward the forest loam. Georgiana could almost smell their sweaty flesh. Again, she marveled at how complete the illusion appeared.

Without warning, the large bay hunter that Brock had ridden pawed at the ground. The other horse, a dainty mare with white forelegs, picked up the hunter's agitation and snorted at the pine boughs. She, too, began to paw at the ground, her dark eyes wide.

Georgiana's brows drew together as her vision flickered. Now she was watching the horses from within the illusion. Whose eyes was she looking through? She didn't know. Nor did she care at the moment. What concerned her more was the horses' agitated movements. She didn't remember this part. The hunter and mare had been calm, the day perfect.

A stronger wind ruffled the man's hair. The little black veil on the end of the woman's riding hat fluttered. Georgiana, watching from afar in her bedchamber, felt the breeze and the heat of the sun's rays. Hounds bayed in the distance.

Confused, she stared at the couple in the center of the illusion. They'd directed their gazes behind them, down the lane they'd been walking along. A niggling sense of unease stole through her. She cast her mind back, trying to remember if their walk had been interrupted by a brace of hounds in pursuit of a fox.

No. They'd remained alone.

The man put his arm around his soon-to-be wife and drew the horses closer. They began to walk faster, casting glances over their shoulders all the while. With each passing second, the baying grew louder and their horses became increasingly agitated, the large bay sidestepping and bumping into the mare.

Fog flooded into the illusion, as though propelled by a giant hand. It obscured the couple's feet.

Georgiana swallowed. Normally a pack of hounds wouldn't indicate trouble, but somehow, she knew these hounds were different. They wanted the couple.

They wanted to *feast.*

Helplessly she flickered into the illusion again and watched as the mare bucked and twisted her head, ripping her reins from the man's hands. The bay also reared, and despite every effort to retain them, the horses ran off into the trees, leaving the man and woman alone.

Run, she silently told the couple in the illusion.

At her side, Brock stood. "Run," he breathed.

Distant banging on the door distracted her. She could hear Sir Anthony yelling. The scene before her and in her mind had transfixed her, however. She didn't move. Neither did Brock.

The man clasped his arm around the woman's waist and together, they began to hurry down the path. The woman stumbled once, clearly twisting her ankle.

Georgiana felt a sharp pain in her own ankle. Startled, she rubbed it. The pain slowly faded.

The hounds cleared a crest behind the couple. Trailing behind them were several white-robed figures. Looking through the eyes of the illusions again, Georgiana couldn't see their faces, but she sensed menace in them. The footsteps were measured, like a march or a funeral procession. They all wore serpent's eggs.

Her gaze locked on the single robed figure who strode before the rest. His robe was black.

"Father," she whispered, her heart filling with dismay. While she couldn't quite make out his features, she knew the Duke of Gloucester had come for her.

"I don't understand any of this," Brock said, gripping her arm. "But I know they have to run. Now. Make them run, Georgiana."

The hounds, a pack of black beasts with reddened eyes, sighted their quarry. A chorus of baying filled the air. They charged forward. The woman in the illusion cried out. The man directed them into the trees bordering the lane, presumably where they wouldn't be so easy to follow.

The hounds would eat them alive.

Georgiana shut her eyes and tried to recreate the illusion in her mind, to affect it in some way. While the pendant around her neck burned with heat, she couldn't get a clear picture of the illusion. It had taken on a life of its own and kept changing with every moment.

Unexpectedly she felt the presence of another in her mind. Someone very powerful, digging deep into her subconscious. It was almost as though a headache of monstrous proportions, one with claws, had seized her temples. And with the pain came the certainty that someone else was directing her illusion now. Someone stronger than she.

The door to her bedchamber banged open. Sir Anthony rushed in and stopped between Brock and Georgiana, his gaze fixed on the illusion she'd created.

"He's found you," the older man breathed. "Don't let him come any closer, Georgiana. If he sees you, he will discover your identity."

"I can't stop him," she cried. "I can't find a way to change the illusion. He has control of it now."

"Fight him." Sir Anthony gripped her shoulders. "Fight him, dammit, or you and Brock are going to die."

She gasped at the urgency of her uncle's grip.

"Let her go," Brock demanded. He pushed Sir Anthony's hands away and positioned himself directly in front of her, so she had to look at him rather than the illusion.

"Close your eyes," Brock said, his tone calm. "I'm going to talk you through this."

Surprised at his confidence, she studied him and realized he could help her, though she wasn't sure where he had gained this sort of experience. Her uncle was equally as startled, judging by his raised eyebrows. Nevertheless, she placed her faith in Brock and closed her eyes, then strained to hear his voice above the hounds' baying, which nearly drowned out the woman's panicked cries.

"There is fog," Brock said. "Do you see it in your mind?"

"Yes."

"Do you see the trees?"

Georgiana nodded. She could see them. She'd molded the fog in her mind to create them.

"There are hounds at the end of the lane, and druids in white robes. One druid is in a black robe. Do you see them?"

Swallowing, Georgiana created the figures from the mist. Her headache grew more intense, pounding at her temples. She groaned and clutched her head.

The other, she thought, had sensed her interference.

"The druids are marching. Slow them down," Brock murmured.

Jaw clenched, Georgiana imagined the druids moving their legs more slowly, their steps taking twice as long to descend as they might in reality.

"You've done it." A note of wonder crept into Brock's voice. "The man and woman . . . they're running through the forest. Hounds are chasing them. Ahead of the couple, there's a path. At the end of the path, their horses have tangled their reins in brush and are trapped."

"I see it," she said, her headache becoming nearly intolerable as she fought to keep control of the druids. She heard a swift snapping sound. "What was that?"

"Nothing," Brock murmured. "The man and woman must find the horses, Georgiana, and disentangle the reins."

She imagined it just as Brock directed, and heard his sigh of relief.

"We're escaping," he reported.

Georgiana immediately released the druids in her mind, her reaction to his words so swift she might have been touching a hot coal. Her headache ended just as quickly, the sudden cessation of pain leaving her dizzy. Legs buckling beneath her, she fell against Brock.

He cradled her in his arms and laid her on her bed. She felt the softness of her ivory counterpane beneath her. Fighting a now-familiar need to sleep, she opened her eyes and stared at Brock.

A raised welt had turned his cheek red.

"Brock, what happened?" she murmured, her eyes closing again, despite every effort to keep them open.

"I ran into a branch."

Her brows knitted together. "But it was just an illusion."

"Or a sign of impending madness—"

"Let her sleep," her uncle cut in, his voice low.

"Will she be all right?" Brock asked.

"She's tired, nothing more. She'll be fine. Today she's had to use a muscle that she's never exercised before, and it's drained her of strength. I'd say you fared far worse than she."

Silence filled her bedchamber, and as Georgiana drifted toward the sleep she so desperately needed, she heard Brock's determined reply. "You aren't leaving Palmer House, Sir Stanton, until you've answered every one of my questions."

The Duke of Gloucester remained perfectly still, the dark walls of Cailleach's tomb forming a cocoon around him. He sensed his advisors hovering around him, their white robes brushing against his own dark one, but paid them little attention. Instead, he bent every ounce of his concentration on the scene unfolding in his mind.

While eating lunch, he'd felt the first mind-splitting vibrations of a powerful illusion forming somewhere in London. Recognizing the new guardian's patterns, he'd called his druids together and had come immediately to the tomb, which concealed his ability much like a stone circle buffered the echoes of magic. There he'd invaded the illusion in an attempt to divine the new guardian's identity.

So far, however, he remained frustrated.

The man and woman in the trees stood too far away for him to recognize. He thought he recognized a few small gardens from Hyde Park, however, and he found that fact rather interesting. Beyond them, he detected a bedchamber—clearly the boundaries of the illusion.

Who had created it?

Grimacing with effort, he tried to hold on to the illusion, to see something more that might give him a clue to the new guardian's identity, but it was fading too quickly.

He focused on the woman and man again and realized their clothes and bearing were clearly that of quality. The tester bed, he saw, was lace-draped, like that of a woman's bedchamber.

As the last of the illusion faded, the duke allowed himself to return to the present. Remembering the lace, a peculiar notion had grabbed hold of him. Silently he considered the idea that the new guardian was a noblewoman, and a very powerful one at that.

Because the first illusion was of Gwynllian, he'd suspected the Glamorgan Druids first. Even now, his brothers in worship were re-investigating each member of the Glamorgan Order. Still, druids were crafty, and he couldn't help but wonder if Gwynllian hadn't been a red herring, designed to throw him off the path toward the true culprits and lead him falsely to the Glamorgan Druids.

If so, which order of druids had found such a new Guardian of Becoming? Many different orders littered the woods of all the British Isles. Could one of them have discovered a female druid with latent ability, and developed it?

He thought that scenario unlikely, considering the power of the vibrations he'd felt. In the past, only the guardians born of parents who *both* possessed the ability had strength such as the kind he'd just experienced. As far as he knew, he and Branwyn were the only guardians who'd mated and produced a child . . . a child, of course, who was dead.

It was a puzzle that defied understanding.

A groaning noise intruded on his thoughts. He opened his eyes and glanced into the cell he and his brothers had fashioned. A bloodied but very much alive footman was finally stirring after a night of unconsciousness.

"Prepare him," the duke commanded.

A white-robed figure scurried over to the cell and began to strip the footman of his clothes. Others began to chant softly. The duke felt a heaviness in his loins, adding to the frustration that had filled him from the first moment he'd discovered the new guardian's illusion. The musty smell in the tomb gained an overtone of mead as someone brought out a jug and poured for all.

The duke selected one of the brass mugs and drank deeply of the sweet liquor. Here, he was master. Here, everyone knew his place.

While the footman was undergoing purification rites, the duke slowly considered and dismissed every person he'd met or heard of who could possibly be a guardian in disguise. Because the illusion had featured Gwynllian, a Glamorgan Arch Druid, his thoughts returned to Sir Stanton and the

Glamorgan Druids. Through the years, they'd all been questioned—subtly, of course. Various whores they'd bedded and a cadre of servants who worked for them had very carefully checked and double-checked their activities. None had appeared worthy of suspicion.

Appearances, however, often deceived, and no one understood that better than the duke, who made a habit of deception. Everyone would remain under suspicion. And while he knew that the new guardian would eventually betray herself through an illusion—it was simply a matter of time—he decided to deploy his spies to all likely candidates.

Behind him, the footman screamed as a white-robed figure drove a knife into his chest.

The duke winced. He hated the screams. But knew they were necessary. Now, more than ever, he needed Cailleach's wisdom.

"Carefully, please," he chided the others. "We need his heart *beating*, not still."

Chapter
8

❧

Once Brock tucked the counterpane around Georgiana, he led Sir Anthony toward the study. His mind still reeled with what he'd seen in Georgiana's bedchamber. A growl of pure disbelief built up in his throat as he directed the older man down the stairs. He stared at the fine carpet covering the wood floor and, for a moment, saw the patterns in its weave turn into snakes, writhing in torment. The world around him, he thought, was crumbling.

An image of his mother—wasted, vacuous, and utterly mad—suddenly reared in his head and stirred a far colder fear inside him. Sweating slightly, he steadied his hands and stared at the carpet until the snakes became mere tufts of wool again. The growl waiting at the back of his throat retreated sullenly.

"Lord Darleigh, are you well?" A few steps down from Brock, Sir Anthony paused and examined Brock with a sharp gaze.

Brock rubbed his eyes, then nodded wearily. "I'll feel even better once we've had our talk. Please, continue on to the study."

Sir Anthony hesitated a moment before obeying Brock's instruction and descending to the first floor. Brock followed, taking deep breaths all the while in an effort to reclaim his composure. Violent expressions of emotion were a sign of insanity, he told himself. He would remain orderly and calm, a veritable scion of good sense.

And yet, despite his efforts, the shout he'd muzzled hadn't lost any of its power. It still waited to be uttered, but now it lurked deep within him, mutating into a refrain that created a background hum for his thoughts.

You are not mad. You are not mad. You are not mad.

Each step he took echoing hollowly within him, Brock entered the study and shut the door. He stared at Sir Anthony and realized he no longer recognized the man. His faded blue eyes, leg-o'-mutton whiskers, and gray-fringed bald head, while giving the impression of encroaching age, had also taken on a threatening aspect. It bothered Brock that he'd never even guessed at the secrets that must lie beneath that unremarkable appearance.

He turned and pressed his back against the door, obeying a half-formed instinct to block the exit. "What in hell did I just experience?"

Sir Anthony walked over to Brock's whiskey bottle and poured himself a glass. He tossed off a swallow, then faced Brock squarely. "Georgiana isn't the person you thought she was."

At the mention of his wife's name, Brock winced. He tried to picture her sleeping in her bedchamber, her cheeks a faint pink, her lips curved in a kissable smile even in sleep—and failed. He didn't know who she was—he simply couldn't fix an image of her in his mind. Just like Sir Anthony's, her sweet face had concealed from him the most shocking of secrets, secrets that evoked an exquisite sense of betrayal within him. "Say something beyond the obvious," he demanded.

"Georgiana expressed to me a desire for you to know everything. And so, I'll answer your questions to the best of my ability. You experienced an illusion that Georgiana created with her mind."

Brock gaped at him. He wanted to deny Sir Anthony's words, but how could he, given his harrowing experience in her bedchamber? The sense of betrayal inside of him twisted, leaving him sickened. "What *is* she?"

"She's not a demon, Lord Darleigh." Sir Anthony examined him with a stiff-lipped frown. "She's a woman with a special gift."

A wild laugh gathered in his chest. He bit down on his lip to keep it inside. "She's a woman with a special gift whom I *married*. She shares my name, Stanton. She shares my home. She's even shared my bed on occasion. And now I discover that the woman I thought I'd married is something entirely different."

"I understand that we've shocked you—"

"Shocked?" Brock threw his arms wide. "Devastated is more appropriate. How could you have allowed us to marry? How did she manage to keep such secrets from me?"

"I know it's difficult to learn that the person you've married doesn't really exist—"

"You can't possibly know," Brock grated.

"Not first-hand," the other man admitted, "but Georgiana has explained her own situation and feelings to me on occasion, so I feel confident that I know how *you're* suffering."

Brock snapped his mouth shut. The desire to laugh returned. Just as ruthlessly as before, he cut the urge off. "How does she create these illusions?" he asked in clipped tones.

"As I said, Georgiana is special. She was born with the ability to create illusions. There are only two other people like her in the world. I'm not exactly sure how she does it, because I don't possess the ability myself." Sir Anthony shrugged, then tossed off another mouthful of whiskey. "It's an inherited trait. Both of her parents could also create illusions."

Brock thought back to the little he knew about Georgiana's youth. Her father and mother, Sir John Wesley and Margaret, had died in a carriage accident when Georgiana was very young. Gwynllian and Sir Anthony had considered the Wesleys close friends and took their orphaned daughter in at a young age. They'd told Brock that Georgiana's parents had both been rather staid . . . a laughable impression, given the new facts. "What were they . . . witches of some sort?"

Sir Anthony placed his whiskey glass on a side table. He rubbed his chin and, after a few seconds, studied Brock with a thoughtful air. "What do you know of druidism, Lord Darleigh?"

"Druidism? Nothing."

"Have you ever heard the word mentioned?" the older man pressed.

"Only in connection with the Hellfire Club. They dabbled in druidism many years back," Brock answered carefully. "There isn't much to recommend it, from what I recall. Jaded aristocrats dressed up in white robes with pointy hoods and attended secret ceremonies, which usually degenerated into orgies. They often tried to call up old Scratch himself."

A frown tugged at Sir Anthony's lips. "Druidism has nothing to do with the occult."

"But it has something to do with Georgiana," Brock guessed.

The older man nodded. "Come away from the door. Sit down, and let me explain."

"Quite frankly, I don't have the slightest interest in druidism. Just tell me about Georgiana." Brock selected a chair by the windows and folded his frame into it. "I haven't the patience for a long, drawn-out tale."

Sir Anthony fixed him with a pleading gaze. "Druidism is so many things I can hardly explain it in a few quick sentences. For your sake, however, I will try."

"Good."

The older man knotted his hands behind his back and paced toward the window. "Druidism is an ancient Celtic religion. It's a collective memory of the heroes that have gone before us, a natural philosophy of life, a connection between the worlds of order and chaos, and an understanding of the spirits and forces which can guide us. Druids are at once simple people devoted to the trees and advisory counsels to kings."

The corner of Brock's mouth quirked bitterly. "Obviously Georgiana is a druid of some sort. If I were a betting man, I'd wager you're a druid, too."

"Druids do not believe that man is superior to the earth and its beasts," Sir Anthony continued, his expression dogged, "as espoused in many other religions. Indeed, we live in a community of nature, where the stag is our guide and the oak tree our protector. We allow the natural world to direct and teach us. It is our ally. It is our past and future. It is us, and we are one."

"One with the forest," Brock muttered.

The older man stopped before the windows.

"Look outside at the trees, Lord Darleigh. Do you hear them calling to you?"

Brock joined Sir Anthony at the window. A sprawling stand of oaks greeted his vision, each one covered in large green leaves and at the height of summer growth. "You belong upstairs, with my mother."

"Please, Lord Darleigh—"

Brock sighed. Clearly he was going to have to play along, at least for the time being. "I see firewood and lumber. I hear my gardener cursing as he wrestles with his scythe."

"The forest speaks," Sir Anthony murmured.

"Oh? What does it say?"

" *'You may have forgotten me, but I know you well. I have enfolded you in my branches since the beginning of time and cushion your feet with leaves as you walk toward the future. Many have searched for me, but I have always been here, hiding among the trees, whispering your name.'* "

Brock lifted one eyebrow. "I see."

"I'm afraid you don't *see* anything."

"You've convinced me you're not all debauched roués looking for an excuse to hold an orgy."

Sir Anthony turned away from the window and reclaimed his whiskey glass. "At least I've gained *some* ground."

"So you are a druid, then," Brock pressed.

"I am."

"And your sister, Gwynllian?"

"She joined the order of Glamorgan Druids, as did I, many years before."

"What about Georgiana?"

"Georgiana has never belonged," Sir Anthony said.

It wasn't the answer Brock had been expecting. He'd assumed her special ability was related to druidism in some way. "Then how can she create these illusions, without the help of druidism?"

Sir Anthony turned away from the window and selected a seat by the fire. His curiosity piqued, Brock followed suit. Soon they were both facing each other—two very sane men holding a conversation more suited to Bedlam.

"Georgiana is a Guardian of Becoming," Sir Anthony revealed. "Not by her choosing, but by birth. Her ancestry stretches as far back as Merlin himself."

"A guardian of what?"

"Becoming. Georgiana, and others like her, stand in the threshold between the worlds of chaos and order. They supervise that which passes through."

Brock shook his head. "I haven't the slightest idea what you're talking about."

"It is difficult, I know. Consider carefully what I'm about to say. Things that appear a mystery now may become more understandable." The older man heaved a deep sigh, and then launched into an explanation about the oldest book of druidry—*Mabinogion*—and the Celtic fairy people. He discussed, in general, the lineage of the guardians and the expectations the druids had of them. Brock listened as Sir Anthony tried to clarify what the worlds of chaos and order were, and how the guardians created their illusions, but he didn't really understand. He didn't *want* to understand.

It reminded him too much of the world his mother lived in.

His throat tightened with a rush of sympathy as he tried to imagine the confusion and shock Georgiana herself must have felt upon hearing Stanton's explanations. A sudden urge to take her away from London and her uncle surprised him with its intensity. He wanted to protect her, to spare her further pain that she was no doubt destined to experience.

At the same time, he wondered if hindsight would prove this urge very unwise. How could he build a life with a woman who could create an illusion to make him believe whatever she wished? It would be akin to living in a world of madness, the same one his mother lived in. He could never be sure what was real, and what was fake.

Even so, when he'd watched her illusion, and seen himself and Georgiana from the past, he'd felt something he didn't understand. It had pulled at him and was far too strong for him to ignore. If he had made different choices, and Georgiana hadn't discovered his true reason for marrying her, would he have learned eventually what that "something" was? Abruptly regretting those lost opportunities, he frowned.

". . . the line of Guardians of Becoming is over a thousand years old," the older man droned on. "Bloodlines are very important to druids, and the Glamorgan Druids insure that they have a continuous line of guardians by mating them together—"

"By mating them?" Brock cut in, thinking the whole thing sounded like a scheme hatched at Tattersall's between two breeders.

Sir Anthony nodded. "Yes. Georgiana was conceived when two guardians mated."

Brock hesitated. This line of thought troubled him in some obscure way. "How many guardians are in existence today?"

"Only three. Georgiana is one of them."

"Who are the other two?"

"David Gwylum and Cadwallon ab Ilfor Bach."

"Two men," Brock said, mostly to himself. "And you say the Glamorgan Druids keep the line of guardians alive by mating them together."

As soon as Brock repeated the thought aloud, the implications hit him like a blow. He turned to stare at Sir Anthony with narrowed eyes. "By God, if Georgiana is the only living female guardian, and the Glamorgan Druids wish to keep the line of guardians alive . . ."

"They are going to want Georgiana to mate with David Gwylum." Sir Anthony regarded him mournfully. "I tried to prevent this."

Brock shot to his feet. "And Georgiana? How does she feel about it?"

"As unfavorably as you evidently feel. Sit down, Lord Darleigh. Let me finish," the older man pleaded. "I haven't yet told you about Georgiana's father."

"I won't sit, man." Brock began to pace. The fact that Georgiana hadn't agreed to this mating soothed him somewhat, but not enough. "I want to hear it all, and quickly."

"I'll be very precise, then. You've always thought that Georgiana's father was Sir John Wesley, a minor Welsh baron. You thought Gwynllian and I took her in when Sir Wesley and his wife were killed in a carriage accident. While Sir Wesley and his wife *were* killed, their baby daughter died along with them.

"Gwynllian and I have been pretending Georgiana was their baby daughter to conceal the fact that Georgiana was born out of wedlock. In fact, her father is Cadwallon ab Ilfor Bach, a Guardian of Becoming."

"Georgiana is a bastard," Brock said, his voice flat.

"I'm afraid so."

"What else?"

The older man raised an eyebrow. "You don't seem surprised. Did you already know?"

Brock's lip curled. He stopped pacing and regarded Sir Anthony with a cool expression. "No, I didn't. And if I don't seem properly surprised, you'll have to forgive me. I've already reached my surprise quotient for one day and haven't any left in me."

"Perhaps you'll dredge up some yet, Lord Darleigh. You know Cadwallon ab Ilfor Bach as the Duke of Gloucester."

The words hung in the air between them for a second or two as Brock tried to comprehend them. The Duke of Gloucester? He shook his head, a cold feeling of foreboding chilling him.

"I assure you I'm telling the truth," the older man insisted.

Brock swore quietly. There were few in the king's court who didn't hate and fear the duke and his unscrupulous practices. Not the kind of man to make merry, the duke appeared exclusively at royal functions . . . and hangings.

Quickly Brock reviewed what he knew about the Duke of Gloucester's past. An older man, he'd come from Wales and quickly gained solid footing with the king, making allies, persecuting enemies, and reclaiming and building his estates. He seemed to live a charmed existence, knowing of plots against him before they hatched, and having an uncanny knack of being in the right place at the right time. Now Brock knew why: the Duke of Gloucester had wizardry at his disposal.

"As far as I know," Sir Anthony continued, "the duke doesn't know Georgiana's identity. We've done our best to hide her from him."

"Why?"

"Many years ago, Gwynllian divined the duke's future and revealed that his daughter—Georgiana—would grow up and eventually prevent him from ascending to the English throne."

Brock nodded uneasily. Everyone knew the Welshman had his eye on the throne. "Does Gwynllian know how Georgiana will accomplish this?"

Sir Anthony shrugged. "Her ability to create illusions is somehow connected. We understand that much, but naught else."

Eyebrows drawn together, Brock mulled it over. "In essence, the duke wants to prevent her from fulfilling her destiny."

"He'll use whatever means necessary," the older man confirmed. "He will kill her if he has to."

"That sounds rather extreme, even for the duke. He'd kill his own daughter?"

"It's quite in character for him, I assure you." Sir Anthony sighed heavily. "Back before Georgiana was born, he used a pack of hounds to hunt Branwyn, her mother. Branwyn managed to birth Georgiana and hide her in the boughs of an oak before the hounds caught and killed her. Gwynllian and I found Georgiana and raised her in secret, to prevent the duke from knowing she lived."

Brock's lips quirked bitterly. "When I married Georgiana, I thought her a simple country girl, an orphan who'd been brought up by a kindly aunt and uncle. She concealed her true nature well."

"Georgiana knew nothing of druidism or her ability to produce illusions until last night. We kept the knowledge from her to protect her. When a guardian produces an illusion, you see, other guardians and trained druids can sense that illusion being produced. In Georgiana's case, her ability is so strong, it's akin to a lighthouse beacon broadcasting its presence.

"We knew if we allowed her to produce an illusion, the duke would sense it and eventually realize that his daughter had managed to escape him. Only a child mated between two guardians could command her level of power."

"But you let her come to London," Brock pointed out. "Weren't you afraid the duke would question the identity of a young woman who lives with you?"

"Until she created the illusion, the duke thought Georgiana had died along with her mother. Since he's a man certain of his own infallibility, Gwynllian and I knew his ego wouldn't permit him to think otherwise. Besides, the past we constructed for Georgiana is without any cracks. We felt Georgiana would remain quite safe."

"He wouldn't recognize her?" Brock pressed.

"As the fates would have it, Georgiana looks like neither her mother or her father. She wouldn't attract his attention on that score." Sir Anthony fixed Brock with a pleading glance. "Georgiana was very unhappy in Wales. A strange restlessness surrounded her always, from the moment she was a young girl. It clouded her eyes and gave her sweet nature a sharp edge. When she came to London, some of that restlessness eased."

Brock nodded unwillingly. He understood a little of what Sir Anthony was saying. Suppressed energy surrounded Georgiana and animated her every movement, as though some demon had lodged inside her and refused to give her peace.

"We wanted her to have the best chance at happiness possible," the older man continued softly. "When she met you, Lord Darleigh, I felt vindicated. I had never seen my Georgiana so happy as I did on your wedding day."

Brock turned to look out the window. Guilt touched him, its caress bitter yet familiar, like that of an old enemy. "We were happy . . . for a time."

"Indeed." Sir Anthony sighed. "On the day of your ceremony, we thought her Welsh identity well and truly buried. All would have remained peaceful if Georgiana hadn't worn that damned pendant last night."

"What pendant?"

"It looks like a red glass egg and belonged to Georgiana's mother."

Brock narrowed his eyes. While Georgiana had already insisted she hadn't taken a lover, he'd still wondered from whom she'd received the pendant. At least he knew now that she'd been telling the truth. "She wore it last night. Is it some sort of druid's amulet?"

"A druid's glass helps beginning guardians focus their ability to create illusions. When Georgiana wore it, the glass helped her to create an illusion."

"Obviously she didn't understand the pendant's qualities," Brock reasoned. "Weren't you running a great risk by giving her the pendant and allowing her to wear it?"

"We didn't give her the damned pendant. She found it in a meadow in Wales and never told us about it."

"That doesn't sound like Georgiana," Brock observed.

"She was a child. A very lonely one. But let's not argue the point." Sir Anthony flexed his shoulders, as though his next revelation was a weighty one. "Georgiana created two illusions of Gwynllian last night, just as she created that illusion of your past a little while ago. In doing so, she's informed the duke of her existence. When she created the illusion of your past, the duke traced the source of the echoes she created and interfered with her illusion. You witnessed the result."

"By God, why didn't you tell Georgiana not to create an illusion, then?"

"I hadn't reached that point in my discussion yet. You barged in, and I thought it best to leave you and Georgiana alone. I had no idea she would test her ability again so quickly."

"Do you think the duke has discovered her identity yet?"

"Probably not. But he must realize her connection to the Glamorgan Druids. Her illusion was of Gwynllian, after all, and Gwynllian is an Arch Druid in our order."

"Did the duke get a look at Georgiana's illusory face when he entered her illusion?"

"He didn't draw close enough to 'see' her through his illusion's eyes. I believe we're still safe. Even so, I don't question that he has people looking for her already. He will scrutinize Georgiana closely, simply because of her association with me and my sister Gwynllian. We haven't much time before he learns who she is and attempts to take her life through more traditional methods as well as through illusions."

Brock touched the cut on his cheek. "It isn't just an illusion, is it? I watched a branch snap against my face in the illusion, and a corresponding cut opened on my real face."

"I'm afraid you're correct on that score. There's a strange connection between mind and body that scholarly inquiry is just beginning to understand. I liken it to the tales of the shaman who curses his enemy with the 'evil eye.' If the enemy knows that he's been cursed by the shaman, often his health will fail and he will die, merely by suggestion. Likewise, you felt a connection with your illusory self, and when you saw the branch cut your cheek, your body responded by creating a corresponding welt on your skin."

Stiffening with dismay, Brock leaned forward in his chair. "Do you mean that the duke was trying to kill us in the illusion, in the hopes that our real bodies would die as well?"

"I'm afraid so. Although I don't think he has any interest in you, Lord Darleigh. Georgiana is, and will always be, his primary target. And it isn't so easy to kill a guardian. In order to truly silence the guardian's spirit, he or she must be buried in a bog."

Disgust made Brock frown. He remembered a story from a few years before. Peat cutters in Gloucester, England, had partially hacked through the body of a bearded man wearing an ancient robe. A garotte made of hazel was still wrapped around his neck and two wooden stakes flanked the body. Conventional wisdom suggested the man had been killed, then deliberately deposited in the bog. "The Duke of Gloucester is known for his ruthless disposal of his enemies," he murmured.

"He is a formidable adversary. Georgiana can't protect herself from him. She needs the help of the Glamorgan Druids. That's why I'm relieved that your marriage to Georgiana is less than happy. Her place is with them now. You might say her very survival depends on it."

Brock stood up abruptly and strode over to the window. He looked out at the sun-washed lawn, his gaze unfocused, seeing only Georgiana's face. He'd entered a new world where illusions and reality entwined in a dangerous mix. How long could he remain in this place without losing his own sanity?

He'd have to find a way. Last night, he reasoned, he'd made love to her. In doing so, he'd added a very difficult element to the situation. Georgiana could very well be carrying his child now. He wasn't going to abandon her to the duke and the dubious protection the Glamorgan Druids would offer her, not until he knew for sure that she wasn't expecting.

And maybe not even then.

"I'll look after her," he said, surprising himself with the strength of his voice.

"So, despite all you've heard, you wish to remain a husband to Georgiana?" Sir Anthony asked.

Brock paused a delicate moment, and then stated baldly, "She could be pregnant."

The older man stared at him, then swore quietly and turned away. When he spun back around to face Brock, his cheeks had a ruddy flush. "Gwynllian and I will manage the situation."

"I'm afraid that's not good enough."

"Think, man," Sir Anthony urged. "A life of illusions brushes very closely to a world of madness. Is that a world you wish to live in?"

"I won't abandon my child."

"If there *is* a child."

Brock nodded, acknowledging Sir Anthony's point. "In any case, I won't leave Georgiana now, unprotected, to face the duke alone."

"What sort of protection can *you* offer?" His tone slightly contemptuous, Sir Anthony raised an eyebrow. "You know nothing of illusions or druidism. And while you're a peer of the realm, you aren't powerful enough to threaten the Duke of Gloucester or use English law against him."

"Georgiana needs someone to guard her, someone who is absolutely trustworthy and is willing to risk his own life to save her."

"And that someone is you?"

Brock nodded. "Yes."

Sir Anthony shrugged. "I'll guard her."

"You?" Brock looked him up and down. "Pardon me for saying so, but your brawling days are over, if they ever existed. You wouldn't last more than a minute in a real fight. I've spent countless hours at Figg's Pugilism Academy fighting Jack Langan, the English pugilistic champion. I'd say I'm eminently qualified. The duke will have to go through me to get to Georgiana."

"Do you know how to handle a knife?"

"Once or twice my opponent has pulled a knife on me. I've handled the situation. Also, don't forget that I helped talk Georgiana through her illusion a few hours ago."

"Perhaps you *are* qualified. Regardless, Georgiana must return to Wales with the Glamorgan Druids."

"Her place is here, in London."

"Ah, if it's a matter of money," the older man said after a delicate pause, "I'll insure that you continue to receive an annuity, even after you and Georgiana are divorced."

"I don't want anything from you," Brock replied evenly. "Nor will I accept even a ha'penny from Georgiana's government securities in the future. I am simply trying to save Georgiana's life."

"As am I. Georgiana and I are leaving for Wales tomorrow," Sir Anthony calmly insisted. "Only there can we protect her adequately, while training her to prevent the duke from gaining the throne of England. Could you imagine what would happen if she turned her back on her destiny?"

Brock swallowed. England under the rule of the Duke of Gloucester would surpass the hardship and misery of even Oliver Cromwell's reign. "I'm not suggesting she turn her back on her destiny. I simply wish her to stay in London."

"We should ask Georgie, no?"

A beat of silence passed between them, during which Brock debated the wisdom of laying his hands on Sir Anthony's shoulders and shaking the hell out of him.

"I've already informed the Glamorgan Druids that Georgiana and I are leaving for Wales," the older man continued. "If I don't bring her, they will come to London and take her back themselves, possibly alerting the Duke of Gloucester in the process. She must go tomorrow, with me."

Brock narrowed his eyes. "Won't her hasty departure draw the duke's suspicion?"

"We have to risk it. Georgiana must learn how to use her ability, and she's safer doing so in Wales, under the protection of the Glamorgan Druids and away from the duke."

"How can she learn to use her ability if the illusions she creates lead the duke to her?"

"She can practice in a stone circle, not unlike the one you call 'Stonehenge.' The stones act as buffers, absorbing the echoes that normally would be broadcast to the entire land."

"A farmer's field not more than a twenty minutes' ride from Palmer House contains a stone circle," Brock pointed out. "She can practice there."

"Georgiana belongs in Wales," Sir Anthony stubbornly insisted.

"We must ask *her*, no?"

Chapter
9

Afternoon sunlight brightened the grass and trees outside Georgiana's bedchamber window. It sifted through the panes, settling upon her satinwood bureau and burnishing it with golden warmth. Nellie bustled around the room, selecting undergarments and a sprigged muslin gown, and helped Georgiana don them. These familiar rituals and the brilliant July sky would have soothed Georgiana at any other time. Today, however, she felt cold down to her very bones and uncomfortably restless.

Nellie's deft fingers worked the buttons along the back of her gown. Georgiana tried to remain still as the lady's maid fastened them, but the need to act had boiled up inside her. She walked toward the window, leaving Nellie with her hands in the air.

"Lady Darleigh?"

Georgiana heard the concern in Nellie's voice, and it tugged at her. Still, she couldn't respond. Suddenly she felt trapped, suffocated, and horribly panicked. She grasped the knobs on the windowsill and drew the window upward, letting heated air into the bedchamber. Her gown fluttered at the sleeves, and as the seconds passed, the breeze swept the worst of her urgency away.

At length she turned to face the lady's maid. "Where are Brock and Sir Anthony?"

Her forehead creased, Nellie moved behind her once again and fastened the remaining buttons. "They're downstairs in the study, ma'am. Shall I send for one or both of them?"

"Not just yet," Georgiana murmured, wondering how she could ever face Brock after what he'd witnessed. "How about a cup of tea instead?"

Nellie cast a glance at the clock on the mantle shelf, then muttered an exclamation. "Good heavens, it's afternoon already. I'll have a luncheon brought up as well."

Georgiana didn't think she could force food past her lips. Still, she nodded and smiled tremulously as the maid smoothed Georgiana's skirts and draped a shawl over her shoulders.

"There, ma'am, you're done and as pretty as a rose, if I do say so myself," Nellie said in cheerful tones. "I'll return in a bit with something for you to eat."

After Nellie had left, Georgiana grabbed a piece

of embroidery, sat down on a settee, and began to pull colorful pieces of silk through ivory damask. She didn't particularly enjoy embroidery and wasn't very good at it, but she needed something to keep her hands busy.

While she worked, she thought about all her uncle had revealed. Her mind still spun with the knowledge that she, and she alone, would prevent the Duke of Gloucester from gaining the throne. It resonated like a forbidding music deep inside. Would she be able to fulfill her destiny?

She tightened her fingers on the embroidery hoop. She felt little other than hatred for the father she'd never known and who'd evidently tried to murder her. Silently she vowed she would do whatever was necessary to keep him off the throne, as fate had intended.

She paused in her embroidery. Yesterday, she mused, she'd been a lady looking forward to a night of entertainment at Watier's Club. Today she was a Guardian of Becoming and the target of the Duke of Gloucester, who would stop at nothing to see her dead. She could hardly fathom the change, it had happened so quickly.

Suddenly, a strange sense of disassociation claimed her. She looked at her hands—white, slender, lady's hands. Whose hands were they? she wondered. And the legs beneath her skirt, and arms that supported the embroidery hoop, and the heart that beat in her chest—who owned them? Tendrils of panic began to unfurl through her anew. Her life, she thought, had run completely out of control. Abruptly she placed the embroidery hoop on the settee, stood, and walked over to the looking glass. Frowning, she studied her image.

A woman stared back at her, one with large, frightened green eyes and a wealth of brown hair. A large red pendant hung from her neck to settle between her breasts. Georgiana felt positive she didn't know that woman. She touched her own cheeks, and the image followed suit; still, Georgiana felt no sense of *knowing*. If not for the weight of the pendant against her skin, she would feel no connection to the image whatsoever. Her hand trembling, she reached out and placed her fingertips on the looking glass.

"Who are you?" she murmured softly.

A large figure moved into view behind her. She dropped her hand. Slowly she turned to face him.

Brock's eyes were dark and his expression solemn, but the tiny lines around his mouth hinted at pain she understood well. She thought he'd never looked more tired, more harassed than he did at that moment. Without even thinking she walked toward him and lifted her hand to smooth his shirt.

He took a step backward, out of her range.

She winced. Her hand dropped to her side. She knew better than he that they had no future together as husband and wife. Brock had been right to step away from her. Anything else would only make their parting more difficult.

"You've talked to my uncle," she said, her voice carefully neutral. "What has he told you?"

"Everything, I imagine." His lips twisted bitterly. "I know you're the bastard daughter of the Duke of Gloucester and the only one standing between him and the throne of England. You are supposed to place your loyalty with the Glamorgan Druids and are expected to mate with one of them."

Her cheeks warming, she looked away. "I didn't wish any of this to happen. I'm sorry, Brock."

"Why apologize? From what I understand, you knew nothing. You're simply a pawn in a game between the Glamorgan Druids and the Duke of Gloucester."

"I'm also the Marchioness of Darleigh. A divorce between us will bring the stain of dishonor upon your name, one you gave me in good faith."

"So you've decided on divorce, then?"

"What other choice have we? Our marriage has been less than perfect. We're hardly husband and wife. And I'm not like you or anyone else you know. I need to be with people who understand me, and they need me as well—"

"And this David Gwylum? Will you mate with him?"

She spun away from him and walked over to the window. "Why must you ask me these difficult questions?"

"I want to know where I stand."

"Where you stand?" Hands clenched, she turned

and looked him directly in the eye. "Now that you know who, and *what*, I am, surely you don't stand anywhere near me."

"Call me stubborn, call me foolish, call me what you will . . . but after two years of watching you and wanting you, I find myself reluctant to let you go." He paused, then added, "Or the baby you may be carrying."

"At least now I know why you're clinging to our marriage," she choked out. "You want your heir."

"I want you. And I won't abandon any child of mine," he admitted.

"A *druid* child, born of a druid bastard." She stared at him, certain he'd lost his mind. "I can create illusions. My father wants me dead. I haven't much to recommend myself, do I? If you had any sense at all, you would wash your hands of me instantly."

Brock stood suddenly and faced her. "You're right. I should disown you. I should divorce you immediately and find another woman to share my life with. But the hell of it is, when I try to think of someone else, I can only see your green eyes.

"Sometimes, when I talk with Lord Carlisle, and he shows me the latest trinket he bought his wife, or explains the waistcoat she's embroidering for him, I become jealous as hell. I wonder what could have been between us, if events had happened differently. Do you ever wonder?"

"Yes," she admitted softly.

"We can't change the past, but perhaps the future—"

"It doesn't matter, not anymore," she interrupted.

Shrugging, he changed the subject. "Sir Anthony wishes you to travel to Wales with him."

She nodded slowly. "I must go."

He slouched against the wall and studied her, the intensity in his eyes giving the lie to his casual position. Silence lengthened between them. Georgiana felt a strange fluttering in her stomach.

"I want you to stay at Palmer House, where I can protect you," he finally said. "Once the Duke of Gloucester no longer remains a threat, I want to start over again."

Her heart gave a quick little thump. "Start over again? What do you mean?"

"I want to erase the mistakes of the past, Georgie. When I court you the next time, it will be for you, and not your money."

"Are you mad?" That uncomfortable restlessness rose within her, forcing her to her feet. She began to pace, then threw a glance at Brock as the silence grew between them.

His face, she saw, had become quite pale. She wondered why for a moment, but her confusion quickly cleared as she realized how she must have offended him when she'd called him "mad." Because of his mother, the word had practically become a slur.

"I'm sorry, Brock," she hastily apologized, "I spoke without thinking. Still, now that I've said it, we cannot ignore the implications."

He stared at her, clearly nonplussed.

She forged ahead. "Your mother lives in a world of illusion. While we've rarely spoken about it, I can see how much her condition pains her. Now, as you know, I create illusions with my mind. Your world, too, could become one of illusion if I chose to place you there. Doesn't that notion alarm you?"

A long pause ensued, during which he assessed her with a measured glance. "It all comes down to trust," he finally said.

"Does it? I could make you think anything I wished. You might see me sleeping in my bed, when actually I'm running around town, from party to party. I could make you think my neck was white and bare, when actually I wore an expensive bauble an admirer had given me."

"You could hide a lover, change the appearance of a friend, or even give Nellie a moustache," he agreed. "But would you, Georgiana? Would you do it?"

"I would never deliberately hurt you."

A ghost of a smile tugged at his lips. "You're not very reassuring. Nevertheless, I intend to chance it."

Determined to make him see the folly of his actions, Georgiana shook her head. "You'll be in danger if I remain here. The Duke of Gloucester wishes me dead. I have no doubt he'd kill you to get to me. I should leave, if only to protect *you*."

"As much as I appreciate the gesture, I believe I'm in a better position to protect you. You need a guard, Georgiana. I'll stay by you, night and day. The duke will have to go through me before he can harm you. And I assure you, that isn't easily done."

She frowned. "All right, let's assume for a moment you risk your life to guard me and, after we dispose of the duke, you court me. What happens if you discover that the attraction between us is a fleeting one, not worth pursuing further? You would have risked everything for naught."

"I hardly consider your life worth naught." He abandoned his casual slouch against the wall and moved to her side, standing so close that she could see the gold flecks sparkling deep within his eyes. "We needn't worry about events that far ahead, though. For now, just tell me you'll stay on at Palmer House while we sort out our next steps."

"Oh, Brock." Her heart aching, she reached out, touched his lapel, straightened it. She needed to feel some part of him. Any part. "If your offer had come a week earlier, or even yesterday, it would have pleased me greatly. But it's come too late. Just last night I discovered that I don't very much like the woman I've become." She stopped, blinked back sudden tears, and forced the difficult words out. "I've had my chance at love. Now, I need to embrace my destiny."

He caught her hand in his own and squeezed gently, warming her skin which had become so very cold. "You can create your own destiny, Georgie. If you want to, you can give us a second chance."

"It's not that easy," she cried. "If I ignore the Glamorgan Druids, a part of me will always resent you for standing between me and my responsibilities. I'll lose what little honor and self-respect I still possess. Don't you see? I *must* go to Wales."

"Is it your destiny to mate with David Gwylum also?"

Unable to reply, she swallowed against the tight knot that gathered in her throat.

He cursed softly, beneath his breath, then challenged her with that dark gaze of his. "You've accused me of being an illusion, Georgiana, and now I charge you with the same. You aren't the person I thought you were when we married. You aren't even the person I've lived with over the last two years. *That* Georgiana would never choose duty over love."

She stared at him, his point hitting home.

"If you won't stay in London, let me come with you to Wales," he offered, his voice husky, her hand still within his grasp. He pulled her against him, his face tanned against the white linen of his shirt, his lower lip full and sensuous.

She still wanted him desperately, as she'd wanted him from the very first moment she'd seen him. "No. You'll only confuse me, cloud my thinking . . ."

"I'll protect you." He slipped his hands around

to the small of her back, until his arms encircled her and cradled her.

She made a sound somewhere between a protest and a denial. She felt so good when he touched her that she trembled with longing. The warmth of his body against hers stirred up memories of every detail of their lovemaking last night. Suddenly she could think of nothing but him, smell nothing but his clean scent, feel nothing but the soft brush of his lips against her forehead as he lowered his head to hers.

"Let me come with you," he whispered seconds before his lips closed over hers.

Desire for him drowned out the protests she knew she should utter. His mouth moved gently over hers, slowly. He seemed to draw her soul up from her body, drinking her until she was weak and her knees buckled. He caught her and held her in his arms, and once he'd steadied her he slipped his hand downward to press against her belly.

She dragged her mouth from his. "You must stay here, in London."

"I'm going with you," he breathed, then lowered his head for another kiss. She stopped him just in time with a finger against his lips.

"Every time I touch you, I want you to make love to me," she murmured. "If you join me in Wales, I'll think of little else. I need to concentrate on learning how to use my ability, and preparing for my confrontation with the duke—"

"You might be carrying my child," he cut in, speaking with gentle determination. "And you need someone to guard you. I'm going to Wales with you, whether you want me to or not."

Brock pushed open the door to his mother's bedchamber several inches and peered inside. The housekeeper snoozed on a side chair, and his mother sat up in bed, her gray hair brushed and held back from her face with a pink ribbon, her wasted frame hidden by a frilly bed gown. He took a moment to assess the lucidity in her eyes, then sighed with relief.

He stepped into the room. "Hello, Mother."

She fixed a bright, birdlike stare upon him. Her lips twitched upward briefly before settling into a frown. "Come in, come in," she invited. "I've been waiting hours for you. You're very negligent, to forget our appointment."

Eyebrow raised, he closed the door behind him and sat in a chair near the bed. Mrs. Steele muttered in her sleep, then resumed snoring.

"My apologies, Lady Darleigh," he said in his most formal tones, wondering who she thought he was this time. Reginald, again? Silently he damned the insanity that had brought her to this point.

"I don't want your apology. Be on time from now on, Reginald."

Brock inclined his head and decided to play along for a minute or so, before broaching the true reason for his visit: to inform her of his journey to Wales on the morrow.

"Well, Reginald, what news is there at court?" she asked in quavering tones.

"The Duchess of Kent has run off with a banker," he reported, wishing he understood more of the people she'd known in her time. He had no idea if anything he said was even slightly plausible. "And the king has apparently suffered another bout of madness. He's confined to his bedchamber and is receiving treatment from physicians Smith and Barfield."

His mother's hand fluttered to her mouth. "Oh, the poor man." After a few moments of respectful silence, she asked in soft tones, "What else?"

Brock struggled to keep his mind on the conversation. Thoughts of Georgiana kept intruding. Their interview had gone well overall. The future, however, didn't look nearly as promising. Until he found a way to neutralize the Duke of Gloucester, Georgiana would remain in danger.

The Duke of Gloucester.

Brock rubbed his chin.

The duke had been his mother's contemporary.

The thought came from nowhere to settle in his mind like an itch that needed scratching.

He gave his mother a thoughtful look. "Have I mentioned that I suspect a plot afoot in the court, to discredit the king?"

"Oh?" She sat forward, her lips pursed. "Who are the principals?"

"The Duke of Gloucester." He paused for a moment, assessing the shuttered look that suddenly invaded her eyes. "Do you know him?"

A sly smile curved her lips. "Ah yes, the duke. Quite a man-about-town."

Disconcerted, Brock sat back in his chair. "How well do you know him?"

"Don't be jealous, Reginald," she chided. "He's not one for me. It took me only one night to discover that much."

Brock swallowed. "You were lovers?"

She tapped him playfully on the arm. "You shouldn't ask your betters such intimate questions."

"What do you know about him? Tell me," Brock urged.

"I know a secret of his," she teased. "But I mustn't tell. If the duke discovers I've given him away, he'll be quite angry with me."

Frustration filling him, Brock tried a more cajoling tone. "I'll keep anything you say in the strictest confidence. Haven't I served you well in the past?"

"I'm sorry, Reginald. I mustn't say."

He heard the note of finality in her voice and nearly cursed aloud. "And I *must* know. Please, think about telling me. In the meanwhile, I am journeying to Wales tomorrow." With a spurt of inspiration, he added, "to find out more about the Duke of Gloucester."

"You *are* jealous," she accused in coy tones.

No, I'm bloody frustrated, he wanted to shout.

Instead, he took a deep breath and fought for a gentler tone. "When I return, I'll give you what information I've been able to dig up on the duke. Perhaps then you'll tell me his secret, and together, we will prevent his attempt to discredit the king."

His mother's eyes grew shadowed. "The duke wishes to do more than discredit the king. He wishes to assume the throne. I can say no more."

Without further ado, she closed her eyes and waved a languid hand his way. "Leave me, Reginald."

"Promise me you'll consider my request," Brock pleaded, his voice low.

When she didn't respond, he realized that she had left him—if not in body, then in mind. Disappointed, he gazed at her for another few seconds, then stood and left the bedchamber.

Chapter
10

❧

$\mathcal{A}$ cavalcade of barouches, their sides emblazoned with the Darleigh crest, lined up outside of Palmer House. Georgiana surveyed their smart mahogany-colored exteriors and wondered how she would manage two weeks inside one of them. The town of Caernarfon, their destination, was some two hundred forty miles northwest of London, including at least one hundred miles of bad road. Even the most expensive rig wouldn't cushion the shocks of deep and far too frequent potholes.

She walked across the cobblestones to stand near the carriage in the lead. Footmen, their uniforms a sparkling green in the brilliant sunlight, loaded trunks onto the coaches. The sun beat down upon her head and the air scarcely stirred, making her hot and uncomfortable in her travelling gown. Brock's and Sir Anthony's scowls as they conferred some ten feet away didn't make the situation any easier.

She fanned herself with an ivory fan and contemplated the carriage's closed interior. Silently she reminded herself that she'd managed to get herself to London three years ago. Somehow, she'd get herself back home as well.

Sir Anthony turned abruptly from Brock and strode in her direction. Dressed somberly in black, his lips drooping into a frown, he looked prepared for a funeral. "Are you sure you won't change your mind?"

"No." Georgiana glanced at Brock, who was speaking to each of the drivers in turn. "He's promised to be on his best behavior."

Her uncle snorted. "God save us all from Lord Darleigh. I can only imagine what sort of trouble he'll stir up."

Moments later, Brock signaled for them to board their respective carriages, then swung up onto a large bay hunter. Despite her misgivings, excitement sparked in Georgiana's veins. She took Sir Anthony's outstretched hand and climbed into the barouche's interior. The smell of freshly-polished leather filled the air. She sat down while her uncle arranged himself on the leather squabs across from her. Within minutes they were off.

Their pace initially was slow and filled with aggravation as they battled the other carriages for space upon the road. With each passing second, Georgiana felt claustrophobia creeping over her. Sir Anthony clearly had no such difficulty; he snored contentedly across from her. She wanted to elbow him. Instead, Georgiana stiffened her spine and endured. She endured for over a week, through London and into the Midlands, past Birmingham and finally to Shrewsbury.

Much to her relief, the nights were comfortable, at inns which had real mattresses rather than straw ticking and hot meals in the evening. Nellie, who was traveling with her, made up for any deficiencies the establishment might have suffered. If not for Brock and Sir Anthony glowering at one another, she might even have learned to enjoy the journey, with its music of rattling harnesses and horses' hooves and the hoot of the outrider's horn.

After more than a week of jostling and bouncing around, they were ready to cross into Wales. They'd stopped for the evening at the Red Hart, an inn situated upon a hill and affording an excellent view of the Berwyn Mountains. Georgiana had dinner in her bedchamber and quickly fell asleep, aware that Brock had stationed himself outside of her bedchamber door. Her husband was determined to guard her . . . and so far, he'd done a very fine job of it. She could hardly take a breath without him knowing it.

She awoke the next morning at the sound of the inn's bootboy warning coach travelers that the carriage to Chester was about to depart. Determined to have a moment to herself, she dressed hastily and slung a shawl over her shoulders. Then she slipped out of her bedchamber, stepping carefully over Brock's slumbering form.

His hand snaked out and grabbed the hem of her skirt, startling a squeak out of her. She hadn't even known he was awake!

"Where are you sneaking off to?" he growled, assessing her with red-rimmed eyes. Clearly she'd roused him from a deep sleep.

"I need some time to myself," she informed him in a whisper.

"I'll not risk your safety."

"Please, Brock, let go of my skirt and allow me some freedom."

"You have five minutes," he allowed, releasing her skirt to straighten his tall form and stand. "I'll watch from the window."

"Thank you," she muttered, his high-handed tactics annoying her even as his concern warmed her from head to toe. Feeling like a naughty child, she crept out the front door and onto the lawn.

Only one other guest was awake and lingering in the yard. If not for the book in his hand, Georgiana would have thought the man completely unremarkable, unshaven and dressed as he was in poor, rough clothes. Idly she wondered how a man in such low circumstances had learned to read. At the very least, she thought, he ought to replace that hole-ridden hat atop his head.

Very much aware of Brock's gaze upon her, she crossed the road to stand on an outcrop of boulders.

Then, from atop her rocky perch, Georgiana dismissed the servant from her mind and took in a deep breath. The scent of heath, much like damp, newly-mown hay with an undertone of rotting stems, brought back childhood memories of running through the fields.

Stretching a little, she glanced at the mountains. A subdued mixture of grays and browns, they formed a natural border between England and Wales, one that Llywelyn ap Gruffud—the last true king of Wales— hadn't managed to enforce. The sky above them was troubled, filled with dark clouds that moved faster than they ought. Regardless, the mountains stretched upward into that swirling mass.

The mountains had no choice, she thought. Fate had thrust them upward into the skies just as it had demanded she keep the duke from inheriting the throne. Shivering, she pulled her shawl more tightly around her shoulders and caught a faint vibration in the air, brushing past her skin almost like a breeze. Her pendant grew warm between her breasts. She knew instinctively that somewhere in Wales, a druid was practicing magic. The notion resonated within her and made her heart beat faster. Would she have the courage to board her carriage later this morning, and take the final step into Wales . . . and her new life?

Her gaze roamed across bare rock and heath that had rooted in decayed moss. To an untrained eye, she mused, North Wales might appear desolate, wild, and severe. But Georgiana saw the light-green moss that clung to the humus, the yellowish fronds of ivy that swept along the ground, the aquamarine moss that dressed up the boulders. Ptarmigan and dotterel clucked contentedly in the heath and silver-studded blue butterflies fed upon its honey-scented nectar.

Wales, she thought, was a land of profound depths. Passionate and severe, beautiful but ungentle, this place offered promise to those who looked into its harsh face, and tragedy to those who dropped their gaze. Would she find promise or tragedy in Wales?

Georgiana lifted her chin. She loosened her shawl and let the breeze catch at it, drawing it away from her body. Cold air cut through her traveling gown and chilled her skin. And yet, her heart grew warm, because she knew Wales and understood it. No matter what this land offered her, she'd embrace it wholeheartedly, for to do anything less would dishonor it.

She was going home.

And she would triumph.

"I've given you a half an hour," a low male voice chided her from a few feet back. "I can allow you no more."

Georgiana smiled to herself, but it was a smile softened by appreciation and happiness. She enjoyed having his dark masculine presence by her side, lavishing her with the attention she'd once longed for. "I know."

"Is all of Wales so harsh?"

Georgiana gathered her shawl close to her body and turned around. Brock stood on the road below, his gaze sweeping across the hills.

"Just as the hills in Yorkshire aren't representative of all England, these uplands are but one face of Wales." Warming to her subject, she pointed to the south. "Swansea is a beautiful little port in South Wales, and Aberystwyth is filled with hill forts dating back to pre-Christian times—"

She broke off when she noticed he'd focused his attention upon her, his gaze curious. "What's wrong?"

He held out a hand, which she took as she stepped down from the outcrop. "You look different."

Aware that the wind had blown her chignon into a mass of stray tendrils and curls, she lifted an eyebrow. The old Georgiana, she thought, would have patted those curls into place and made some witty rejoinder designed to draw a compliment from him.

The old Georgiana was gone.

"In what way?" she asked, releasing his hand to walk back toward the inn with him.

"You seem more at ease." He rubbed his chin with two fingers, then added, "and stronger."

She smiled again, but said nothing.

"I don't know who you are anymore, Georgie."

Brock sounded mystified. They paused as a drover crossed their path, a sheepdog gamboling at his heels. Then he shrugged and slipped his hands into his pockets. "I suppose I never knew you."

Georgiana ducked her head and continued toward the inn. "We never knew each other."

He hurried to catch up, his gaze on the peculiar servant, who no longer held a book but still lingered in the yard. "Will you ever allow me into your life again?"

Her lips formed the word *no*. She had already chosen her duty to the Glamorgan Druids over Brock, and he deserved the truth. Nevertheless, something entirely different came out. "I don't know, Brock. I can't say."

Damning herself for her lack of courage, she entered the carriageway outside their inn and stopped near her barouche. The drivers and outriders were making last-minute preparations before starting off again. She'd missed breakfast.

Brock moved to her side, his hair ruffling in the breeze. He picked up a small basket and handed it to her. The tantalizing scent of cocoa and hot biscuits wafted toward her. "When will you know?"

Basket clutched in her arms, she looked away. "Thank you for thinking of my breakfast."

"When will you know?"

Cornered, she gave him the only answer she could, one she felt certain he didn't want to hear. "Once I've fulfilled my destiny."

Cursing softly, he turned from her and mounted a chestnut-colored thoroughbred that a groomsman held for him. He took the lead in front of their carriages and, throwing her a pained look, started down the road toward Gwynedd County.

Her hands trembling, she boarded her carriage and settled down across from her uncle. As much as she disliked admitting it, she very much wanted Brock at her side. The realization troubled her. While she said aloud that she'd made her choice in favor of the Glamorgan Druids, her need for Brock suggested she still straddled two worlds. He was her one weakness, her crutch.

Georgiana pressed her face against the windowpane. Thoughts like these left her feeling very grim indeed. Unfortunately they couldn't be dismissed. If she continued to stand between the two worlds, she knew that very soon she'd find herself torn apart.

Brock rode about a half-mile ahead of the carriages. The clouds above him, some of them dark and angry-looking, gradually lightened as the sun crested the horizon and began its ascent. He scented the air and smelled rain. Soon he'd have to take shelter in one of the barouches. The thought left him nonplussed. He wanted to see this land that was taking his wife away from him, mile by mile.

Frowning, he reined his horse closer to the edge of the road to peer at a stone cairn. Like everything else about Wales, the cairn hinted at great antiquity, at battles and quarrels and grievances between

Wales and England which had ended in death.
Indeed, he was feeling very English at the moment,
an outsider passing through a pessimistic land with
a flair for the dramatic. Everywhere he looked, he
saw stones and dried-up heath and mountains
looming in the distance. How different it all was, he
thought, from England's orderly, well-tended gardens.

Over the last week or so, while he'd guarded her
faithfully, he'd asked himself plenty of times if he
really stood a chance of winning her back. As
they'd traveled farther away from England he'd
begun to think that the odds weren't in his favor.
Georgiana had virtually transformed into a different woman with every turn of the carriages' wheels.
She'd seemed to age—not physically, of course; she
was still as beautiful as ever—but instead she
showed a new introspection, a mystery in her
silences that she would have filled before with light
chatter. He couldn't even guess at what she was
thinking and the notion nearly drove him crazy.

At least he could comfort himself with the fact
that she remained safe.

Would he still feel comforted a week from now,
though? Or a month from now? What if a year
passed and things still hadn't changed between
them? He didn't know how long he could go on like
this, guarding her and needing her so badly he
wanted to shout from the pressure of it.

Brock pulled his horse up. He looked down the

path he'd just traveled. In the distance, several carriages jingled their way toward him. How easy, he mused, it would be to turn around and ride for Palmer House. His heart lightened at the thought of England and his gentlemen's club and Carlisle's easy company. Obeying a sudden impulse, he kicked his horse into a light trot and started toward the carriages.

The footmen and outriders tugged at their caps as he reached the carriages and passed them. He spotted Georgiana and Sir Anthony's carriage and quickly tried to think up a likely excuse as to why he was returning home: the estate finances, his mother, a business deal he had simmering. . . .

Sir Anthony stuck his head out the window of his barouche. Evidently he'd seen Brock coming. "Is there a problem, Lord Darleigh?" he asked, his faded blue eyes sharp.

Brock opened his mouth, then closed it again. The words which had come so easily to his head a moment before refused to be uttered. He allowed his horse to fall into step with the carriage.

Sir Anthony studied him for a few seconds, then said firmly, "No one will question you even once if you decide to return home."

Brock cleared his throat. "I was thinking—"

Georgiana chose that moment to look out the window. Her green eyes were sad and knowing in that perfect oval face of hers, and behind them he saw that spark of restlessness that had always been there.

Just looking at her tugged at him. He remembered anew that moment they'd shared in the forest, while he'd been courting her. He'd lost so many opportunities since then, made so many wrong choices. . . .

Clutching the sill, she leaned out the window. A flash of red caught his attention. He realized the rubies on her ring—the ring that he'd given her the day they'd married—were sparkling in an errant ray of sunshine that had somehow managed to break through the clouds.

"My uncle will take care of me," she insisted.

Something inside Brock twisted. Hard. He grimaced. "Who said I'm returning to England?"

Her expression lightened suddenly, and she released the windowsill. Sir Anthony frowned.

"I was thinking we might cut our traveling short today, for Georgiana's sake," Brock said, his voice harsh. He was angry at himself for staying. Why hadn't he simply surrendered her into Sir Anthony's care?

Because you love her, a tiny voice said.

Scowling, Brock dismissed the voice as foolish and sentimental. "We've been pushing hard and I thought we could all use some rest," he growled.

"Thank you, Lord Darleigh." Georgiana smiled, and abruptly she looked like the woman he'd married. "Still, I'm eager to see my aunt and would prefer to travel until nightfall."

"As you wish." Brock prepared to turn his horse

around, and then hesitated. His current position, atop a small hillock, afforded him a bird's-eye view of the road they'd just traveled. There, at least a mile back, a figure in rough clothes with a brown hat drawn over his face rode atop a horse.

Brock knew he should expect other travelers on the road. And yet, he thought he remembered seeing this same servant days ago, back in Birmingham. The hat was unusually ratty and he remembered wondering why the man had bothered to wear it. And how had such a poor man acquired a horse?

Suspicion stirred in his gut.

The Duke of Gloucester, Brock mused, was known for his thoroughness. The man would explore every possible lead in his search for Georgiana's identity. Perhaps when the duke had learned they'd left London with Sir Anthony, he'd designated a minion to follow them.

Brock frowned. Obviously he would have to keep a very close watch on the situation. Suddenly feeling very justified in his decision to guard Georgiana, he turned his horse in behind the last carriage and brought up the rear. A cold drizzle began to fall. He estimated the temperature couldn't be much higher than fifty degrees and turned the collar of his jacket up.

As they crossed into Wales proper and made for Llangollen, he reflected that Georgiana wasn't the only one who was walking destiny's path. He had this strange sense that all roads would lead to

Georgiana and Wales, no matter what choice he made or where he rode. An unseen hand seemed to be guiding him toward a future that had already been decided and merely needed to be played out.

His mood growing worse by the hour as the servant continued to follow them, Brock trailed the carriages over the River Dee and into Llangollen, where the land was lower and forests prevailed over boulders. Most of the street and shop signs were in Welsh. Brock had difficulty deciphering them, as the Welsh language seemed to lack vowels. He had even more trouble following conversations because the shop and inn proprietors talked to him in a strange variety of English he could hardly understand. Brock thought he saw muted triumph in Sir Anthony's eyes when the older man finally took over the negotiations for rooms, underscoring the fact that Brock was a stranger—a frustrated stranger—in a foreign country.

Keeping his attention on the servant who continued to follow them at a discreet distance, Brock followed the carriages through a myriad of landscapes, some forested, some mountainous, and some overrun with sheep. They passed north of Mount Snowdon, its peak reaching far into the sky, around Swallow Falls, and through the Pass of Llanberis. Late one evening, near the end of the second week, they saw the Menai Straits glittering in the setting sun.

Brock let out a sigh that their trip was almost completed, safely, without any interference from their servant follower. The previous day he'd noticed that the man had left the road, perhaps for some local village. Despite all of Brock's imaginings otherwise, the man was naught but a Welshman traveling home.

Even so, as they wound their way down toward Caernarfon, a whole new apprehension gathered inside him. Just outside of town, at Gwynllian's cottage, the Glamorgan Druids awaited Georgiana's arrival. They were his rivals, intent on taking her away from him. Would they succeed?

He narrowed his eyes.

Not if he could help it.

They came to him a few minutes after he'd donned his nightshirt and nightcap and climbed into bed. He supposed they thought him at his most vulnerable, tired after a long day and likely sleeping. They didn't know that he absolutely adored the night and lived for the darkness, and spent several hours in bed each night, relaxing and expanding his awareness . . . but not sleeping. Never sleeping.

The Duke of Gloucester simply didn't sleep.

He didn't like the dreams that sleep sometimes brought him. Dreams about hounds.

At the mere thought of it, the scars on his leg began to ache. Ignoring the throb, he rolled out of bed and crept behind drapes which concealed French doors. His hand on the doorknob, he glanced out over the terrace and scanned the estate grounds. He detected none other than the two who were already in his bedchamber.

Smiling slightly with anticipation, he began to create the illusion. All around him order ebbed and flowed in a cold, predictable way, while chaos bubbled its siren song. Eagerly he embraced the chaos and began to sculpt it into an illusion of himself, lying on the bed, eyes closed.

The two druids at the window froze, apparently sensing the vibrations from his illusion. Just as quickly they spread out, moving away from the illusion he'd created on the bed and toward his hiding place behind the drapes.

Grudging admiration filled him. These two were well-trained. The match would prove more even than he'd thought. Quickly he created another illusion of himself, this one standing behind the drapes, and moved to a location next to his bureau. Now there were three targets for the assassins: himself, and two illusions. Would they pick the right one?

When the druids approached the drapes, locking onto the second false target, he gave the illusion a candlestick and forced it to scuttle away, the quick reformation of order stirring the drapes and adding to the effect. At the same time, he forced the fake duke on the bed to sit up, a pistol in hand.

The two would-be assassins looked at the fake duke on the bed in confusion.

Nearly chuckling with glee, the duke created yet another illusion, this one of himself standing near the door, fully dressed, brandishing a sword. One by one, he moved the illusory dukes until they stood facing his attackers.

Backing away, the druids stared at each of the illusions, their attention shifting from one to the other. They clearly felt the telltale vibrations, but they weren't skilled enough to know which duke was real, and which ones were fake.

The duke maneuvered all three of his illusions around the two druids. As one, the illusions spoke. "Do you wish to die by pistol, sword, or candlestick?"

Their eyes widening, the two men continued to back away. The duke could smell their confusion, an acrid scent that excited him all the more. Clutching his cane, he deliberately backed the would-be assassins toward his real self; and when they drew close enough, he lifted his arm high and swung it at them horizontally, so when the cane struck the first druid it broke his head open like an overripe melon.

The second man, covered with gore from the first, had little time to react before the duke brought his cane down again, striking him on the shoulder. A cracking sound filled the bedchamber. The assassin crumpled to his feet, crying out in agony.

The duke lowered his cane. This one he wanted alive.

Eyebrows drawn together, the duke placed one of his slippered feet on the assassin's neck and pressed, hard, until the assassin began to choke. After several moments, he lifted his foot, certain that the would-be killer now understood his place.

"Who sent you?"

Rubbing his throat, the assassin stared at him.

The duke lifted his cane and bashed the man's kneecap, drawing a howl from him. "Must I take you to Cailleach's tomb?" He drew back his arm and smashed the man's other kneecap. Blood spattered the wall. "Who sent you?"

The assassin leaned forward to clutch his knees. Suddenly, a knife appeared in his hand. Before the duke could stop him, the man plunged it into his stomach, his eyes lighting with unholy triumph.

"You devious little bastard," the duke muttered, and yanked the knife from the assassin's stomach. Still, he was too late. Life had already leaked from the assassin's gaze. He kicked the corpse gently. Too bad. They wouldn't be able to harvest his heart later.

Frowning heavily, the duke threw the knife onto the corpse and paced over to the window. Over the last two weeks he'd had no success at all discovering the new guardian. He'd examined every one of the known Glamorgan Druids for a second time, to no avail, and all of his spies had reported ordinary findings. Before these two had appeared in his bedchamber, the duke had feared the trail leading to the new guardian had gone cold.

The fact that someone had sent assassins after him indicated he *was* closing in on the new guardian. But which spy had drawn close? The duke groaned aloud with frustration. This latest difficulty was yet another example of things going wrong lately. He had actually made a mistake. He should have sensed the assassin's intention to kill himself. He should have stopped him.

He should have found the female guardian by now.

Was it his destiny ultimately to fail?

Shaking his head, the duke muttered an emphatic *no*. He reminded himself that whoever had concealed her had done an excellent job of it. His own brothers had spent painstaking hours re-examining notes on all of the druids known to them and had found nothing.

Nevertheless, she was out there. Somewhere.

And he had to find her, soon.

Before her ability and skill grew beyond his and threatened his very life.

Sighing heavily, the duke surveyed the blood and bodies covering the floor of his bedchamber. *Quite a mess*, he thought. But a necessary mess. Rogue druids needed to be taught their places.

He pulled on the bell cord to summon his butler,

also one of his most accomplished druids, then collapsed onto his bed. Exhausted from the effort of maintaining three illusions at once, the duke closed his eyes and surrendered to an unusual bout of sleep.

He dreamed of hounds.

Chapter
11

❧

Georgiana stuck her head out of the carriage window as they pulled around to the front of Cadair Abbey. Her aunt stood outside, a gray cloak around her slender frame, her hand in the air and waving. Several footmen dressed in mismatched clothes stood nearby.

"Gwynllian was never one for ceremony," Sir Anthony muttered from his perch across from her. "Look at how those footmen are dressed."

"Yes, isn't it wonderful?" Georgiana's smile widened as they rolled to a halt. Gladness filled her at the sight of her aunt and all her quirky ways. Rather than wait for a footman to open the door, she turned the latch, jumped out, and raced across the cobblestones to her aunt's open-armed embrace.

"Georgiana, my dear," Gwynllian murmured, her hand brushing across Georgiana's hair to settle in the small of her back.

"Aunt Gwynllian, I've missed you so much."

Her aunt loosened the embrace and allowed Georgiana to step back a pace, so they might look at each other. Georgiana saw a sheen of moisture in Gwynllian's gaze, and felt tears in her own eyes as well.

"We've much to discuss," her aunt said in a mock-censuring tone.

"Yes, there's much you've kept from me."

Gwynllian made a shooing gesture. "There's time for talk tomorrow. I want you to rest from your journey."

Georgiana's smile faded. "When do I meet the Glamorgan Druids and David Cwylum?"

"Later. Perhaps tomorrow."

Before Gwynllian could elaborate further, Brock pulled his horse to a halt next to them and dismounted. He had a coating of dust on him and stubble on his face, making him appear thoroughly disreputable, and extremely male.

After giving the reins to a footman, he slapped at his pants and jacket, but his attempt to clean up had little effect. Privately Georgiana rather liked the way he looked. A marquess who occasionally got his hands dirty was a man with a lively disregard for convention. For all of his staid upbringing, Brock had lately proven himself both unpredictable and exciting.

He let his hands fall to his sides and surveyed Cadair Abbey. "This is a cottage? I was expecting a little timber-and-wattle structure."

Gwynllian smiled. "I wasn't expecting *you*, Lord Darleigh. Welcome to Wales, and to my home. It's called Cadair Abbey."

Eyes narrowed, he tilted his head. "I believe I've heard of it before. The name sounds familiar."

"Cadair Abbey was home to Benedictine monks back in the sixteenth century. It came into our family in the seventeen hundreds." Unable to stop herself from touching him, and claiming him in her own small way, Georgiana placed a hand on his arm and directed his attention toward the south. "It's named after that mountain, Cadair Idris. When standing in the abbey's bell tower, you can see its peak quite clearly."

Her gaze lingering on the hand that Georgiana had placed on Brock's arm, Gwynllian's smile disappeared. "You both must be exhausted. Why don't you go inside? Georgiana, you know the way to the dining room. I've had the servants lay out an informal supper for you."

Self-consciously, Georgiana allowed her hand to fall to her side.

"Thank you, Miss Stanton," Brock said in formal tones. "You're very kind to put up an unexpected guest."

Gwynllian measured him with a narrowed gaze. "Accustomed as you are to Palmer House and all of London's frivolities, I'm sure you'll find your stay here provincial as well as boring. How long were you planning to remain in Caernarfon?"

Brock shrugged. "For as long as Georgiana needs me."

Feeling the tension gathering around her, Georgiana stepped between the two and put her hand on Brock's arm again. "Lord Darleigh kindly offered to escort us here. Throughout the journey he's guarded me faithfully. We can't send him home without giving him a chance to rest, no, Aunt Gwynllian?"

Her aunt's eyes took on a shuttered look. "Of course not."

Sir Anthony clambered down from the carriage. His attention lit upon Gwynllian and, while a smile touched his lips, his brows drew together in the manner of someone worried or sad. Their gazes locked for a few seconds.

"Gwynllian, my dear sister, how are you?" he finally said, and then the two were hugging fiercely.

Georgiana turned away from the pair, to give them their privacy, and led Brock up the stairs to Cadair Abbey. Tears were filling her eyes all over again. Wiping at them with her handkerchief, she murmured some nonsense about the abbey's architecture as they entered the main hall, where monks had worshipped centuries before.

Once inside, they paused to give their traveling coats to waiting footmen. In the past, Georgiana had found the main hall daunting, with its stone walls and windows stretching up to a ceiling some twenty feet high. Today, however, she was simply glad to be home and looked upon everything with a kindly eye.

"This part of the abbey is not the most comfortable," she admitted happily, glancing at the ponderous mahogany side tables and bureaus pushed up against the walls. As usual, Gwynllian had decorated them with vases of late-summer flowers, giving the musty air a sweet undertone. "Let's go into the presbytery, and find that supper my aunt spoke of."

Brock nodded. "Like everything else about Wales, your aunt's home has an aura of days long gone by."

Sensing that he felt a bit out of his element, she tucked his hand into the crook of her arm and led him into the dining room. There, they snacked on pigeon pie, boiled beef, and a great loaf of bread served on a wooden trencher. All were smoking hot and delicious.

Gwynllian and Sir Anthony joined them shortly afterward, and with much chitchat and talk about their journey, they filled their stomachs. The wine served, a rich burgundy, was of the finest quality, and afterward they all sipped the traditional Benedictine liqueur, a strange-tasting, herbed cordial which Sir Anthony claimed was imbued with secret healing qualities. Gwynllian took special care with Brock's cordial, telling him she wished to give him the finest drink the cellars of Cadair Abbey had to offer.

Once the sun had set completely and the tall case

clock had chimed eight in the evening, Gwynllian asked a footman to take them to their bedchambers. Feeling quite mellow after drinking to everyone's health, Georgiana noted that her aunt had placed Brock in a bedchamber at the opposite end of the hall, as far away from Georgiana as possible. Obviously she didn't approve of Brock's presence or Georgiana's need of him. A twinge of guilt reminded her that her aunt was right . . . she ought to send Lord Darleigh home.

Unsettled, she entered the bedchamber she'd grown up in as a child and maneuvered around the trunks of her fashionable London gowns. Gwynllian, she noticed, hadn't changed anything. The silver backed hairbrush and the bottle of French perfume her aunt had given her for her fifteenth birthday still sat atop her polished oak bureau.

She'd thought she'd feel peaceful and comfortable in her old bedchamber. Instead, she realized she'd been gone so long it no longer seemed to belong to her. Her dismay growing, she allowed Nellie to prepare her for bed and spent the next hour trying to fall asleep. At last she succeeded, but it was a restless sleep, with images of Gwynllian and the robed druid, whom she now knew as David Gwylum, swirling in her mind.

Someone began to shake her gently. She opened her eyes to find her aunt gazing at her and the room around her pitch-black. She thought she was having a nightmare.

"Come and meet the others," Gwynllian murmured. She placed the candle she'd been holding on a side table and shook out a long robe made of cotton. "They're waiting for you in the sacred grove."

Sleep deserted her instantly. She wasn't having a nightmare after all. Regardless, she felt a chill that had nothing to do with the night air. "Now? In the middle of the night?"

"Our ceremony must remain a secret." Gwynllian held the robe up, silently urging her to put it on.

Georgiana tried to make her limbs move. They trembled too hard to obey her.

Gwynllian's eyebrows drew together. "I would never let anyone hurt you, dear," she murmured. "By the same token, I can no longer stand in the way of your destiny. You must meet David and the Glamorgan Druids. As it's a fairly cool night, I suspect they'd appreciate your immediate appearance."

"I don't know what they expect from me," she stalled.

"They expect nothing. Do only what you wish." Gwynllian shook the robe. "Let me see some courage from you, Georgiana."

Her aunt's prodding finally had the desired effect. Georgiana directed her body to sit up, and surprisingly, it listened. Soon she was dressed in the robe with only the scantiest of underthings beneath and a soft pair of slippers on her feet. Gwynllian's pleased nod encouraging her onward, she led the way from her bedroom and into the hallway.

Brock stretched out in his simple pine bed and tried to focus on the ceiling. A series of large plaster tiles formed a pattern above him, their arrangement made all the more interesting by the fact that they kept slipping out of place. He didn't know how much of that monk's liquor one had to drink before becoming accustomed to it, but he felt damned groggy, unusually so, and he wasn't the kind of man who couldn't hold his cordial, for God's sake. If he didn't know better, he might even suspect Gwynllian had slipped him a bit more than cordial.

Of course, she hadn't. Gwynllian wasn't the type to drug unsuspecting males. And she must know he needed no help dropping off to slumber this eve, especially after all that travel. So why did he have such a muddled head?

By God, his limbs felt like dead weights. Grumbling, he pulled himself into a sitting position and, when the room stopped spinning, hoisted himself to his feet. There he stood for several seconds, gripping the bedpost, determined to walk off whatever demon had got hold of him, before he passed out in his sleep and died.

Christ Almighty, he felt like hell. Glaring, he surveyed the bedchamber Gwynllian had put him in. Not only had she selected the room farthest from Georgiana for him, she'd barely given him enough space to turn around in. Only the oriel window saved the room from utter closeness. The fact that the furniture was made of pine—the cheapest wood available—wasn't lost on him, either. She had clearly registered her displeasure over his presence without saying a word. As far as Brock was concerned, however, she could go straight to Hades. He wasn't abandoning his wife and possibly his child to a bunch of harp-playing rustics who prayed to the trees.

He stumbled over to the oriel window which jutted a good three feet out into the night, making a ledge of sorts for him to stand in. The window was big but the view disappointing. It overlooked a deep, impenetrable forest—the Coed y Brenin Forest, Georgiana had called it, spouting off one of those damned Welsh names. *Tywyn, Llanwrtyd, Eglwyswrw*—he'd challenge any self-respecting Englishman to think up something more cryptic.

He sighed and pressed his forehead against the windowpanes. The cold glass cooled his skin, and the room spun more slowly. Already he was feeling better. He just needed to walk. Rubbing his eyes, he pushed back from the window, blinked twice, and focused on what appeared to be a torch out there on the abbey grounds. Who in God's name, he wondered, would skulk around the lawn at this time of night with a torch? These Welshmen, they had strange customs. . . .

He shook his head and stared at the torch, which

became two torches, then four. No, the torches weren't multiplying. Nor was he hallucinating, despite the liquor. Instead, more people with torches were joining the leader. He glanced at the clock on the mantelshelf. It read half-past midnight.

His curiosity perked up. It was only the middle of July, too early for a harvest celebration. Regardless, the hour was extremely late. What in hell were they doing?

Misgivings filled him. His thoughts strayed inevitably to Georgiana. Was she somehow involved? Maybe Gwynllian *had* slipped him a special drink this evening—to prevent him from interfering in some arcane druidic ceremony.

An impulse grabbed hold of him and demanded he dress and follow the druids. Provided he skulked after them quietly, without alerting them to his presence, he should be able to satisfy his curiosity and assure himself that Georgiana wasn't in harm's way. Stifling a groan, he shuffled over to the wardrobe and found a pair of wool trousers his valet had unpacked earlier that day. After falling over twice and much cursing he managed to pull them on, and a shirt besides. He opted for boots, given the rough Welsh terrain, and shrugged into a jacket. Then, dressed if not stylish, he stumbled into the hall and walked past Georgiana's bedchamber, pausing long enough to open the door and glance inside.

Her bed was empty.

Not at all surprised, Brock made his way down

the stairs to the great hall. *Where the monks once prayed*, he reminded himself wryly.

The house was very still. All of the servants had evidently gone to bed. Attempting to be as quiet as possible, but afraid he sounded more like a lumbering elephant, Brock found the front door and let himself out. Cold air slapped him in the face and sobered him even more. He took in a deep breath, his nose tingling, and wondered which way the druids had gone.

Scanning the countryside, he noted a large expanse of lawn to his right, and darker shadows to his left. Otherwise everything remained pitch-black and indecipherable. Unlike the others he'd seen, he hadn't brought a torch, and the darkness left him with a severe disadvantage. His eyes were open but he couldn't see a damned thing. He would have to rely on his senses of hearing and touch.

And his mind, despite its current foggy state. That patch of unrelenting darkness, he reasoned, must be the forest. He walked to the left, examining both the abbey for his oriel window—which would tell him he was entering the forest at the right point—and the shadows for evidence of a path. After a good five minutes of frustrated wandering and stumbling, he located his oriel window, then started off toward the darker shadows. He picked up a stick along the way, and felt the ground with it like a blind man, so he might avoid those roots which stuck up out of the ground.

The idiocy of his plan to find the druids in the forest soon presented itself to him in all its glory, for when he reached the trees, he discovered they formed a barrier he'd need a sword to penetrate. Without his own torch, he'd never find a path. Softly he cursed. Still, at the very least, his midnight walk had driven the peculiar grogginess away. His effort wasn't a complete loss.

Grumbling, he turned back toward the abbey. And froze.

There, hurrying erratically across the lawn, was another source of light . . . not a torch this time, but something smaller. A lantern maybe, with its wick turned low. The lantern stayed near the bushes, then rushed across open space before taking shelter behind a large tree.

Brock ducked behind a gorse bush and, eyes narrowed, watched the lantern make for the woods. The furtive aspect of the lantern motions suggested its carrier wasn't on an evening stroll. Indeed, Brock guessed that the figure planned to follow the druids and had prepared better for the endeavor. His smile grim, Brock decided that he would trail after the lantern-carrier and discover why the druids worshipped trees at such an odd hour.

He skulked along the edge of the forest until he reached the point where the lantern had gone into the woods. Sure enough, he found a path after only a few tries. Several feet down the path a tiny orange light grew smaller by the moment. Owls hooted and crickets hummed within the trees, inviting him in. Hastening onto the path, Brock followed the lantern's glow.

Made of dirt and crowded on either side by leaves, bushes, and other forest detritus, the path was extremely treacherous. Roots stuck up at haphazard angles and tripped him, while brambles pulled at his clothes. Even so, he managed to conceal himself from the lantern-carrier, for the little orange glow continued to move steadily down the path.

Brock walked through the trees for almost five minutes before he noticed a brighter shine beyond the lantern's glow. The trees seemed to be thinning out as well. Tensing, he realized they had finally come upon the druids. He kept his attention on the lantern as he crept from bush to bush, working his way closer to a clearing. The torches, he saw, stood in wooden stakes that served as holders and ringed the clearing. When he'd inched close enough, he selected a thick stand of bushes—without thorns—and crawled into them. His gut tight with excitement, he parted the branches and peered at the druids.

The forest floor sloped downward as it opened onto the clearing, placing him above the ceremony. Rectangular stones of great size, obviously manmade but worn down by rain and snow, encircled the clearing and partially obstructed Brock's view. The forest, he realized, must have grown up around the stones after they'd been placed in this location.

Figures of varying heights, dressed in off-white robes which covered their head and shadowed their faces, had formed a loose circle inside the stones. He strained to see what they were doing. Far to his left, the little orange glow had grown smaller, but remained motionless, suggesting the lantern-carrier was spying as well.

As odd as the gathering appeared, Brock didn't receive a sense of evil, malice, or even superstitious doings from the druids. They blended with the landscape and moved as gracefully as a branch blowing in the wind, bringing to mind wood sprites and fairies, rather than witches. Intricate designs in gold and copper thread embroidered their robes, giving them a luxurious quality.

Remembering what Sir Anthony had told him about druidry, he had an idea that druids tapped into wholly natural forces which, through time, men and women have forgotten existed. In fact, a primeval aura surrounded them, speaking of rich and ancient traditions. Brock mused that he might have been peering back in time, at pre-medieval lords and ladies attending a spiritual gathering.

One by one, the figures stepped to the center of the circle and made throwing motions. Steam rose from between them and filled the air with a light herbal scent. He realized they had a cauldron boiling away at the center.

Three figures stood closer to the cauldron than the rest. Judging by their sizes, he guessed their cloaks hid two women and a man. He watched as the largest figure threw leafy branches into the cauldron, followed by the smaller figures, who each dropped a block of some sort into the liquid. Eyes narrowed, he stared at the smallest figure's left hand. As he'd suspected, a tiny flare of red sparkled in the torchlight.

Georgiana.

His mood slipped several notches downward. Part of him had hoped she'd change her mind, turn her back on druidism, and return to London as Lady Darleigh. Although he had no real basis for that hope, he couldn't help himself from daydreaming. But that would have made the situation too easily resolved. God knew Georgiana never resolved *anything* easily.

The larger figure began to speak in Welsh, his words incomprehensible. All of the others joined in . . . except Georgiana, whose gaze remained fixed on the fire. Their chanting became singsong, like a story to music. Then, without warning, all of the robed figures surged forth and put out the fire beneath the cauldron with gourds of water. A great hiss filled the clearing, along with a billowing rush of steam that swirled in eddies as it exploded toward the heavens.

Instinctively Brock drew back into the bushes. Within moments, the air cleared, and he leaned forward again. Georgiana and her two companions stood very near the cauldron, staring intently at its contents. Brock's raised position allowed him to see some sort of oiling substance pooling on the liquid's surface, along with pieces of branches.

What in *hell*, he wondered, were they cooking?

Minutes passed. They continued to stare into the cauldron. The others sat quietly in a circle around them. Brock began to grow restless. He shifted in his nest of bushes and noticed that the lantern-carrier had more endurance than he; that hearty still remained utterly motionless.

Suddenly, the larger figure spoke in a demanding masculine voice.

"Choose your name."

Brock twitched. For an elderly man, Sir Anthony had a certain power to his voice. *Druid's power*, no doubt. Dislike for Georgiana's uncle left him with a sour taste. Sir Anthony claimed he had her best interests at heart; if so, how could he insist on indoctrinating her into this fantastic cabal?

"I have chosen," she sang out in a clear voice, interrupting his thoughts.

"The name you have selected is to be hidden forever from all but yourself," Sir Anthony said in sonorous tones. "It is yours to use when you need strength and courage."

Georgiana bowed her head. "Thank you."

The third figure standing near the cauldron spoke up. "The waters have given me a name and a

sign. We will call her Gobaith, the last hope of the
Glamorgan Druids. Hold out your hand, Gobaith."

Brock recognized the third figure's voice as
Gwynllian's.

Georgiana held out her right hand. Using a pen
or stick of some sort, Gwynllian drew something on
Georgiana's palm. Once finished, the older woman
bid Georgiana to memorize the symbol. Nodding,
Georgiana stared at her palm for almost a minute,
then closed her hand into a fist.

Sir Anthony raised his arms and spread his
hands. His voice rang out clear and true:

Slowly the chosen awakens from her dream.

Behold, Gobaith has been reborn.

The Guardians of Becoming will rule once more,

And bring a long lost peace."

Silence rang out in the clearing.

Brock kept his attention on Georgiana, sensing
more to come.

A fourth druid moved next to her, this about Sir
Anthony's size, but skinnier. He took her hand and
held it waist-high, revealing their linked hands to
all. They both closed their eyes. An expectant
silence fell over the entire group. Around them, the
standing stones began to glow with an unearthly
blue light.

A green sprout emerged from the earth in front
of Georgiana. Slowly the sprout grew larger, sway-
ing and stretching like someone who'd slept in a
cramped position for far too long. It thickened into

a sapling and lengthened until it reached above their heads, developing branches without leaves. The trunk grew in diameter and roots pushed into the ground, creating fissures. Branches snapped and the earth groaned in protest.

Eyes wide, he felt a superstitious awe curl through him.

A soft cry went up among the druids. Some took a step away from the tree, which he felt certain was an illusion Georgiana had created. Braver souls pressed closer and gaped.

The tree, he realized, was an oak. Its trunk had grown to ancient proportions, far too wide for a man to encircle with his arms and towering above them. The mere size of it inspired him. Still, it had no leaves. It was a tree of winter, of frost and death. Suddenly, the scent of freshly-scythed grass filled the air and the tree burst forth with green shoots unfurling like flower petals and trembling as they formed into leaves, creating a dry rattle that drowned out the earth's groans.

It was a beautiful specimen: unblemished, in perfect health, vigorous, at peace with the landscape around it. Brock suspected it was a symbol of the world Georgiana wished to inhabit. *A fantasy world,* he mused.

He didn't think she could make the illusion any more complete, but she did, creating acorns on the ends of the branches that glowed a golden brown in the torchlight. A fierce but warm wind swept through the little clearing, shaking the leaves, and acorns dropped from its branches to land on the grass.

Abruptly, the tree vanished. Georgiana released her companion's hand and swayed; Sir Anthony grabbed her arm to steady her. The standing stones returned to their natural gray color. Gwynllian, who'd been hovering behind her the whole time, moved quickly to where the illusion-tree had grown. She reached down, scooped something off the earth, and held it up between two fingers for the others to see.

An acorn.

A chill went through him. Was it coincidence, or had Georgiana somehow managed to create reality from dreams?

Soft cries echoed around the clearing as the druids recognized what Gwynllian held in her hand. One by one they faced Georgiana and bowed their heads. They obviously thought she'd created it, but Brock just couldn't convince himself that they hadn't been tricked by a bit of advance planning on Gwynllian's part.

Visibly trembling, Georgiana fought to stand on her own. Nevertheless, her voice rang out when she spoke. "We're together again, and are strong in our unity. I'm a Guardian of Becoming, and I'll do my best to protect you. In return, I want you to treat me like any other. We are all but a little part of the whole of nature. Those who think more of them-selves are damned."

A pause ensued, during which they all raised their heads as she'd bid. Then, a few at a time, they threw back their hoods and went up to Georgiana to congratulate her. Only a few women among them, the druids nevertheless looked quite normal and well cared for, obviously Welsh aristocrats for the most part.

He didn't see the baskets propped up against the standing stones until the druids fetched and opened them. A celebration commenced, with much laughter and feasting on whatever they'd brought in those baskets. Glasses emerged from hiding, their crystal stems sparkling in the torchlight. One young-looking druid with blond hair— the same who'd held Georgiana's hand while she'd created the illusion—poured wine for all.

Brock sat back on his heels. He might have been watching a soirée at a London townhouse. While the robes were questionable, the manners and merriment appeared quite natural and familiar. Georgiana was smiling and laughing along with them.

Knowing instinctively that the blond youth hovering around Georgiana was none other than David Gwylum, Brock allowed himself a brief smile. Worry that had grown heavier with each passing mile from England suddenly eased. So, the druids expected Georgiana to mate with a lad? He wondered how she felt about *that*.

Gwylum's very youth underscored the necessity of Brock's presence. The lad didn't appear strong enough to swat a fly, let alone protect Georgiana from any assassins the duke sent her way. God knew Sir Anthony wasn't exactly in fighting form.

He backed out of the bushes. Quietly he returned to the path. Tomorrow he would have a word or two with Gwynllian about his determination to protect his wife. Whether she liked it or not, he was going to stay at Georgiana's side and guard her for the remainder of his time in Wales.

Glancing at the lantern-carrier, he noticed that the little orange flame was on the move again, heading toward him. Evidently the spy was returning to the abbey. Brock decided it wouldn't hurt to ask him a few questions. He positioned himself behind a thicket of brambles.

When the orange glow grew close, Brock stood perfectly still. A light moisture formed on his brow and his chest rose and fell in short breaths. His eyes narrowed, he focused on the man and judged his size as less than his own. His confidence rose. The second after the figure passed, Brock stepped onto the path and placed a light hand on his shoulder.

"Who are you?" he asked, his tone quiet, yet intense.

The other man reacted as if prodded with a hot poker. He spun around with the lantern swinging, and landed a glancing blow against the side of Brock's head. Before Brock could react, he drew back his arm and hurled the lantern downward again.

Stunned, Brock threw his arms up and grabbed the lantern, more to protect himself from another blow than to retaliate, but his movement had the second effect: the stranger, already propelled by the lantern's motion, stumbled forward into a tree when Brock grasped it and pulled. The other man's momentum quickly yanked the lantern from Brock's grasp, however, forcing him to let it go. It fell to the forest floor. The orange light flared as oil leaked from its reservoir, lighting up the other man's face.

Recognition made him tense. The servant who had followed them from Shrewsbury had turned up at last. Yet he had no time to think anything else, for the man sprang to his feet and jumped at him, hands outstretched. Brock had a precious second or so to read his intention, and lifted his leg to block the attack. Evidently well-versed in fisticuffs, the servant anticipated his move and lowered his hands to grasp Brock's ankle.

Brock felt the man yank his leg and twist it, in an attempt to bring him down. He yielded to the twist, his leg muscles on fire, and bent over, supporting his weight with his palms against the ground. Then, with a deep breath, he brought his free leg up and threw it backward, jamming it into the servant's groin.

With an explosive breath the servant went careening backward into the trees. The sound of branches breaking filled the forest. Brock landed on his chest and lay still for a moment, seeing stars instead of branches.

Wiry arms snaked around him from behind and began to choke him, dragging him backward. Brock coughed, the stars in his vision beginning to spin. By God, he thought, this man was going to kill him, with nary a word exchanged between them. He'd seen the servant, and now he apparently had to die. Obviously the duke had sent one of his minions after them.

Summoning the last of his strength, Brock bent his arm and sent his elbow smashing into the man's face. The hands at his throat loosened, but didn't release him. His lungs began to burn. Panic filled him. Back arched, heels scrabbling against the forest floor, Brock felt around for anything that could be of use. When his fingers touched a cold stone, he curled his hand around it. It barely fitted into his palm. Groaning now, he hefted the rock in his hand and swung at the servant's skull. The sickening sound of bone breaking echoed between them. Abruptly Brock could breathe again as the man's hands fell away.

Gasping, choking, Brock staggered to his feet and stared at the other man. Light flickered on the trees in front of him, creating shadows on the man's face. Realizing he had company, Brock spun around. The golden-haired youth—Gwylum, most likely—stood directly behind him, Georgiana at his side.

"Georgiana," Brock gasped, and took a step toward her.

Brows knitted, she lifted her hand. "My God, Brock—"

Gwylum stepped between them, his Adam's apple working. He lifted his lantern high in the air, revealing the servant's face and the ugly gash on his forehead. Tiny pieces of bone flecked the wound.

"You've killed him." The youth's voice cracked on the last word.

Rubbing his throat with one hand, Brock turned to look at the corpse. "I saw him sneaking around the grounds outside the abbey, and followed him. He led me here. I wanted to ask him a few questions, but he attacked me before I even said a word."

"You don't need to defend yourself, Lord Darleigh." Gwylum lowered his lantern. His expression was unusually grim for one who hadn't even yet grown a beard. "We know him. He's one of the Duke of Gloucester's emissaries."

Georgiana maneuvered around Gwylum and touched Brock's wound, her brows drawn together. "Brock, I'm so sorry this has happened to you. Let me take you back to Cadair Abbey, so I might tend to you."

Frowning, his eyes narrowed, Gwylum gazed at Georgiana. He appeared more hurt than angry, Brock thought. Had the lad expected Georgiana to fall into his arms, simply because others told her that her destiny demanded she do so? The poor sod, he was in for terrible disappointment.

"A glass of whiskey wouldn't go amiss," Brock admitted, his throat on fire from the strangling he'd received. He focused on the younger man. "So, tell me, Gwylum, what do you suggest we do with the duke's emissary?"

Chapter 12

❦

Bury him." Sir Anthony, his gray hair almost white in the torchlight, came up behind them. Frowning, he walked a tight circle around the dead man. "Make him disappear. We don't want the duke to know you finished him off. In fact, the less attention drawn to Georgiana, the better."

Brock nodded slowly. He knew Sir Anthony's suggestion made sense. And yet, his gut churned as something inside of him balked at concealing the event. "Do you think the duke knows Georgiana's identity now?"

The older man shrugged. "If the duke knew who Georgiana really was, he would have sent ten men after her, not one. And they wouldn't have failed."

Georgiana clutched Brock's hand, as though she had to reassure herself that he remained alive. "Still, when his spy doesn't return, won't the duke suspect us?"

"The duke will know his spy met with a foul end, at the hands of the Glamorgan Druids," Sir Anthony allowed, his attention on the corpse. "That doesn't mean much, though. All of the duke's spies meet with a foul end when they stick their noses in Glamorgan business. The duke may simply assume we caught his man and are holding him in a cell somewhere."

Eyes narrowed, Brock stared at Sir Anthony, wondering how he'd never even guessed at this cold-blooded facet of the man's nature, or the longstanding feud between the English and Welsh druids.

"How long have you and the duke been enemies?" he asked.

Gwylum piped up. "We've been fighting each other for almost twenty years."

Brock measured him with a glance. "You don't look twenty years old."

The lad thrust his chin forward. "I'm sixteen."

"He's a fine young man," Georgiana interrupted in a soothing voice. Still, when Brock focused upon her and raised an eyebrow, she grimaced and her cheeks grew darker in the torchlight. Brock would almost wager she'd blushed. And who wouldn't blush, when expected to mate with a sixteen-year-old?

Sir Anthony sighed. "We can become acquainted later. For now, I want Georgiana and David to commit the spy's features to memory."

Gwylum gestured for Georgiana to precede him toward the dead man. Nose wrinkled, she stepped forward, and Gwylum lowered the lantern close to the man's face to illuminate his features. Once she'd finished, he lifted it and they both stepped back.

Carrying a lantern, Gwynllian came up behind them. Farther back, several of the druid merrymakers had gathered. They all wore worried expressions.

David spoke to her first. "Lord Darleigh intercepted one of the Duke of Gloucester's spies. As you can see, he dispatched the spy with admirable efficiency."

Gwynllian paused by the dead man and examined him.

"We should have anticipated this," Sir Anthony joined in, refusing to meet anyone's gaze. "When the duke doesn't hear from his emissary, he'll send more. We'll have to be very careful from now on."

"I noticed the man as far back as Shrewsbury," Brock revealed, struck by the peculiar notion that Sir Anthony acted guilty of something. "I should have acted upon my suspicions immediately and questioned him."

The older man frowned. "We'll need to come up with a plan. But not here. Let's go back to the abbey." He gave Brock a disgruntled look. "To discover that spy, you must have been spying upon us yourself. Do you realize, my lord, that our stone circle is forbidden to anyone unsanctioned for entry?"

"I didn't enter the circle," Brock pointed out.

"Ah, a fine distinction. Regardless, you have desecrated one of our most sacred ceremonies."

Standing near Georgiana, Gwynllian shook her head at her brother. "We should thank Lord Darleigh for exposing the duke's spy. Perhaps his bid to guard Georgiana has merit. If he hadn't interfered, the spy would have returned to London and shown the duke *this*." She held up the acorn between two fingers.

Sir Anthony's frown smoothed out. He took the acorn from Gwynllian and examined it. "You are, as always, right on the mark," he murmured.

A hush fell over the five of them. Suddenly, Georgiana spoke up. "Where did the acorn come from, Uncle? Did David and I make it?"

He nodded, his expression somber.

"But I thought that Guardians of Becoming only created illusions."

"Most of them could only create illusions," he clarified. "There is one who learned to do more: Merlin. It was his lifetime's work."

"I'm not Merlin." She crossed her arms over her breasts. Her chin jutted forward ever so slightly. "I hardly know anything at all about creating illusions. I shouldn't have been able to create an acorn."

Confused, Brock rubbed his temples. "Wait a minute. Are you telling me that a Guardian of Becoming can create *real* objects from nothing?"

"Not from nothing. From chaos." Sir Anthony

edged toward the path, clearly eager to return to the abbey. "Do you remember when I told you about the worlds of chaos and order, and how the Guardian of Becoming sits between the two, monitoring that which passes between them?"

"Vaguely."

"Well, Georgiana gathered up the fabric of chaos and shaped it into something with an orderly form, something we, as humans, recognized."

Brock shook his head. "If I hadn't seen it. . . ."

No one replied. A soft breeze whispered around them.

At length, Gwynllian spoke. "Georgiana didn't create the acorn alone. She and David had linked hands and combined abilities. While he isn't nearly as strong as she, he has a lot more experience, and was able to shape her raw power into a tiny bit of reality. Together, they are strong indeed."

The youth, who'd been silent up until then, suddenly smiled. "She's quite . . . stupendous."

Brock silently groaned at his worshipful tone.

Georgiana heaved a very audible sigh. "I'm tired. I want to return to the abbey. Tomorrow we can mull over the implications of the evening's events. Will anyone escort me?" She looked pointedly at Brock.

Brock hastily stepped forward and collided with Gwylum, who also moved to her side. He exchanged glances with the lad and saw youthful determination in his eyes, coupled with outrage.

"It seems we both wish to escort you," Brock observed.

"Then I shall have two escorts." She bent a strained smile on them, allowed each to take her arm, and began walking. "I feel like I'm between two worlds, not two . . . men," she murmured.

"You're between the past and the future," Gwylum insisted.

Sir Anthony and Gwynllian fell in behind them at a discreet distance. In the clearing, lights bobbed as the druids began to disperse as well, two of them pausing to lift the body and carry it off. Someone brought a torch for Sir Anthony before vanishing into the woods. The older man held the torch high, illuminating the path they walked along.

Brock bent his head closer to Georgiana's. "What sort of ceremony were you attending?"

"Say nothing," Gwylum counseled, before Georgiana had a chance to reply.

Georgiana looked from the youth to her aunt, her expression clearly annoyed.

"You may tell him," Gwynllian told her.

Gwylum stiffened. "Gwynllian—"

"Lord Darleigh is Georgiana's guardian," the older woman interrupted. "She may tell him."

Scowling, Gwylum fell silent.

Georgiana focused on Brock. "You witnessed my initiation ceremony. We were celebrating the Ritual of Naming . . . or *re*naming, depending on how you perceive it. When an initiate joins a druidic order, she is given a chosen name, one that the other members of the order know her by, and a secret name used in personal rituals."

"Your chosen name is Gobaith, no?"

She sucked in a little breath, as if the word had the power to startle her. "Yes, it is. It is a token of my new relationship with the world, now that I am a member of the Order of Glamorgan Druids. I can't tell you my secret name."

They walked quietly for a time.

"The ceremony looked interesting. Enjoyable, even," Brock eventually said. Without warning, inspiration struck. He smiled, anticipating the reaction to his next request. "Would I be allowed to join the Glamorgan Druids?"

"No," Gwylum and Sir Anthony said in unison.

Georgiana slanted a glance toward Brock. Her lips curved upward, too. "I'm afraid my uncle and new friend don't trust your motives."

"All organizations have certain requirements," Sir Anthony pointed out. "As a member of several gentlemen's clubs in London, you must surely recognize that fact. I'm afraid you will never meet our requirements."

"The young boy Arthur didn't meet the requirements of knighthood. And yet, only *he* could draw the sword from the stone." Brock knew his analogy was outrageous, but he just couldn't help himself.

"Gentlemen, now is not the time for debate," Gwynllian chided. "Cadair Abbey is just ahead.

Why don't we all retire for the night and discuss our situation on the morrow, as Georgiana suggested? Besides, she needs a very good sleep tonight, for tomorrow she starts her training, and she won't get any rest with all this bickering around her."

"Thank you, Aunt," Georgiana said as they rounded a bend in the path and emerged onto the lawn surrounding Cadair Abbey.

His head beginning to throb again, Brock reflected that *he* had little to thank Gwynllian for. While it pained him to part from his wife's side, his desire to have a few words with the woman who'd drugged him was stronger. He let go of Georgiana's arm and fell back a few paces, until his stride matched Gwynllian's.

"Georgiana may thank you," he murmured. "Be assured, I will not. I am well aware that the cordial you gave me earlier contained more than Benedictine."

The older woman looked him straight in the eye. "I was testing your strength of purpose," she said, then moved off before he could question her further.

Georgiana woke late the next morning and didn't feel rested at all, despite managing at least six hours of sleep. The attack on Brock last night had underscored for her how much danger they all faced. Almost two weeks had passed since she'd created her first illusion, two weeks for the duke to search for her. Was the spy who had attacked Brock just one of many emissaries fanning out across the Isles, or had the duke discovered her identity? Her uncle had insisted they remained relatively safe, but Georgiana wasn't so certain.

Brows drawn together, she went down to breakfast amidst the fragrant smells of herbs, eggs, and freshly baked breads. She discovered her uncle, her aunt, David, and Brock already sitting around the dining room table. She nearly turned on her heel and marched back upstairs. This group mixed as well as oil and water. She wasn't certain she could withstand any more sharp words.

Marshalling her courage, she nevertheless entered and claimed the seat she'd always occupied as a child. The dining room, part of the presbytery and therefore not as high-flown as the rest of the abbey, had a low, timbered ceiling and walls painted the color of mellowed whiskey. Bricks surrounded the fireplace and provided an atmosphere she'd normally describe as cozy. Today, however, the mirror that decorated the largest wall reflected strained faces.

David greeted her from across the table, and Brock from the far end. Situated an equal distance from her, they both watched her every move. Feeling like a bone caught between two dogs, Georgiana surveyed the platters on the sideboard. Welsh griddle cakes sprinkled with caster sugar, marinated cockles, Anglesey eggs, laver bread and

Glamorgan sausages created a fragrant smell that quickly set her mouth to watering. It had been a long time since she'd enjoyed a traditional Welsh breakfast.

Still, she didn't feel like eating much, not with David and Brock staring at her like that. She picked at the Anglesey eggs, scooping a tiny portion of the grilled cheese topping, and stole another glance at Brock. Now he was frowning at his sausages.

"Welsh food not to your taste?" she asked him, her voice tart.

"I've never tasted sausages like these." Eyebrows drawn together, he appeared bemused.

A very handsome bemused, she silently added. Dressed in soft gray trousers and a black jacket, his shirt white and starched against tanned skin, he looked very dark and very English.

"They've no meat in them," David said, obviously trying to show his contempt for Brock, but simply sounding petulant.

She'd known from the moment she'd set eyes on the youth that she'd never produce the child the Glamorgan Druids were hoping for. How could they expect her to mate with a lad? And yet, even if David were as attractive as Adonis himself, she wouldn't have bedded him. Unfortunately, Brock continued to hold her heart in his hands. Most likely, he always would.

Still, that didn't mean she would neglect her other obligations toward the Glamorgan Druids.

Her life was with them now, not with Brock. She'd had her chance to find happiness in English society and had not only failed utterly but grown to dislike the woman she'd become. Without the Glamorgan Druids, she would have no chance at redemption, and no purpose in her existence. None at all.

"Well, that explains it," Brock said, pulling her from her thoughts. "We Englishmen need hearty fare to start the day." He pushed the sausages to one side, instead focusing on a pile of cockles.

The sound of dishes clanking and silverware scraping filled the dining room for a time. Sir Anthony finished his breakfast and opened the first letter on a stack the footman had delivered earlier.

His unexpected gasp startled them all.

"What's wrong, uncle?" Georgiana asked, alarmed.

"This letter was delivered by courier earlier this morning," he told them, his tone urgent. "Two of the members of my London order of druids were found dead the day after we left for Wales."

Gwynllian sat up straighter. "How?"

"They were bludgeoned," he revealed, his features screwing up with disgust. "Someone strung the bodies up in a grove of oaks. Rumor has it that their deaths had been part of a druidic rite."

Georgiana muffled a shocked gasp.

"London is in an uproar," Sir Anthony continued. "The king has placed a bounty on the head of any man who practices druidry. My man writes that they've all gone underground to hide."

Brock regarded Sir Anthony with narrowed eyes. Remembering Sir Anthony's guilty attitude from the night before, he toyed with his fork for a moment, then said, "Did you send these men after the duke?"

His cheeks unexpectedly flushing, Sir Anthony nodded. "I might as well admit all of it. I wanted to eliminate the duke on my own, to spare Georgiana, so I sent my men after him. They were the most accomplished druids I'd trained in London."

Brock muffled an exclamation. "You sent a bunch of tree-worshippers after the duke?"

"Don't be so snide. These druids knew how to fight. Indeed, I'd been preparing them for this assignment over many years. David made certain they would understand how to deal with the duke's illusions, and I taught them druidic fighting techniques. Evidently they still failed."

"Druidic fighting techniques?"

"There are certain methods of toning—"

"Toning?"

"Speaking in such a way that the listener must obey—"

"Do you mean to say that your assassins tried to talk him to death?" Brock shook his head. "A creature like the duke responds only to brute force and violence. I'll send a few of my friends from Figg's Pugilism Academy after him, instead."

"If you wish your friends to die, then send them." Sir Anthony leaned back in his chair and rested his hands on his stomach, his fingers entwined.

"My brother brings us truly shocking news," Gwynllian broke in. "Emotions are riding high. Let's not allow this to weaken us by making us squabble amongst ourselves. Rather, I demand that you both promise to avoid sending any more assassins after the duke. We cannot fight destiny. Georgiana will ultimately be the one to thwart him."

While Gwynllian's plea hung on the air between them, the knowledge that she must defeat the duke began to weigh very heavily on Georgiana's thoughts. How was she supposed to thwart a man whom two accomplished druids couldn't even touch? What was the plan?

"How am I to thwart him?" she blurted, breaking the silence of accord that had begun to grow in the room.

Sir Anthony slowly put down his fork, then fixed his attention on her.

"Well, Uncle?" she prodded. "How am I going to stop him?"

"A lot of that depends on you," the older man replied.

Brock scraped his plate with a piece of laver bread, polished it off, and sat back in his chair to observe them, a cup of coffee in his hand.

"What do you mean? For God's sake, don't shilly-shally and speak in cryptic sentences. Tell me in plain language what I must do."

Sir Anthony looked at Gwynllian and spoke as though no one else were in the room. "The youth of today, they have no patience."

"Explain as best you can, Anthony," the older woman soothed.

A gimlet eye fixed on Georgiana, Sir Anthony took a deep breath and let it out slowly before he continued. "As you know, the Duke of Gloucester is a Guardian of Becoming. He has the ability to create illusions, like you and David. We have our own spies in his camp, and we have discovered that while the duke can create illusions, he has not advanced to the next stage: the ability to create reality from chaos."

While dressing, Georgiana had slipped the acorn from the previous evening into her pocket. Now, she touched it with her fingertips.

"The acorn is the key," she murmured.

Nodding, Sir Anthony continued. "You and David created reality from chaos and wove it into your illusion. The oak tree became so real that it nearly fooled even me, and I knew what you were doing. In this manner, you and David will fool the duke, and make him think he is existing in reality, when actually, he is existing in an illusion of our creation."

"For what purpose?" Brock asked.

The older man diverted his attention to Brock. "We must trap him in an illusion."

Brock frowned. "Drive him mad, you mean."

"Exactly. If we can convince the duke he is functioning in the world of reality, when actually he is caught in an illusion, we can trap him—permanently."

"Permanently?" Georgiana shook her head. "Do you mean that David and I would have to keep the illusion that traps the duke going forever?"

"Not forever. For some time, though," her uncle admitted. "At least until his mind becomes so dependent on the illusion that he refuses to leave it and begins to sustain it on his own. After restraining him, we'll bring him to Wales and, ah, bury him in the bog outside of Caernarfon."

Brock set his cup of coffee down and announced, "Your plan has a flaw."

"Oh? How so?"

"Won't the duke sense Georgiana's illusion the moment she creates it? You can't expect him to walk into her illusion and think it's real with his head ringing."

"We must create an illusion within an illusion," David said. "When he enters our illusion, he will see another one, which will explain the vibrations he feels."

"It all sounds rather complicated," Georgiana observed.

David nodded. "The duke is wily and very knowledgeable. Our illusion will have to be sound indeed to fool him."

"That's where the practicing comes in," Sir Anthony cut in, reclaiming their attention. "David and Georgiana must go to the stone circle and work on creating an illusion that will fool the duke. Gwynllian and I, for our part, will think of some scenarios that might lure him in."

"How can I help?" Brock asked.

"You can't," Sir Anthony promptly replied.

Gwynllian placed her fork and knife next to her plate and folded her hands. "Perhaps he *could* help out. Lord Darleigh has a particular knowledge of madness, through his mother. He will not be easily fooled. If David and Georgiana can convince him that an illusion is actually reality, then we can assume they've grown quite skilled in their ability."

Paling, Brock rubbed his jaw with two fingers.

"Go back to London," the older man urged him again.

"I'll be your test subject if you wish it," Brock offered.

Georgiana's insides suddenly felt hollow. "Sir Anthony just said that one could be trapped in an illusion and go mad. I won't allow you to risk yourself like that, Brock."

"Are you afraid I'll go mad, Georgiana?"

"Well, of course not—"

"Then don't interfere."

Sir Anthony stood abruptly and looked at each of them, an angry frown pulling his face downward. "This has gone far enough! Lord Darleigh is not a druid, a Welshman, or even an invited guest. I

will not allow him to interfere in Georgiana's training—"

"Uncle, please," Georgiana cut in.

Gwynllian lifted an eyebrow. "Calm yourself,
brother. You'll bring on an attack of apoplexy."

As if Gwynllian's prediction were coming true,
the older man's face grew flushed. "Sister . . . he
must go back to England."

All faces swiveled toward the dark-haired
woman with the gray eyes. She, in turn, examined
each of them, her gaze lingering on Brock in particular. When she finally looked away from Brock, her
eyes grew unfocused. A tea cup in hand, she
absently swirled its contents and glanced downward.

Without warning, the older woman focused on
them again, her eyes as sharp as ever. "He stays."

Sir Anthony threw his napkin down in evident
disgust. "I'm leaving for the stone circle. I'll see you
there later." Turning on his heel, he strode from the
dining room.

Georgiana didn't realize she'd been holding her
breath until her chest began to ache. She took in
some air but gained little relief. Perhaps it was her
heart that ached. She knew her uncle had been
quite correct to insist Brock leave, and that as long
as he remained in Wales, he would continue to put
himself in danger. And if Brock died, she would be
dead, too.

Without warning, Gwynllian patted her hand.

"Go put on your druid's robe," her aunt urged. "You too, David Gwylum. We'll leave in half an hour."

Both Georgiana and David stood. Her aunt had that effect on people, Georgiana thought. If one had any sense, one obeyed instantly. She preceded David out the door, and with a murmured comment about meeting him later, watched him bound up the staircase for his bedchamber.

Shaking her head at his youthful energy, Georgiana prepared to start across the hall. Brock's low voice arrested her in midmotion.

"Your brother told me you can see the future," he said.

The dining room door, she saw, remained open about an inch. David hadn't closed it entirely when they'd left. Lower lip caught between her teeth, Georgiana glanced up and down the hall to make sure she wouldn't be observed, then sidled close to the door. She strained to hear Gwynllian's reply.

"Sometimes, when conditions are right, I can," her aunt admitted.

Georgiana heard a scraping sound, as though Brock were pushing his chair back. "You've seen mine."

Silence filled the dining room. Georgiana wondered if Gwynllian had nodded or simply refused to answer.

"You need me, don't you? In this plot against the duke? I obviously play some role, or you would have sent me back to England." His tone became cajoling. "Tell me, Gwynllian, so I might prepare myself."

More silence followed.

"Why won't you tell me? Are you trying to protect me?" The chair scraped some more. "Am I going to die?"

From her hiding spot behind the door, Georgiana sucked in a breath.

"You're a nice man, Lord Darleigh," her aunt answered, "and I sense that you truly care for my niece. I wish I could say that without you, we will fail in our plot against the duke. I'd like to tell you that you rescue Georgiana from dire circumstances and ride away on a white charger, with her arms clasped around your waist. But my reasons are much more prosaic."

Georgiana leaned closer. She'd heard Gwynllian use this tone before. It usually meant her aunt planned to deliver a wallop.

"If we send you away, Georgiana will resent us always. She'll wonder what would have happened if you'd stayed. In short, we'd make a martyr of you, and she and David would never mate. You must go on your own. Only then will she turn to the man with whom she is destined to spend her life."

Brock answered with calm determination. "Georgiana will never mate with him, regardless of my presence. Nor will I go away on my own. Georgiana must send me away."

"Then you'll remain at risk." Gwynllian sighed. "Do you remember how to reach the stone circle in the woods?"

"Yes."

"I'll see you there in a half an hour, then."

Chairs scraped again. Georgiana jumped, but not quickly enough. Brock walked quickly through the door and nearly ran into her. They both faced each other, Georgiana aware of warmth flooding her cheeks.

"Eavesdropping, Lady Darleigh?" he asked, emphasizing her married name. Apparently he intended to remind her of their vows at every opportunity.

"Guilty as charged," she admitted, then looked through her lashes at him, feeling suddenly shy. "You were right, you know. I'll never mate with David Gwylum."

A sudden intensity in his gaze made her heart beat faster. He took her arm and led her away, into an alcove which a tapestry partially concealed. When he pulled her close to him, his breath fanning softly against her forehead, logical thought fled her mind. She felt only the hard length of his body against hers; smelled only the delicious maleness of him; saw only his eyes darkened with determination, and a spark that awakened even deeper needs within her. She pressed her cheek against his broad chest and, for the first time in weeks, felt truly safe.

His arms went around her, cradling her. "Come home with me, to England," he urged in a whisper. "Allow me to deal with the Duke of Gloucester in my way. I promise you, I'll set you free to create your own destiny. Hell, we'll create it together."

He sounded so convincing that the word *yes* nearly flew from her lips. Had she ever wanted anything more? True happiness, she sensed, would lie only with Brock.

And yet, she also knew if she surrendered to him and neglected her duty to the Glamorgan Druids, she'd dishonor not only herself but her mother's memory. Forever she'd resent him. How could they ever be truly happy in such a circumstance?

The push and pull on her, between duty, honor, and love, was so strong it felt real. In fact, it was tearing her apart. She could feel her heart pounding and tears gathering in her eyes as she fought the compulsion to lay her head on his shoulder and allow him to solve all of her problems.

One by one, the tears began to run down her cheeks.

Evidently he sensed her pain, for he pulled back a little to peer into her face. "Oh, Georgie," he breathed a moment later, and crushed her to him.

He knew. She didn't have to tell him.

She began to cry in earnest, but quietly, so they wouldn't be overheard. "I'm so sorry," she choked out between sobs, wishing with every ounce of her being that things were different between them.

Softly he cursed. "Damn the Duke of Gloucester. Damn him to bloody hell. If he hadn't come between us—"

"Please, Brock, don't torture me. We both have to accept my destiny."

"I don't accept anything of the sort. We can make our own destiny, Georgie."

Her tears flowing even faster, she wrenched herself from the warm, safe circle of his arms. "We can't. Don't you see? If I ignore my destiny I'll dishonor myself and everyone who loves me."

"Georgie—"

Before he could argue any further, she turned from him and ran toward the stairs leading to her bedchamber. She could take no more.

"Georgiana," he called out again.

She reached her bedchamber, slipped inside, and shut the door on his pleas.

Brock watched as she turned at the top of the stairs and ran for her bedchamber. Again he cursed, louder this time. He took the stairs after her, determined to talk this thing through, but paused at the door when he heard her sobs from inside. He knew she wouldn't listen to him, no matter what he said. She'd gotten it into her head to fulfill this destiny of hers, regardless of the sacrifices it forced her to make.

The Duke of Gloucester, he mused, stood at the very center of Georgiana's destiny, and consequently at the center of all of Brock's troubles. He and Georgiana would be free to love if the duke were eliminated. Granted, the duke wasn't an easy man to eliminate; Sir Anthony had already tried and failed. But Sir Anthony had sent a bunch of priests after the duke. Brock felt certain the duke wouldn't so easily protect himself from men of a more physical variety.

Like the ones he'd met in some of the rougher fights at Figg's Pugilism Academy.

Brock continued on past Georgiana's bedchamber and entered his own, a plan growing in his mind. If he found a way to hire a few fighters from the academy, without revealing his or anyone else's identity, he could send them after the duke. He hadn't the slightest doubt that these men, skilled as they were, could restrain the duke long enough to hand him over to the Glamorgan Druids. Indeed, he'd challenge anyone to go a couple of rounds with these men and come out of it without a black eye and a few missing teeth.

But he wasn't in London, so how could he hire them?

Rees. He would write a note to Rees, and in the note, enclose another letter for Jack Langan. Langan, one of the craftier individuals to walk London's fine streets, was smart enough to hire the appropriate men, without ever revealing who had selected them for their task. Unfortunately, the boxer rarely stayed in one place, requiring Rees's help in forwarding the letter.

His excitement growing, Brock sat down at the pine desk near his window. He would succeed where Sir Anthony and his druids had failed, and then, he and Georgiana would be free to live, and to love. With dusky sunshine falling across his face, he selected a piece of parchment, opened his inkwell, dipped his quill in ink, and began to write.

❧

The first two weeks in Wales passed quietly for Georgiana, her days consumed with druidic training, and her nights spent with Brock and the others, at dinner and then in the salon. By August first, the day of the festival of Lughnasadh, they'd all fallen into an uneasy truce, one in which David had stopped whining and Sir Anthony had ceased to insist Brock return to London.

That morning, Georgiana went to the stone circle to practice creating illusions. She knew she was supposed to be focusing on the relationship between all things, both animate and inanimate. Understanding that relationship was key to creating reality from chaos. And yet, the azure sky called to her, as did the small trout stream that ran about a hundred feet back from the stone circle. *A perfect day,* she thought, *for daydreaming.*

She selected a grassy spot heated by the sun and

sat down, aware the warm weather would soon give way to cooler temperatures. The first of August had brought a hint of autumn to the air; Georgiana could smell the crispness of the clouds and the faint scent of newly-mown hay. She wondered if their good fortune was equally in jeopardy.

So far, they'd remained safe in Wales. But she suspected it was only a matter of time. By now, the duke must be wondering why he hadn't received a report from his emissary. While she didn't think the duke would risk his own person by traveling away from London to investigate the situation, she didn't doubt he'd send another emissary to see what had happened to the first.

Perhaps he'd send an army of druids to finish her off.

Still, the duke's spies occasionally had a habit of disappearing, when her uncle's order or one of the other druidic orders managed to capture them. She hoped the duke wouldn't place too much significance in the disappearance of his first spy, until he'd sent another to investigate and received a report back.

Gwynllian took her cloak off and laid it on a standing stone which had fallen over in eons past. "You have to concentrate, Georgiana. Before you can draw from the world of chaos, you have to understand fully the world of order. And to understand, you must first have awareness."

Georgiana sighed. She'd grown tired of learning

about druidry and her own unique ability. She wanted to walk, to explore the woods, to think about the Lughnasadh festival planned for that evening.

Brock was off helping Sir Anthony prepare for the festival by bringing firewood to the festival grounds, erecting dance floors, and the like. The knowledge that he'd been given permission to attend was a guilty pleasure to her. Excitement stirred inside her at the thought of the bonfires, and the mead, and the singing and dancing.

"We could study the Ogham instead," her aunt threatened, mentioning the secret alphabet that the druids had once used to communicate with.

Georgiana waved her hands at Gwynllian. "No, please. That would be pure torture."

Mouth in a firm line, Gwynllian drew on a gauntlet. As soon as she lifted her arm, a falcon flew down from the treetops to clutch the glove. "Good day, pretty one," she cooed in Welsh. "Will you help me convince Georgiana to practice?"

The bird fixed its black gaze on Georgiana, then began to preen her brown and ivory feathers with a short beak.

"I quite agree. She has done very well so far," Gwynllian said to the falcon.

Georgiana sighed again. She didn't know if Gwynllian could really understand the bird, but she'd learned long ago that her aunt had a limitless ability to nag. "Give me a few moments to reach awareness."

The older woman smiled. "Excellent."

She closed her eyes and began with the basic exercise Gwynllian had taught her. She imagined that she had no head. Where her shoulders stopped, the world began, and the world itself was her head. When she had this concept firmly fixed in her mind, she opened her eyes and looked around. She saw trees, and standing stones, and Gwynllian with her falcon, but they no longer were separate entities. Now that her awareness extended beyond her own body, they had crossed the natural barrier of isolation she'd erected around herself and become part of her.

Gwynllian suddenly lifted her arm and urged the falcon into the sky. "Go with her."

The bird took flight, lifting slowly to the treetops. Georgiana stayed with her. Since it had become part of her awareness, the falcon couldn't leave her behind, just as Georgiana couldn't forsake an arm or a leg. They flew as one, circling high in the sky, catching an updraft and spiraling to breathtaking heights before swinging down to the clearing again, which from above looked like a small circle of green amidst a lawn of trees.

Georgiana could almost feel the wind ruffling her feathers. She wanted to laugh aloud. As one, the falcon flapped downward, slowly, to land on Gwynllian's arm. A slight throb built behind her temples, a result of her effort to maintain awareness, but that throb had grown less painful with time. She had nearly mastered this skill and found it particularly enjoyable.

It wasn't without its negatives, however. With an expanded awareness came an increased chance for pain and suffering. If the falcon had been shot with an arrow, she would have felt the tip pierce its skin. If someone chopped down a tree within her sphere of awareness, she'd feel the axe cut into its bark. In short, she suffered along with anything and anyone that had become part of her. That fact alone sometimes made the exercise a bit dismaying.

"Your awareness does not judge," Gwynllian intoned. "It does not fight or struggle or change. It accepts and loves." Her litany had become so familiar Georgiana was nearly saying it in her sleep.

Listening carefully, she focused on a distant tree and felt the sun shining upon its leaves. It was part of her, like a child. A rush of affection for this slow-growing, nearly inanimate creature surprised her with its intensity.

"Can you feel the different vibrations in your awareness?" her aunt asked. "Do you see how one resonance leads to another?"

While the resonance had little to do with audible music, Georgiana liked to think of it that way. The tree, she mused, resonated in a deep key, like a series of slow drumbeats. On the other hand, the falcon was light and airy, more like a harp. The two couldn't be more different. Even so, when she focused on the tree's resonance, the pattern of its drumbeats intermingled perfectly with the falcon's, creating a peculiar music that would sound off-key if either were missing.

"Beneath these patterns is a sound without pattern or purpose," her aunt continued. "It simply exists. Do you hear it?"

"Yes," Georgiana murmured. It was the sound that had haunted her dreams, and frightened her with its aimlessness, like the buzzing of disturbed bees.

"That is the sound of chaos. Allow it to wash over you. It won't hurt you, Georgiana. It is as much a part of our world as the more familiar things you know and love."

Dropping her mental guard, Georgiana placed her faith in her aunt and allowed the sound to fill her mind. It made the throb behind her temples hurt more. She groaned.

Gwynllian's voice became more urgent. "Chaos is simply noise, and while it is loud, it cannot drown out the patterns that exist in the world of order. Mold the sound of chaos, Georgiana. Give it a pattern. Make it blend with the other vibrations which exist in your awareness. Do it now."

Brow furrowed, Georgiana took the aimless noise of chaos and tried to break it into distinct vibrations. She attempted first to make it sound like the deep drumbeats of a tree. For a while she thought she had it . . . the wildness of chaos began to smooth out.

She couldn't hold on, however. As always, the oddest sensation began to creep through her body, a strange restlessness, as though chaos were molding her to something without form or pattern even as she molded it to match a tree's resonance. Repelled, she loosened her mental grip, allowing the deep drumbeats to return to aimless noise, and then tried again, this time copying a falcon's resonance.

That strange feeling of possession washed over her again. When it threatened to overwhelm her and her headache became too much, she retracted her awareness much like a clam retreating into its shell. She even felt its closing snap like a stab of pain in her mind. This is where their lessons always ended . . . in failure.

Frowning, she opened her eyes and locked gazes with Brock. He must have returned from his preparations for the festival and decided to watch her lesson with Gwynllian. She thought she detected admiration in his eyes. *For who, and what?* she wondered. Certainly not herself, after that dismal performance.

She daubed the moisture from her brow. "I don't have the strength to do this."

Her aunt smiled. "Did you see, Lord Darleigh?"

His deep baritone also held a hint of humor. "The tree? Or the falcon? They were both very real-looking. She damned near did it that time."

Eyebrow quirked, Georgiana examined them both. "I did nothing other than give myself a headache."

Brock stood and walked to her side. Towering over her, his expression suddenly serious, he took her hand. "The tree you created was a masterpiece; its detail, incredible. I touched its leaves with my own hand. I could feel its need to come into existence. A moment too soon you switched to the falcon, and I could hear the tree's cry as it dissolved into chaos once more. Why did you give up on the tree, Georgiana?"

"Because if I hadn't, chaos would have claimed me."

"What do you mean?"

"When I am trying to mold chaos into something from our world, it tries to mold me. I feel almost . . . possessed and stop before it overtakes me."

"You're allowing fear to overtake you," Gwynllian said. She sent the falcon into the air and removed her gauntlet. "You're afraid you can't control chaos. You fear it. But when your awareness is expanded, chaos is part of you, like a child or a loved one. You must accept it for what it is and shape it with loving hands. Only then will you succeed in creating order from chaos."

"I'm trying. I really am," Georgiana protested.

"I know you are, dear."

"Creating illusions seems so easy when compared to this."

A quick smile crossed Gwynllian's lips. "What we are asking you to learn in one month, most don't learn in a lifetime."

She picked up her cloak and surveyed them

both, her attention lingering on their joined hands. "I think we've done enough for now. It's nearly tea time. Lord Darleigh, will you join us for tea and Bara Brith?"

"I'd be delighted."

"Good. I have a few things to do. Will you take Georgiana back to Cadair Abbey? I'll be along in a while."

"Of course." Brock nodded and, his hand wrapped around Georgiana's, led her down the path toward Cadair Abbey.

She swung their hands gently, enjoying the brisk afternoon and the pleasant company. Through the weeks she'd grown to enjoy his subtle wit and tolerant observations very much. To her surprise, she'd discovered a new Brock in Wales, a Brock she had only imagined existed. "You've been good to me, Brock."

"You're my wife." He said the word *wife* like a caress.

"All of this is because of our marriage vows?" she teased him.

"I want you to be safe. And happy."

"Why?"

He didn't answer. Rather, he glanced at his boots and murmured some nonsense about the weather.

Suddenly shy, Georgiana also glanced at the ground. "Did you fix up the old barn for the Lughnasadh festival?"

He rolled his shoulders, presumably to get the

kinks out. "A couple of rounds at Figg's Pugilism Academy with Jack Langan is child's play compared to plugging up that barn."

She watched his muscles bunch beneath his linen shirt and felt a hot stir of desire within her. He was sweaty, the veins on his neck standing out, and his arms looked very strong. She wanted to kiss him, to make love to him the way they had in London. "Did my uncle have you wielding a hammer?"

"We blocked the worst of the holes with bales of straw," he explained. "Your uncle made certain I hadn't a chance to sit down. He's still trying to chase me back to London, I suppose."

A sudden prick of tears in her eyes forced Georgiana to look away. He was doing this for her, she thought. He had fit himself into her life and sacrificed even his pride for her. Warmth spread through her at the notion. She blinked rapidly to clear the tears before returning her attention to Brock.

"When *are* you going back to London?" she whispered.

Brock twined his fingers in hers. "When I'm certain you're safe."

Filled with happiness, she said nothing more as they walked back to Cadair Abbey in companionable silence. The silence between them grew deeper as they approached the front door. She preceded him into the great hall, and there they paused. Sunlight flooded the cavernous room, dispelling shadows that normally caught in the corners. Even so, Georgiana couldn't help but wonder how much longer Brock could continue to sacrifice his life as an English nobleman for her and not resent her for it.

"Will I see you tonight?" she asked.

"According to Sir Anthony, we're to gather in the courtyard at around five o'clock. From there, we'll ride together to the barn." Brock pressed a kiss against her hand, then released it. "Until then."

Her cheeks flaming almost as much as the desire licking along her veins, Georgiana watched him go.

"Georgiana." His eyes dark, David emerged from the stairwell, where he'd obviously been eavesdropping.

Georgiana jumped, then spun around to face the youth, furious. "It isn't polite to observe a conversation without revealing your presence," she chided, feeling absurdly guilty.

"I'm glad I concealed myself," he insisted, his voice wavering. "I saw how you keep him here with your pretty smiles and soft sighs. Why don't you look at me that way, Georgiana?"

Georgiana pressed a hand against her temple, which had suddenly begun to ache. "I'm sorry, David," she said gently, "but I don't love you."

"You love him," he accused.

"I'm afraid so."

"But what about the duke? He's going to find you and kill you eventually. And what about us?

We're supposed to . . . mate." A ruddy flush suffused his cheeks.

"Oh, David." She took his hand and led him to a settee, where they both sat. "Lord Darleigh has my heart. He always has. But that doesn't mean that I can *follow* my heart. Sometimes, no matter how much two people want to be together, circumstances keep them apart. In my case, I'm well aware of my duties to the Glamorgan Druids and plan to see them through . . . all except our mating, that is."

He stared at the floor, a muscle in his jaw twitching.

"I'm too old for you, David. You need a young woman."

"I need *you*, Georgiana. Please, come to me tonight. To the stone circle. Let's talk there, where I might have a better chance at persuading you otherwise."

Georgiana lifted an eyebrow, curious despite the emotion behind his plea. "Why the stone circle?"

"There, any child we make will be imbued with the magic stored in the stones."

"I've never heard that before."

"It's true, I assure you."

Shaking her head, she warned him, "Perhaps you're right. In any case, I can't join you in the stone circle tonight. I don't want to raise your hopes."

"Please, Georgiana," he begged. "If you don't come, I'll sit there by myself all night, in the cold, and I'll likely catch an illness. You know you can't defeat the duke without my help. What good am I to you if I'm dead?"

She barely prevented herself from rolling her eyes heavenward. "All right. Because we're a team, I'll come, if only to haul you back to the festival."

David rewarded her with a smile. Without warning, he swooped down, placed a light kiss against her lips. Then, his cheeks absolutely flaming, he hurried off down the hall.

Brock pressed himself against the wainscoting in the presbytery hallway. He was trying very hard not to laugh. He had to admit, Gwylum had proven an earnest suitor. Georgiana had her hands full trying to keep the youth's ego intact, while forcing him to realize he wouldn't have his first sexual experience with her.

Brock remembered his own youth. Christ, once he'd walked around with an erection for days, until his father had taken pity on him and brought him to the Red House, a brothel on the edge of fashionable London. Someone had to do the same for Gwylum, before he drove Georgiana mad.

Or pawed her again.

His amusement evaporating, Brock glanced around the corner and saw Georgiana climbing the stairs, most likely for her bedchamber. What would Gwylum try next, when Georgiana joined him in the stone circle? Another kiss? Perhaps an ill-considered dip into her bodice? Lips tightening at the mere thought of it, Brock emerged from his hiding place and walked across the hall. Apparently he was going to have to bring Gwylum to a lightskirt. Tonight. But how?

Brow furrowed, he wandered into the dining room, where the obligatory tea and cakes were laid out, and grabbed a piece of Bara Brith. He had to admit the bread was tasty. Wales wasn't such a poor place to live . . . if you hadn't a Welsh lad sneaking around behind your back, trying to lay your wife.

Indeed, he'd made many friends over the last month, and heard many tales between swallows of wine and rough country bread. He'd even managed to persuade a few townfolk from Caernarfon to keep an eye out for strangers checking in at the local inns and hostelries . . . for a price. He didn't want another one of the duke's spies coming anywhere near Georgiana.

His gaze flickered past a bottle of Benedictine, the stuff that Gwynllian had once drugged him with. Idly he considered drugging Gwylum in the same manner, then discarded the idea.

He walked over to the bottle and smoothed his fingers over its brown contours. Most of the villagers had never tasted the stuff. John and Edward Eifion, two brothers that he'd grown to know the best, had once wondered aloud about its reputed healing properties. His drugging experience uppermost in his mind, Brock mentioned that he hadn't appreciated it. The brothers reflected that an Englishman wouldn't know the difference between piss and whiskey, to which Brock had responded with an insult of equal kind—all good-natured ribbing, of course.

He wondered what the pair would do for a bottle of Benedictine. Detain Gwylum, perhaps, so he couldn't join Georgiana on his midnight rendezvous? A sudden smile crossed his lips. With a little preparation on his part, the scheme could prove quite rewarding. Gwylum would make love tonight, he thought. But not to the woman he was expecting.

Chapter

14

Since the Lughnasadh festival was not strictly a druidic one, Georgiana passed over her druid's robe in favor of one of her round gowns. Made of canary-yellow silk and sporting a tasseled ribbon beneath her bosom that drooped in an eye-catching bow, the gown had relatively few frills and was perfect for a simple country get-together. She selected a crocheted shawl to ward off the chill that the night sometimes brought, and carried a tasseled navy bag to match. Once Nellie had finished coiffing her hair into curls intertwined with strings of tiny pearls, Georgiana felt almost . . . English again.

She examined her image in the looking glass. Her hair was a rich chestnut brown, and anticipation warred with impatience in her green eyes. Excitement over seeing Brock while dressed in her English finery had lent her cheeks a soft blush, and

the dress's heart-shaped bodice dipped to an allur-
ing point, exposing enough of her bosom to keep
any man's attention.

Perfect, she thought.

Her gaze centered on the druid's egg, which
hung like a big ugly mistake against her breasts.
That wasn't going to work at all. She slipped the
pendant into her bag and replaced it with a pearl
suspended from a gold chain, one of the trinkets Sir
Anthony had bought for her when she'd first come
to live with him in London.

Then, her tasseled bag in hand, she descended to
the first floor. At the entrance to the hall, she paused
and assessed its occupants. Brock, David, and Sir
Anthony milled about the old hall, waiting.
Stomach fluttering, she entered the hall. They all
noted her approach immediately and bowed.
Seeing the admiration in their eyes, she laughed
and told them not to stand on ceremony, then
joined them in light banter.

Brock placed a hand on her arm. "You look gor-
geous."

Seconds later, Gwynllian arrived, looking stunning in a gray gown of watered silk trimmed with
sky-blue velvet. An India silk shawl covered her
arms and shoulders, and a beautiful aquamarine
pendant nestled against her bosom.

"As does your aunt," he added, earning a smile
from both her and Gwynllian.

Her aunt took Sir Anthony's arm and shepherded them all toward the carriages waiting in the courtyard. Brock, David, and Georgiana climbed into the first carriage. David managed to squeeze onto the seat next to her, leaving Brock no choice but to occupy the seat across. To his credit, Brock simply appeared amused at the lad's antics. Georgiana, however, fumed that the youth continued to lay claim to her despite her objections.

Once they'd all seated themselves, they were off. Caernarfon's town council was sponsoring this year's festival and had designated an old barn on the hill as the party's location. Rumor had it that Llywelyn had once quartered himself, his men, and their horses in that old barn, to plan an attack on Edward I and Caernarfon Castle.

Whatever the case, Brock apparently knew the barn well enough. He'd spent many an hour there preparing for the festival and earning his right to attend. Again, love for him and the effort he'd made on her behalf crept through her. Even as David pressed his arm against hers, forcing her to retreat to the far corner of the seat, she wished fate hadn't dealt her this particular hand of cards. If only she hadn't been born a druid, if only she hadn't a duty to fulfill, if only, if only . . . she would drive herself mad if she wasn't careful.

The ride took far too long, in Georgiana's opinion. She couldn't wait to get out of the carriage and away from the eager youth. At length, when they began the trek uphill and bonfires flashed passed the window, she knew they had nearly arrived. As soon as the barouche rolled to a halt, she was out without assistance, even though she hiked up her skirt in an unladylike manner in doing so.

Faces that had become familiar glowed in the light of many bonfires. The barn's holes and cracks, the ones too high up to be plugged, poured out light and sweet scents that tantalized her nose. Druids and the local town gentry stepped up to greet her and exchange pleasantries, laughing and talking with the excitement and spirit of the festival.

Georgiana felt that anticipation, too. Tonight, they stood at the beginning of harvest time, when the land would surrender its produce to keep them alive through the winter. For one evening, they would dance and feast and make merry; but it was a bittersweet sort of merriment, because they knew that a veritable mountain of work awaited them in the following weeks.

The wheat and barley had to be reaped, the hay they'd gathered for the livestock needed to be stored, the vegetables need to be preserved, and the cattle would be let loose to trample and manure the denuded fields. Georgiana likened the festival to taking a deep breath before one plunged into great industry, and feeling satisfaction in the work already accomplished.

She looked upward at a troubled sky, which hung so low that the light from the bonfires seemed to give them a pallid gleam. Purplish and moving far more swiftly than they ought, the clouds predicted a heavy downpour, which they sorely needed. Summer had proven unusually dry, affecting both the size and quantity of the harvest.

Smiling, she made her way into the barn with David at her side and Brock a little to her left. Gwynllian and Sir Anthony brought up the rear and were treated like royalty by all. A lot of bowing and scraping went on, testimony to the unquestionable authority they wielded—and the many donations they'd made to the town council coffers.

Several small bonfires were crackling merrily throughout the barn, adding to the heat created by the press of bodies. Huge tables laden with Welsh fare were pressed up against one wall and a small musical ensemble had begun to tune up their instruments in the corner. A wooden dance floor occupied the far end of the building, and a few chairs ringed the floor for those too old, too tired, or unable to dance. Torches placed in strategic locations lent an ambient glow to the gathering.

A large, bubbling cauldron served as the centerpiece of the barn. Smiling and red-faced, a Welshman she didn't recognize stood near the cauldron with a ladle, serving its contents into pewter mugs the partygoers carried. Judging by the way he stumbled over nothing, he'd had more than his share of the cauldron's contents.

She knew what the cauldron contained. The smell of wine, honey, and spices in the air revealed the mystery to all. Ceridwen, the darkly smiling goddess of mysteries, once had a cauldron of wisdom in which she mixed wine, honey, malt, and water, to make mead. As the tale went, any who drank Ceridwen's mead would gain secret knowledge and renewed energy. Georgiana knew that those who imbibed from the festival's cauldron would act like they had secret knowledge, only to awake with a roaring headache on the morrow.

Shrugging, she accepted a mug from a woman with a wreath of angelica atop her head, and stepped up to the cauldron to have her share. Looking for Brock, she sipped mead and discovered him on the far side of the barn, talking to a very attractive brunette. The mead suddenly tasted like vinegar. Eyes narrowed, she took a step in his direction, when a hand dropped heavily onto her shoulder and held her in place.

"Stay here, Georgiana," a youthful male voice whispered against her ear.

She sniffed the air suspiciously and smelled whiskey. Frowning, she turned around and faced David. A ruddy flush colored his cheeks. "You shouldn't be drinking, David. You're going to make yourself ill."

"Stop acting like my older sister."

"That's what I feel like," she insisted.

"You're still going to come tonight, right? You won't leave me sitting out there alone, in the rain?"

"Keep up this drinking and I *will* leave you

alone," she threatened. "Why don't you go and talk to some of the other young ladies in the room? You're a handsome lad. I'd wager any one of them would love to speak to you."

"Stop calling me 'lad.' "

"When you're a man, I'll call you mister. For now, you're a lad," she told him in annoyed tones. With that, she left him with a bemused expression on his face.

Aware that Brock still conversed with the attractive brunette, she wandered over to a smaller bonfire where the unmarried women were throwing nuts into the fire.

"Would you like to test your luck?" a wizened old woman asked, a sack of nuts at her feet.

Georgiana shrugged. "Why not?"

"But she's already married," a young girl with ringlets and pink ribbons in her hair complained.

The old woman shook a finger at her. "Mind your own business, missy."

Ringlets and ribbons flounced off in a snit.

Clearly satisfied, the old woman reached down, selected three nuts from the bag, and placed the first one in Georgiana's palm. "This one is you."

Georgiana nodded.

"This one is your husband," the old woman murmured, setting the second nut into her palm, "and this one is your lover." She placed the final nut into Georgiana's hand and stepped back. "Throw them into the fire. If the nut blazes, the man it represents will be enthusiastic. If it jumps, he will be unfaithful. If your nut burns together with one of the other nuts, then you and he will be together forever."

Lips quirked, Georgiana tossed the three nuts into the fire and fought to keep track of them amidst the flames. For a moment, the nuts remained unaffected by the blaze. Then, without warning, two began to burn violently, as though a hidden hand had doused them with lamp oil.

The old woman quirked an eyebrow at Georgiana. "Your lover is too young for you. Stay with your husband."

Amused, Georgiana nodded and took a step away. She would have tripped if not for the warm male body she bumped against. Ready to turn around and chide David for dogging her every move, she found herself staring into Brock's dark eyes instead.

"Are you going to listen to her?" he asked with a grin.

She took his arm and steered him away from the old woman. "It's just a game."

"A game I rather like."

Shaking her head at him, she allowed him to lead her toward the dance floor.

"When will you be leaving?" he asked.

"Later. Much later." She considered telling him that she had to meet David in the stone circle, so she might return his drunken carcass to the festival. In the end, she decided to stay quiet on the matter. She wouldn't embarrass David by revealing his foolishness to Brock.

"When you're ready to go, inform me," he insisted. "As much as I enjoy a good party, I'm afraid I'm a bit fatigued after lifting all those bales of hay. I'll leave with you."

She raised an eyebrow, thinking he didn't look the least bit tired. Indeed, she had the peculiar impression that he was baiting her. Whatever the case, now she had to think of a reason why he shouldn't wait for her, but plan on returning to Cadair Abbey alone. She, after all, had an appointment with David in a stone circle. "Why don't you leave now? I'll make excuses for you."

"No, I'd rather wait for you."

"Well, I—" The sound of male voices raised in song saved her from replying further.

Indeed, the whole barn grew quiet when a triple harp and the fluttering notes of a recorder joined the choir and together they created a beautiful rendition of *Ships of Caernarfon*. Georgiana knew there wasn't a dry eye in the house, her own included, when the last note trailed off and silence reigned. Then, amidst furious applause, the choir sang *Ar Lan y mor*, *My Little Welsh Home*, and other traditional folk songs that Georgiana remembered from her childhood.

The mood inside the barn quickly became maudlin as those who'd drank too much mead wept openly. The musicians, appreciating the need for party spirits tonight, of all nights, dismissed the choir to mingle with the townfolk, and began to play a rousing country dance. A violin and drums joined the lighter notes of harp and recorder, and soon it seemed as if half the population of Caernarfon was stomping around on the dance floor.

Georgiana led Brock onto the dance floor and, despite his protests, began to weave in, out, and around him in a Welsh folk dance Gwynllian had taught her. To his credit, he picked up the steps quickly, and soon was matching her pace and even showing some ingenuity as he spun her around and around in an unexpected move.

Throughout their dance, Georgiana felt her heart beating fast, not just from exertion but with the closeness of his body to hers, the warmth of his touch, the dark promise that she saw in his eyes. Wild and free with the mead flowing through her veins, she pouted at him, wanting him to kiss her. When his head swooped close to hers, she closed her eyes, her entire body tight with longing for him—

And then he released her.

She stumbled against a chair and had to hold on to its back for support. Brows drawn together, she looked for Brock . . . and saw David in his place.

"I've cut in," David informed her, glowering.

"You are trying my patience, David." Teeth clenched, she wanted to murder him.

He grasped her clumsily by the arm and shepherded her onto the dance floor, where he proceeded to step repeatedly on her toes. For a time, she allowed herself to be mangled—for David's sake—but kept an eye out for Brock, who'd disappeared.

At last she saw him in the corner, his head bent toward two Welshmen. He produced a dark brown bottle from beneath his jacket, and at that moment he marked her attention. He lifted the bottle to her, as if to say, "Cheers," and then handed it to the two men. Brows drawn together, she wondered what he was doing, and watched as he left the barn without a backward look.

"Georgiana, David," an urgent voice said in her ear.

She and David broke apart to stare at Sir Anthony's flustered countenance.

"The duke has sent another one of his men," the older man murmured. "He's over there, by the cauldron. Do you see him?"

Tendrils of fear curling through her belly, she turned to assess the man her uncle had indicated. He seemed of moderate fortune, wearing clothes that matched the style and quality of just about everyone else present.

So he would blend in, she thought.

"He is likely here to discover what happened to the duke's first emissary, a man named Peabody. You must create an illusion of Peabody and convince him all is well. Remember: the duke's spies are likely very well-versed in spotting an illusion, so it *must* be believable."

"Won't the duke's emissaries sense the vibrations coming from our illusion and suspect us even more?" David asked.

"We'll have to draw him outside, to the small stone circle we excavated in the fields last year. The stones are broken, but will likely prove adequate to absorb the illusion's echoes."

She took a deep breath and stared at David, who had grown very still. He returned her stare, his blue eyes several shades darker than normal in the flickering light.

"Are you ready?" he asked.

"Yes. We'll do exactly what we practiced in the stone circle."

"I'll have one of my men lure him out there." Sir Anthony offered Georgiana a lantern. "Go, now, and wait for him."

Georgiana and David hurried out into the night. They raced away from the barn, through a hedgerow, and into a farmer's field just beyond town.

"Over here," David said, pointing to the far end of the field, where a heap of dirt lay near another hedgerow.

Georgiana followed him toward the mound. "These stones are old," she said when she saw the broken megaliths.

"The field is riddled with cairns. This place was powerful once. I hope it remains powerful enough to buffer our illusion."

Georgiana grabbed his hand and held it, as much for his benefit as for her own. "Let's begin," she whispered. "Not only must we conceal ourselves, but we also have to create an illusion of the duke's first emissary. By God, I hope this works."

They spoke no more. Instead, Georgiana closed her eyes and reached awareness, but only after several tries. She was damned scared and not at all certain they were going to create something believable.

All around her, she felt vibrations. She could even feel her own, and David's, which wound through hers, creating a music unique to the two of them. She remembered the dead man's face, and from the fog that slowly swirled around the corners of her mind, she shaped his image. David was helping her, she could feel him there, directing, adding detail. Abruptly she was very glad she had him at her side.

All too soon they saw the silhouette of another man approaching the dilapidated stone circle, his steps very slow and cautious. When he saw the illusion of Peabody, his pace increased, until he entered the stone circle. He stared at Peabody, and glanced around, his expression wary.

"You've been in Caernarfon for two weeks. Why haven't you sent a missive to the duke recently?" the stranger asked the illusion. "He damned near has an army massed at the border to Wales and is preparing to engage the Glamorgan Druids."

Georgiana, focused on maintaining the vibrations in her mind to mimic that of the dead man's, hadn't an answer. Her heart beat wildly in her chest. They were going to fail.

"I haven't anything to report," the illusion said. "I've found nothing suspicious."

"You stupid ass. Don't you know that you're supposed to send a missive even if you're visiting paradise itself?"

"He didn't tell me that. I'll send a missive right away."

The duke's second emissary narrowed his eyes. "You don't sound right, Peabody."

"I'm fine," the illusion insisted. In counterpoint, Georgiana could feel David tensing next to her.

"Hold out your hand."

"Why?"

The second man withdrew a knife from his sock. "Hold it out. Now."

Sweat broke out on Georgiana's brow. Her eyes squeezed tight, she imagined Peabody extending his hand.

Without warning, the second man swiped the knife downward, toward the illusion's hand. Georgiana reacted instantly, imagining the hand was made of blood and flesh. To her utter shock, a cut opened on the illusion's palm, one so real-looking her own palm ached in sympathy.

David, for his part, made Peabody cry out.

"What was that for?" the illusion complained in a loud voice.

Her temples began to throb. Blood, she thought.

She had to create blood. Biting hard on her lower lip, she drew some of her own blood and tasted it. It was enough to give her a feeling for its structure in the world of order. She heard the directionless, formless sounds of chaos on the edge of her consciousness and brought it forth. It took her over, trying to reduce her to chaos even as she tried to rearrange it into blood.

Her stomach clenched and she thought she might be sick. Still, she held on, and embraced the chaos for one split second, long enough to create a few drops of blood. A few drops was all she needed.

The illusion reached out and grabbed the other man's hand, smearing it with dark stains.

Smirking, the other man backed away. "Just wanted to make sure you were . . . really you. I'll return to the duke and tell him you're an idiot. If I were you, I'd get that report to the duke right away. And I'd think twice about coming within ten miles of him."

He left without another word.

Chapter
15

Georgiana pressed herself against the barn wall and surveyed the crowd. She and David had returned from the farmer's field almost an hour before, and now, she felt almost drunk with excitement and triumph. It hadn't been easy, but they'd somehow managed to fool the duke's second spy. Perhaps, with more practice, they'd even outwit the duke.

Gwynllian and her uncle were seated in the far corner of the barn. They'd both looked at her and David with pride when they'd learned the illusion had proven successful.

"You two were meant to be," her uncle had gruffly counseled, taking away some of Georgiana's elation.

Now, a group of townfolk surrounded them and were listening to the stories they told. Georgiana knew the time was ripe to make her escape. She started toward the door, then glanced one last time at her aunt. To her surprise, their gazes locked. A secret smile formed on Gwynllian's lips before she returned her attention to her audience.

Georgiana glanced around for David, but couldn't find him. She assumed he'd already left for the stone circle and was waiting for her to bring him back. Her mood was too good, though, for the notion to annoy her. Warm from drinking too much mead, she slipped out into the night, had a carriage brought round, and climbed inside. Shortly thereafter they were off to Cadair Abbey.

During the ride, she glanced out of the carriage window. The dark, purplish clouds still hung far too low, but they were moving so fast they didn't seem to have time to stop and rain on them. With a little luck, her meeting with David in the stone circle would prove dry, if not warm.

As soon as they reached Cadair Abbey, she stepped onto the carriageway, took a lantern from the driver, and told him to wait until she returned. Then, the wind blowing hard at her back, she hurried across the lawn and entered the woods. It took her a scant ten minutes to reach the edges of the clearing which protected the stone circle. There, she stopped, and carefully surveyed the circle.

David sat upon a blanket he'd spread out in the middle of the circle. He wore a druid's robe, with the hood drawn up over his head. Hesitantly she approached him, and when he saw her coming, he patted the blanket beside him.

She thought he appeared larger than normal. "David, what are you doing? Stand up. Don't force me to drag you back to the festival by your ear."

"Extinguish your lantern," he whispered.

"What? We aren't enjoying a tryst. I'm here to prevent you from growing cold and wet, remember?"

"Sit down next to me." Again he whispered in a gravelly voice.

"You've had too much whiskey," she murmured. "You're drunk. I expected as much." Even so, she placed the lantern on a boulder, selected a spot near to him, and sat. "Do you want to talk for a moment?"

He fumbled with his cloak. "Damn, its cold. I've brought extra blankets. Lie down and I'll cover you."

"David, what's wrong with you? You know full well I have no intention of making love to you—"

Without warning, he cupped her chin, cutting off the remainder of her sentence. "My beautiful Georgiana," he murmured a second before his lips descended to hers, shocking her even as the pleasure of his kiss made her body ache with longing.

His tongue tangled with hers, bold and demanding. Georgiana's thoughts raced wildly. Somehow, she managed to drag her lips from his. "Where is David?"

"He's fine," Brock whispered, then went back to kissing her.

Eyes closed, she surrendered to the power of his mouth upon hers. And yet, worry about David was ruining her enjoyment of the sensations coursing through her. Feeling almost giddy, she pulled her lips from his. "Where *is* he?"

Brock nuzzled her neck with his lips. "Do you think I'd hurt him?"

Breath caught in her throat, she stretched her head sideways, to give him fuller access. It had been so long, and felt so good. "*I've* certainly considered it. You didn't lock him up somewhere, did you?"

"I had him, shall we say, detained. But I don't imagine he's suffering too badly." Chuckling, he ran his hands down her waist, and then back up again. He cupped her breasts, kneading them, making them ache with soft insistence. "He might even thank me tomorrow."

She pushed up on one elbow. "What *did* you do to him?"

"I'm fulfilling his fantasies, although not quite in the way he imagined. I had him brought to the town lightskirt."

She choked, then laughed softly. "You are very, very bad." Secret admiration for her husband's daring filled her.

"And you," he said, kissing her ear, "are my wife."

A nonsensical reply formed on her lips. He stole those words before she even said them by kissing her again, then trailing his lips along her neck, blowing gently against her ear. She wondered why it had taken so long for her to realize that Brock waited for her, not David. The masculine, spicy scent of him and the rough tension in his voice, even at a whisper, should have given him away.

He curved his hand around her bottom to fit her even closer. "I need you, Georgie. So damned badly."

She drew in a shuddering breath and slid her palms against his neck. She may have had other priorities in her life right now, but being in his arms felt so right, so perfect that she couldn't deny him or herself any longer.

Eyes closed, she opened her mouth against his, fierce anticipation flaring along her nerves every time their tongues touched. His kisses were deep and long, their pleasure so potent that her insides felt seared by desire. She knew she could never have enough of him, even if they were to remain locked together all night.

Vaguely aware of the clouds whirling and rumbling above them, matching the turbulence inside her, Georgiana opened fully to him. He explored her mouth eagerly, ruthlessly, like a half-starved man finally offered food, his raw need for her heightening the ache between her thighs. She felt very powerful and confident, knowing how much he desired her, and when he lifted his mouth from hers and began undressing her, she teased him by stretching her body and wriggling as he tore each piece of clothing off her.

Then, her heart beating so hard that each thump reverberated throughout her body, she lay still before him, naked, the blankets bunched up at her feet.

A fissure opened between the clouds, allowing pale moonlight to flood the clearing. Brock pushed back from her and studied her from head to toe, his face tight in the pallid glow.

"You're so beautiful," he breathed.

A cold breeze shivered across her skin, making her nipples contract. Groaning at the sight, he swooped downward and covered one with his mouth, his warmth so different after the cold that she cried out at the delicious contrast of it. Too quickly his tongue left her nipple to burn a path across her breasts. Seconds later, she felt him cover her other nipple with his mouth and suck gently, until her thighs were slicked with moisture and her desire for him to fill the hollow space inside her almost overwhelmed her.

"Brock," she breathed, saying his name like a question and a plea all in one. She felt his erection pressing against her thigh and wrapped her palm around him, making him gasp.

He lifted his mouth from her nipple and threw his head back, clearly giving in to the pleasure she was giving him. Gently she stroked him, pulling until the tip of his erection grew moist, and then taking some of the moisture on her finger and caressing the tip. His low groans told her what pleased him the most, and please him she did, taking secret delight in the sharp intensity of his face as she drew him closer to the edge of release.

"Ah, Georgiana," he moaned, and slipped his hands under her bottom. Squeezing gently, he moved until she was under him, his erection nudging against her belly. She spread her thighs, desperate for him to fill her.

Instead he slipped downward, trailing a path of kissing across her ribs and down her stomach, pausing to kiss the beauty mark just above the curls between her thighs, then dipping lower until he found the center of her pleasure. An unfamiliar, sensual sound filled the stone circle and she realized she had cried out. She clutched his shoulders, her fingertips digging into his muscles, and arched her back as he began to lick her, gently, patiently, making her moan.

The sensation was peculiar and wonderful; and when he entered her with his tongue she thrust against him, unable to help herself, twisting her hips against his mouth. He grasped her hips, holding her steady as he divided his attention between licking her and plunging inside her with his tongue. Somehow, the fact that she couldn't move made his caress all the more exquisite. She cried out his name frantically, her legs tensing as she hurtled toward release, her entire body awash in a pleasure so taut it felt like pain.

Abruptly he lifted his mouth from her, arresting the pleasure which had been building inside her in midmotion. She writhed against him, gripping his buttocks and squeezing, thrusting her hips against his erection, knowing she would do anything he wished, if only he would fill her and ease the terrible throb between her thighs that tortured her with the potential for fulfillment. She would beg, she would cry, she would promise.

He looked at her, and in his eyes she could see knowledge of all these things she felt. He could use her now, if he desired it, manipulate her, force her to promise to return to London with him . . . but he didn't. Groaning her name, he shifted upward until his chest rubbed against her breasts. Her legs wrapped around his waist, she grasped him and guided him to her.

Kissing her deeply, he pushed inside her, as far as he could, stretching her with his largeness, soothing the emptiness which had made her ache. For a moment, he remained still inside her, and she wanted to scream because he felt so good; and yet, a whole new sort of tension grabbed hold of her, and soon she was twisting against him again, needing him to bring her to completion.

His mouth never leaving hers, he began to move inside her, thrusting gently, in a slow rhythm that made her wild with longing. Her breath came in short little pants. She knew she couldn't withstand much more and thrust against him more quickly, trying to set the pace. He obeyed her silent command, plunging deeper, and faster, his arms tight bands of iron around her as a wave of pure urgency carried her upward. Suddenly, she tensed, her body trembling as the wave crested and shattering pleasure seemed to break her into a thousand pieces. She jerked against him and cried out and felt certain she'd swoon, so intense was the feeling.

Seconds later, he stiffened and growled deep in his throat, thrusting quickly into her and then collapsing atop her, most of his weight braced against his elbows. She felt warm and cuddled and totally drained, the bone-deep pleasure still ebbing and flowing inside her as her heart slowly returned to its normal rate.

Still clutching him around the waist, she lifted herself upward to place a kiss against his lips, one he fervently returned before rolling onto his side. He pulled her close, until her bottom pressed against his thighs, and draped an arm over her. They remained snuggled together for a long time.

At length, he sighed and lifted her hair. "I love how you smell, right here," he said, nibbling the back of her neck.

She rubbed her bottom against him, at the same time grasping his arm and wrapping it around her, so that his palm cupped her breast. Her eyes half-closed, she stared at the stone circles ringing the clearing and noticed they had a faint blue glow.

She opened her eyes wider. Sure enough, the

stones were glowing with a light that faded with each second. She wriggled in his grasp until she was lying on her back and Brock was facing her from his side. "Do you see that?" she breathed.

He nuzzled her hair, a relaxed smile curving his lips. "See what?"

"The stones," she whispered. "They're glowing." As soon as she spoke, she knew she'd waited too long, for the glow had already dissipated into the shadows.

His gaze focused on the stones; he shook his head. "They look a pale gray to me."

"They were glowing a moment ago."

His eyebrows quirked thoughtfully. "Do you suppose it's a sign of approval?"

She smiled despite herself. "*I* certainly approve."

He laughed, then pulled her more tightly against him. "I have a question for you now. We've been in Wales for over a month. Have you had your monthly courses?"

Georgiana stilled. She hadn't thought much about it. Silently she calculated the last time she'd bled and realized she was due. "No, I haven't."

"Hmm. What do you suppose that means?"

"Nothing," she told him, blushing a little. "I'm not very, ah, regular."

"You must tell me immediately if you discover you're expecting."

"Of course I will," she assured him, distinctly uncomfortable with the turn their conversation had taken. "May we talk about something else?"

"Such as?"

"Such as David. Who, exactly, took him to the town lightskirt?"

"Two brothers I met, John and Edward Eifion, offered to detain him for me." He gave a nefarious chuckle and nuzzled the hollow of her throat, sending chills across her skin, before his lips moved to her ear, where he nibbled delicately.

Wanting to chide him, she laughed instead. "How did you bribe them?"

"With a bottle of Benedictine . . . one of Gwynllian's finest," he offered, his eyes clear of any remorse. "And several English pounds to pay for David's entertainment."

"You are a rogue." Playfully she swatted his naked buttocks.

He offered her a mock groan in response, and grabbed her hand to kiss it. "My governess was the only one who'd ever spanked me, and as she was uncommonly pretty, the punishment never had the desired effect. It still doesn't."

Shaking her head, she laughed again. "Do you know what the Eifion brothers *did* with David?"

"They said they would ply him with mead all night long. They even promised to embarrass him into drinking, if necessary. Then, when he was properly softened up, they offered to bring him to their house, where they had a lovely little lady waiting for him, one who often services the men of Caernarfon."

"You men are all very predictable," she observed,

her voice tart. "Wine and women will make you forget everything, even your principles."

He shrugged. "You've certainly made me forget everything."

"As have you, at least for a while. I wish we could stay here all night."

"Why don't we?"

She stared at him, mute, the pull between love and duty making her ache inside.

He kissed her gently, and when he pulled back to look at her, she saw the softness in his eyes and wanted to cry. "You're with the man you married. Isn't that the way it's meant to be?"

She pulled away from him a little, away from his tormenting words. A sliver of cold air crept between them. "In a perfect world, yes, that's how it should be. By God, I wish it were so."

"Then *make* it so, Georgiana. Leave tomorrow with me for London."

"I can't." Her heart aching, she reached for her robe.

"Can't, or won't?"

"You're asking me to pretend I'm naught more than an aristocrat's wife, entertaining and attending charities and all the things aristocrats' wives do," she said, drawing her robe over her head. "While I would have played that role very happily once, I'm different now. I can't pretend I wasn't born a druid with a peculiar ability, and I can't forget that I've a mortal enemy in the Duke of Gloucester. The thought of going to London and returning to my former life is an impossible one now. I have a destiny to fulfill."

"You should determine your own destiny, not let others determine it for you," he said, rather bitterly.

"I'm to prevent the Duke of Gloucester from gaining England's throne. Until I've defeated him, we can have nothing."

"And after that?"

"You seek promises from me, Brock, that I'm not willing to give."

He grasped his robe and pulled it on. "We should start back." He sounded disappointed.

Mourning the loss of their intimacy, she slipped shoes on her feet and stood. "Tonight was wonderful. While I don't entirely approve of how you detained David, I'm terribly glad you did."

He turned to her with a unexpected smile. "Shall I detain him again sometime?"

"At first opportunity," she agreed, her lips twitching upward.

Together they folded the blankets he'd brought. Then, wadding the stack under one arm, he took her hand and led her back to Cadair Abbey.

Chapter
16

❧

Georgiana didn't fall asleep until late that night, her thoughts consumed by images of Brock making love to her—memories of the way his face had looked, and how gently he'd touched her as he brought her indescribable pleasure. When sleep finally came to her, it claimed her completely. She woke at nearly eleven o'clock the following morning, long past the time breakfast was served.

Even so, the dining room wasn't empty when she made her way downstairs. It contained one red-eyed, clearly annoyed youth.

David clenched his fists when she entered. "Did you enjoy yourself at the festival?"

Her cheeks warming, she turned and busied herself at the sideboard, which contained the usual selection of Welsh cakes, eggs, and sausage. She didn't know whether to pretend ignorance or admit her knowledge. In the end, however, David saved her from making the decision.

"Gwynllian mentioned she saw you and Lord Darleigh emerge from the woods long after the festival."

In the middle of scooping eggs out of a dish, she froze.

"You're supposed to be mine, Georgiana." A petulant frown curled his lips.

She finished scooping her eggs and sat down. "David, we've gone through this before. While I have every intention of honoring my duty toward the Glamorgan Druids, you and I will never mate."

"But why? Am I ugly?"

"God, no. You're a very handsome lad, destined to become very sought-after by the ladies in town."

"Why do you reject me, then?" He paused, a flush brightening his cheeks. "Do I smell?"

"David, stop it. You're a perfectly desirable and handsome youth, but you're simply not for me. I lost my heart to Lord Darleigh long ago. I couldn't help it at the time, and I can't help it now. There is something between Lord Darleigh and I, some sort of sympathetic response on a primal level."

He slammed his fork down, stood, and began to pace across the room. "Your mother chose to do her duty. *She* mated with the Duke of Gloucester. If she hadn't, you wouldn't be here now."

His argument hitting home, Georgiana swallowed. "David, I—"

"Never mind. Let's just continue our practicing in the stone circle," he interrupted, clearly unhappy with her.

She took a deep breath. Should she pursue this argument further? In an instant she decided to let it go. It was so unpleasant, and wouldn't change a thing. "We'll start right after breakfast," she agreed.

"After we practice, I have a place I'd like to take you to. It's on the edge of the woods, a mile or so along the edge of Cadair Abbey's grounds."

Georgiana touched her snake's glass pendant, which lay against her chest. "The meadow? Why?"

"I have something special to show you."

Her curiosity piqued, she finished her breakfast quickly. Then, in silence, she walked through the forest with David. Clouds scuttled across a gray sky above them, and wood smoke fragranced the air. Everything had a dry, dead look, and Georgiana had a sense of endings, of a door closing that she would never pry open again.

Upon reaching the stone circle, she sat on a boulder and rubbed her hands together to keep them warm. David preferred to stand and pace a little, claiming it helped his concentration. Together, they combined their abilities in various ways, in an attempt to produce the most realistic illusions possible.

Outside of their illusion at the festival last night, they'd been working on illusions of forests and trees. Georgiana seemed to come closest to creating order from chaos when she tried to mimic those particular items. She'd given the situation some thought and decided it must have something to do with the stone circle she stood in. According to Sir Anthony and Gwynllian, most of the magic worked in that circle had been nature magic, and when Georgiana and David created illusions, the stone circles naturally influenced them and buffered the echoes of their abilities.

At length, when she began to ache inside and knew she had nearly come to the end of her resources, she announced that the time to quit had arrived. David agreed immediately to suspend their practicing and led her down a path away from Cadair Abbey. With the wind at their backs, they walked for ten minutes before the woods brightened and Georgiana realized they were about to emerge from the trees. Moving more slowly, David steered her off the path and guided her around thorn bushes and boulders, until they emerged into a grassy meadow.

Georgiana surveyed the meadow. She knew this place well. She'd found her pendant here years ago. Back then, the meadow had swayed with a riot of wildflowers whose colors—purples, blues, yellows, and pinks—were so vivid they nearly hurt the eyes. A warm, sweet fragrance had hung heavily on the air. Now, filled with brown, dried stalks, it looked barren. The drought had shriveled up anything of beauty, and the air smelled of parched nothingness.

A fence ran along one side of the meadow. In the

distance, a stand of trees hemmed in the other side of the meadow. She could barely see a swathe of brown clay near the edge of the trees, suggesting a dried-up streambed.

David paused and glanced at her, his manner unusually grave. "What do you think?"

"I see nothing unusual," she ventured carefully. "This *is* the special place you wished to take me to?"

He nodded.

Eyes wide, she gave the meadow and its surrounding landscape another look. Even after careful study, she could see nothing extraordinary, except perhaps the old oak tree which grew in one corner of the meadow, where the fence met the stand of trees.

She'd found her pendant near that oak. It didn't surprise her that her mother had chosen that spot to hide the snake's glass. Oaks were trees of great magic and protection. They were the trees of Taliesin, on whose works the Glamorgan Druids had been founded.

"I've always found the oak tree rather interesting," she allowed. "I discovered my mother's snake's glass near it many years ago. Tell me why you've brought me here."

"You were born here," he informed her baldly. "Your mother died nearby. That oak tree protected you until Gwynllian found you."

Georgiana stared at him. Her heart gave one wild thump in her breast, then settled down into an uncomfortable rhythm. "Gwynllian told you this?"

He nodded. "Didn't she tell *you?*"

"No. My uncle simply said my mother had died in the fields surrounding Cadair Abbey."

Trembling, she followed him through the meadow. Burrs caught in her robe and an arid wind whipped through her hair, loosening tendrils that obscured her vision and stung her cheeks. Tips of stalks stabbed at her hands. The bare trees and distant mountains suddenly looked very dull, very gray. Her gaze was watery, but her throat felt bone-dry, as if every bit of moisture in her body had pooled in her eyes.

This is near the place where her mother had died.

"Please, David, tell me what Gwynllian said," she pleaded, her voice trembling.

He sent her a questioning glance. "It's rather . . . harsh."

"I know."

Shrugging, he gave in to her. "Gwynllian said that the duke sent hounds after your mother. Branwyn ran along that stream, there." He pointed to the dried-up stream bed. "You were born by that oak tree. She hid you in its boughs, and managed to run another mile into the forest before the hounds got to her, far enough so they wouldn't scent you. Gwynllian found you and brought you back to Cadair Abbey before the duke discovered otherwise."

Her eyes welling up with tears, Georgiana stared out across the field. Slowly the tears dripped down her cheeks. She didn't bother to wipe them. She didn't care if David saw them. An unimaginable sort of pain was filling her.

"Branwyn was a smart woman," David allowed in his youthful voice. "She had a lot of courage. Even a pack of dogs couldn't frighten her. She knew how important you were, and sacrificed herself to save you."

"She loved me," Georgiana said. The tears were flowing freely now.

"She also knew you had a destiny to fulfill," David pressed. "Through you, the balance between good and evil would be maintained."

"How did she know about my destiny?"

"Gwynllian told me once that she'd warned Branwyn against the Duke of Gloucester. Branwyn refused to believe that the duke would try to kill both herself and her unborn baby."

"He is evil," she breathed, hatred joining the sense of loss which ached inside her like a rotten tooth.

David kicked a rock, sending it skittering through the grass. "Last night, the Eifion brothers told me a very strange tale. I wish I had heard it earlier."

"About the Duke of Gloucester?"

"About Cadwallon ab Ilfor Bach. That's the duke's Welsh name. The older Eifion brother, John, was one of the duke's contemporaries. They grew up together. Deep in his cups, John told me last night that he'd once done something very terrible to the duke, when they were both younger."

"Why did he tell *you?*"

David shrugged. "I never pass up an opportunity to ask about the duke. You never know when you'll discover something you can use to your advantage."

Taking a deep breath, Georgiana tried to fight off a fresh wave of tears. She nodded, silently encouraging him.

"When John was a boy," he continued, "his parents raised hounds. Irish wolfhounds, in fact, the biggest dogs alive. His father trained the dogs to hunt in a pack and took them on hunting trips.

"According to John, in those days people considered Cadwallon an oddity. Some people even feared him in spite of his age. It didn't matter to anyone that he was heir to the dukedom of Gloucester. He was considered Satan's emissary and had to endure a lot of taunting, persecution, and the like."

"He must have created a few illusions at the wrong time and scared the townfolk half to death."

David shrugged. "Who knows? In any event, John said that he saw Cadwallon walk into the woods one day. He loosed the wolfhounds on the boy in a cruel practical joke. When they found Cadwallon the following day, his hair had turned a silvery white. He was clinging to the highest branches of an oak tree, and one of the wolfhounds sat patiently near the base of its trunk. Bite marks on the boy's leg oozed blood. Later, they became infected."

She nodded. "The few times I've seen him at court, he's limped. The bites must have permanently scarred him. While I feel for the child, though, I revile the man."

"I think it's peculiar that the duke used hounds to hunt your mother. He killed her in the way he most feared dying himself."

Her stomach clenched. "He is vile."

"After his experience, he must have a fear of hounds," David offered. "When we create our illusion intending to trap him, we should use dogs. They might set him off balance."

Georgiana's gaze roamed across the meadow, imagining a woman stumbling along through flowers, hounds baying in the distance. She pressed a hand to her forehead and closed her eyes. "David, I can't think about the duke any longer. Please, return to the abbey. I'd like to be left alone here for a while."

"Can you find your way back?"

"Yes." *Physically, yes.*

Emotionally, however, she was lost. "Thank you, David. For bringing me here."

His eyes sad, he turned and disappeared into the woods.

Brock spent most of the day after the festival in the town of Caernarfon, checking with his contacts, insuring that unusual visitors hadn't surfaced in

any of Caernarfon's inns and hostelries. After he'd
satisfied himself that Georgiana remained secure,
he returned to the abbey and glanced through a
stack of mail that had been delivered during his trip
to town. Expecting to hear from Rees, he found
nothing addressed to himself. He hoped his young
cousin had followed his instructions and forwarded
the enclosed note to Jack Langan.

Dinner later that evening was a quick affair, with
only Gwynllian and Sir Anthony for company. He'd
seen neither Georgiana or David during the times
he'd been at the abbey, and he wondered about it
through every course, including dessert. When he
asked Gwynllian about their absence, however, she
simply shrugged and said they'd had work to do.

Retiring alone to the salon after dinner, he stayed
and drank a glass of port. Gwynllian had piqued
his curiosity with her cryptic statement, and now it
ate at him. What sort of work were they up to, that
they had to miss dinner? He couldn't even guess at
an answer, and spent most of the night tossing in
his bed, wondering. A feeling of loneliness came
over him, and more than a touch of jealousy.

When the ormolu clock on his nightstand
announced the arrival of midnight in little tinkling
notes, Brock knew he'd never sleep. He'd been tossing around the idea of visiting Georgiana in her
bedchamber anyway, to steal a few more kisses;
now he couldn't think of a more important task
needing his attention. He would go to her bed-

chamber, find out what she'd been doing all day, and then caress her until pleasure made her cry out, regardless of who heard her.

His loins tightening, he grabbed a candle to light the way, slipped out of his bedchamber, and shut the door behind him quietly, with a click. Then, walking close to the walls to avoid the floorboards that groaned the loudest, he followed the corridor to the end and made a right. Facing a vaulted foyer, he knew from previous scouting missions that Georgiana's bedchamber was located in the passageway beyond.

He crossed the foyer and started down the passageway. When he'd drawn within a few feet of her bedchamber, he stopped. Her door stood open an inch. Prudently he took a second to peer through the crack and saw her sleeping peacefully on her bed. Alone.

Smiling to himself, he pushed the door open and walked inside. A feeling that he couldn't name swelled inside him, tightening his throat as he crossed the room to his wife's side. Had any man wanted a woman more than he wanted Georgiana? He didn't think so. But it was more than wanting. She'd awakened a soul-deep longing in him that he couldn't control. His life would be nothing without her.

He paused by her bedside and held the candle aloft so he might gaze at her. His smile immediately slipped into a frown. Tears had left tracks down her cheeks. Dark shadows circled under her eyes, and even now, she whimpered softly.

He looked away from her, his gut twisting with guilt. He'd brought her to this point. If he'd simply divorced her as she'd requested, the choice between her duty to the Glamorgan Druids and himself wouldn't be tearing her apart like this. Indeed, every time he held her in his arms, he hurt her more.

Quietly, he tucked the counterpane around her, so she wouldn't grow cold, and backed out of her bedchamber. With regret like ashes in his mouth, he returned to his own bedchamber and struggled with his conscience. He ought to leave now for London, and trust in Sir Anthony to guard her. He ought to break the ties between them and give her the peace of mind she needed. He ought to do a lot of things . . . but he just couldn't.

When morning arrived, he went downstairs to the dining room in a surly mood. Fortunately, the room remained empty of anything other than a steaming breakfast, sparing him the need to join in conversation. A few letters, he noticed, lay on a salver near the coffee pot.

Scowling, Brock poured himself a cup of coffee and snatched a scone from a plate of pastries. He hadn't slept at all, and he wasn't liking himself much, and he didn't know how much longer he could continue on in Wales without slamming his fist through a wall. In this state of limbo, he sorted through the letters and found one for himself, from Lord Watkins, the "Neddy" fellow Georgiana considered a friend. Wondering what Watkins could possibly have to say to him, he opened the letter and read the first few lines.

Rees had gone missing, for almost a week now.

Forehead creased with worry, Brock looked up from the letter to fix his gaze, unseeing, upon the carpet. He wondered if Rees had gone on some drinking or gambling binge that had landed him in the wrong section of London. Was he lying in an alley somewhere, drunk and broke?

No, Rees wouldn't stoop to that level of behavior.

Perhaps he'd found a mistress instead, and had spent the week in a bedchamber somewhere. Brock thought the second scenario more likely. Still, he couldn't quite believe it. Frowning, he refocused on the letter, scanning its contents. A sentence two-thirds of the way down leapt out at him.

. . . servants reported seeing peculiar figures in long, white robes . . .

The letter dropped from his suddenly nerveless fingers.

His heart beginning to pound, he grasped the letter and read quickly through the rest.

. . . the king suspects druids involved, perhaps the same involved in the killings earlier this month. He has posted a reward for anyone with information leading to Lord Hammond's location. I've contacted Lord Hammond's parents, who are no doubt on their way home from their estate in Scotland. I thought it only proper for me to inform you as well.

The letter went on to explain how Neddy had determined their location in Wales through a few comments Rees had made and Georgiana's various reminiscences of Cadair Abbey outside of Caernarfon. Brock impatiently read through the rest, his attention locking on Neddy's final sentence:

I fear the worst for Rees.

Tucking the letter into his jacket, Brock pushed away from the table, ran to his bedchamber, and called his valet. Then he began to pack a few necessities and dress in clothes that could withstand several days of riding, nonstop. All the while he cursed himself. He'd been foolish to involve Rees, however innocently, in his scheme to subdue the duke.

Brock could easily surmise what had happened. Obviously Rees had passed the letter Brock had sent him on to Jack Langan. Langan, as requested, had hired a few local toughs to subdue the duke. The duke must have fended off the boxers' attack and forced them to reveal the names of the people who had hired them. When Rees's name surfaced, the duke had simply kidnapped him. Perhaps the duke was torturing Rees even now, in an effort to gain more information. Indeed, the duke might already have learned Georgiana's identity from Rees.

Suddenly Brock realized how naive he'd been, hiding up here in Wales, "guarding" Georgiana. He couldn't guard her from the duke. The man would find a way to kill her when he chose to, despite

Brock's efforts to the contrary. The only way to truly eliminate the duke's threat was to eliminate the duke. After, of course, he'd found Rees. God willing, his cousin was still alive.

Purpose stiffening his spine, Brock yanked on his riding boots, shrugged into a serviceable jacket, and strode out the door. He was leaving for London. Now.

Chapter
17

Georgiana awoke and gazed around her bed-chamber, noting the soft haze of sunshine that filled the room. Dawn had long since come and passed. She sat up and loosened the ribbon at the throat of her pristine white cotton nightgown. After spending most of the day before in the meadow where she'd been born, she'd returned to Cadair Abbey recommitted to the Glamorgan Druids, as David had no doubt intended.

She'd put on the white cotton nightgown and, half-expecting Brock to visit her in the middle of the night, tied the ribbon at the throat securely, as if that might imprison her own need of him. Then, exhausted, she'd fallen asleep and remained undisturbed the entire night.

Obviously, despite her apprehensions, Brock had decided not to come.

Her head was already aching as she dressed with

Nellie's assistance and descended the stairs to breakfast. Yesterday, she'd spent hours in that meadow, trying to feel her mother's presence, to imagine what her last minutes had been like. It bothered her that she must have visited the meadow a hundred times in her youth and never knew what had occurred there. She'd climbed the oak tree and walked along the stream until finally she'd fallen to her knees and wondered why, why her mother had died. It didn't seem fair.

Later, when she'd returned to the abbey, she'd realized David had made his point quite clearly. So far, she'd proven that her mother was made of tougher fabric than she. Branwyn had sacrificed and shown great courage in the face of a horrible death; while she, Georgiana, continued to selfishly long for a man who had no place in her life.

Georgiana entered the dining room in a very poor mood indeed, and discovered all of the usual parties seated, with one exception: Brock. Lord Darleigh's place remained conspicuously empty.

Nodding to Sir Anthony, Gwynllian, and David, she selected a plate of breakfast fare from the sideboard and sat down at the table. Her gaze slid to Brock's vacant chair as she joined in desultory conversation with the others. He hadn't yet missed an opportunity to breakfast with her and pry a laugh out of her. She'd found it a wonderful way to start the day. So where was he this morning?

Inexplicably, worry flared inside of her. When a

pause in the talk provided her an opportunity, she raised an eyebrow and schooled her tone into one of casual curiosity. "Where is Lord Darleigh this morning?"

"Returned to London," Sir Anthony replied, his gaze never leaving the stack of mail he was reading.

Georgiana stilled. "When?"

"Early this morning."

A sinking sensation gathered in the pit of her stomach. The moment seemed to drag on forever. *Brock was gone.* And he hadn't even bothered to wish her good-bye. "Did Lord Darleigh mention to any of you that he planned to leave today?"

"He said nothing," Gwynllian murmured. "He had gone before any of us were awake."

"I suppose an emergency with his estate in London drew him away."

Her aunt shrugged. "Quite possibly."

"He left you a note," Sir Anthony added, gesturing toward a salver on the sideboard.

Georgiana rose hastily from her seat and retrieved the note. She unfolded it and studied the smooth, masculine script.

"Dearest Georgiana,
    Rees is missing, and I fear I'm responsible for his disappearance. He innocently passed on a letter I'd written to a friend of mine, who then set in motion a scheme to subdue the duke. I'm afraid the duke uncovered the scheme and kidnapped Rees to

learn who originally wrote the letter. I am return-
ing to London immediately to discover my cousin's
whereabouts. I pray he still lives. Please remain in
Wales until I return for you.

Yours always,

Brock."

She cried out and clutched the letter to her chest.

Sir Anthony jumped out of his chair and rushed to her side. "Georgiana, what is it? What's happened?"

"Brock's cousin Rees is missing. Brock thinks the duke may have taken him. That's why he left so precipitously for London!" She shoved the note into Sir Anthony's hands.

Her uncle scanned the note's contents, his face growing pale. "Lord Darleigh is going to go after the duke. Alone." Quickly he relayed the contents of the letter to David and Gwynllian.

"We can't let him face the duke alone." Georgiana clasped her hands and began to pace. Her heart seemed to contract in her chest until it became a cold, hard stone. "The duke will break him as easily as you or I can break a branch."

"Georgiana's right," David chimed in. "We must leave for London at once, and stop Lord Darleigh before he gets himself killed and gives away Georgiana's identity in the process."

Sir Anthony rubbed his forehead. "The duke

may very well know her identity by now. Indeed, he could have broken this Rees fellow and already be on his way to Caernarfon."

"No, I don't think so."

Everyone turned to stare at Gwynllian. Her statement hung on the air between them, bringing silence to the room.

"What do you know?" Georgiana breathed.

Gwynllian stood, moved to Georgiana's side, and embraced her in a quick hug. "We'll do what we can for your husband," she murmured, and then said more loudly, "Haven't you all been reading the gossip pages? The king has been planning a welcoming reception for visiting royalty from Austria. Prince Blücher-Sydow is an important ally on the Continent, and all of the king's advisors are certain to attend the function."

"Advisors such as the Duke of Gloucester?" David asked.

Gwynllian nodded. "I'd wager my life on it. The duke wouldn't let such an opportunity to cozy up to the king pass him by. And since he'll want to deal with Georgiana directly, he'll wait to act until the reception has concluded."

"Why will he want to deal with me directly?" Georgiana asked.

"Because you're strong, my dear. Very strong. He knows only a druid of his skill and power has a chance at defeating you."

"I don't feel very strong."

"Think of Brock," Gwynllian counseled.

Georgiana lifted her chin. "You're right. I'd do anything for him."

"This reception sounds like the perfect opportunity to trap the duke," Sir Anthony observed. "When does it take place?"

"In two weeks from now, giving us just enough time to reach London." Gwynllian turned her attention to Georgiana. "Georgiana, do you think you'll be ready by then?"

"I'm ready *now*. I don't want to live another day with the duke's threat hanging over my head."

Sir Anthony looked at David. "And you?"

The lad nodded. "I'm ready."

"That settles it, then," Gwynllian said. "We'll leave for London within the hour. Sir Anthony, can you secure us invitations to Prince Blücher-Sydow's reception?"

"I'll send a courier ahead to retain them," Sir Anthony promised.

A hard smile curved Georgiana's lips. This truly *was* harvest day. While she felt satisfaction at the skills she'd learned in Wales, the difficult task had yet to come.

Brock stared into the burgundy depths of the liquor he swirled in his snifter. Across from him, the Duchess of Winterbury lounged in a velvet-backed chair, her wide blue eyes not so innocent. They sat in his study, enjoying a surprise tête-à-tête among the financial papers that had once summed up his life as "bankrupt" and now declared him as "fully solvent."

He had promised to escort Amelia to Lady Nichols' ball this evening, but hadn't expected her to appear on his doorstep early, offering to join him in predinner festivities, as she'd termed it. He supposed he *should* have expected her advance. He'd taken her to the opera and theater three times since he'd returned from Wales, all in an effort to gain information about the duke. Rumor had it that Amelia was the Duke of Gloucester's cast-off mistress, and Brock had hoped she might give him some insight into the man.

He'd managed to learn nothing on his own.

The first few days upon returning from Wales, he'd spoken for hours to the local constabulary and the Bow Street Runners. He'd questioned Rees's servants and assembled a mass of servants and friends to scour the streets of London for a clue to Rees's disappearance. All attempts had failed.

The duke had been very thorough in removing Rees without implicating himself; and yet, Brock knew the duke was responsible. All of the people involved in his scheme to rough up the duke had either disappeared or been found murdered. Jack Langan had inexplicably embarked on a journey north, according to the regulars at Figg's. Brock suspected the boxer's body would soon surface in the Thames. The two thugs Langan had hired had both been dumped in an alley in Haymarket, right near Figg's. And Rees . . . honorable, dependable Rees . . . had been the unwitting courier who'd set his scheme in motion.

His gut wrenching with guilt, Brock rubbed his temples. Not a minute passed when he didn't silently castigate himself for risking anyone but himself. He simply hadn't realized how extraordinarily wily and powerful the duke was. The man must have had spies everywhere in order to discover the plot against him. Indeed, Brock had begun to suspect that the duke had planted a spy in Palmer House. One of the servants, perhaps.

He tore himself from the unpleasant thoughts and forced himself to smile at the duchess. "I'm pleased that you've come by early this evening, Amelia."

The duchess laughed softly and stood. Trailing her fingers across tables and the tops of chairs, she sauntered in his direction, her lips in a pout. "You've led me on an interesting chase, Darleigh, and made it quite enjoyable. And yet, I think we've both grown tired of playing fox and hound." She paused by his side and twined her fingers through the ends of his hair, pulling on his scalp.

He felt rather than saw her circle around him, her hands creeping up into his hair. Dispassionately he recognized that the duchess was easy on the eyes. A peach-colored complexion and soft blond hair complemented her blue eyes and gave her the appearance of an angel, one wholly at odds with her true nature. Her husband, a doddering old rake in his seventies, had no idea that he'd married a lady of voracious and notorious tastes. Regrettably, she'd also proven unbelievably closed-mouthed. Desperate, he'd worked very hard to pry some information from her, all to no avail.

While her touch did nothing to stir him, he nevertheless faked a groan and leaned into her fingers. He didn't want to hurt her feelings.

"We've been together for almost a month now," she continued, moving to stand in front of him. Despite her multitude of petticoats, she managed to perch on his knee. "I wish I had known you much earlier. In the past, you had always seemed . . . rather dour."

Brock shrugged, his gaze straying to her bosom, almost completely revealed by her low-cut bodice. The sight did nothing to tempt him. "My estates took up much of my time."

"Whatever the reason, I'm glad you've finally decided to allow yourself some pleasure. With me. I assure you, my appetite is fully whetted. Why don't you go over to the door and lock it?"

He wanted to tell her to get off his knee, so he might stand up, but guessed that such "dour" practicality might ruin the mood she was working so hard to create between them. Instead, he gave her a slow smile and slipped his hand beneath her cushy buttocks, so he might shift her weight off him. The move required more effort on his part and, while it drew a soft moan from her, it also made him realize the duchess needed to cut down on the bonbons she devoured every afternoon.

Standing once again, she blew him a kiss, then turned toward a nearby couch, presumably to sit. At that moment, Brock noticed the white face peeking in from behind the study door.

He froze, taking in the large green eyes and wealth of brown hair atop her head. Georgiana, in London? He withdrew from the duchess as though she'd transformed into Typhoid Mary, earning a quick frown from her.

Brock paid the duchess little attention. His mind was racing. Why hadn't she stayed in Wales as he'd asked? She remained in danger in Wales, but in London, she was a walking target.

Amelia clucked. "Oh, how tacky. You didn't mention that your wife was returning from Wales, Darleigh."

Georgiana pushed the door open and stepped into the room. Her clothes wrinkled and stained from travel, she looked exhausted. Brock wanted to rush over to her and take her into his arms. He didn't, though. He'd worked hard to cultivate the duchess and still hoped he might pry something of interest out of her. Georgiana, he thought, would understand once he'd explained it to her.

"I didn't know she was returning," he murmured, standing.

Amelia raised an eyebrow, a faint smile on her lips. She didn't appear even slightly fazed by Georgiana's presence. He suspected this wasn't the first time she'd been caught between a husband and wife.

"I've interrupted you both," Georgiana said, her tone flat. "I should have written to inform you of my visit. Please forgive me." She began to back out of the room.

To his horror, Brock suddenly couldn't find his voice. He watched helplessly as Georgiana turned away.

Amelia studied him with narrowed eyes. She frowned, clearly unhappy with what she saw, and transferred her attention to Georgiana.

"Pardon *me*, Lady Darleigh," she said, her husky voice halting Georgiana's retreat. "Your husband had kindly offered to escort me to Lady Nichols' ball, as a favor to His Grace, who is feeling ill this eve. I see I must release him from this duty, so he might welcome his wife home."

Georgiana turned around very slowly. "Lord Darleigh may do as he wishes."

Eyebrow raised, Amelia looked at him, waiting for his response.

"I'll send a friend, Lord Carlisle, around to escort you there, and meet you later myself," he offered, knowing her pride wouldn't allow her to accept.

Amelia's smile grew more cynical. "Prince Blücher-Sydow of Austria has already offered to escort me, should I require him. Don't worry yourself over me, Darleigh. I'll send him a note." She leaned close to Brock and whispered, "I don't share my men. When I have your full attention again, send for me. But don't keep me waiting too long."

Choking out an acknowledgement, Brock escorted her to the door with a hand against the small of her back. There, he directed his butler to find the duchess's maid and both their cloaks, and to see them on their way.

"Good-bye, Darleigh," Amelia said on her way out.

His gut tight with dismay, he spun around and faced Georgiana. "What you just saw . . . it isn't what you think. I mean, the duchess, she's not—"

"Where's Rees?" she cut in, her voice cold. "Have you found him, or did you give up your search for him in favor of the duchess?"

"He's still missing. I asked him to give a letter I'd written to Jack Langan, a friend of mine. In this letter, I instructed Langan to discreetly hire a few toughs from Figg's Pugilism Academy. The toughs were supposed to subdue the duke long enough for your uncle's London druids to work their magic on him, or whatever they planned to do." His voice began to tremble. "Instead, Langan has gone on an extended journey, most likely to the bottom of the Thames; the two toughs from Figg's are dead; and Rees is missing."

"I've heard the gossip, Brock. You seem more

concerned with the duchess's social schedule than with finding Rees."

"Georgiana, I—"

"I saw how you fondled her backside," she choked out, her eyes blazing. "How could you? Rees is still missing, and I've been traveling for two weeks now to reach you, and one of our horses went lame, slowing us down, and . . . and . . ."

"And?" he asked, torn between dismay at her accusations and a sense that she was hiding something that he very much needed to know.

"And I'm pregnant!" she wailed, her face screwing up into a tight knot of misery. Seconds later, she began to sob and buried her face in her hands.

"Oh, Georgie," he breathed. Sudden joy filled him. His lips twitched into a smile, one he quickly reigned in. He rushed to her side and gathered her into his arms, where she sobbed unabashedly against his shirtfront, wetting it with her tears.

He let the storm run its course, and when her sobs became mere sniffles, he held her back at arm's length. "When did you discover it?"

"On the way from Wales," she admitted, blowing her nose into a square of linen he supplied. "It's been a month and a half since we made love. My courses have never run that late, and besides, I've been sick in the morning."

"A rocking carriage could make anyone sick," he reminded her cautiously.

"I'm not wrong about this, Brock. I feel different."

"Are you happy?"

"Deliriously so!" A smile appeared briefly upon her lips, but was quickly replaced by a frown. "Have I spoiled your fun with the duchess?"

"I have no interest in the duchess. I'm simply cultivating her in an attempt to find out where the duke has Rees. She's the duke's cast-off mistress and I thought she could help me."

Her voice trembled when she spoke. "I wish I could believe you."

"I know I've lied to you in the past, but haven't I proven myself to you since then, Georgie?"

She measured him with a wide-eyed gaze, then nodded slowly. "When I think of all that has gone between us in the last month, I realize you've proven yourself to me repeatedly. I trust you, Brock. I . . . I love you." Quickly she laid her head against his chest, as though she were afraid of what she might see in his face after such a declaration.

"Look at me," he murmured.

Her green eyes wide and vulnerable, she fixed her attention on his lips.

"I love the fact that you're going to have my child," he told her, his voice soft. "I love the way you smile at me in the morning, I love the lilt in your voice when you talk about Wales. I love *you*, Georgie. God, I've missed you so much."

Her eyes began to fill with tears. Without warning, she jumped against him, nearly knocking him over as she wrapped her arms around his neck and squeezed him tightly. Smiling, he wrapped his arms around her waist and hugged her back. He felt buoyant inside, as though he'd shed a hundred unwanted pounds. They stood like that for a long, long time.

At length, however, his thoughts returned to their baby. Separating from her a little, he placed a palm against her abdomen. "This changes everything."

Smiling tremulously, she wiped her eyes. "How so?"

"I'm going to have to hide you somewhere until I've dealt with the duke."

"Until *you've* dealt with the duke? That's my task."

"You're expecting my child. You can't possibly intend to challenge the duke to a druidic duel, and place both your lives at risk."

She pulled away from him a little more. "I will indeed face the duke—with David. If I don't, my life, and our baby's life, are worth nothing. Remember, the duke had my mother eaten alive by hounds, even though she carried his own child. Do you think he will show me any mercy, now that I'm expecting?"

Already he missed the warmth of her body snuggled into his. "Your uncle and I will pool our resources and defeat him ourselves."

"My uncle sent two druids after the duke. They died. You sent two thugs after the duke. They also died. Now you're going to pool your resources with him? I wouldn't wager a tuppence on your success."

"I won't allow it, Georgie."

"And I must follow my destiny, Brock. Don't you understand? My entire life has been moving toward this moment. Despite your objections, David and I remain the only chance of defeating the duke. We must do as fate has decreed, and fight the duke until either he, or we, die."

Even though he saw the logic in her argument, he still balked at it. "My life would be over if I lost you."

"Until I eliminate the duke, we have nothing." She clasped his hand in her own. "Come with me to my uncle's townhouse. Together we'll decide upon the best strategy to defeat him."

"You wish to work together?"

"Yes."

"Your uncle agrees?"

"He suggested it." A hesitant smile curled her lips. "Now that he knows he's going to be a great-uncle, his attitude toward you has softened considerably."

Brock shook his head, bemused at the thought of Sir Anthony giving him his blessing. "Any plan we decide upon will have to be very convincing, and very unpredictable. The duke seems to have eyes everywhere. Furthermore, I won't agree to anything that puts you at the slightest risk."

"We'll thrash it out together, with the others,"

she hedged. "Have you heard about the state reception the king is holding for Prince Blücher-Sydow tomorrow night?" she asked.

"Who hasn't? It's the talk of the season."

"Gwynllian thinks the reception might be the best time to attack the duke. We're all going to attend: my uncle, my aunt, David, myself, and you." Her gaze softening, she brushed her fingers across his cheek. "During our ride to London, we came up with an interesting strategy. Come with me to my uncle's townhouse. We'll discuss the particulars there."

Chapter
18

❧

The night of the fête for Prince Blücher-Sydow began with royal fanfare, at Windsor Castle, some twenty-odd miles west of London. Georgiana arrived and hurried into the throne room, just in time to see George IV fit his huge body into a gold and velvet chair. Amid a flourish of trumpets, the king welcomed the prince formally to England and gave a small speech on the prince's many admirable qualities, as well as those of Austria.

Her limbs aching with nervous energy, Georgiana stood near the rear of the throne room and tried to see over the heads of the other aristocratic attendees. Ostrich feathers, gray wigs and smartly-dressed locks combined with a dazzling array of ball gowns and evening coats to neatly block her view. She moved to the left and peered between the shoulders of a portly woman in a turquoise dress and an old man wearing breeches outmoded many seasons before.

Where was he?

Prince Blücher-Sydow embarked on a lengthy discussion of the advantages of maintaining an English-Austrian alliance, but Georgiana barely heard him. Instead, she slanted a glance at Gwynllian, who stood behind her and to the left. Gwynllian caught her gaze and nodded toward a tall man near the dais.

Her heart stuttering in her chest, Georgiana studied the man. He wore a fine black evening coat and trousers, and gold thread entwined on his waistcoat, giving him the look of wealthy elegance. His hair was silvery gray, and his light blue eyes had a piercing quality that seemed to see through the skin to the soul. Handsome in his own way, the Duke of Gloucester sent shivers of revulsion across Georgiana's skin.

Still, she couldn't quell the fascination that kept her attention locked on him. She felt as though she were seeing him for the first time. This man was her father. He was also a murderer. He had killed her mother and wanted her dead, too, so he might sit upon the throne of England. She tried to see some aspect of herself in him, some stray mannerism or detail in his appearance that would link them to each other, and found nothing.

She watched him smile at a comment the prince made, one designed to draw laughter from his audience. Dutiful chuckles emerged from the people around her. Lips compressed, Georgiana remained quiet. A strange ambivalence was growing inside her like an illness. Some idiot part of her mourned his loss and wished he would acknowledge her presence. It wanted him to tell her he regretted forsaking her and desired to know her better now.

She wanted him to love her.

Unexpectedly, tears filled her eyes.

A hand settled on her shoulder. She glanced behind her to meet Brock's stare. He looked so very tall and handsome that she caught her breath; and when she saw understanding in his dark eyes, that small bit of sympathy from him was her complete undoing. Her cheeks grew wet with tears.

His arm encircled her waist and pulled her close. Ducking her head to hide her discomposure, she allowed him to escort her away from the center of the crowd, to a nook hidden by two potted palms. Everyone seemed oblivious to her retreat, except the Duchess of Winterbury, who observed them with a narrowed stare.

"Will you be all right?" he murmured against her ear.

Sniffling a little, she nodded her head. "I never expected to know anything but hate for the duke. And yet, when I look at him, I feel so lonely."

"You're in a hellish situation."

Instead of replying, she savored the warmth of his large body so close to hers, and let him comfort her with his presence.

"Where is David?" he asked.

Georgiana sighed. "In the crowd, behind me."

"I think last night's meeting at your uncle's townhouse went rather well between us all, don't you?"

"I could have done without the insults David threw your way at first. I still find it amazing that you two managed to bond by dawn."

"In the end, David had to admit that he enjoyed Blue Belle. She's quite . . . accomplished, from what I hear."

Georgiana sighed. She supposed last night wasn't the first time that a discussion of sexual exploits had brought two warring males together.

"Where are Gwynllian and Sir Anthony?" Brock asked.

"In their assigned positions."

"Good."

Looking over Brock's shoulder to exchange glances with David, Gwynllian, and Sir Anthony, she discovered the duchess's attention upon their alcove. That august lady didn't look pleased, judging by the frown that drew her pretty face downward.

"I fear I've caused trouble between you and the duchess," she murmured, snuggling against Brock's chest. Quite happy to deliver her husband from the clutches of that very sensuous woman, she would have caused him more trouble if possible.

Brock murmured against her ear. "The duchess will shortly find someone new, and forget me."

"She won't forget you. No woman could."
Georgiana discovered her tears had dried up,
replaced by a feeling of hope matched only by the
ache he roused inside her. By the end of the night,
she might be free to love Brock as she wished to.

She might also be headed for a bog.

Ever aware of her father's light blue eyes scanning the room, she fit herself against Brock's tall
frame and tried to look as inconspicuous as possible. At the same time, the unexpectedly long-
winded prince finished amidst rousing applause,
not so much for the content of his speech, but more
for the fact that he'd released his audience.

The king stood tentatively on his gouty leg and
indicated they should all retire to the Waterloo
Chamber for a buffet, and afterward, to the Grand
Reception Room for dancing and card playing.
Georgiana, who'd never visited Windsor Castle
before now, allowed Brock to lead her through the
hall, and noticed many other disoriented faces
along the way. She made certain to remember each
room's decor, orientation, and furnishings, knowing that she'd use the recollections later.

Ill health had forced the king to forsake St.
James's Palace for Windsor Castle, and now he
rarely stirred from these stone walls. Instead, polite
society now came to him, and although George IV
remained popular, his illness was an inconvenience
for all. Brock, who'd attended a state reception at
Windsor Castle as a child, quickly garnered a fol-

lowing behind him, as others realized he was one of the few who knew where to go.

"Lord Durleigh," a deep voice called out.

Brock's steps slowed until he halted, but he didn't turn around. Inexplicably, his hand clasped hers and squeezed. Her mouth suddenly dry, Georgiana slowly spun around. Brock finally moved with her.

She stared directly into her father's piercing eyes.

"Good evening, Lord Darleigh, Lady Darleigh," the duke said.

Georgiana's lips twitched in a perfunctory smile. Inside, however, she'd become empty, weightless. Hollow pangs contracted her stomach and her throat grew tight. At the same time, her heart pounded. A hot flash washed over her and she knew in that instant she was going to swoon.

"Good evening, Your Grace," Brock replied, his hand tightening on hers to the point of pain.

Georgiana forced herself to speak, but she hadn't any air behind her words. "The prince's reception has proven quite delightful, no?"

"Indeed." The duke lifted an eyebrow. "You seem out of breath, Lady Darleigh. Are you well?"

Frantically Georgiana searched for a suitable excuse. Her mind remained empty of anything but a need to run and hide. She felt her eyes widen and knew she looked both trapped and guilty.

Brock came to her rescue once again, assuming

jovial yet confidential tones. "We have very happy news, Your Grace. Lady Darleigh is expecting."

Nodding dumbly, Georgiana pressed a hand against her midsection. Her cheeks flamed at Brock's casual revelation of her situation, even while she applauded his quick thinking.

The duke stood back and examined her. "How wonderful for you both. You have my congratulations."

"Thank you," Brock said, and stuck out his hand for the duke to shake it. After a slight hesitation, the older man clasped Brock's hand and the two men shook.

"As you doubtlessly know, her condition is very delicate and subject to many uncomfortable symptoms, including excitation and breathlessness," Brock continued. "But don't fear, our family physician is monitoring her very closely. Naturally we'd appreciate your keeping our news in the strictest confidence, until the happy day grows close."

Georgiana forced herself to breathe evenly. She wanted very much to join in the conversation, if only to allay his suspicions further. "I must apologize, Your Grace. I find this breathlessness comes upon me without warning."

The duke clucked in sympathy. "Your journey from Wales must have been very uncomfortable, then."

"You've heard about my recent travels?"

"Very little escapes me," he said in dry tones.

Georgiana's heart quickened. "The trip was long, but not wholly uncomfortable."

"Of course . . . you had young David Gwylum to amuse you."

She nodded. "You *are* very well informed about my travels."

"Sir Stanton, your uncle, is an . . . old friend of mine. We grew up together in Caernarfon and keep abreast of each other's activities. How is he?"

"Very well."

"And Miss Stanton?"

"In good health." Georgiana swallowed. "They're here somewhere. Perhaps you might talk to them yourself."

Eyebrows arched, he nodded. "I'll look for them. In the meanwhile, you must tell me about your time in Wales. Did you enjoy yourself?"

"Immensely."

"And you, Lord Darleigh?"

"I enjoyed seeing the places Georgiana knew as a child," Brock offered in an innocent voice.

"Good." The duke's gaze swiveled from Georgiana, to Brock, and back again. Her skin prickled at the weight of his stare.

"I've often considered returning to Caernarfon for a visit," the duke said, "but George IV requires constant attention, as do all kings. You see, I've made it my life's work to allow nothing to come between me and the throne. You must agree that no sacrifice is too great for England."

Brock nodded in agreement. "The king is lucky indeed to have such a man as you standing behind him."

Standing with a knife in your hand, Georgiana thought.

His lips curving in a smile that didn't match the cold assessment in his eyes, the duke inclined his head toward both of them. "Enjoy the evening," he murmured, before moving off into the crowd.

Georgiana swayed and clutched Brock's arm for support.

A smile pasted on his face, he slipped his arm around her waist and half-carried her to a chair, where she collapsed. She felt light-headed, almost giddy with relief.

Brock grabbed a glass of lemonade from a passing footman and sat next to her. Gratefully she sipped the cool drink. Moment by moment, the room stopped its rolling motions and breathing became easier for her.

"Do you think he knows?" she eventually managed to whisper.

"The duke isn't a man to waste time. If he knew who you were and what you planned, we would both be dead."

"I damned near died talking to him," she admitted. "I had no idea his presence would affect me so."

"Even though it was painful, your meeting up with the duke was probably the best thing that could have happened to you. Imagine if you'd suffered that sort of reaction while creating your illusion. Your plan would have come crashing down like a building condemned."

"True. Now that the shock of talking to him for the first time has dissipated, I'll know better what to expect from him and myself, and might be more capable of restraining my emotions."

"Let's hope so," Gwynllian spoke up from behind her.

Georgiana turned around and discovered her aunt hovering a few feet behind, her gray eyes intent.

"Did the duke betray any knowledge of our plan?" Gwynllian asked Brock.

"None whatsoever. He spent some time prying into the time Georgiana had spent in Wales, but he doesn't appear to have found any cracks in the false background you created for her all those years ago. He appears completely certain that Georgiana is Sir Wesley's orphaned daughter."

"Excellent." Gwynllian took Georgiana's hand and rubbed it briskly. "You're freezing cold, dear. Have courage. When this night is through, the duke will be a threat no longer, and you will be free to pursue a destiny of your own choosing."

Have courage.

Not so easily done, Georgiana thought.

Without warning, an image of the meadow where her mother had birthed her formed in her mind. She saw the oak tree, the stream, and the bare, spindly branches stretching toward the sky. Somehow, her mother had prevailed against the duke.

She would too.

Georgiana smiled and clenched her hand around Gwynllian's. "We're going to win this battle, Aunt."

Gwynllian returned her grip with one equally as determined. "You *are* my sister's child."

A warm glow of contentment crept through Georgiana. "If I die this evening, I'll have no regrets. I will die with honor."

"You're not going to die." Brock covered their clasped hands with his own. "I won't allow it."

Eyeing him with a strange expression, Gwynllian slipped her hand from theirs. "Are you certain about that, Lord Darleigh?"

His chin firm, he nodded. "Absolutely. May I escort you both to supper?"

A ghost of a smile curving her lips, Gwynllian nodded. "You may."

Her mood soaring at the calm determination in Brock's voice, Georgiana allowed him to clasp her arm. Gwynllian took his other arm and, together, Georgiana walked into the Waterloo Chamber with the two most important people in her life.

The Waterloo Chamber was one of the grandest rooms in Windsor Castle, sporting not only the largest seamless carpet in the world, but also a gallery of Thomas Lawrence's portraits of the leading figures in the Napoleonic wars. At any other time, Georgiana might have felt a burst of pride upon seeing the Duke of Wellington, George III, and other English heroes staring down at them from their positions on the wall. Today, however, she found their eyes coldly measuring, as if they wondered whether or not she would succeed in her duty, as they had succeeded in theirs.

In consequence, she ate very little of the lavish supper spread before her. Aware of the duke presiding near the end of the table, just a few feet from the king, she could only toy with the piece of underdone beef which still leaked blood. David, she noticed, shot confident little glances toward the duke, displaying a self-assurance that belonged only to those too young to realize how easy it was to die. Nevertheless, she admired his cool poise and hoped it would carry them through the night.

Once they'd finished an incredible array of gourmet foods, including salmon consommé, thick soup, trout, cutlets of chicken, saddle of lamb, roast pigeons, green salad, asparagus in white sauce, a fruit macédoine in champagne, ham mousse, and lemon ice cream, they all moved to the Grand Reception Room where a ten-piece orchestral ensemble was practicing the opening strains of a waltz. Georgiana kept Brock close to her after dinner, taking comfort in his presence.

When the ensemble struck up a melody suited to a cotillion, however, Georgiana moved onto the dance floor with David, giving him the first dance. With a courtly flourish the youth performed the steps, providing a glimpse of the attractive and sophisticated man he would someday be. He seemed completely at ease. Even so, she worried about him. She worried that she'd broken his heart and in doing so, put their plan to trap the duke in jeopardy. How could they create a seamless illusion with David resenting both her and Brock?

A sudden flurry of conversation caught her attention. David paused, clearly on the alert as well. There, at the entrance to the Waterloo room, a woman had just entered.

Not a woman, Georgiana corrected herself. A girl, judging by the wide blue eyes and flawless complexion. She was quite pretty, with jet-black hair that shone almost blue in the blazing candlelight.

Just then, the dance ended. She and David made their way to the edge of the dance floor, stopping near Gwynllian, who observed the black-haired girl with a raised eyebrow.

David, Georgiana thought, seemed quite besotted. He couldn't quite drag his attention away from the girl. She smiled to herself. She hadn't broken his heart, not by any means. A red-blooded male just coming into his prime, David would replace her quicker than she could blink an eye.

The notion couldn't have pleased her more.

Moments later, Brock paused by her elbow and asked her to dance with him. She forgot about the

black-haired girl and gave herself over to the pleasure of his embrace, the masterful feel of his hand at
the small of her back.

Thinking of the duchess, she whispered against his
ear, "I'm sorry for doubting you, even for a moment."

The dance separated them before he could reply,
but when they touched the next time, she added,
"After tonight, we start anew. We forget the past
and focus on the future."

"On a destiny of our own choosing," he agreed.

Her smile intimate, she nodded gracefully and
finished the dance. Brock escorted her to the edge of
the dance floor again and when she looked into his
eyes, she saw the love she'd dreamed about and
longed for. The dangerous mission ahead of her
made her bold, and before she had quite thought it
through, she was dragging Brock into an alcove and
kissing him full on the lips.

His eyes wide, he remained passive beneath her
mouth for but a moment. Then, his strong arms
encircled her and fit her to his body and she
thought she might swoon from the pleasure of it.
These moments, she mused, could be their last; and
yet, when she stood close to him, anything seemed
possible, even the duke's defeat. His touch was a
taste of heaven, a taste of the perfect life awaiting
her, if only she could fulfill her destiny and prevent
the duke from gaining the throne of England.

Suddenly Georgiana wanted it over. She just
wanted to finish with her duty, her destiny, and the

Glamorgan Druids. She wanted to be free to love Brock as she sensed they could love. Stiff-lipped with determination, she stared him directly in the eye and said, "We have to find David."

Brock stiffened, clearly surprised. "I thought you wished to execute your plan after the moon had risen fully. It's not even midnight yet. We have at least another hour to pass."

Georgiana gritted her teeth. "I cannot wait a moment longer."

"You have to wait." He brushed her hair back from her temples and pressed a kiss against her forehead. "Shh, Georgiana. It's almost over. Have patience."

Somehow, she managed to heed his advice. Casting frequent glances at Brock's watch fob, she cooled her heels until the hour passed midnight and approached one in the morning. As each minute passed she grew more tense. At last, when Gwynllian signaled to them with a discreet nod, Georgiana thought she might scream with relief. Grabbing Brock's hand, she hurried him through the Waterloo Room, the foyer, and out the front door.

Velvety black night settled in around her. She clasped Brock's hand in both of her own and murmured, "Be careful."

"You as well." Unexpectedly, a smile softened his face. He placed his palm on her midsection. "We'll have much to talk about after we're finished tonight."

A knot formed in her throat. She nodded and, seized by an impulse she couldn't deny, she reached up on tiptoe to press her lips against his. His answering kiss was far too brief and bittersweet; she couldn't be certain they'd ever kiss again.

"Until later," she murmured, and started off into the woods.

Chapter
19
❧

The Duke of Gloucester stood on the outskirts of the Waterloo Chamber, surveying the aristocrats who filed slowly into the Grand Reception Room. As they passed him, they bowed their heads, as if they, too, had seen the future. He nodded, accepting their worship as his due.

Soon, England will be mine, he thought.

And frowned. He felt jittery. Out-of-sorts.

Even the feel of the snake's egg against his chest couldn't restore his confidence.

Something was wrong.

He'd known since this morning, when he'd woken up entwined in Lady Wellborough's arms, sweating, his heart pounding, the vestiges of a nightmare clinging to him. A nightmare about hounds.

Always the hounds.

He remembered the sound of baying. They were coming for him, just as they'd come for him as a child.

The duke swallowed. The scars from his bite wound began to ache. They'd ached before. He'd seen a physician about them several years ago. The physician had said he was completely healed and shouldn't feel anything.

But he did.

The bite wound was still infected, somehow.

Those damned hounds.

His reaction to the nightmare had been very violent. He'd nearly broken Lady Wellborough's arm in an effort to get away from the hounds. She'd screamed and cried at first, nearly blathering with panic, but he'd slapped her, and she'd quickly remembered herself and begged his forgiveness.

Heat gathered between his legs at the memory. The red welt on her face had looked so damned . . . appropriate. It was the mark of a woman who knew her place. She might be a bitch in heat, but she knew how to grovel.

Therein, he mused, lay the problem with English society. Not all people knew their places. The Glamorgan Druids clearly had no sense of their place in society relative to his. They kept launching those sly attacks on him, and investigating him, trying to find his weak points. Instinct told him they were about to launch another attack. Evidently he needed to teach them their places, too. Was there a bog in Wales large enough to hold all of the Glamorgan Druids?

If not, he'd make one. Because he was angry. No,

not just angry. Gut-boiling angry. At everyone in this room. In this castle. In all of England. He was even angry at himself, for taking so long to discover the identity of the little slut he'd fathered. If Lord Hammond hadn't finally gibbered out Lord Darleigh's name, he might still be wondering from which direction the attack would come.

Ah, but Lord Hammond *had* come up to snuff; he'd revealed that the letter hiring that rabid dog Jack Langan had come from Lord Darleigh. The duke knew Lord Darleigh wouldn't have set thugs upon him unless the man was protecting someone . . . his dear wife, in fact. Georgiana Darleigh.

The duke realized he was clenching his fists. He felt one of his worst rages coming on. It had taken him years to learn how to control them. Moisture popped out on his brow. He dabbed it away and imagined slamming a lid down on a boiling pot and clamping it shut. The visualization worked, but just barely. He could still feel the rage inside him, waiting for a chance to get out.

Why not let it out?

The thought came from nowhere, insidious, sibilant, the whisper of a snake. He touched his shirt front, feeling the snake's egg grow warm against his skin. *Soon*, he promised. *Soon*.

Smiling at the last few stragglers to leave the Waterloo Chamber, he relaxed his hands and followed them into the Grand Reception Room. He immediately scanned the crowd and located Edward and Henry, his two bodyguards. Normally he wouldn't attend a state reception with bodyguards, but the sense that something was wrong had forced him to take unusual measures. His mood souring even further, he positioned himself near the refreshment table and looked for Sir Stanton.

The Glamorgan Arch Druid, he noted, was standing next to his sister. A smile lifted his mouth. He wondered if Gwynllian Stanton would prove as entertaining as Branwyn. Silently he promised to take her for a mistress as soon as he gained the throne. He'd like to mark her with a few welts. At least he would know just by looking at her that *she knew her place.*

The duke winced suddenly, and nearly clutched his temples. An intense concentration of vibrations had assaulted his mind. He knew well what the vibrations represented. A Guardian of Becoming was creating order from chaos, if only on a temporary basis. Judging by the intensity and patterns of the vibrations, the guardian at work was none other than his dear daughter.

Protecting his mind from the worst of the onslaught, he glanced through the room, looking not only for David but the illusion his daughter had created. His admiration for Sir Stanton had grown a hundredfold when he'd deduced his daughter's identity. The little orphan's history had been so carefully constructed it had fooled even his men . . . and that wasn't easy.

He'd known for a few days now. Still, he'd held off an attack, waiting for the right moment, a time when he might get close to her without raising the suspicions of others. This was a task he had to accomplish himself—he wouldn't trust it to anyone else—and he didn't want any witnesses. Tonight appeared to be the perfect opportunity he'd been waiting for. In a little while, when the wine flowed more copiously and people had immersed themselves in merrymaking, Edward and Henry would escort Lady Darleigh away for an audience with the king.

Edward and Henry suddenly stepped from the crowd to flank him. They knew they were here to capture the duke's daughter, but the duke hadn't yet revealed her identity to them. He never gave out information unless it was absolutely necessary.

"There's no danger to me," the duke murmured to his bodyguards, both accomplished druids in their own right and able to sense illusions. "Spread out through the crowd. Find David Gwylum and Lady Georgiana Darleigh. Bring them both to me."

"Lady Darleigh?" Edward's tone held a quaver. "She can't possibly be—"

"My daughter," the duke confirmed.

Edward gaped like a beached fish for a time, then found his voice. "But we checked her background time and again. We've had people watching for years. She never once did anything to raise suspicions."

"Are you questioning me?"

"No, Your Grace," the man humbly offered.

While the duke felt admiration for Sir Stanton, he felt nothing for the daughter he'd never known. He wondered how Branwyn had managed to hide the baby all those years ago, so the hounds wouldn't discover it. That was Branwyn, resourceful to the very end. "Still, now she's revealed. I simply need to find her, tie her up, and bring her to the bog."

The two men nodded, their nostrils flaring and eyes bright with excitement.

Like hounds readied for the hunt, the duke thought. He assumed a severe expression. "If you fail me, you will die."

Fear joined the excitement in their gaze, a perfect combination for getting things done. Nodding their heads, they vanished among the partygoers.

The vibrations still strong in his head, he resumed his examination of those in the Grand Reception Room. Couples swirled and flirted on the dance floor to an airy little melody, while old maids and dowagers watched with expressions of longing. Men with high collar points and perfectly tailored jackets gambled at green baize tables, or tossed off shots of fine Scottish whiskey. Indulging himself for a second, he assessed their clothes and knew none matched the quality and elegance of his own.

A flurry of conversation near the door to the Grand Reception Room caught his attention. Several people were gazing at a pale woman who stood unmoving in the foyer outside. As soon as his gaze touched upon the woman, she beckoned to him with a lazy motion.

He only needed a few moments to realize the woman's identity. Branwyn, the mother—*dead* mother—of his child. Smiling, he wondered why Gwylum and Georgiana would have bothered to create such a clumsy illusion. Obviously they wanted to lure him outside, perhaps into a trap.

The duke squared his shoulders. He would very much like to go outside. The fact that Gwylum and Georgiana had separated themselves from the pack made his task easier. The king had hounds that were very well trained in locating whomever they scented. More important, they were not fooled by illusions. While he couldn't run a brace of hounds through the partygoers, he could certainly track down Gwylum and Georgiana Darleigh outside with the hounds. He signaled to Edward and Henry to return to his side.

"Go get six of the king's hounds, and meet me outside," he murmured. "We're going to have the pleasure of a hunt this evening."

Grinning, the men turned and hurried from the room.

They didn't bow to him, the duke noticed, or even nod their heads before they left.

They had forgotten their places.

Tomorrow, he'd help them remember. For their own good.

Saddened at the thought of having to teach Edward and Henry manners, but knowing he had no choice, the duke ducked into an alcove. Columns around the niche concealed him almost thoroughly from the others in the room. There, in privacy, he closed his eyes. He felt the cold ebb of order in him, and the more exciting bubble of chaos. Even though the laws of the natural world demanded that he transform chaos into order to create an illusion, he'd often thought it would prove even more interesting to turn order into chaos.

Perhaps, after he was king, he would explore the notion more fully. For now, he would create an illusion of himself, to follow the illusion of Branwyn. If the others did have a trap waiting for him, he wouldn't jeopardize his real self. Focusing on chaos, he slowed its bubbling down until it reached the lazy ebb and flow of order—in particular, until it matched the flow of his own body. As the pressure in his mind built, he could feel the illusion forming around him. When he judged the time as right, he snapped his eyes open and stared into his own face.

Pleased, he sent the duke-illusion out of the alcove and through the crowd. Pride filled him as he watched lords and ladies step out of the way to let him pass. He was a ruler, a superior intellect, a leader who naturally incurred the respect of those around him.

Still, to insure his destiny, he had to throw a few particular bodies into the bog. Striving to maintain the illusion and see what the illusion saw, he slipped out a side door without anyone the wiser.

His eyes wide, he saw very little of St. George's Hall as he crept toward the door. Instead, he concentrated on what his mind's eyes saw. Branwyn continued to beckon, her body very real-looking. Gwylum had never been able to accomplish such a fine illusion. His daughter's ability, he guessed, must be great indeed. But why would he expect any less? She was, after all, a child of his loins.

Branwyn and the duke-illusion stepped outside and began to walk around the castle, toward the stables. The duke followed them, slipping out onto the grounds. Cool night mist settled on his skin, and the bottom of his trousers became wet with dew. Shortly after he rounded the side of the castle, he heard a snuffling, choking noise. For a moment he thought the hounds of his nightmares had somehow materialized to find him, and his heart began to pound.

Then Edward and Henry walked into view, with three hounds apiece. The dog's throats worked wildly but no sounds emerged. They'd had their vocal chords cut long ago, to prevent them from alerting their prey. Panting slightly, the pair paused by the duke.

The duke took deep breaths until his heart returned to a normal rate. "Do you have Gwylum's calling card?"

"Yes, we brought it, Your Grace," Henry said.

"Allow each dog to smell it."

Henry reached into his pocket and drew out Gwylum's calling card, which he'd wrapped in a square of linen. He held it in front of each hound, who sniffed it eagerly.

After all the dogs had smelled the card, the duke gestured toward them. "Give me two of them. Each of you take two as well. We'll search the grounds until we find Gwylum and Lady Darleigh."

Inexplicably, Edward and Henry remained still. In contrast, the dogs lunged on the ends of their leashes.

"Did you hear me?" the duke asked.

"They're hungry, Your Grace," Edward said. "The lad who tends them in the royal kennels said the king hasn't fed them for nigh unto three days. He plans on hunting tomorrow with the prince, and wants a good show."

"So?" The duke bristled.

"We know you don't like hounds much—"

"Give me their leashes," he demanded, stung that they dared mention his weakness. Silently he vowed that after tomorrow's lesson, Edward and Henry would never question their lord again.

Reluctantly Edward handed the duke the leashes of two of the dogs. "At the first smell of blood, they'll go crazy," he warned.

Tracy Fobes

Wrapping the leather bands around his palm twice, the duke savored every jarring leap the hounds made, every whispering bellow they attempted to utter. These dogs didn't frighten him. Indeed, their violence wouldn't be directed at him, but at Gwylum and his daughter, just like they had once been directed against Branwyn. And after the dogs had savaged the two traitorous druids into unconsciousness, he would bind them and bring them to a bog just south of Caernarfon in Wales, one that held the bodies of all his enemies.

That's where he put the people who didn't know their places.

He sneered at the hounds, hoping Edward and Henry would see that they'd misjudged him, and yanked on their leashes, drawing choking noises from them. After a second or two of displaying his prowess with the dogs, he snarled, "Start searching the grounds."

"But Your Grace, shouldn't we stay together? What if there's others in the woods, waiting to ambush you—"

The duke glanced pointedly at the hounds panting at the end of their leashes. "Who would dare? Now go!"

His two bodyguards jumped to obey, scurrying off into the woods with the hounds lunging in front of them. Annoyed that they'd questioned him yet again, the duke forced himself to focus on the images flooding his mind. His illusion, he realized, was entering the woods behind the royal kennels, following Branwyn down an overgrown path. Noting the two boulders that marked the path's beginning, he yanked his hounds into the proper direction and off they went, slavering and snuffling and anticipating dinner, no doubt.

They paused at the edge of the trees so he could search for the boulders. He found them almost instantly. In the meanwhile, he looked through his illusion's eyes and saw something very curious: Branwyn had begun to fade out. Surrounded by trees, she'd become grainy. He could see branches right through her. So, his daughter wasn't as powerful as he'd thought. Already her illusion was weakening. The notion boosted his confidence. Soon, he'd find her and remove the last obstacle between himself and the throne.

Far to his left, he noticed Henry charging off in the direction of the stables, the hounds straining terrifically on their leashes. For a moment, the duke wondered if they'd found their quarry. But then his own hounds grew excited, their tails wagging in short little bursts, their ears straight up, their mouths drooling saliva. They tried to drag him into the woods, so eager were they to feed their empty stomachs.

The duke smiled. It felt good to be in control of the dogs. He opened his druid's senses and listened to the trees. They spoke of four intruders. Four? He paused. Somewhere, deep in the forest, they'd set a trap for him. But what sort of trap?

Cautiously he moved down the path, into the woods. Every step carefully placed to avoid making excess noise, he allowed the hounds to lead him. He hadn't gone very far before he heard a snuffling noise to his left, following by a muffled grunt and the sound of branches and bushes breaking.

"Your Grace," a familiar voice called out softly.

Limbs charged with excitement, the duke moved toward Edward's voice. Jumping excitedly, the hounds were nearly impossible to control. The duke yanked on their chains, choking them to inform them of their master's displeasure, and stopped near Edward.

His shadow dark and misshapen, Edward stood over a large bundle. The duke saw a pale white face and realized it wasn't a bundle, but a body instead. He drew close, peered at the face and saw a large gash on the man's forehead. He rocked back on his heels. "Well, well. Lord Darleigh. What happened?"

"He was hiding a few feet off the trail, no doubt planning to ambush us. We scuffled. He should have stayed in the ballroom," Edward informed him. "He's dead."

The duke clucked. "Poor Lady Darleigh; now her baby has no father. Give me your dogs, and take Lord Darleigh's body back to Windsor Castle. Hide it in my coach. We'll return him to my estate for a . . . proper burial, along with his cousin Rees." He'd been keeping Viscount Hammond alive, just in case he'd needed a token for blackmail. It amused him to think he would be burying the two cousins with each other. What was that old saying? Plot together, brave together, later in the grave together?

"What will you do if there are druids in the woods, waiting for you?" Edward asked.

"I sensed four people: you, Lord Darleigh, my daughter, and Gwylum. There aren't any more."

"And if Gwylum and Lady Darleigh try to confuse you with an illusion?"

"The dogs are unaffected by illusions, you idiot. Now stop questioning me, and do as I've bid."

The other man handed the dogs over, bringing the duke's set up to four—almost too much for anyone to handle. Then he began dragging Lord Darleigh's body away.

Satisfied that he'd foiled at least the first trap Lady Darleigh and Gwylum had set for him, the duke started into the forest. The hounds quickly took him off the path and into the brambles. With each second they grew more excited, stopping to sniff the air and then lunge forward. They came to a small clearing ringed with trees. Moonlight cast a milky glow on bushes and the ruins of a small gazebo. Studying the clearing, he thought he saw something move.

There. He saw them again, their silvery coats glistening with a pale radiance. *Wolves.* Bellies to the ground, they were creeping up on him, their teeth bared and skull-white.

The duke caught his breath. Were they real? He still detected the vibrations of an illusion, but they could have been a result of the Branwyn illusion, which grew weaker by the moment.

He glanced at the dogs. They snuffled happily at the ground, clearly unconcerned.

An illusion, then. A grim smile tightened his lips. If the wolves had attacked him and he thought they were real, his physical body would have borne the scars of their attack. But he had the hounds, and the hounds knew better.

His dear daughter had made her first mistake. She hadn't counted on the hounds.

He strode forward boldly. The wolves uttered threatening growls. Even though he knew they were illusions, the sound still raised hairs on his arms. As soon as he walked amidst the wolves, though, they dissipated like fog upon a wind.

He chuckled to himself.

The hounds took a sudden turn to the right. The duke gave them their heads, knowing they had nearly run their quarry to the ground. His own blood quickening with the excitement of the hunt, he moved faster with them. A few minutes passed. The hounds became almost frenzied. They were very, very close.

Ahead, another hint of movement caught his eye.

He pulled the hounds up. They choked and gagged with disappointment.

A druid in a long white robe stood in the middle

of the path. The druid was holding a bow. He had his fingers wrapped around an arrow, nocked and drawn back, ready to fly. Gaze sliding from the druid to the hounds, the duke assessed the druid's reality. Again, the hounds didn't appear to see the druid. The duke froze, a nasty thought surfacing in his mind. Had the druid cloaked himself using some sort of invisibility spell, and fooled the dogs?

No. The dogs might not see him, but they would smell him.

Another illusion.

The druid let the arrow fly. Fascinated, the duke watched the arrow come toward him and strike him in the heart. It dissipated on impact.

Very clever, he thought.

Still, his daughter had made her second mistake.

He vowed she wouldn't have the chance to make a third.

Striding through the illusory druid, the duke chuckled to himself. This little hunt was proving rather enjoyable. Although the four hounds were a handful to manage, their enthusiasm had infected him. He could almost smell the blood in the air.

A grove of oak trees stood directly ahead. Utterly silent yet baying ferociously, the dogs strained on their leashes, nearly yanking his arms from their sockets. They dragged him into the oaks and suddenly paused, flanks quivering, noses pointing at a far tree.

The duke examined the tree that had caught the hounds' interest. He saw nothing. Still, the vibrations of an illusion echoed in his mind. Gwylum and Lady Darleigh were hiding themselves.

"Reveal yourselves now," he ordered, "or I'll release the hounds."

The far oak tree abruptly wavered and dissipated. There, Lady Darleigh and Gwylum stood with hands clasped. They looked so small and young that he wanted to laugh aloud. Had they really thought they could defeat someone as powerful and experienced as he?

"Well, Georgiana, we meet at last as father and daughter," he said.

She raised her chin and stared at him. He couldn't see the expression in her eyes; he hadn't enough light. Still, he imagined they held defiance and more than a little fear. "You aren't a father to me. You killed my mother. You tried to kill me."

The illusion of Branwyn walked from the trees to join Lady Darleigh and Gwylum. The duke shook his head. "Why don't you stop the illusion?"

"I want my mother here with me," Lady Darleigh insisted. "I want her to hear why you killed her."

"She's not real."

"She is to me."

Sighing, he shrugged, thinking Lady Darleigh teetered on the edge of madness. "I hadn't a choice. Your aunt told me you would somehow prevent me from gaining the throne. England occasionally requires sacrifices of its subjects. You, my dear, are *my* sacrifice, as was your mother."

"You plan to kill me?"

"People die every day, Georgiana. You *will* be buried in the bog, just like Branwyn. Perhaps your body will come to rest near hers. I'll try to place you in the same location," he said, offering what little comfort he could.

"And me?" Gwylum asked, his voice cracking on a high note.

"You've made a poor choice and allied yourself with the wrong people. I'm sorry, Gwylum, but you'll have to go too."

"I won't let you do this!" he cried.

"You can't prevent me. These hounds have your scent. As soon as I let them go, they'll come for you."

"Where is Rees, Viscount Hammond?" Lady Darleigh suddenly asked. "Is he dead?"

"He will be shortly."

"So, he's still alive," she breathed.

"Indeed." Tiring of the conversation, the duke loosened the dog's leashes. They lunged forward, eager to know her a bit more thoroughly. Her eyes wide, Lady Darleigh pressed a hand against her breast and took a step backward.

The duke nodded, understanding her fear. "When Edward brought me these hounds, he told me that the king hadn't fed them for three days. Apparently he wished to prepare them for a royal hunt tomorrow morning. They are trained to scent blood and are very hungry. They won't stop eating until they reach bone. You will die quickly, my dear."

"Please, no! You're my father. You must feel something for me," she moaned, tears welling up in her eyes.

"I do feel something for you—sadness, that you must die," he lied. "But we must think of England."

"If you let me live, I'll align myself with you," she babbled. "I'll forsake the Glamorgan Druids and come to live with you. I'll do anything you wish, anything at all."

Gwylum sucked in a breath and stepped away from her. "Georgiana!"

"I'm sorry. I don't want to die, not like my mother!"

Deciding not to prolong her pain any longer, the duke loosened his fingers to release the dog's leashes. "Good-bye, Georgiana."

A moment later, a blinding pain cut through his arm. He gasped and staggered, his fingers closing around the leashes by reflex. The dogs, yanked to the side by his stumbling fall, snarled and choked.

His arm a mass of pain, he turned to see who had attacked him. And gasped.

"The hounds are trained to scent blood, no?" Lord Darleigh murmured. The gash on his forehead had disappeared.

The duke made a noise somewhere between disbelief and anger. Evidently the little slut he'd fathered had managed to fool him. He hadn't seen Lord Darleigh's dead body before; he'd simply seen an illusion. He'd been waiting for someone to ambush him in the woods, and they'd satisfied his expectations, making him comfortable with the game. Comfortable and falsely confident.

Clutching his arm, he turned with wide eyes to gaze at the hounds. Their leashes were still wrapped around his hand. He shook them off, aware that the dogs were looking at him with a baleful light in their eyes. Why weren't they charging Gwylum?

Without warning, he knew the answer.

They smelled his blood.

They were very hungry.

And he was the injured one of the pack, the easiest to bring down.

A low, stuttering moan gathered in his throat. He took a step backward, away from the dogs.

The dogs took a step forward. One slunk around him. They were going to surround him.

His stomach clenched. He thought he might be sick. The scars on his ankle throbbed. Suddenly he was six years old again, and the hounds were chasing him. They wanted to eat him. He had to escape. He had to find a tree!

Gibbering with fear, the duke continued to back away, faster and faster, until finally he turned around and ran as fast as he could, tripping on exposed roots, thorns grabbing at his fine evening suit, branches slapping him in the face. He didn't care about any of that; he only wanted to escape the hounds.

His lungs burning, he dodged boulders, listening for their baying, and abruptly he could hear their throaty cries . . . had other hounds joined the first pack? He didn't know, he couldn't tell—

One of them clenched its jaw around his leg. He cried out and fell down. Pain shot through him. He beat the hound away with his fists and stumbled off. Ahead, a tree beckoned to him, its branches low enough and big enough to support his weight. Aware that tears ran down his face, he jumped onto the lowest branch and held on tight. Just as he pulled himself to a higher branch, the first dog arrived and began to snap wildly at the base of the tree. The duke scrambled upward. Another dog joined the first and threw its body upward in an insane effort to climb the tree.

They were very hungry.

The duke didn't dare come down.

Instead, he stared at the red light in their eyes and waited for his father to come and rescue him.

Chapter
20

Georgiana knew she was sitting on a bed of pine needles. She couldn't see them, smell them, or feel them. She understood that David, Gwynllian, and Sir Anthony stood somewhere nearby. The knowledge had little impact on her; her grasp of reality was growing more amorphous with each passing second. Chaos had flooded her, invading every pore as it sought to claim her with its buzzing presence.

She welcomed chaos with open arms. She brought it into herself and reveled in its presence. Without her total immersion in chaos, she wouldn't have been able to create such a convincing illusion of hounds, the same hounds which had led the duke through the forest and which now cornered him in the illusion David had created: a tree.

David had also supplied the other illusions necessary to confuse the duke. He had left her free to create hounds as lifelike as possible, for if the duke questioned their reality, their plan would fail. Unexpectedly, she'd found her task quite easy. Anger and a sense of betrayal had fueled her ability and made her desperate. In the end, giving herself over to chaos had seemed a small price to pay for cornering the duke in an illusion.

Even now, she knew Sir Anthony and Gwynllian were restraining the duke. That had been their plan. After the duke was fully restrained, David was supposed to let go of his illusion, and she of hers. By then, the duke's memories of the hounds that had trapped him as a child would have replaced the illusions, making them unnecessary. Then her aunt and uncle would take him to the bog near Caernarfon, where they would deposit him . . . may the old gods make him suffer for what he'd done.

In some lost part of her mind, Georgiana knew the time had come to surrender her illusion. Still, she held on. Chaos buzzed inside her like a hive of angry bees, driving out reason, urging her to embrace it even more fully. She wasn't a person anymore, but instead a hound, sitting at the base of the duke's tree, staring up at him, wanting to taste his flesh, wanting him to die.

She hurt too much to let go. She longed for her mother too much. The duke had killed Branwyn, and now she would stay here until he rotted on his branch . . . or fell, in which case she would eat him.

After all, she hadn't eaten for three days.

*   *   *

Concealed behind an outcrop of boulders, Brock raced into the clearing as soon as Sir Anthony gave the signal. Georgiana lay on a bed of pine needles, her chest rising and falling slowly, as though she slept. David sat on her left, staring at nothing, his face very white and vulnerable. In the distance, the duke cowered in a tree, four very real-looking hounds crouching at his feet.

Sir Anthony and Gwynllian followed him into the clearing and paused behind him. Sir Anthony grunted, whether with distress or satisfaction, Brock couldn't tell. The three of them had tracked into the woods behind the duke a few moments earlier, arriving in time to witness the final confrontation between Georgiana, David, and the duke. His heart in his throat, Brock had watched Georgiana put herself at the duke's mercy and nearly charged into the clearing to protect her.

Only Sir Anthony's viselike grip on his arm had stopped him.

With fear like ashes in his mouth, Brock hurried over to Georgiana. Kneeling by her side, he ran a hand through his hair. "Georgie, can you hear me?"

Her green eyes stared straight at him. Through him. They saw nothing.

"Georgiana!" He chafed her palms, rubbed her fingers. She felt terribly cold, her skin smooth and dry, reminding him of the way his mother felt. When he, David, Gwynllian, Sir Anthony, and Georgiana had talked over this scheme last night, he'd felt nothing but misgivings. Evidently his concern had been justified. Indeed, the way he felt right now, his misgivings had degenerated into outright panic.

He hadn't wanted Georgiana within a mile of the duke.

They'd overridden his objections, however, and put him in charge of smuggling the real dogs off the castle grounds, so the duke's men would take the illusion-dogs instead. He'd also kept the duke's men away from the woods, giving Georgiana and David the chance to trap the duke. Both tasks he'd completed with admirable efficiency.

Georgiana, though, had performed her task too well. Her lifeless stare was scaring the hell out of him. He brushed her hair back from her forehead, then shook her a little. "You have to let go now. Let David take over. Think! Think of the baby."

Gwynllian placed her hand on his shoulder. "Georgiana is gone," she murmured.

"Gone? What do you mean, gone?"

"She allowed the illusion she'd created to overtake her mind, just as the duke's mind was overtaken."

Brock glanced at the duke. The silver-haired man was still clinging to a tree branch high above the illusory dogs. A few druids had emerged from the woods to gather around the trunk, no doubt considering the best way to bring the duke down from the tree without shattering his make-believe world. "Her mind was overtaken?"

Moisture gathering in her eyes, Gwynllian looked away. "She is, you might say, in the realm of madness."

"No." Brock shook his head. "No. She'll come back to me. I know it."

"Be proud of her, Lord Darleigh," Gwynllian urged. "She sacrificed herself for the Glamorgan Druids and the good of all England."

"She is not dead."

"No. But she's not with us any longer, either." A tear slipped down Gwynllian's cheek. "We will take care of her."

"Take care of her? How?"

"We'll place her in her bedchamber at Cadair Abbey. I have a woman who will see to her needs."

Brock shuddered. "She's going to come back to us."

"I would give my own life to make it so," Gwynllian vowed.

"What about him?" Brock nodded toward David. While the lad's gaze was vacant, he stood on his own and walked with a bit of urging from Sir Anthony.

Behind Sir Anthony, the druids had brought down the duke from the tree and were trussing him up like a spring chicken destined for the oven. Drool leaked from the corner of the duke's mouth, and his arms curled in a strange manner, as if he were still clutching a branch.

"David is also immersed in the illusion, but he

remains aware of our world. His task was easier than Georgiana's. He simply needed to convince the duke that his tree—an inanimate object—is the stuff of reality.

"Georgiana, on the other hand, had to convince him of the authenticity of a living creature, requiring that she mimic every part of that creature's essence. She's lost herself in the hounds' spirit. Or perhaps she doesn't *want* to return to us. The duke has made her suffer terribly."

"So they're both mad, the duke and Georgiana?"

"We will take care of her," Gwynllian repeated, her gaze ineffably sad. "Your child will continue to grow inside of her. When her time comes, we'll deliver the baby, and send for you."

"No!" Brock began to pace. "Can I help her?"

"In what way?"

"I've helped my mother in the past—drawn her from her madness into lucidity. Maybe I could do the same for Georgiana."

Gwynllian shook her head. "She is not mad in the traditional sense—"

"She sounds close enough to me." Brock stiffened with determination. "Leave me, so I might talk to her and say what I need to without an audience."

The older woman touched his arm. "Be truthful to her. Be honest. Perhaps you *will* get through. Indeed, I'm not certain she's yet fulfilled her destiny."

"What? There's more?"

Gwynllian's eyebrows quirked. "I've seen something very odd. A young girl. I don't understand it. Please, try to wake her, Lord Darleigh."

"I'm damned well going to try."

Nodding, Gwynllian walked away, toward Sir Anthony, David, and the other druids.

Georgiana reclined against a bed of pine needles, her face so white it had the sheen of death to it. Brock took a deep breath and let it out slowly as he sat down next to her. His heart clenching, he lifted her slight form and settled her into his lap. She was so small, and vulnerable, and so beautiful that he ached just to look at her.

Carefully he thought over the times they'd shared together and knew many of them had been bad. They'd fared better in Wales, but Brock knew that true happiness would continue to lie just out of their reach unless he admitted to her what he held in his soul.

Gathering his courage, he brushed the hair back from her face and pressed a soft kiss against her cheek. "I miss you, Georgiana. I miss you already, even though you've only been gone a short time. You are, and always will be, the best part of me.

"I remember the first day we met. You were like the sunshine. Warm, happy, smiling, you drove my grim thoughts away. You may not believe me, but I think I fell in love with you then. I fell in love with your sweet scent and your quick smile and your innocent kindness.

"Indeed, I fell in love with the person that you are, but I was simply too stupid to realize it. My estate had gone bankrupt, and my determination to save it drove out all other considerations. Still, when I married, I wanted you for my wife, even though I could have had many others, title-hunters who would have handed over their fortunes gladly. It was you that I wished to spend my life with. It was always you."

Brock felt his eyes filling with tears. Ashamed, he let them come anyway. He would hide nothing from her. He would bow his head and sob openly if it would help. "Losing you after we married hurt me more than anything I'd ever felt before. On that day, I cut out a piece of my own damned heart and have yearned for you ever since. Now I understand that my happiness is dependent on yours. I live to hold you, to love you, to protect you. You are my light, my life. Without you I am lost."

He choked back a harsh sound that might have been a sob. "I need you so badly, but I drove you away. By God, when I think of the opportunities I've missed, and the days we could have spent together, I want to shout with loneliness. If only I knew of a way to turn the clock backward! Sometimes, I feel like I've misplaced a part of *myself*."

Without warning, she murmured softly. Brock wasn't certain if he'd really heard the sound or imagined it. Had his words finally penetrated her madness? Could he bring her back to him, as he'd so often talked his mother into abandoning her demons?

He bent closer to her and spoke more quickly. "Georgie, I love you so much my heart aches with it. When I look at you, I see not your green eyes and brown hair but rather the beautiful woman you are inside, the woman I married, the woman I love. I want us to have a family, and grow old together, and spend our dying moments in each other's arms. Please, Georgiana, don't leave me."

Her eyelids flickered.

The tears flowed freely now, running down his face to splash against her cheek. He didn't care who saw them. Only Georgiana mattered now. He clutched her to his chest. "Come back to me. Leave that place of anger and pain and let me show you how much I love you. Let me make up for all of the pain I've caused you. Return to me, and we'll create a destiny of our own choosing."

Feeling the warmth flowing back into her body like warmed honey, he knew he'd won. His heart clenched again, this time with joy. Slowly he lowered his lips to hers and kissed her, gratitude and happiness aching in his throat.

Her eyes opened. "Brock? I love you."

"I love you too, Georgie," he whispered.

Georgiana awoke in her tester bed in Palmer House. The second she opened her eyes, she saw

Brock's face, leaning in close. She still tingled with the memory of the soft words Brock had whispered to her in the forest, words of love that she'd so longed to hear. Swooning shortly after she'd emerged from the illusion, she hadn't had the chance to tell him what she held in her own heart.

She would tell him now.

"Brock, I—"

Four concerned faces suddenly peered at her from above, cutting her off. Sir Anthony, Aunt Gwynllian, David . . . and Brock. They all looked tired, with dark shadows under their eyes, but Brock appeared the worst of all. His cravat was disheveled, almost untied, and his skin had a terrible pallor to it.

"Georgie," he breathed.

She struggled to push up on her elbows.

Brock rushed to place an arm around her shoulders, helping her to sit up. Sir Anthony shoved a glass of water near her face, and David's face lit up with a silly grin.

Her eyes moist with tears, Aunt Gwynllian took her hand. "You're going to be fine, Georgiana."

"How long have I been sleeping?" she asked no one in particular, amused by their overly solicitous expressions and yet feeling slightly crowded.

"For more than twenty-four hours now," Brock answered. He made an expansive gesture toward the window. "The sun is just coming up."

"It's the dawn of a new day," Sir Anthony added.

"A day without the duke and his threats hanging over our heads."

Gwynllian shooed them all back from the bed, then moved forward to claim Georgiana's hand. "I'm proud of you, dear. I'm certain your mother is proud of you, too. You've destroyed the duke and ended Cailleach's reign over this little portion of England."

Sir Anthony nodded. "You've served the Glamorgan Druids well. We are all in your debt."

"And those dogs you created, Georgiana," David enthused, his voice cracking, "were first-rate! I wish I could do that."

"Keep practicing," Georgiana advised him, smiling. A warm glow filled her, erasing the tiredness that fought to drag her back into sleep. She caught Brock's gaze and held it, certain he would be very happy to hear what she had to say next.

"I've satisfied only a part of my destiny," she reminded them, "by vanquishing the duke, and leaving the Glamorgan Druids free to pursue a life of knowledge unencumbered by violence. The Glamorgan Druids must proceed on their own from now on. Without me."

Sir Anthony glanced from Brock, to Georgiana, then frowned. "Georgiana, are you telling me you plan on forsaking a life of druidry for Lord Darleigh?"

She smiled at her uncle, the warm glow inside her becoming tinged with joy as she saw the answering glimmer in Brock's gaze. "I've fulfilled my responsibilities to the Glamorgan Druids as much as I plan to. You, Aunt Gwynllian, and David will have to lead the order. I'm staying in London, with Brock. We're going to create our own destiny."

"But—"

Gwynllian silenced Sir Anthony with a gently-placed hand on his arm. His face reddening, the older man looked away.

"You were meant to stay with Lord Darleigh," Gwynllian murmured, brushing Georgiana's hair back from her forehead. "I wouldn't have allowed you to marry him if I hadn't foreseen true happiness for you both. You've traveled down a difficult road, but take pride in the fact that your destination is a place not many couples reach."

Coloring a little at the warm promise in Brock's eyes, she clasped his hand in hers.

"And we never could have mated anyway," David informed her in a confident voice. "You're simply too old for me."

Georgiana stared at the youth for a second or so, and then they all laughed—all except David, who didn't seem to see any humor in his statement.

Sir Anthony, his good mood restored, put an arm around his sister. "Come with me, Gwynllian. You too, David. Let's leave Lord Darleigh alone with his wife."

They all filed out of the bedchamber. Gwynllian was the last one out. As she reached the threshold, she paused and glanced back at Georgiana and

Brock. Her eyes had a faraway look. "I wasn't going to mention this, but after further consideration, I feel I must tell you that there is yet one portion to your destiny that you *will* fulfill, Georgiana."

A shiver passed over Georgiana. Eyebrow quirked, she stared at her aunt. "Whatever do you mean?"

"England's throne is not yet secure," Gwynllian murmured. "Your services as a druid are still required, although when, I cannot say. My advice to you is to stay with Lord Darleigh in London. Indeed, I sense that it's imperative for you to do so."

Without further explanation, Gwynllian crossed the threshold and closed the door behind her.

After casting one last concerned look toward the door, Brock caressed her cheek with his palm and asked, "Georgiana, my love, how are you feeling? Do you need more sleep? Would you like something to eat?" His hand slipped down to her abdomen, pressing lightly.

A horrible thought grabbed hold of her. "The baby—"

"Is fine," he reassured.

She sighed, deeply. "Thank God. What do you suppose my aunt meant by suggesting I would yet fulfill my destiny?"

"I don't know, and I prefer not to think on it."

"Let's forget it, then."

He nodded his agreement, his hand still pressed against their baby.

And yet, even as she luxuriated in the new, loving closeness between them, she still felt as though a dark cloud were hanging over her. Why? The duke was vanquished, her baby was fine, Brock was at her side, they loved each other and were free to pursue a life together. . . .

Rees.

The name popped into her mind from nowhere. She broke off, her happiness dissipating like fog in the sun's strong rays. "Have you found Rees yet?"

A quick frown curved Brock's lips. His brow furrowed and he looked away, his pain almost palpable. "Found his body, do you mean?"

She stiffened, remembering abruptly her final confrontation with the duke. My God, Rees was still alive somewhere!

She grabbed his shoulder. "Rees is alive."

Brock covered her hand with one of his own. His frown grew deeper. "David told us that the duke claimed Rees was still alive. We've searched Tamerly, the duke's estate, and every other building the duke ever inhabited, and found nothing."

Georgiana groaned softly. Her hopes for happiness plummeted like a brick thrown into the ocean. Through no fault of his own, Rees's death would always stand between them, would always remain a festering sore that the slightest wrong move would tear open.

"You've searched everywhere?" she asked.

"We've turned the town upside down. We can't find him."

"What if he's still alive?"

Cursing softly, Brock stood up and began to pace. "By God, I've done little else but torture myself with thoughts of Rees, of how he might be alive somewhere, waiting for me to rescue him. I'm so damned frustrated I could put my fist through the wall. I've searched everywhere, and talked to nearly a hundred different people. I've offered a reward for information. I've gotten down onto my hands and knees and prayed. What else can I do?"

Frowning, she stared at her husband. "You've missed something."

"You're goddamned right I missed something. But what?"

"I don't know. We could drive ourselves mad, trying to think of all the possibilities." Georgiana pushed the covers back and stood on shaky legs. Brock circled around behind her to offer support. She clung to him for a moment, then rang for Nellie. "I'm going to dress, and then you're going to tell me every place that you've searched, and the names of every person you've talked to, even if we *do* drive ourselves mad doing so."

Brock released her, his eyebrows quirked thoughtfully. "Drive ourselves mad, you say."

"I'll do anything to find Rees."

"My mother is mad," he said, obviously following his own train of thought.

"What of it?"

"Last July, right before we left for Wales, my mother said something very peculiar. She mentioned she had once been the duke's lover and knew a secret of his."

Georgiana shivered at the mention of the duke's name. He was on his way to Wales by now, with David, Sir Anthony, and Aunt Gwynllian; but no matter how far from her he traveled, she would always feel a lingering sense of menace. "Do you think she really was the duke's lover, or was her claim a manifestation of her madness?"

"I don't know. Whatever the case, she refused to tell me her secret. She claimed the duke would be very upset with her if she spoke of it."

Georgiana slapped her palm lightly with a clenched fist. "We have to pry this secret from her somehow."

"I'll go and talk to her right now." Without further comment, Brock turned and left the room.

Once Nellie had finished helping her dress, Georgiana walked to the Dowager Lady Darleigh's bedchamber. The door was open a crack, allowing her to see into the room. Brock sat in a hard-backed little chair, a frown tightening his lips. He looked positively frustrated.

Apparently the dowager was refusing to tell her secret.

Georgiana turned away and pressed her back against the wall. She scoured her mind for a likely method to pry the necessary information from

Brock's mother. An utterly repugnant idea occurred to her rather quickly. Dislike it as she did, she forced herself to consider it. The discomfort it would cause her was nothing compared to the joy she'd feel if she found Rees alive.

Nodding, she decided she really only had one viable option.

The Duke of Gloucester would have to pay a visit to the dowager.

Georgiana cleared her mind of all extraneous thought and focused on the vibrations of chaos and order. Now that it had gotten its claws into her once, chaos flooded her more quickly. Her insides clenched with a moment of panic and she thought she might descend into madness again, but then, she remembered the words Brock had whispered to her last night and knew nothing—not even chaos—would drag her from the happiness that she sensed could be hers.

Chaos buzzed and swirled like a fog in her mind. Painstakingly she formed it into an image of the duke, one branded into her mind from the previous night. Nausea rolled inside her at the mere thought of him. Swallowing, she created the duke as best as she was able and sent him inside the dowager's bedchamber.

Closing her eyes, she watched the scene unfold through her illusion's gaze.

As soon as the duke entered, Brock jumped to his feet and gaped. Georgiana could well understand his reaction. Smiling, she had the duke put a hand on Brock's shoulder and murmur "I love you" into his ear.

Looking dazed, Brock fell back into his chair.

The dowager, for her part, gasped upon seeing the illusion, and quickly smoothed the bedcovers down in the manner of a lady smoothing her skirt. "Your Grace," she murmured. "I wasn't expecting you."

Georgiana thought she sounded quite lucid and whispered a silent prayer of thanks.

"I thought it high time I paid you a visit, Lady Darleigh," the duke said in warm tones. "We were good friends once. I've neglected you for far too long."

Looking down at the bedcovers, Brock's mother fluttered her eyelashes. "How kind of you to remember me."

"You're looking quite well."

"Thank you, Your Grace. As are you."

"We had some fine times together, didn't we, Anna?"

"We did."

Looking through the duke's eyes, Georgiana would swear a blush colored the dowager's cheeks.

"Have you kept yourself busy?" the duke asked.

"Yes, very. Reginald here has been managing my schedule. He is extremely trustworthy and knows all my secrets." The old woman waved airily at Brock. "I'm quite in demand, no, Reginald?"

Georgiana lifted an eyebrow. *Reginald?*

"Lady Darleigh is very kind with her time; she has many charities she contributes to," Brock smoothly replied.

Intrigued, Georgiana wished she had the time to ask more about this Reginald character. Instead, she focused on the duke's "secret."

"Ah, Lady Darleigh has always been a charmer." The duke smiled. "She stole my heart years ago."

"Oh, nonsense, Cadwallon," she chided, using his first name. "I was a pleasant interlude, no more."

"Regardless, we had our secrets, did we not?"

She lowered her gaze. "We did."

Brock managed a casual tone. "Secrets?"

"Oh, yes." The duke let out a sigh. "One in particular was rather interesting, I thought. It's a secret no longer, of course."

Eyebrows lifted, Brock's mother perked up. "You've told, Cadwallon?"

"Of course."

"May I hear it?" Brock asked.

The dowager shrugged. "If the duke will allow it."

"If it amuses you, Lady Darleigh, tell him," the duke offered magnanimously.

"All right, then." A sparkle brightened the old woman's eyes. "The duke has a secret underground chamber at the back of his estates in Tamerly. You took me there once, didn't you, Cadwallon? It was quite . . . gruesome."

Stiffening, Brock leaned forward in his chair. "Where, exactly, is it located?"

"In a large meadow behind the stables." She examined Brock with a curious expression. "Why, Reginald, you've gone pale. Is something wrong?"

"No, not at all." Brock stood, bowed to the duke's illusion, and pressed a kiss against his mother's cheek. "I must be leaving, Lady Darleigh. Your Grace, will you come with me? I'll escort you to the door."

The duke glanced at a watch fob tucked into his waistcoat. "Thank you for the offer, Reginald. How quickly the time passes when one is enjoying oneself. I see I must leave, too."

"Are you both leaving, then?" the dowager asked plaintively.

"I'm afraid so, Anna." The duke gave her a smart bow. "We'll visit again. Until then, I wish you the best of health."

Brock slipped out of the bedchamber, waiting for the illusion to follow him out, and then closed the door. Georgiana allowed the illusion to dissipate, and immediately found herself swept up into her husband's arms.

"You were marvelous," he breathed against her lips, seconds before he kissed her.

After taking a few seconds to indulge herself in the feel of his warm mouth against hers, she pulled away.

"We have to find Rees first."

"God, I hope he's alive." Brock took her hand

and rushed her down the stairs. As soon as they reached the foyer, Brock asked the butler to have his gig brought around. Shortly thereafter Georgiana found herself en route to Tamerly Estates, Brock speeding through the streets of London with consummate skill. Even so, the trip to the duke's estate seemed to take forever. When they finally pulled into the long carriageway leading to the great house, she breathed a sigh of relief.

A footman met them near the front porch, which loomed over them with great marble columns and a multitude of windows.

Breathing quickly, Brock climbed out of the carriage and helped Georgiana disembark as well. Then, he turned to the footman and said, "Quick, man, point me to the stables."

Eyes wide, the footman gestured toward a gravel path on the left. "Shall I announce you, my lord?"

Rather than answer, Brock and Georgiana hurried down the path.

"Excuse me, my lord, but no one may roam the duke's properties without his consent," the footman called out.

Brock and Georgiana ignored him. There, in the distance, the stables loomed, and behind them a meadow spread out, looking very dry and bleached in the late summer sun. And yet, as Georgiana charged into the meadow, she saw the first few shoots of green returning to the earth. She knew in that moment they would find Rees. Alive.

Brock had raced several feet ahead of her. Suddenly he shouted to attract her attention. He appeared to be standing on a small pile of rocks, but as she grew closer, she realized the rocks were the roof of an ancient burial mound, one often used by the druids of old. He circled around the rocks and, without warning, disappeared.

Georgiana reached the mound and discovered a tunnel leading into the earth. She followed it downward, the pitch-blackness complete except for the flickering glow of a torch that had nearly burned down. A horrible decaying smell wafted from deeper within the tomb.

"Rees!" Brock cried out, somewhere ahead.

Her heart pounding with excitement and anxiety, Georgiana stumbled deeper into the tomb, past a huge bronze cauldron and a heap of animal horns. A moment later, Brock was staggering toward her, a man slung over his shoulder. Georgiana turned around and hurried back to the surface, Brock close behind her. When they reached daylight again, Brock set Rees gently on the ground.

Georgiana sucked in a breath. Rees's eyes were closed and his breathing was very shallow. Dark circles ringed his eyes and his cheekbones stood out prominently. Cuts marked his face and neck. Her gaze dropped to the bandages on his hand. What had the duke done to him?

At least he lived.

She dropped to her knees and cupped his face

with her hands. "Rees, dear, we've found you. We're going to take you home."

The younger man's eyes flickered, and then opened. "Georgie?" he whispered.

Tears filled her eyes and began slipping down her cheeks. She held out her hand toward Brock, so she might pull him closer to Rees. "Yes, Rees, I'm here. Brock is here. We've come to take you home."

"The duke?" Rees whispered.

"Is dead." Brock took her hand and clasped it tightly. He sounded suspiciously hoarse. "I owe you everything, Rees. I can never repay you."

"Just get me a decent meal," the younger man quipped, then started coughing.

Georgiana laughed, but the tears kept coming. "Let's take him home, Brock."

Epilogue

❧

The perfume of cherry blossoms filled the air, mixing with warm March sunshine to create the perfect fragrance of spring. Wild daffodils that grew in the naturalized sections of St. James's Park swayed in a gentle breeze. Georgiana lay back on the blanket spread out beneath her and contemplated an azure blue sky.

Brock lay back next to her and linked his hands behind his head. "Do you approve of my secret picnicking spot?"

"Heartily." She rolled onto her stomach and, careful not to place too much weight on the baby, who was due within the month, plucked a stem of grass. "How many other women have you taken here?"

"You're the first. I found it only last week."

"I presume I'll be the last, too." Trailing the stem along his face, she tickled him mercilessly and giggled when he caught her hand and kissed it.

"Wretched woman," he growled. "You like to tease me, don't you?"

"More than anything else."

He chuckled, but she quickly muffled the sound with a kiss, opening his mouth with hers and sending her tongue on a thrilling exploration. He let her do as she wished, remaining passive beneath her and challenging her femininity.

She knew it was a game, one they played occasionally. He would lie there and pretend not to be affected, and she would become increasingly bold in her effort to "arouse" him. She didn't stop, not even when his erection was throbbing in her hand and her thighs were slicked with moisture. And when he could withstand no more of her pleasuring, he would take her, thoroughly, and quench the desire that had stripped them both of their natural reserve.

They had some other games, too, but she liked this one the best. She always tortured him, and always won. Indeed, if they were in their bedchamber at Palmer House, she mused, she would tease him now. She would gaze at every inch of him, and when he was aching to feel her touch, she'd kiss him softly, everywhere, and watch his desire for her grow so hot that it melted every inhibition he possessed.

Ah, he was putty in her hands.

She smiled against his lips.

He broke away from her kiss and eyed her thoughtfully, at the same time sliding his hand beneath her skirts, which had bunched upward around her thighs. Burying his nose in her hair and breathing deep, he dragged his warm palm along her thighs, then touched the curls between her legs, gently massaging the center of her pleasure.

She moaned, quietly. He seemed to know exactly how to bring her to the peak with the smallest effort. After a moment or two of his own brand of sweet torture, she found herself wondering if they dared make love here, in this secluded Eden. . . .

His finger slipped inside of her. Gasping softly, she thrust against him, wanting . . . no, *needing* more. She lifted her face up to his and kissed him wildly. If society expected a well-bred woman to politely tolerate a husband's lovemaking, then she guessed that made her a whore, because she simply couldn't have enough of what her husband offered her so masterfully.

"Shall we return to Palmer House?" she moaned, between kisses.

He raised a thoughtful eyebrow. "You don't like our secluded spot?"

"It isn't . . . private enough."

"Why? What did you have in mind, Lady Darleigh? Something more than an afternoon nap?"

"You know well what I want."

He chuckled, deep in his throat. "I prefer to make you wait until tonight."

"What?" Georgiana wasn't certain she'd heard him right. "You are a beast, Brock."

"And you're spoiled." Nodding thoughtfully, he gave her a toe-curling grin. "You're definitely going to wait."

She punched him lightly on the shoulder, then pouted at him, all to no avail. And yet, even while she resented the delay of the pleasure only he could bring her, she had to admit, waiting only increased the delight. Her thighs were already slicked with moisture and she knew anticipation would keep them that way until he finally took her.

Smiling, Brock lay back and put an arm over his eyes. "Curl up next to me," he encouraged her. "We'll have a nice nap."

Grumbling, she did as he'd bid, and after a while she found herself drifting off. Her pregnancy had made her more sleepy than usual, and Brock often made certain she had a nap when she needed one. Apparently she'd needed one today.

Was he always right?

Some time later she awoke and discovered the sun had begun its descent toward the western horizon. Brock still slumbered peacefully on the blanket and didn't stir when she sat up. Taking a moment to feast upon his strong, lean form with her gaze, she stood and decided to take a walk through the park while waiting for him to awaken.

Bluebells and astilbe swayed beneath maple and oak trees which were just beginning to sprout leaves. Birch trees, already well into their spring blooming, provided a kelly green backdrop for masses of honeysuckle and trumpet vines that clung to a fence. Birds swooped and dived among the branches and a few spring butterflies flitted from flower to flower. Georgiana took a deep breath, let it out slowly, and knew she had never been happier than she was at this moment. Rees was completely healed, and her aunt and uncle had returned with David to their London townhouse.

The duke, of course, was in the bog outside of Caernarfon.

With my mother, Georgiana thought bitterly. Frowning, she forced the thought away. She would allow herself peace, now that she'd satisfied her obligations to the Glamorgan Druids.

The sound of sobbing caught her attention. It seemed to be coming from behind a stand of birch trees in the distance. Curious, Georgiana followed the sound and discovered a young girl, maybe eight or nine years old, hidden behind the trees. Judging by the girl's well-made dress, she was a daughter of the aristocracy.

She approached cautiously. "Are you hurt, little girl?"

Her eyes watery and red, the girl focused on her, then looked down. "Go away," she ordered between sniffles.

Georgiana hesitated. Perhaps she *should* leave, and give the girl her privacy. Then she saw a carpetbag at the girl's feet. Understanding dawned inside of her.

The girl was running away.

Georgiana knew she had to stop her. The perils awaiting a small, wealthy child wandering alone through the streets of London were legion.

"What's your name?" she asked, her tone gentle.

The girl's chin thrust forward pugnaciously. "Why do you want to know?"

"Maybe I can help you."

"I doubt it."

"Why are you running away?"

The girl shot her a suspicious glance. "How do you know I'm running away?"

"You have a carpetbag near your feet," Georgiana pointed out dryly.

"Are you going to try and stop me?"

"No. I simply want to know why you're running."

"Because they want too much from me," the girl hissed. "Victoria, you must learn your letters. Victoria, memorize the history and lineage of each of England's kings. Victoria, listen to your Greek teacher, and your Latin teacher, and learn the languages they speak! I cannot do what they ask of me. So I'm running away."

Victoria. Georgiana searched her mind for any recollections of an aristocratic daughter named Victoria. Without warning, she remembered a miniature she'd once seen in St. James's Palace. "You're the Duke of Kent's daughter, aren't you?"

"I am. Are you going to tell on me?"

"No, I won't. I'm Lady Georgiana Darleigh. A pleasure to meet you, Lady Victoria."

The girl crossed her arms over her chest and rolled her eyes heavenward.

Georgiana smiled. "You may choose not to believe me, but I know something about duty. I once had a burdensome duty myself. Would you like to hear my story?"

"Is it a real story, or a fairy tale?"

"A little of both," Georgiana said. "May I sit down?"

"All right. Please do. Tell me what you must, Lady Darleigh."

Amused by the girl's commanding tone, Georgiana proceeded to tell Victoria about the Glamorgan Druids and what they'd wished of her. She mentioned her own personal villain—the duke—and her prince, Brock. But most of all, she concentrated on explaining to Victoria how she'd once wanted to run away too, but in the end, had done what others expected of her. While her duty had been painful, it had brought her honor, and made her respect herself—two of the most precious gifts that any person could ever receive.

Victoria remained very still while Georgiana told her story, the expression on her face rapt. When Georgiana finished, the girl raised an eyebrow and said, "I think your story is more fairy tale than true. No one can create illusions."

Smiling, Georgiana shrugged. "Regardless, the feelings I've expressed to you are very true."

The girl nodded thoughtfully. "Perhaps I won't run away after all."

Suppressing a grin, Georgiana held out her hand. "May I take you back to the palace?"

"Indeed you may." Her movements graceful, Victoria put her hand in Georgiana's. "My father says I might be queen some day. Do you think you might agree to become one of my advisors?"

For one startled second, Georgiana froze. She remembered what Gwynllian had said—that the throne of England was not yet secured—and wondered if this simple moment with a young girl had been her destiny all along. If she hadn't rescued Victoria, the girl might have been lost in London, even killed. Perhaps Victoria, not herself, stood between the duke and the throne. By rescuing the little girl from the woods, she may have insured Victoria's, rather than the duke's, accession.

Georgiana shrugged to herself. She would probably never know for sure, one way or the other. Muffling a chuckle, she decided to play along. "Of course, Your Majesty. I would be honored."

Breathtaking romance from

TRACY FOBES

FORBIDDEN GARDEN

HEART OF THE DOVE

TOUCH NOT THE CAT

Sonnet Books
Published by Pocket Books

3025

Return to
a time of romance...

**SONNET
BOOKS**

Where today's

hottest romance authors

bring you vibrant

and vivid love stories

with a dash of history.

PUBLISHED BY POCKET BOOKS